SOMEBODY'S DARLING

LINDA FAUSNET

To my daughter, Celia, who enjoys a handsome hero as much as her mother. Someday you'll be old enough to read this book....

My books contain steamy sex, bad words, and human beings of all sorts, include gay people. If you're not a fan of those things, you may want to stop reading now. If you're cool with that stuff, come take my hand and join me on this journey...

This book is a work of fiction. References to real people, events, establishments, organizations, or locales are intended only to provide a sense of authenticity and are used fictitiously. All other characters, and all incidents and dialogue, are drawn from the author's imagination and are not to be construed as real.

Published by Wannabe Pride 2016

Editing by Katriena Knights

Cover Design by Chuck DeKett

FIRST EDITION.

Library of Congress Control Number: 2015919166

❦ Created with Vellum

1

The living don't realize the dead walk amongst them.

On this warm evening in April, the dead were sitting on the steps outside Hunt's Battlefield Fries on Steinwehr Avenue in Gettysburg, Pennsylvania. Though they could choose to be invisible to the living whenever they liked, right now Jesse Spenser of the First Texas Infantry and Fillis Mungin, a runaway slave from Virginia, were content to have the tourists see them plainly.

Though their clothing would have looked bizarre anywhere else, the two were taken for reenactors or tour guides. Jesse wore, or at least appeared to wear, gray wool pants, a white cotton shirt with suspenders, and a brown slouch hat. Fillis wore a long, pale blue cotton dress. Their clothing fit in perfectly in the historic town of Gettysburg.

Jesse never failed to attract attention from the female tourists, as many women loved a man in uniform. He had brown hair that had grown just long enough to start to curl and warm, blue-gray eyes that added to his allure. He never thought of himself as attractive, though. He was just a poor farm boy from Texas.

A dead farm boy from Texas.

He had died on the second day of the famed battle of Gettysburg more than one hundred and fifty years ago. Even if he did turn a woman's head, it would do her no good. She wouldn't even be able to touch him. That didn't stop him from flirting, though. Having human interaction like that made him feel alive again.

A group of teenage girls walked by, and one of them made eye contact with Jesse. He nodded his head and said, "Ma'am," in greeting. The girls giggled and blushed. Jesse's accent and Southern manners never failed to charm the ladies. He thought it a shame that people seemed to have abandoned such old-fashioned ways, especially here in Yankee country.

Jesse also thought it somewhat shameful the way some of these young girls dressed nowadays. Not that he wanted women to go back to dressing the way they did when he was alive, pretty much covered from head to toe, but there had to be some kind of happy medium. Girls had such terrible role models these days; people like those awful Kardashians. *Dreadful.* Whatever happened to classy women like Lauren Bacall and Audrey Hepburn? Jesse had seen it all through the years. Times had certainly changed.

A ghostly Union soldier walked by and nodded to Jesse, who nodded back. The Yankee was currently invisible to the living. Jesse could tell because the soldier's image was transparent. He could see the soldier, but he could also see *through* him. The vast majority of spirits chose this path—to walk unseen among the living.

Jesse chose to be visible more often than most spirits because he felt lonely when no one but other ghosts could see him. Still, there was always the risk of frightening people. How he hated when a woman would shriek with terror when he was careless about when and how he disappeared, or when one of them would accidentally bump into him and feel a wisp of frigid cold instead of warm flesh. It hurt so much when a pretty lady's expression turned to horror at the sight of him. Worse still were the children. Jesse's ghostly heart ached when he remembered the handful of times he had inadvertently frightened a child. He loved children dearly and couldn't bear the thought of becoming the subject of their nightmares when all he wanted to do was play with them for a little while.

Another Yankee drifted by, nodding at him. Jesse was on good terms with most Union soldiers around these parts. So many years had passed since the Civil War had ended, and most Yanks and Rebs got along now that everyone was dead. Though many of the deceased soldiers had gone on to heaven or wherever they were supposed to go, there were a fair number still left behind wandering the battlefields and the town of Gettysburg. It was a lonely existence for sure, so there was no sense in remaining enemies when there were few friends to be found. Jesse's friendship with Fillis would have been quite odd back when they were still alive. Jesse, a Rebel fighting for the South, and Fillis, a runaway slave.

Fillis, who had died in her fifties just before the battle of Gettysburg, adored Jesse. She was like an adoptive mother to many of the soldiers who sought her counsel and comfort. She referred to herself as their "Second Mama," not wanting to take anything away from their real mothers, who had died long ago. Jesse was Southern through and through and would always remain loyal to his beloved Texas, having taken up arms to defend his home and family.

In death, he'd become close with Fillis and had learned the truth about the horrors of slavery.

"Mmmm. My, my, my..." Fillis muttered as she watched an attractive woman in a low-cut blouse walk by. Jesse chuckled softly. That was one thing the black woman and the white soldier had in common.

Girl watching.

They both missed the physical companionship of women, that was for sure. Fillis had far more actual experience with that sort of thing than Jesse had. She had lived on a plantation in Virginia until the master of the house discovered Fillis's indiscretion with his wife. Fillis had run away and had died of tuberculosis not long before the great battle.

Jesse was still a virgin when he died. There were a handful of women back home that his parents had hoped he might marry, but there was no one who really took his fancy. It had been hard for him during those long nights at camp knowing he had no sweetheart back home waiting for him. Though he would never have wished to cause some poor woman suffering and mourning, it still hurt sometimes to know that there had been no girl thinking of him as he lay cold and dead on the rocks of Devil's Den.

Though he had no physical heart anymore, he still felt a horrible ache in his chest when he thought of his mother getting the news of his death. Perhaps it was for the best that he had no other love waiting for his return.

Still, it annoyed him that he'd died before he'd ever been with a woman. He'd had many opportunities while he was a soldier. Prostitutes were not hard to come by, but he never regretted passing them up. Even now that he was dead, he fantasized about what it would feel like to make love to a woman, but he still couldn't imagine being so intimate with a stranger.

The streets were crowded tonight. That was how Jesse knew the weather must be warm and comfortable. He could hardly remember what it felt like to be cold or hot anymore. He wished he could smell the fresh air as he watched the people walking by. Yankees and Confederates in uniform were scattered on the streets here and there; some were real, dead soldiers and some were living people in costumes. Jesse was amazed at how seriously some of the reenactors took their duties as pretend soldiers. When a ghost opted to remain fully visible, as Jesse was now, it was hard to tell who was alive or dead. Jesse could usually tell a real soldier when he looked into his eyes and saw the weary, haunted look of someone who'd been wandering around for a century and a half.

Though most of the restless soldiers who still drifted through the streets and battlefields got along well or were at least civil to one another, there was one feud that had never died. Jesse's eyes narrowed when he spied his archenemy, Joel Casey of the 124th New York Infantry, walking toward them. Jesse hadn't seen him for quite some time and he'd been hoping the Yank had finally crossed over.

"YEEEEEEEEEEEOOOOOOOOOOOOWWWWWWWWWW!" Jesse let loose with a fierce Rebel Yell. He ignored the odd looks from tourists while he savored Joel's gut reaction of visible terror.

Jesse relished the way that sound still seemed to make Joel's blood run cold even though he no longer had blood in him. That sound was so frequently a prelude to slaughter on the battlefield that it wasn't something you ever forgot, no matter how long you existed.

"Good to see you, baby. Where you been?" Fillis asked,

greeting Joel far more warmly than his nemesis had. There was a hint of disappointment in her eyes, and Jesse knew she had also hoped he had crossed over. Fillis loved Joel as much as she loved Jesse. She had died in Gettysburg shortly before the battle and had witnessed the three-day ordeal as she wandered around in spirit form. She had a tender spot in her heart for all those boys who fought and died that day.

Ignoring Jesse, Joel smiled at Fillis. Joel was even more dashing in uniform than Jesse. He wore a dark blue, four-button wool coat and blue wool pants. He had light blond hair, and the color of his Yankee uniform set off the blue in his eyes, giving them a startlingly bright look. It was not uncommon for a woman to forget what she was saying when she turned and looked into those eyes.

"I just, you know, needed a break for a bit," Joel told her. Fillis nodded, understanding. It was not uncommon for a ghost to disappear for a time. *Vanishing* was what they called it. Vanishing was different than simply being invisible. Invisible meant you were still hanging around, but only other spirits could see you. Vanishing meant you were not conscious. It was kind of like a ghost's form of sleep. It would be simply unbearable to be endlessly conscious all night and all day for decades, even centuries, at a time. Spirits could fade away for a bit and then come back after they'd rested for a while.

Unless they crossed over to the other side. Then they didn't come back. Jesse had known many spirits who had crossed over. He'd actually seen it happen a couple of times. A bright portal appeared when you were ready to move on. Sometimes you could tell when someone's time was coming near. Jesse remembered a soldier who was eighteen years old, a baby really, when he died on the Wheatfield on the second day of the battle. A member of the famed Irish Brigade, his name was Daniel Sheehan. In the days leading up to his crossing over, he seemed calm, tranquil. Something in him had changed, and he was finally ready to go. Off in the distance on the same part of the battlefield where Daniel had died, Jesse saw the young boy's portal open, and then he was gone. He was a good kid. Jesse missed him.

Jesse wished a portal that led to the extreme Deep South would open up and swallow Joel, and he told him so. "Thought mebbe you'd finally gone down to hell where you belong," Jesse informed him, his strong Texas accent becoming even more pronounced when he was angry. Known as the Immortal Enemies, all the ghosts in Gettysburg knew that Joel and Jesse couldn't stand the sight of each other.

"Well, it wouldn't be hell without you there, Secesh," Joel said, shooting Jesse a steely glare.

"Boys..." Fillis admonished gently. She hated when they fought, which was constantly.

"Mudsill," Jesse muttered.

"Traitor!" Joel shot back. A few of the tourists stopped to watch, thinking their bickering was part of some reenactor show. Johnny Reb vs. Billy Yank. "Bunch of pansy-ass, stupid hicks. All of ya."

"My stupid hicks beat the tar out of your delicate lil' Orange Blossoms," Jesse said. Joel's regiment had been nick-named the Orange Blossoms because most of them came from Orange County, New York.

"Yeah?" Joel said, blue eyes blazing. He jerked his head toward an American flag that was flying just above his head at one of the souvenir shops. "Which *flag* do you see flying now?"

Jesse's reaction to the word "flag" was as pained and full

of horror as Joel's had been when he'd heard Jesse's eerie Rebel Yell.

"Joel!" Fillis said sharply, shooting him a warning look that said he'd gone too far. She quietly added, "That's enough out of both of you."

"Sorry, Fillis," the boys said in unison, like two brothers who were in trouble with Mom for fighting.

"Good to have you back, honey," Fillis told Joel. Jesse sneered at him, but stayed silent for Fillis's sake.

"Thanks, Second Mama. Missed you, too," Joel said. He took a seat next to her on the steps.

"See ya later, Fillis," Jesse said as he got up. He could only be civil with Joel for so long, so he figured it best to leave. Fillis's sad expression pained him, but he couldn't stand to be near that filthy Yank a moment longer. One of the worst things about being a ghost was that he couldn't punch Joel's lights out. That was the one thing the two soldiers could agree on. They would give just about anything to finally be able to beat the living—or dying—crap out of each other.

As Jesse wandered off down the street, he decided to vanish. He'd disappear for a short while, just until the next afternoon when he could see one of the few bright spots of his dreary existence.

His beloved Lucy Westbrook.

2

J esse drifted through the town of Gettysburg, slowly but not aimlessly. He was headed to pay a silent visit to the most beautiful woman he'd ever known. He had time, though, since Lucy's shift didn't start for another half hour.

Currently invisible, he was free to wander anywhere he liked. He watched the tourists and residents of the town as he glided. He suddenly stopped short when he caught sight of an older woman with her gray hair pulled back into a loose bun. A bolt of irrational hope coursed through him. *Mother.*

Jesse felt stupid as he watched the woman walk past him. Of course it wasn't his mother. She had to have died more than a hundred years ago, miles and miles away in Texas. Still, he was quite shaken up. The resemblance was so strong—at least from a distance.

Jesse pictured his loving mother with her gray hair pulled back, wearing a worn, cotton dress. She'd been weeping the last time he saw her. It was the summer of 1861 when he left for battle. Jesse was her only child. After he was born, she was never able to have another. His father was old and sick, and Jesse had always wondered how long the man had survived after Jesse left to fight for the Confederacy. The thought of his mother being left alone was unbearable.

Fortunately, there had been lots of cousins nearby to help with their small farm, but Jesse knew no one could replace him in his mother's heart. Even after all this time, Jesse missed his mama. Fresh guilt surged within him as he wondered for the millionth time if he'd made a mistake in joining the war effort, thus destroying his precious mother's whole world.

Jesse shook off the sad memories and tried to focus on happier thoughts, and there was no happier thought for him than lovely Lucy. She worked at Meade's Tavern, a bar and grill that Jesse had avoided for years, mostly due to its name and theme. Who needed to see artwork of General Meade and all those other Yanks all over the place? Then one day while he was drifting around the town, aimless and invisible, he had seen a group of fifth-graders climb out of their school bus. Jesse loved when kids came to visit Gettysburg. He loved the sound of their laughter and enjoyed watching them play, fight, and tease each other. Jesse followed them into the restaurant and sat in the back to watch them.

It made him smile to see them horsing around and shooting at each other with those little pop guns they sold around here. He never really minded when kids joked about the battle. It was only natural for them to be curious about the blood and guts of the war. However, it bothered him when the older, punk kids reveled in the especially gruesome stories of the fight. They eagerly told horrible tales of bodies blown apart by cannonballs and entrails splattered on the fences. Those kids didn't seem to understand that this wasn't some fictional horror movie. Those body parts were all that was left of somebody's child.

Jesse had sat, invisible, in the back of the restaurant. He noticed Lucy immediately. She was a pretty, petite girl in her mid-twenties. She had gentle, brown eyes and long, richly dark brown hair that flowed all the way down her back. Jesse loved the way she looked in her waitress uniform—a knee-length black skirt and white button-down blouse.

While the other servers whined about the kids and the mess they were sure to make, Lucy greeted them with a warm smile. Jesse was instantly smitten with her. It wasn't just that she was a pretty girl. It was more the way she interacted with the kids. She was calm and patient and seemed happy they were there. Jesse felt the same way about the children and had felt a familiar pain in his heart that day. The one that reminded him that he would never be a father.

Not all of Jesse's thoughts about Lucy were so pure. Since the day he first saw her, he regularly fantasized about making love to her right there on the wooden bartop. He imagined carrying her over there, laying her down, and climbing on top of her. In his fantasy, she wrapped her arms around him and cried out his name in pleasure.

Yeah, right.

Jesse didn't know the first thing about pleasing a woman. All he knew about sex was what he saw in those porn movies businessmen sometimes watched at the Days Inn across the street. Jesse couldn't imagine knowing how to make a woman scream like that. Not that it mattered. He wouldn't be able to touch Lucy even if she let him. His hands would go right through her, leaving only an icy feeling behind. Even if he were alive, he knew a smart, classy girl like her couldn't possibly be interested in an uneducated farm boy.

Already convinced she was wonderful moments after he laid eyes on her, he became even more enamored when she spoke about the war.

"So, if you'd fought in the Civil War, which side do you think you would have been on?" she asked the kids as she set down cups of ice water in front of each child. The kids answered excitedly.

"The good side!"

"The blue ones. The ones who fought with Abraham Lincoln."

"The Union side, cause they're the ones who were trying to stop slavery."

Lucy nodded. "I see. So you think the gray guys were bad guys?"

"Yeah, they were bad. They hated black people! They made them be slaves!"

"Well, it's true that some people in the South were mean to black people," Lucy told them. "But did you know that most of the soldiers who fought for the South were very poor and didn't own slaves? A lot of them felt like they were fighting to protect their homes and their families."

Jesse's ghostly heart melted as he listened to Lucy defend the Southern soldiers. That was a rarity, especially around these parts. Jesse felt like she was talking about him. How he had given his life for the South. For his home, his parents, his community.

The children's teacher, a woman in her late forties or so with slightly graying hair, smiled at Lucy. "Very impressive. It's nice to hear someone discuss history in less than black-and-white terms, no pun intended."

Lucy's smile broadened. "Thanks. I love history. I'm a

student at Gettysburg College. My major is Elementary Education."

"So you're going to be a teacher. Wonderful! I'm sure you'll make a great one."

Jesse smiled at the thought. She *would* be a wonderful teacher, though he could never have concentrated on the lessons if he were her student.

He had visited her at the tavern many times since that day. Watching her, fantasizing about her, made him forget his empty existence for a while. He watched her interactions with customers and would often follow her into the kitchen when she grabbed a quick study break. Sometimes he would sit right beside her. Lucy would shiver suddenly, not knowing why.

Jesse would have loved to have a chance to talk with her, but he didn't dare take that risk. If he did, it would only be a matter of time until she found out the truth. Though it was painful for him to be literally invisible to her, he couldn't bear the thought of her thinking of him as some kind of ghoul when she found out he was dead. It was better to watch her in secret. His fantasies of her were one of the only joys he had left anymore.

Jesse did have one real interaction with Lucy. He'd been people-watching with Fillis one night when a kid, maybe five or six years old and wearing a blue Union cap, walked by him.

"Oh, no! It's a Yankee!" Jesse had cried out in his thick Southern accent. "You can't git me!" he said, winking at the kid, basically telling him to shoot him. The kid giggled and aimed his little popgun at him. "Aggghhhhh!" Jesse cried, and fell flat on his back in a spectacular death right there on the pavement.

"Ha-ha, I got you!" The kid said in a singsong voice.

"You sure...did," Jesse said, groaning for effect as the kid giggled wildly.

When Jesse opened his eyes, he was horrified to find Lucy standing over him. At first, he felt like a complete fool in front of her, but then she graced him with a beautiful smile. She looked over at the kid, and then back at him. She laughed softly, and then offered her hand to help him up. A bolt of fear had shot straight through him.

"Oh, that's all right, Ma'am!" Jesse said as he jumped to his feet. He saluted her and she smiled at him again before turning and heading off to the tavern.

It always amazed him how physically strong emotions still were, even after death. He had felt electrified, completely lit up inside when she smiled at him. It was terribly tempting to try to speak to her again, but he couldn't do it. He couldn't bear the thought of her finding out the truth and then being afraid of him.

That was the thing about Lucy. She was absolutely petrified of ghosts.

Lucy was also quite sensitive to the paranormal. She often saw shadows out of the corner of her eye, visions of spirits that others failed to notice. Jesse knew she tried to convince herself that it was just her imagination, but it had happened too many times to ignore. Jesse always knew when she'd glimpsed a ghost, because she often went pale and her hands shook. He ached to comfort her, to ease her fears, but there was nothing he could do.

Lucy hated walking out on the streets of Gettysburg late at night after her shift when it was dark and silent. She always had someone walk her to her car after work. Jesse didn't like the idea of her walking out to her car by herself anyway. Lucy was terrified of ghosts, but they couldn't hurt her. It was the living she should worry about, and Jesse didn't think any woman should be walking around in a parking lot at night by herself.

Though there were plenty of male servers there who were willing to walk her out, they teased her mercilessly about her fear of ghosts. Like almost every building, store, and restaurant in Gettysburg, it was rumored that Meade's Tavern was haunted. Well, of course it was. There were ghosts and spirits everywhere.

Craig, one of the cooks, was a fairly good-looking guy in his twenties with brown hair, blue eyes, and a lady-killer smile. He loved toying with Lucy when it came to her ghost phobia. Jesse hated when Lucy's coworkers tried to scare her. With Craig, it seemed almost a form of flirting, which annoyed Jesse even more. Craig and some of the bartenders would often make the kitchen door squeak behind her when she thought she was alone as she cleaned up the main dining room after closing. Sometimes they would slowly tromp down the stairs when there was supposedly nobody up there. Lucy had caught on to their tricks a long time ago, but not before being frightened out of her wits several times.

It angered Jesse to watch those guys upset her, but there was nothing he could do to stop it. They were only teasing, and they seemed to genuinely like Lucy, but they had really scared her a few times, and Jesse didn't find it the least bit amusing. That was no way to treat a lady as far as he was concerned.

Now Jesse sat in the back, lost in his memories of when he first saw Lucy. When she arrived at work, his mind wandered to his favorite sex-on-top-of-the-bar fantasy. As always, she looked so pretty in her waitress uniform. Jesse could practically feel his heart pounding when he saw her. It felt so real, like he still had a physical heart that actually pumped blood faster when she was near. He loved the way she made him feel. Sometimes, when she happened to glance at the back of the room where he sat, he could pretend she could see him. He wished so much that he could talk to her again. So far, *"Oh, that's all right, Ma'am!"* were the only words he had ever spoken to her.

Jesse was disappointed that Lucy never seemed to sense that he was near. He reasoned it was because he didn't move around too much; he just sat quietly and watched her. It was probably for the best. If she sensed him, she might be frightened by his presence and he wouldn't be able to watch her anymore.

Jesse watched her all during her shift. It was Saturday, so the place was busy. He felt badly that she had to work so hard. It must be tough to work and be a college student. She shared an apartment nearby with her best friend, Theresa Hetty. Theresa was a friendly, outgoing girl with pretty strawberry-blonde hair and light blue eyes. Jesse had seen her in the restaurant a few times, and he was fond of her because she was a loyal friend to Lucy. All Jesse knew about Lucy was what he could learn from her conversations here at Meade's Tavern. Sometimes he wished he could follow her home to her apartment, but it was too far away.

He had tried. Many times. Each time Jesse had wandered outside of the town of Gettysburg, he would simply vanish in the same way he did when he needed a break like the one Joel recently took. It was probably a good thing that he couldn't go that far. Jesse knew it would be terrible of him to follow Lucy to her private home. Not that he would *ever* violate her by watching her changing her clothes or anything like that. It was one thing to watch her, unseen, here in the restaurant when there were lots of people around. It would be quite another to watch her when she was alone in her own home.

Jesse knew that Lucy had earned a scholarship to school and her parents paid for the rest, but she had to work so she could afford the apartment she shared with Theresa. He felt terrible, watching her work so hard on her feet for hours and hours. It felt so unnatural to watch a woman work while he just sat there. His manners as a gentleman dictated he should help, but he couldn't do a thing.

It was getting late, and the bar was nearly empty at closing time. Jesse watched Lucy with concern as she helped wrap up the last tabs for the remaining customers, then locked the front door. This was the part of the night that she hated the most. When the place was empty, dark, and silent. She didn't need her coworkers to frighten her; she was already scared. Jesse could see it in her eyes. She usually wound up tidying the dining rooms by herself, while the manager wrapped up the receipts in her office and Craig cleaned the kitchen. Every creak, every noise startled her. There was no escaping ghost stories around here. There were dozens of ghost tours out on the streets on a nightly basis, and not a day went by when customers didn't ask if she'd ever seen a ghost.

"No, I haven't," Lucy always told them with a smile. "But I know a lot of people who have." That was her stock answer —a better one than just telling them no. That way they weren't too disappointed. Jesse knew Lucy didn't want to admit to herself that she had caught glimpses of spirits. She didn't want to believe ghosts were real.

Lucy scanned the room, looking for the dustpan that went with the broom in her hand. She spied it on the floor in the back of the room. Without giving Jesse enough warning that she was coming his way, she walked right through him.

A sudden, frigid chill went through her as she walked through Jesse. She gasped and rubbed her shoulders.

Still invisible, Jesse froze. He hoped to God he hadn't frightened her. Everyone had heard stories about feeling a chill when ghosts were near. She paused for a moment, then shrugged off the chill and continued her work.

Jesse narrowed his eyes and glared at the slightly cracked-open kitchen door where he saw Craig and a teenage busboy named Brayden watching Lucy. They were plotting something. They watched as Lucy picked up a beer glass from a table and set it on the bar. Then she left the room and went into the other dining area with her broom and dustpan.

Snickering, Brayden snuck into the dining room.

"Just put it back exactly where it was before!" Craig whispered from behind the kitchen door. Brayden grabbed the glass from the bar and put it back on the table where it had been before Lucy moved it. "Hurry up!" Brayden rushed back into the kitchen, and the two idiots stayed there, waiting for Lucy's reaction.

Jesse's ghostly hands clenched in fury. Lucy was such a sweet girl, and he couldn't understand their need to torture her. Jesse had half a mind to scare the hell out of those two bastards. It wouldn't be hard. They were so damned cocky, convinced there was no such thing as ghosts; it would be nothing for Jesse to simply appear right in front of them. He'd growl at them like a monster, and they'd likely piss themselves. It would be glorious. Trouble was, there was really no way to do that without terrorizing Lucy in the process. She would know by their panicked reaction that they weren't making it up this time.

Jesse stared at the glass on the table. If only he could move it back to the bar. It was technically *possible* for him to do it, but it was extremely difficult. It took a great deal of concentration for a ghost to move or touch anything, and it left a spirit very weak afterward. The weakness was no big deal. It simply meant he wouldn't have the strength to appear visible for a short while. The annoying thing was, the angrier and meaner a spirit was, the stronger he was. If Jesse were a complete jerk, he would be able to overturn tables in the restaurant. But like most spirits that still haunted Gettysburg, he was sad, lonely, and tired of existing. That kind of attitude would never get the job done. Still, if it could keep Lucy from being scared, it was worth a shot.

Jesse walked over to the table where the glass sat. He closed his eyes and gathered all the strength he could muster. He concentrated, visualizing himself carefully picking up the glass with both hands and somehow getting it all the way to the bar where Lucy had placed it. He opened his eyes to see what he was doing and reached for the glass. A thrill shot through him as he was able to make physical contact. He could actually feel the coolness of the glass. Jesse slowly yet firmly grasped it and lifted it from the table.

He prayed to God that Lucy wouldn't come in and see the glass hovering by itself in midair. Holding it with both hands, he methodically turned and began to walk toward the bar.

Jesse didn't even realize he had dropped the damn thing until he heard the glass shatter when it hit the hard, wooden floor. The sound of breaking glass would have barely registered if it was midday and the place was full, but in the still of the night, it rang out like a gunshot.

Great, he thought as he surveyed the shards of glass, which Lucy would now have to clean up.

Simultaneously, Craig and Brayden walked into the dining room from the kitchen and Lucy came in from the other room. Lucy walked around, looking at the ground for the source of the crash. Jesse watched her carefully, his heart sinking as he waited for her terrified expression when she saw the glass. She spied it, and then looked up at Craig with annoyance.

"It-it-it wasn't me!" Craig sputtered, staring at the glass on the ground.

"Mmm-hmm. Of course it wasn't," Lucy said. "Nice try, boys." She sighed, and then got to work cleaning up the mess.

Craig and Brayden stared at each other. They looked around the room, searching for a reasonable explanation for what just happened. They couldn't find one, and they exchanged uneasy looks. Jesse grinned. It wasn't the terror he would have liked to see, but at least he had managed to frighten the boys while leaving Lucy unscathed.

Lucy continued her work, and Jesse again wished he could help her. He also wished there was someone other than Craig who could walk her to her car at night. Craig was big and strong and could protect her in case someone tried to rob her—or worse—but Lucy deserved someone who would be more sensitive to her feelings. If it were Jesse, he would walk close to her and talk to her on the way to the parking lot. He knew the deadly silence of the streets near where thousands of people died unnerved her in the middle of the night, so his chatter would have kept her from feeling afraid. But no. All she had was that jackass Craig.

Then again, it would be terribly painful for Jesse to watch if Lucy did have the kind of boyfriend she deserved.

Jesse wanted her to be happy, but if she started dating someone, he would have to stop hanging around Meade's Tavern. There was no way he could handle watching her with another man. The idea of her kissing someone else made his heart feel like it would rip in two. He knew he was being selfish. Just because he was forced to be alone, that didn't mean Lucy had to be. He couldn't possibly be with her, so he knew he should hope and pray that she would find someone wonderful to be with.

Still, there was no way anyone else could possibly love her as much as he did.

3

Like so many other dead soldiers, Joel Casey frequently tortured himself by visiting the place of his death. After vanishing for a while, he knew it was time for him to head back to Devil's Den.

He visited at daybreak. At that hour, it was peaceful and there were few visitors. Aside from the occasional jogger, Joel was alone. As always, his thoughts turned to the horrific violence of that first weekend in July of 1863. Some soldiers, like Jesse, stayed away from the place where they died. Others, like Joel, were drawn to the bloody fields where they took their last breath.

Invisible to the living, Joel sat on one of the rocks in Devil's Den. He recalled so clearly the day those rocks dripped with blood.

He thought back to the days at camp, when they were all rudely awakened by the sound of the bugle far too early in the morning. And the drills. Oh, lord, the drills. It was a wonder they didn't march in their sleep. It wasn't all hard work, though. War was very much a "hurry up and wait" affair, with flurries of frenetic activity followed by lots of downtime.

Joel had been lucky that his best friend from childhood, Charles Clearwater, had volunteered for the 124th Infantry. The two, known as "the brothers" in camp, were inseparable. It was not uncommon for someone to ask Joel to "tell your brother to shut up. I'm trying to sleep!" as Charles had a habit of singing constantly. In the evenings around the campfire, his loud and jolly voice was welcome, as it often reduced the soldiers to uncontrollable fits of laughter. Charles had a tendency to sing about things that would make even the most hardened soldier blush. He also led the troops in boisterous patriotic songs, which helped raise their spirits when they needed it most.

Joel and Charles were like brothers in every way. They teased and harassed one another, and they shared the same competitive streak. On long days in camp when the soldiers would organize a baseball game, the two always played on opposite sides. They spent the long nights gambling, and it was not uncommon for one of them to lose his shirt—literally—to the other when they played poker.

Most importantly, they kept each other sane when the fighting got intense. Chancellorsville had been particularly horrific. They had lost many friends that day, and the ferocity of that battle had been a shock to all of them. They had witnessed fellow soldiers, who had been singing and laughing with them just days before, literally blown apart before their eyes. Only those who had lived through the horror could possibly understand, and it had solidified their brotherly bond all the more.

Then came the battle of Gettysburg. Now Joel sat, transfixed in the early hours of the morning, staring at the rocks where they had faced the bloodiest fighting yet. In addition to horrifying cannon fire and the hail of distant bullets, there was a lot of hand-to-hand combat that day. Dear God, you could see the faces of the men you killed. Joel could still see them. He and Charles had fought side-by-side, doing their best to stay together during the battle. The cannon smoke was so dense and the din of the bursting shells so loud it was difficult to see and hear one another. Yet they had somehow stayed close right up until the end.

The color bearer of the 124th New York Infantry was shot down right in front of Joel. It was horrible, but no surprise. Color bearer was a suicide mission. Carrying that huge regimental flag, you were a moving target to the enemy who would love nothing more than to capture and destroy the flag. It was like a macabre version of a childhood game. One that ended in death.

Joel had managed to catch the flag of the 124th New York before it hit the ground. He remembered the surge of adrenaline and raw fear that had charged through his body. A war raged within him. *I don't want to lose our flag, but I don't want to die.* He had grabbed the flag and held it high as the smoke thickened around him. Through all the noise and confusion surrounding them, Charles somehow managed to catch Joel's eye and grinned at him, giving him the strength to carry on.

When the smoke finally thinned, Joel and Charles found themselves face-to-face with a line of Rebels. Fighting hand-to-hand, their bayonets were so close they could have been impaled with one jab. A fellow soldier took several bullets to his back and slammed into Charles as he fell dead to the ground. The impact had knocked the musket out of Charles's hand. With a panicked look, Charles raised his hands in surrender.

And that goddamned, twisted, sick Rebel soldier looked

Charles right in the eye and rammed his bayonet straight through him. Joel watched helplessly as his childhood friend was gutted right beside him.

In that moment, he saw not the twenty-five-year old man before him, but the face of twelve-year-old Charles. The one who had "died" a hundred times as they played cowboys and Indians.

Joel had been filled with a primal rage and sorrow he could never have imagined possible. War sends a man's emotions into overdrive, to heights the civilian man could not possibly understand. His eyes blazed with fury and his body surged with adrenaline. Joel looked into the Rebel's eyes, then aimed his musket and shot him in the head. He watched the man fall to the ground, and then looked over at Charles lying dead right next to him.

How will I survive the rest of this war without him?

As it turned out, Joel would only live for a few more hours. The end was mercifully quick. He was blown apart by a cannonball, shot from a distance. He was still holding his regiment's flag.

When Joel could no longer bear the horror of his battlefield memories, he allowed his mind to drift to far better times. Memories of his wife, Emma. Even after a century and a half, he remembered her face as if he had seen it yesterday. Her warm yet mischievous blue-green eyes, her long honey-blonde hair. Joel stared out at the battlefield, but instead of the grass and rocks, in his mind's eye he was reliving his time with Emma. Time that had been cut so short.

Joel thought about his days working as an apprentice in the shoemaker's shop that Emma's father had owned. Richard Arlow had liked Joel right away because he was a hard worker. Emma Arlow was just eighteen years old when

Joel first laid eyes on her. When she visited the shop the first time, Joel felt like he already knew her. Richard had spoken at length about his wonderful, virtuous daughter. He had three sons, too, but it was clear that his sweet Emma, the baby of the family, was the apple of his eye.

Emma was indeed virtuous, but she had a flirtatious streak, which showed when her father wasn't around.

"You're quite a handsome man, Joel Casey," she informed him the moment Richard had stepped out of the room. "Such pretty blue eyes."

Joel, who was hardly pure and virtuous, found himself blushing and stammering. "Th-thank you, Miss." She had laughed softly, and seemed amused that she had flustered him.

Emma was constantly catching Joel's eye whenever her father had his back turned. It thrilled him that she found him attractive, and her boldness aroused him. He adored her combination of sweet yet sexy.

Joel was desperate to be with her, but he was terrified of what his boss might think of him courting his beloved princess. One day, he finally got the nerve to ask Richard if Emma had a suitor. Joel knew she didn't, but he figured it was a subtle way to let her father know that he was interested in her.

Richard had broken into a huge grin and said, "Son, I thought you were never going to ask."

Joel eagerly courted her, and they fell in love quickly. No woman had ever made him feel the way she did. Emma loved to read and learn, and he found her intelligence alluring. She lit a fire within him; his entire body tingled with desire whenever he saw her. She was determined to remain n a virgin until marriage, mostly in deference to her loving father. Even so, she made it clear that she desired Joel as much as he did her. They talked at length in private about how much they were looking forward to their wedding night.

They waited to get married until Joel had saved enough money to get a small house for them in New York, not too far from her family's home. The wedding had been lovely, and Emma had looked so beautiful—and so sexy—that Joel could hardly stand the wait anymore.

Finally, the time came for them to consummate their marriage. He eagerly carried her over the threshold and laid her down on the bed. Breathlessly, they tore at each other's clothes, expressing their feelings with "I love you" and "I need you." After waiting for so long, the explosion of pleasure Joel felt upon first entering her was beyond anything he had imagined...and he had imagined it *a lot*.

He'd had his eyes closed at first, and when he opened them he was horrified to see tears streaming down his beloved wife's face.

"Oh, my God. Am I hurting you?" Joel asked.

Emma nodded silently, the tears still coming.

"Oh, Emma," Joel whispered. "I'm so sorry." Charles had warned him that the first time could be painful for a woman. He'd reminded Joel that he would essentially be tearing something inside her, and that he should try to be gentle. How could he have been so careless?

Joel wiped the tears from Emma's face and very gently eased out of her. She began to weep openly.

"I'm sorry. I'm so sorry. After all this time...I've ruined it!" Emma said between sobs.

"Emma! You didn't ruin anything. This is my fault. Entirely my fault. I should have realized..." Joel stroked her cheek gently. "We have time, my love. All the time in the world." Joel looked down at the bed sheets and saw that she had bled a little. A surge of guilt ripped through him as he couldn't help but feel disappointed. It had been so exciting to finally see Emma's beautiful, naked body and he was still quite aroused. He felt horrible for even thinking such a thing with Emma lying there in pain.

"You just rest. I'm going to get you some hot tea. I'll be right back!" He kissed her mouth gently and got up. She was still crying.

Joel quickly went to the outhouse, where he leaned against the wall and stroked himself until he found relief. He wanted to take care of his wife, but he had been so aroused that he could hardly think straight. He sighed, slumping against the wall and catching his breath. He rushed back into the house to fetch the tea.

He found Emma the way he had left her, in bed, sobbing. Joel set the tea next to the bed and gathered her in his arms.

"Shhh, my love. Shhhh," Joel said, gently stroking her hair. "It won't hurt anymore. I won't ever hurt you again."

"You didn't...it's not your fault—" Emma argued.

"I love you, Emma. I love you." Joel grinned suddenly.

"What?"

"You're my *wife*!" Joel exclaimed, as giddy as a schoolboy. "Do you have any idea how wonderful that is? This is the happiest day of my entire life. I can hardly believe it. It's real. It's happened. I can't believe you married me, Emma Arlow!"

Emma smiled and said softly, "No. Emma *Casey*."

Joel's grin widened. "Of course. Mrs. Casey."

Joel took her in his arms, and he felt her relax. She was safe there. They held each other until they both fell asleep. Perhaps it wasn't the wedding night he had imagined, but it was still wonderful.

After allowing Emma some time to heal, they more than made up for the initial disappointment of their wedding night. They spent hours exploring each other's bodies and learning how to please each other. Joel loved that Emma enjoyed sex as much as he did. She loved pleasuring him, and nothing made him feel more like a man than when she cried out his name when they were making love.

It was no surprise when Emma got pregnant soon after they were married. She was a fairly small woman and had a low tolerance for pain, so childbirth had been difficult. The sound of her agonized cries tortured Joel, but he was proud of her for soldiering through it bravely. One of his favorite memories was the day the two of them wept together as they held their son for the very first time. Little David had Joel's piercing blue eyes, as did his little brother, Mathew, who arrived just two years later.

Joel's memories turned darker. He recalled the last time he and Emma had made love before he went off to war. It was a somber event, both knowing it could very well be their last time together. The only physical pain Joel could feel anymore was that familiar ache in his chest where his heart had been when he was alive. He still felt it every time he thought of the last time he had held Emma in his arms. Joel remembered stroking her hair as she tried her best to keep from breaking down in hysterics in front of their children, aged only four and six when he went off to war.

The sharp pain in his chest worsened as he thought of his precious little boys. He could still hear Mathew's voice. *Where are you going, Daddy? Where are you going?*

Joel jumped up from his perch on the hill. He simply could not bear these thoughts anymore. This horrible place where not only his body but his dreams and hopes for the future had been exploded by that cannonball.

4

Joel needed to find Fillis. She always knew what to say to make him feel better. They would sit and watch the tourist women walk by. They'd talk and laugh, and he would forget for a while. The memories would return, but he could shut them off when distracted by the living.

Still invisible for the moment, Joel walked—drifted, really—north. He headed toward the main part of the town of Gettysburg where there were likely to be lots of people walking around, shopping, grabbing lunch.

Joel's emotions still churned within him, but he started to calm down as he floated around Cemetery Hill and looked out onto the expanse of the open field. Many people had died there, but no one Joel had known personally, and he had not been on this field during the battle. It was still a somber place to visit, but it didn't wield the intense power over him that Devil's Den did.

It was always interesting to watch tourists as they surveyed the battlefields. Joel had seen pretty much every kind of reaction possible from them over the last 150 years.

He'd seen people crack jokes, break down sobbing, and fall asleep from boredom during the tours. He'd witnessed drunk teenagers daring each other to venture onto the fields after dark, hoping to catch a glimpse of a ghost. He understood their fascination with death, but Joel despised the idea of people being afraid of him. He'd never wanted to be the ghost of a Civil War soldier. He'd just wanted to be Joel Casey. Emma's husband. David and Mathew's daddy.

One of the rarest, most bizarre reactions he'd seen had happened only a few times over the years. Someone would actually feel the battle wounds of a soldier. It never caused any lasting physical damage, but the pain was quite real. It seemed to happen to people who were particularly sensitive, the ones who could sometimes sense Joel's presence even when he was invisible. Joel remembered one young man who had cried out in agony and collapsed on Culp's Hill, terrifying his poor family. Just a few minutes before, the family had been talking about how they had a relative who fought on Culp's Hill and probably died somewhere close to where they were standing. They thought he was suffering some kind of life-threatening emergency, and Joel had wished like hell that he could comfort them and explain that everything was going to be fine.

Joel figured it was a combination of events that caused a person to experience the death wounds of a soldier. The victim had to be fairly sensitive to paranormal things, have some kind of connection to the person who died, and happen to be on the battlefield at the exact time of day the soldier had been killed.

It was a peaceful day on Cemetery Hill, and the tourists wandering around were mostly quiet and respectful. Joel was angry and depressed after spending the morning torturing himself with memories, and he needed a quiet walk to help him calm down and clear his head.

What he didn't need was to run into Jesse Spenser.

IT WAS inevitable that Joel and Jesse saw each other often. After all, they were both eternally trapped in a small town they couldn't escape. For the most part, they either ignored each other or fired off a few insults as they passed, but not today. "Son of a bitch..." Joel muttered as he saw Jesse walking toward him.

"The pleasure's all mine, Yankee Doodle," Jesse said, looking equally thrilled to see him. He was already in a foul mood because he'd gone to see Lucy only to find she'd switched shifts with someone and had the day off.

"Why the hell are you always in my face, you stupid hick?"

"Oh, you own this town now?" Jesse fired back.

"I got more right to be here than you do, Secesh. This is my country, not yours. You're the one who hates America."

"Oh shut up, you Yankee slime," Jesse drawled. "You folks up North just don't git it and you never will. All you care about up there is makin' money."

"You're right. It's much better to make poor black folks do all your precious farm work for you."

"You know goddamn well I never fought against no black folk!" Jesse said, his voice rising. "You think I'd have made somebody like Fillis work for me? I never did nothing like that and never would!"

"You leave Fillis out of this!" Joel roared back.

"She's the one I was looking for anyway. Not you. So get the hell out of my face, Bluebelly!" Jesse yelled.

"I'm looking for her, too, so why don't you get the fuck out of my face!" Joel screamed back.

"It's so quiet, so peaceful out here on the battlefield," a tourist woman in her sixties remarked to her husband as they looked out over Cemetery Hill. They had no idea that two invisible Civil War soldiers were engaged in a shouting match right beside them. Those two tourists were clearly not the "sensitive to paranormal" types.

The soldiers stared at each other, seething. It was the ultimate in frustrating cruelty that they were unable to beat the shit out of each other. A conversation like this should have ended in an all-out brawl, with both boys landing punch after punch until only one of them was standing. It wasn't physically possible, and it drove them both almost to the brink of madness.

"You ain't nothin' but a kid-glove boy," Jesse said. They were so engrossed in dredging up the past that they lapsed back into 1860s language, forgoing modern speech in the heat of the moment.

"At least I'm not a cold-blooded murderer!" Joel said, getting right in Jesse's face.

"What was your part of the war effort? Sewin' dresses and writin' poems? You killed plenty of folks!"

"Not while they were surrendering, you heartless bastard!"

"*He was not surrendering!*" Jesse hollered. They'd had this damned conversation hundreds of times since they'd died. Joel swore that Charles had his hands up in surrender when Jesse had killed him, and Jesse swore that he hadn't. It was possible that Charles had tried to surrender and Jesse couldn't tell due to the thick cannon smoke and the deafening roar of battle. Jesse did not enjoy killing people and would never have hurt anyone unless he felt he absolutely had to, but Joel would never see him as anyone but the monster who killed his best friend.

"Screw you. I'm going to find Second Mama," Joel said.

"So am I!"

And that was how they found themselves both stalking toward the main street of Gettysburg where they were sure to find their adopted mother. She tended to stay around that same area, so her boys would always know where to find her.

"Oh, lord..." Fillis muttered as she saw Joel and Jesse storming toward her.

"Hey, Fillis," Joel said, ignoring Jesse.

Fillis studied the look on Joel's face. "You been to the Den again, haven't you? Baby, why you do that to yourself?" she asked gently.

Joel shrugged. "What else is there to do around here?"

"Here. Come sit next to me," she said, as she gestured to the sidewalk next to her. The three were invisible, and since they didn't feel anything physical, sitting down was more a habit than a necessity. If you wanted to blend in among the living, you had to learn to act the part, and it was just easier to be consistent even when people couldn't see you.

Joel took a seat next to Fillis while Jesse just stood there, glaring.

"Come on, now. You, too," Fillis said, gesturing to the other side of her. "Joel won't bite. Well, mebbe he would, but he can't. So sit."

Still glaring at Joel, Jesse took a seat on the other side of Fillis. He crossed his arms, looking like a toddler in the midst of a tantrum. Fillis chuckled softly, and then turned to Joel.

"You all right?"

"Yeah. Yeah, I'm fine."

"Let's see what the view is like today!" she said brightly. "Slim pickins so far, let me tell you."

That wasn't surprising. It was afternoon on a weekday, which meant most of the people on the streets were retired folks out touring the battlefields or people who worked at local businesses. If you wanted to see more interesting people, specifically attractive women, your best bet was Friday and Saturday night. If the weather was nice, there were lots of people at the taverns and walking out on the streets.

"Bo-ring," Fillis sang as they watched the thin crowd of mostly men.

All three heads turned when a tall, leggy woman in shiny black pumps and a short skirt walked briskly by before disappearing into an attorney's office.

"Mmmm, that's a little better," Joel said, making Fillis smile.

"Yeah, like you'd ever be able to get a woman like that," Jesse said.

"And you could, Romeo of the backwoods? Doubt you saw much action from the ladies back in the day," Joel said.

Jesse couldn't imagine how merciless Joel would be if he knew Jesse was a virgin. He figured Joel had quite a history with women. Bastard.

"Oh, and you did?" Jesse said, hating that he couldn't think of anything more clever to say.

"Well, my wife was beautiful, that's for sure."

"Yeah, right. I bet she was a troll," Jesse shot back.

Joel's eyes grew stormy, but Fillis beat him to the punch.

"Jesse!" she said sharply. "You leave Emma out of this."

"Yes, ma'am," Jesse said, suitably chastened. It was unlike him to say something nasty, especially about a woman, but Joel brought out the worst in him. He was a gentleman, and he knew better than to say something insulting about another man's wife. Even if that man was Joel.

"I'm sure she was lovely," Jesse said, offering an olive branch. "Far too good for you, I'm sure."

Joel's expression softened. "Well, that's something we can agree on." There was an intense sorrow about him when he spoke of Emma, and Jesse felt his anger ease a bit. As much as he despised Joel, Jesse knew precious little about him. He did know that Joel was fiercely devoted to his wife. Everybody around here knew that.

"Well, you just got lucky then. No way could you get a hot girl like that one," Jesse said, jerking his head toward where the sexy lady had been. Though he felt bad about what he had said about Emma, he felt defensive about his own inexperience and, as usual, was spoiling for a fight with Joel.

"Oh yeah? Care to put a wager on that, cowboy?" Joel said, eyes narrowing.

"Sure, let's make a bet," Jesse scoffed. "I bet you can't possibly get a woman to have sex with you. Because it's not humanly possible, you dumbass!"

"Of course it's not. We can still talk to girls, you know. I bet you I can get any random woman to say she'd choose me over you."

"Bet what? What could you possibly have to give me when you lose?"

Joel fell silent for a moment. Jesse had a point. They were spirits. What could they possibly bet? "There must be something we could do. I know damn well I'd win. No question."

"Fine. We *will* make a wager then!" Jesse said, his voice

rising. He would give anything to win a bet like that with Joel, but he wasn't at all sure he could do it. What girl would prefer a raggedly old farmhand to a dashing Union soldier? Everybody around here thought the blue men were the good guys. Oh, but if he did win...he'd make sure Joel never heard the end of it. Jesse's eyes lit up. "I know exactly what we can bet!"

"What?" Joel asked, eager to hear the challenge.

"If I get a girl to say that she would pick me over you, you have to stand in the middle of Lincoln Square—*fully visible*—and sing 'Dixie.'"

Fillis chuckled. "That's a great idea."

"And when I win, which I will, then *you* have to sing 'The Battle Hymn of the Republic,'" Joel said, jabbing a finger at Jesse.

"Fine. But only if I can sing it like Elvis," Jesse said.

Fillis laughed again. "I believe I'd like to see that."

"Too bad, Second Mama. You won't get to hear it because I'm gonna win!" Jesse said, suddenly filled with determination. He would beat Joel if it killed him, never mind the fact he was already dead. "And I get to pick the girl."

"The hell you do! You'll pick some woman in a rebel flag bikini."

"Damn, that would be pretty hot..." Jesse said. "Well, I'm not letting you pick!"

Jesse and Joel turned to Fillis.

"Oh hell, no. I'm not gettin' involved in this."

"Now what? We flip a coin?" Joel said.

A coin toss was pretty much impossible. One of them might be able to summon the strength to momentarily pick up a coin, but having the coordination to be able to hold it and flip it was highly unlikely.

"We don't have to flip it," Jesse said. "All's we gotta do is find a coin on the ground. Won't be hard around here."

Joel nodded. With people traipsing up and down the streets day and night, there were bound to be coins on the ground. "Heads I win, tails you lose."

It took Jesse a moment to process Joel's statement. Then he said, "Nice try. If it's heads, I pick the girl. Tails you do."

"Fine!"

Fillis shook her head as the boys walked away, searching the ground for coins like little kids looking for treasure.

"Hey, no fair goin' so far ahead!" Jesse called out to Joel.

"What do you care where I am?" Joel asked.

"Cause the deal is we go with the first coin we find. If you find one heads up, you ain't gonna say nuthin'. Git back here!"

Grumbling, Joel floated back to where Jesse was and came to a halt right in front of him. "Happy now?"

"Delighted," Jesse said. They walked together, practically shoulder-to-shoulder to ensure no cheating. "There! Heads up! Hah!"

Joel groaned as he looked at the shiny coin, heads up, on the ground. "Oh, and look who it is!" he taunted. It was a penny, so it was Lincoln's face looking up at them. Jesse stomped his foot down on the former president's face. Of course, the penny was no worse for the wear as Jesse's ghostly shoe went right through it.

"So go pick somebody already!" Joel said irritably.

Jesse was elated to finally beat Joel at something, even if it was just a silly coin toss. He couldn't imagine what it would be like to hear a woman say *I choose Jesse* right in front of Joel's damned, smug face.

"Gimme time. I got to think about it!" Jesse said. He did have some serious thinking to do. The question before him was obvious—Lucy or not Lucy? Joel didn't have any idea who she was, so he wouldn't argue if Jesse "randomly" chose her for their bet.

However, if they did involve Lucy in their bet, he would get a chance to talk to her. He felt like a schoolboy with a crush. What he wouldn't give for her to look him in the eye and say his name *just once!* Jesse was so much in love with her. Was it too much to ask for her to know who he was?

But what if she picked Joel?

Jesse couldn't imagine how crushed he would be if she chose his most hated enemy over him. Joel would never let Jesse hear the end of it. He'd taunt him endlessly even though he didn't know that Jesse loved her. Jesse would never be able to look at her again without remembering that she had rejected him. One of the only things that made his current "life" bearable was his fantasy. The one where he was her hero. The place in his vivid imagination where he held her and kissed her and made passionate love to her. If she chose Joel, he would have nothing to get him through his otherwise meaningless existence.

"I'll pick somebody tomorrow," Jesse said in true, Scarlett O'Hara fashion.

5

"So pick somebody already," Joel said gruffly. He and Jesse were sitting outside Meade's Tavern watching people go by. It was no coincidence that Jesse told Joel to meet him here around ten a.m. when Lucy was due to arrive for her shift.

However, after much internal angst and debate, he had decided not to choose her. He could never expect her to return his love, even if he were alive, but the thought of her being scared of him was enough to keep him from ever speaking to her. It was best to leave things as they were—lonely, unrequited, but with the fantasy still alive.

Then he spotted Lucy walking toward them. His ghostly heart swelled as he watched her long, brown hair blowing in the breeze.

"Her," Jesse blurted out, instantly forgetting his resolve to choose someone else. Watching the love of his life walk toward him, he knew he would never be able to court any other woman. Sure, he flirted harmlessly with tourists, knowing full well they would continue on their way and he would never see them again. This was different. He found he simply could not turn down the chance to talk to her. A thrill went through him when he imagined her pretty brown eyes looking right at him instead of through him.

Joel looked her up and down as she headed toward them. "She's cute," he said.

She's not cute. She's the most beautiful woman in the world, Jesse thought. He knew Joel's assessment was probably more accurate. She probably wasn't traffic-stoppingly beautiful to everyone, but she was to Jesse.

Before Jesse knew what was happening, Joel got up and headed straight toward her. Jesse hadn't expected him to take the lead. He hadn't thought about how this whole thing was going to work. Lucy would probably think they were crazy. One thing was for sure—Jesse had to put on his best poker face. He didn't want to tip his hand to Joel that he knew Lucy, and he also needed to hide his feelings from her. He was used to being invisible, when he could stare at her as dreamy-eyed as he liked. It would be hard, but he had to act as if he were meeting her for the first time.

Joel headed her off just before she went into the tavern. "Excuse me, Miss?"

Lucy turned, and a surge of excitement shot through Jesse.

"Yes?" she asked.

"Can I ask you a question?" Joel asked her.

Lucy glanced down at his uniform and then looked back up at his face. She looked into his eyes just a moment too long, and then nervously pushed her hair behind her ear. She clearly found him attractive and was flustered.

Jesse's heart sank as he realized he had made a huge mistake by choosing Lucy. There was no way he could compete with Joel. Broad-shouldered, blue-eyed, Union soldier Joel. He looked so strong and masculine. Jesse was just as tall and broad-shouldered, but much skinnier. Food had been scarce for many of the Southern soldiers, and Jesse had been underweight when he died. They were both weak as kittens since they were ghosts, but there was no way for Lucy to know that. It would be agony for Jesse when she chose Joel, and there was nothing he could do to stop it from happening.

Jesse wanted to run and hide so Lucy would never see him. His uniform was rough and worn, not like the crisp blue Yankee ones. There was a reason his regiment, the First Texas, was known as the Ragged Old First. His fellow soldiers were strong and brave, but they were also poor and hungry. It was obvious that Lucy found Joel strikingly hand-some. Jesse dreaded to see the look on her face when she finally turned to look at him.

"Between the two of us..." Joel pointed at Jesse, and Lucy finally turned to look at him. She looked at Jesse curiously. She looked down at his uniform and then back into his face the same way she had with Joel. Only this time, she didn't exactly look like she was about to swoon.

Jesse was devastated. She had looked at him like he was some kind of scientific curiosity. The best he could hope for now was that she would pick Joel quickly and get it over with. It would never be over, though, because Joel would never let him forget it.

"Which one of us would you choose?"

"What? What do you mean?" Lucy asked, understand-ably perplexed.

"Me and my...*friend*...here have a bet. We decided to pick a girl at random and ask which one of us she would choose. So, between the two of us," Joel said, practically batting those blues eyes of his, "who would you pick?"

"Why me? Why did you pick me?" Lucy asked uncertainly, as if she expected the two men to start laughing at her at any moment.

"We just decided to pick the prettiest girl we could find!" Joel said, turning on the charm.

Lucy looked uneasy and asked softly, "Is this some kind of joke?"

Oh, God. Jesse thought. *She thinks we're making fun of her.* He should have anticipated that. He was never sure why, but Lucy never believed it when a man told her she was pretty. She always looked uncomfortable and slightly afraid, like she feared she was being mocked.

"Oh," Joel said gently. "You're one of those girls who's pretty but doesn't know it."

I could've told you that, Jesse thought. Lucy never noticed when men checked her out, which was frequently. Jesse noticed. He shot daggers at any guy eying her up, even though they couldn't see him.

"No, ma'am," Jesse said, finally finding his voice. "No joke. It's jus' a silly bet between my friend and me."

Lucy looked at him curiously again. "You look so familiar. Where do I know you from?"

Sudden panic gripped Jesse. He'd hadn't forgotten to go invisible on one of those days when he'd spent hours staring at her, had he?

Her face broke into a soft smile. "I remember now. I saw you get shot by a junior Yankee."

Jesse stared at her a moment, before smiling warmly back. "Sounds like me," he said. *I can't believe she remembered.*

"Wait a minute," Joel said suspiciously. "You guys know each other?"

"No, no," Lucy said. "I just saw him once on the street."

Maybe they didn't technically know each other, but Lucy

was clearly charmed by the memory of him playing with a little kid.

Jesse relished the way Lucy looked at him. He had been nervous talking to her, but she had a way about her that put him at ease. Like even if he said something stupid, she wouldn't think less of him. He knew Lucy was much smarter and more educated than he was, but she didn't make him feel inferior. She looked at him like he was someone of worth. It was a relief to not feel invisible for once.

"So what tour group are you guys with?" Lucy asked Jesse.

"Ah-ah..." Jesse stammered. If he still had blood in his body, he would have blushed. He was caught completely off guard by her question. He hadn't thought to make up a backstory.

"Not a tour group," Joel answered with confidence. "We work at the reenactor store down the street. The Regimental Quartermaster."

Lucy nodded, and Joel smirked at Jesse. Jesse knew he looked like an idiot who didn't know where he worked, while Joel came across smooth and suave.

"I'm Lucy Westbrook, by the way."

Jesse smiled and touched near the tip of his hat and bowed slightly. "Private Jesse Spenser of the First Texas Infantry." It drove him *crazy* that he couldn't remove his hat in the presence of a lady. Appearing to tip his hat and bow was the best he could do with his ghostly body to show the proper respect.

Lucy laughed. "Well, I'm very pleased to meet you, Private Spenser," she said, playing along. Or so she thought.

"I'm Joel Casey of the 124th New York," Joel said, saluting. Offering a salute was his way of avoiding a handshake. "You know, the guys who actually *won* the war."

Lucy laughed again, and Joel grinned at her.

"Oh, quit braggin', Yankee Doodle," Jesse said with annoyance.

"Screw you, Secesh!"

Lucy blinked, and then looked at them both curiously. "Wow, you guys are hardcore."

"You have no idea," Joel said, glaring at Jesse.

"So. Which one of us would you choose?" Joel asked her.

Both Jesse and Joel looked at Lucy, and she blushed and looked down. Jesse felt a surge of protectiveness toward her. He knew how shy she was, and that she wasn't used to male attention. She still seemed worried that this might be a mean joke at her expense. How could she not realize how attractive she was?

Lucy looked up again, glancing first at Joel, then at Jesse. Her face didn't betray any preference, though both boys scrutinized her expression. "I can't choose just by looking at you!"

Thank God for that, Jesse thought.

"Sorry, but I really have to get to work," Lucy said, looking over at the tavern.

"But we have to know your answer!" Joel said, offering her a winning smile.

She smiled back. "Maybe tomorrow." She turned to smile at Jesse, too, before she headed into work.

Lucy walked away, shaking her head slightly. She really wasn't sure who to choose. She found them both entertaining, especially seeing how into "character" they both were as they acted the parts of soldiers. Joel was, without question, the better looking of the two. He was breathtakingly, kneeweakeningly handsome, but there was something alluring about Jesse, too. He had a kind smile and he exuded a sense of warmth and affection. Lucy liked the way he looked at her. She felt so plain next to Joel, but Jesse made her feel beautiful somehow. His accent was adorable, although it was probably just part of his Confederate soldier act.

They were both charmers, that was for sure. They seemed nice. She needed to stop assuming the worst when cute guys spoke to her. She used to be an ugly duckling; scrawny, dorky, with glasses. She'd been bullied a lot growing up, and she still felt like that awkward girl. Though she didn't exactly have men falling at her feet, she had to remember they weren't necessarily making fun of her when they approached. This wasn't high school anymore. Not everybody was out to hurt her.

6

"She's nice," Joel said. He watched Lucy walk away, looking her up and down like he was undressing her with his eyes. "Hmmm. *Very* nice."

Jesse shot him a fierce glare. He didn't like anyone looking at Lucy like she was a piece of meat, but it really raised his ire when Joel did it. Sure, Jesse had sexual fantasies about Lucy all the time, but he was in love with her. That was different.

Joel grinned at Jesse. "Did you see her checkin' me out? She was too nice to choose me right away. I guarantee you, she's made her choice. She's just stalling to spare your poor male ego."

"In your dreams, Blueballs," Jesse retorted. He tried to appear confident, but he knew Joel was right. Lucy had been taken in by those damned blue eyes, and Joel had come across as cool and confident. Jesse had looked like a blithering idiot. He hadn't thought ahead about what he would say to "the girl" in their contest, and he hadn't planned on choosing Lucy until the last moment. He was embarrassed at the way he had stumbled when she asked him a simple question about where he worked.

Joel started humming "The Battle Hymn of the Republic." "You know the words, farmboy? Better start practicing your singing." He cackled, then walked off singing the Union's most popular rallying song. Jesse couldn't help but notice that Joel had a good singing voice. It figured. That asshole was good at everything.

Jesse looked around to make sure no one was looking, then went invisible. He didn't have the energy to pretend to be happy for the tourists. He wanted to sulk in solitude.

He closed his eyes and thought of Lucy. He wondered what it would have been like if she'd been alive in the 1860s. If she'd known him back in Texas, would she have liked him? Would he have been able to court her? Jesse imagined getting love letters from her while he was in camp. What a comfort it would have been to know he had a sweetheart back home who was missing him. Joel always bragged that Emma wrote to him all the time. It was one of the things that got him through all those lonely nights. Jesse had had no such comfort.

Jesse glanced toward the tavern, but decided against going in to watch Lucy. It hurt too much to think about her choosing Joel. It had been a horrible mistake to pick her for their wager. He never should have let Joel into his sacred world with Lucy. Jesse's daydreams of Lucy were fast turning into nightmares of Joel taking over as her hero.

BOTH SOLDIERS SHOWED up in front of Meade's Tavern at ten a.m. the next day.

Lucy spied them waiting outside as she walked toward

the tavern. Shakily, she tucked her hair behind her ear. She'd thought a lot about the boys since yesterday and wondered if they would show up again. They were so handsome and friendly. She had hoped she would get to see them again, yet she was still nervous when she walked up to them.

"Not giving up, are you?" Lucy said to Joel and Jesse. They both grinned when they saw her approach.

"No way. Not until you've chosen the best man," Joel said. He pointed to his chest and mouthed "me."

Lucy chuckled. "I'll need to get to know you better before I choose."

"That seems fair," Jesse said.

Lucy smiled warmly at Jesse. "I'll tell you what. I take my lunch break around two o'clock. You can meet me here if you can get away from work for a bit."

Both Jesse and Joel started talking at once, but Jesse spoke louder and drowned Joel out.

"That would be fine. I'm sure we can take a break at two," Jesse said, looking at Lucy and ignoring Joel.

"Sounds good. I'll be out here," she said, gesturing at the outdoor tables, "if the weather's nice."

"See you soon!" Joel called after her as she went inside the tavern.

Lucy shook her head. They were rather strange, those faux soldiers. She couldn't help but feel flattered that they were fighting over her. Sort of. It was just a game, and they could just as easily have picked any other girl, but it still felt good to have them arguing for her favor. Lucy usually felt invisible around men, especially since she was so shy, so this was a nice change. She didn't want to be forced to choose a winner, but she'd worry about that later. For now, she'd just enjoy Joel's pretty blue eyes and Jesse's sexy Southern accent.

∼

LATER, when Lucy came outside with her salad and iced tea, Joel and Jesse were already sitting at one of the outdoor tables.

"Do you guys want anything?" Lucy asked as she set her lunch down on the table.

"Nah, we're good," Joel said.

"The food is great here, though," Jesse said. He was much more prepared to talk with Lucy today. In the past, he'd never really thought about what to say to her because he never thought he'd get the chance.

"Oh, yeah?" Joel said, grinning. "You been here before?"

"Of course," Jesse said confidently.

"Funny Lucy doesn't remember you," Joel said, smirking. He was trying to catch Jesse off guard.

Jesse smiled at Lucy. "She's never been my server. I'd remember a beautiful girl like her."

Lucy smiled and blushed. Joel frowned.

"What's good to eat here, then?" Joel asked, trying again to make Jesse look stupid.

"I love the buffalo fries with pork," Jesse answered easily. *Nice try,* he thought. Ghosts rarely paid any attention to food. They were never hungry and couldn't even smell food anymore, but Jesse knew the Meade's Tavern menu backward and forward. He could name every appetizer, every drink special, every entrée. Joel would probably think Jesse had just brushed up on the menu in order to be prepared, but he knew it all from watching Lucy for so long.

"Too bad they don't have Southern-fried possum for ya," Joel muttered. That earned a small chuckle out of Lucy.

"Shut your mouth, my tender little orange blossom," Jesse said mock sweetly. He turned to Lucy. "His regiment was called the Orange Blossoms because they were so sweet and delicate."

"Because we came from Orange County, New York," Joel correctly him sternly.

"So, tell me a little about yourself," Lucy said, changing the subject and not addressing the question to either man in particular.

"I grew up in a small town in Texas. I worked on my family's farm until I joined the Confederate army," Jesse said, winking at her.

Lucy laughed. "I see."

Joel glared at Jesse. Since Jesse had told her the truth about his background while pretending it was just part of his soldier "act," Joel couldn't do the same. Lucy obviously found Jesse's "backstory" charming. If Joel followed suit and told her how he'd come to join the Union army, he'd just look like was copying Jesse's strategy for currying her favor.

"I'm from Goshen, New York. I'm interested in history, so that's why I live in Gettysburg now," Joel said. At least the part about hailing from Goshen was true.

Lucy looked up, interested. "I love history! I'm a student at Gettysburg College. My major is Elementary Education, but my minor is history."

"So you're going to be a teacher!" Joel said, smiling.

Lucy looked happy and a little nervous talking to Joel. Jesse watched Lucy sorrowfully. It hurt so badly to see the way she looked at Joel. He couldn't let that stupid Yank run away with the conversation, so he said, "I think you'd make a wunnerful teacher."

"Thank you," Lucy said, her eyes lighting up. "I really want to teach junior high or maybe high school. I'd love to get kids that age interested in history, you know? I want them to understand it doesn't have to be boring. It's not just dates and dry facts—it's about real, living people."

"I couldn't agree more," Joel said.

Jesse snorted. "Suck up."

Lucy had just taken a bite of salad and nearly choked from laughing. She took a sip of iced tea, then glanced at Jesse with amusement. It made him happy that she thought he was funny.

"Shut up, Secesh."

"You shut up, Yankee Doodle!"

Lucy watched them curiously as they argued.

"Traitor!" Joel said, his eyes narrowing.

"Tyrant!" Jesse shot back.

"Grayback!" Joel hollered.

Lucy stared at the two of them. Jesse was suddenly embarrassed, realizing how crazy they must sound to her. They were supposed to be modern guys who were only posing as soldiers. Jesse struggled for something to say, to somehow explain their behavior. Lucy spoke first to break the tension.

"What's wrong with grayback? I mean, why is that an insult?" Lucy asked. She gestured at Jesse's uniform, which included gray pants with his white shirt and suspenders. "Rebels wore gray, right?"

"It means lass," Jesse explained.

"Lass?" Lucy asked, more confused than ever.

"*Lice,*" Joel translated.

Lucy threw her head back and laughed. "Oh, I see!" She looked at Jesse, giggling, and he felt like the stupid hick Joel always said he was. That was, until Lucy spoke again.

"Is it real? Your accent?" She sounded hopeful.

Jesse grinned. "It's real, darlin'. I really am from Texas."

"Good. I like it," she said with a shy smile.

Joel groaned. Jesse knew his accent was his strongest asset when it came to the opposite sex. The one area where Joel simply could not compete.

Jesse leaned over and looked deeply into Lucy's eyes. He spoke in an exaggerated Southern accent. "Alabama. Y'all," he leaned in closer and said seductively, "*Grits.*"

Lucy clapped her hands and laughed. Jesse chuckled, too. He loved hearing her laugh. Joel scowled, which made him even happier.

"You are too much, Private Spenser," she said.

"Thank ye, ma'am," Jesse said, "touching" the tip of his hat.

"Hey, I'm from Noo Yawk. I can tawk in an accent, too," Joel said. Lucy laughed at his joke, too.

"Impressive," she said. "But somehow it doesn't quite have the same effect."

"Hey, I tried," Joel said, grinning at her and throwing his hands up in the air. He suddenly looked thoughtful for a moment. Sad even. "Your laugh reminds me of my wife's laugh."

Lucy looked shocked. She seemed a bit disappointed as well as surprised. "You're married?" she asked, looking at him quizzically.

"Sort of," Joel said, sadly looking down. All his spirit friends in Gettysburg knew about his beloved wife. It had been a long time since he'd had to tell anyone about her. Since she was long dead by now, he said, "Widowed."

Lucy gasped. "Joel, I'm so sorry! You're so young..."

"Well, I'm not as young as you might think," Joel responded. "But I was twenty-six when I lost her."

Jesse nodded sadly. That must have been Joel's age when he left for the war. Who knows how long Emma had lived after that, but he never saw her again after he became a soldier. Jesse couldn't help but feel compassion for Joel. Now that Jesse was in love, he could understand how hard it must have been for Joel to leave his wife, not to mention his children, to go fight with the Union army. He couldn't imagine having had to tell Lucy goodbye when he joined the Confederates.

"It's okay, sweetheart," Joel said softly, looking at Lucy's sorrowful expression.

"I'm so sorry for your loss."

"Thanks," Joel said.

They sat in silence while Lucy finished her salad. Finally, she said, "I have to get back to work."

Lucy stood up, and Joel and Jesse stood up with her.

"Well?" both soldiers said at once, looking at her expectantly.

"You really want an answer now?" Lucy asked, amused by their hopeful expressions. "I need more time. Maybe tomorrow."

Joel groaned, but smiled at her.

"It was really nice talking to you," Jesse said. He touched his hat and bowed his head.

"Sure was," Joel said, bowing slightly.

"Till tomorrow," Jesse called after her as she went back to work. "I won't stop till I've won your heart!"

Lucy's face broke into a lovely, shy smile as she walked back into the tavern.

Jesse watched her go and was able to forget for a moment that Joel was even there.

"I can't wait to rub it in your hillbilly face when she picks me," Joel said, ruining the mood. "Still, I kind of hope she takes her time telling us her decision. I like talking to her."

"Me, too," Jesse said. *I just wish I could talk to her without you around.*

"It's so nice to not feel invisible for once," Joel said wearily.

"I know what you mean," Jesse said, before the two walked off on their separate ways.

7

D ue to their hectic work and school schedules, Lucy hadn't seen Theresa, her roommate and best friend, for several days. They had a lot of catching up to do.

"So!" Theresa said as she flopped down on the fluffy, beige couch in the living room of their apartment. "Got any new gossip I should know about?" She pulled her shoulder-length, strawberry-blond hair back in a ponytail as she looked at Lucy.

"Yes, I do! I gotta tell you about these two guys I met."

"Two! You met *two* guys?" Theresa asked, her eyes lighting up. She had a boyfriend herself, but she was eager to get Lucy hooked up with a great guy. Lucy's last boyfriend, Eric, had been so horrible to her that Theresa was always saying she was overdue for some happiness. And some good lovin', as Theresa called it.

"Yes, there's these guys that—"

"Hold up! I gotta get prepared," Theresa said. She darted into the kitchen and grabbed a glass of wine. When she came back to the living room, Lucy held up her empty hands.

"Really?" Lucy asked.

"Sorry!" Theresa set her own glass down on a coaster on the coffee table, then ran back to the kitchen to get Lucy some wine. Once they were settled with their drinks, Lucy filled her in on what had been going on with Jesse and Joel.

"Okay! So, I'm walking to work the other day, and completely out of nowhere, these two reenactors come up to me. One's a Johnny Reb and the other's a Billy Yank. They claim they're friends, but I'm pretty sure they hate each other. Anyway, they have a bet going that they pick a random girl, and she has to say which one she would choose between the two of them. And they picked me."

"Are they cute?" Theresa asked.

"Oh, my God," Lucy said, dramatically putting her hand over her heart.

"Nice!"

"Theresa, you'd love them. They're always wearing Civil War military uniforms."

"Yummy..."

"I knew you'd say that. You practically drop your panties when you see a guy in uniform," Lucy said.

Theresa laughed. "Oh, baby. Ain't that the truth?" Her boyfriend wasn't a soldier, but she had a weakness for men in uniform. She practically swooned over men in camo.

"So who did you pick? The Yank or the Reb?"

"I haven't decided yet. I really don't want to. I like them both, and I don't want to make anybody feel bad."

"What did they bet?"

"You know, I don't know!" Lucy said. She hadn't thought about it. "I'll have to ask them. They keep hanging around the tavern and asking me to choose. It's kind of nice. They sat with me at lunch the other day."

"So who do you want to choose?"

Lucy sipped her wine, put it down, then leaned back on the couch. "I don't know."

"C'mon. You gotta have a preference. Who's cuter?"

"That would be Joel. Definitely. He's the Union guy. 'Resa, seriously, he's *gorgeous*. I get so nervous just talking to him. You don't see guys that hot in real life, you know? He should be in the movies."

Theresa swirled her wine. "Oh, damn. I gotta meet this guy. He seeing anyone?"

"No, but *you* are," Lucy reminded her.

"I know, I know. I meant for you."

"Yeah, right," Lucy scoffed. Then she said softly, "He's a widower."

"You're kidding! How old is he?"

"About our age. Maybe a little older."

"How awful. Poor guy," Theresa said mournfully. "What about the Rebel? What's his deal?"

"I don't know if he's seeing anyone," Lucy said. "His name's Jesse."

"Hmmm," Theresa said. "Interesting."

"What?"

"I saw that look. You'd pick Jesse, wouldn't you? I can tell just by the way you said his name."

Lucy laughed. "I don't know. Joel's better looking, but Jesse's cute, too. But it's more than that. There's just something about him. He's from Texas and has this *adorable* accent. And he's just...he's so *sweet*. He's like a real Southern gentleman, you know? Tips his hat to me and everything."

"Aww, that is kinda sweet. Not many gentlemen left anymore."

"Don't I know it," Lucy said, shaking her head. "It's not like they're really hitting on me, though. I have to keep reminding myself of that. For all I know, they both have girl-friends. Just because Joel's widowed doesn't mean he has to stay single forever. And Jesse..."

"What?" Theresa asked,

"I have to admit, I hate the idea of him seeing somebody else. Is that dumb?"

"Of course not! It is possible that one or both of them is interested in you, ya know. Why is that so hard for you to believe?"

Lucy shrugged and looked down.

"I want to meet them!" Theresa said suddenly. "I can find out if they're single."

"No way!"

"Why not?"

"Because I know you. You'll be totally blunt." Lucy mimicked Theresa's voice. "*Lucy wants to know—what's your deal? Are you single or what?*"

Theresa laughed and put her wineglass down on the coffee table. "You know damn well I would never do that to you."

Lucy nodded. That was true. Theresa usually spoke her mind but was never unkind. She probably would be able to find out if the boys were single.

"It's so odd, though. All I really know about them is their made-up backstories. When I asked about him, Jesse told me he was Private Spenser from the First Texas."

"That's cute," Theresa said, grinning.

"It really is! And their uniforms are so authentic. Joel wears this nice, blue, button-down uniform..."

"Mmmm," Theresa said, as if she had just tasted something delicious.

"Oh, yeah. You'd love him," Lucy said, chuckling. "And Jesse wears this ragged old uniform that the poorer Southerners would have worn. He wears a slouch hat and suspenders, and he really looks like a farm boy. That's the thing. I keep thinking of him as this sweet farm boy from Texas, because that's all I know about him. And it's not even true! I mean, he is from Texas. He promised his sexy accent is real."

"Good."

"That's what I said. But I doubt he actually grew up on a farm. I just wish I knew more about him." She sighed. "I admit it. I like him. I *really* like him. But who is he really?"

Theresa grinned at her. "That's what you've got to find out."

8

L ucy told Theresa that the guys usually showed up at the tavern at around two p.m. when she took a break. Theresa didn't have any classes scheduled during that time, so she agreed to put in an appearance.

Lucy was still working when the door to the tavern swung open. She was disappointed to see that it was a couple in their sixties who had come in for lunch. She smiled broadly when she saw that Joel and Jesse were following close behind them. She quickly smoothed down her hair and straightened her blouse. She'd taken extra time with her makeup this morning, wanting to look her best for them. Especially for Jesse...

Midday in the middle of the week was slow at the restaurant and Lucy was rolling silverware since she didn't have any customers at the moment.

"Thought you might show up," Lucy said. "Nice to see you."

Theresa wasn't there yet, but would be shortly. Lucy was eager for her help in asking them questions she was too nervous to ask, but she was also a little worried about what her friend would say. Where Lucy was shy, Theresa was fearless.

Joel and Jesse each took a seat at the table where Lucy was organizing all the utensils and wrapping them in napkins.

"How you doin', sweetheart?" Joel asked with a smile.

Having a grown man, especially one as handsome as Joel, call a woman *sweetheart* should have been insulting, but somehow it wasn't. Something in the way he said it just didn't sound derogatory. It sounded gentle and kind.

"Good. Not too busy today," Lucy responded.

"So you up for a little chin music?" Jesse asked.

"What's that?"

"It's the, uh, old-fashioned term for talkin'," he told her.

Lucy laughed. "Ah, I see. You guys really know your 1860s stuff, don't you?"

"Sure do," Jesse said with a wink. "By jingo, you sure do got a lot of the oil of gladness 'round here, don't ya?" Lucy followed his eyes as he surveyed the dozens of alcohol bottles displayed behind the bar. "You gotta be pretty sound on the goose to afford all of that!"

Lucy laughed warmly as she wrapped another set of utensils. Jesse loved seeing the amusement in her eyes when he used nineteenth-century terminology. He tried to think of some more old words to use.

"Can I offer you boys something to eat? Fried bacon? Hardtack?" Lucy asked. She knew from her studies that was what Civil War soldiers had subsisted on.

Joel laughed. "Even if I was starving on a desert island, I don't think I could ever choke down another piece of hardtack."

"Thank ye, ma'am," Jesse said. He patted his stomach. "But my bread basket is full at the moment."

Lucy chuckled again, but she couldn't help but wish Jesse and Joel would be more honest with her about who they really were. She found their characters immensely entertaining, but what she really wanted was to know more about the real people underneath the costumes. Where did they really come from? What did they like to do? Did Jesse have a girlfriend?

Lucy glanced over at the door, wishing Theresa would hurry up and get there. Distracted, she accidentally tipped over the basket of forks, sending them clattering to the floor.

"Shoot," she said, looking at the mess and blushing at being so clumsy in front of the men. She hoped Jesse wouldn't realize that part of her nervousness was due to his presence.

Joel didn't miss a beat. He looked over at Jesse and said, "Well, what are you waiting for? Help the lady!"

Jesse glared at Joel, but didn't move.

Lucy eyed Jesse curiously. After waiting a moment, it became uncomfortably clear that Jesse wasn't going to help.

"That's okay," Lucy said a bit dryly. She crouched on the floor and gathered all the forks, finding it quite odd that her favorite, chivalrous Southern gentleman wouldn't help her with the task.

The door to the tavern swung open with a bang. Lucy was still on the floor, but she could tell by the clacking of heels that it was Theresa.

Theresa looked a bit surprised to see her friend on the floor, then she spied the forks.

"Having fun?" Theresa asked.

"Always," Lucy said. She walked back behind the bar to put the now-dirtied forks in the sink. She picked up some clean ones and returned to her seat.

Theresa surveyed Joel and Jesse, making no secret of the

fact that she was checking them out and that she liked what she saw.

"So these are the famous soldiers stalking you. Yankee Joel and Rebel Jesse."

Joel looked at Theresa with interest. She had beautiful skin, and her reddish-blond hair, reaching just past her shoulders, set off her lovely, light blue eyes. She wore a fairly low-cut, light blue blouse, tight jeans, and high-heeled pumps.

"Yes, ma'am." Joel said before Jesse could say it. "I'm Private Joel Casey of the 124th New York. Victors of the War of Southern Rebellion!"

Theresa looked Joel up and down, and Lucy could imagine all the naughty thoughts that were running through her head.

"And I'm Private Jesse Spenser of the First Texas Infantry," Jesse said, tipping his hat. "Proud to be a soldier in the War of Northern Aggression!" He shot Joel a fierce look.

"Pie eater!" Joel said.

"Little coot!" Jesse shot back.

Theresa looked back and forth between the two, then over at Lucy. "Damn, you weren't kidding. They're crazy!"

"Yeah, but they're beautiful to look at and they keep me entertained, so I like having them around," Lucy said, glancing at Jesse before looking down at her hands. Her face felt hot.

The soldiers stopped glaring at each other and smiled at Lucy, pleased at her compliment. Theresa put her hands on her hips.

"Don't you boys think Lucy's pretty?"

"*Theresa!*" Lucy admonished, her cheeks turning a deeper pink.

Jesse looked longingly at Lucy. "I think she's the most beautiful woman I've ever laid eyes on."

Lucy looked at him, surprised both at his words and the passion with which he'd said them. He really knew how to turn on the charm. Lucy waved her hand in the air dismissively. "Oh, come on."

"Lucy," Jesse said firmly. "It's the truth."

Lucy looked into Jesse's eyes, not quite sure what to make of him. He was always in character as a Confederate soldier, so he was obviously a great actor. Still, he seemed so genuine.

Theresa narrowed her eyes. "So what exactly are your intentions with my friend here?"

"I assure you, our intentions are entirely honorable," Joel told her. "I just want this fair maiden to admit that she would choose me over this rebel rube."

"Shut up, ya blowhard," Jesse said.

"Cram it, you stupid hick."

Lucy shook her head and laughed.

"Did it ever occur to you that she might have a boyfriend?" Theresa asked. "A jealous one that might not like her hanging around you strange yet gorgeous young men?"

Joel looked at Lucy curiously. "Good point. A girl as pretty and smart as you is probably already taken. Say it isn't so!" He put his hand dramatically over his heart.

Lucy smiled at Joel, then looked at Jesse shyly. "No, I'm not seeing anyone."

Theresa eyed Joel up and down. "Well, I am. So don't get any ideas."

"Oh, I'm gettin' ideas all right," Joel said, eying her figure approvingly.

"Keep it in your pants, mister," Theresa said with a flirtatious laugh.

"Theresa!" Lucy said.

"No promises," Joel said. "Lucy, you don't wanna choose the enemy, now do ya? You gotta stand with the Union! You're a Yankee lass, after all."

"How do you know I'm not a copperhead?" Lucy asked. Jesse grinned. A copperhead was a Northerner with Southern sympathies.

"Right! Besides," Jesse said, looking into her eyes with a mischievous smile. "Forbidden love is more excitin', don't you think?"

Lucy laughed softly, but didn't turn her gaze from his for once. Sure, Joel had dazzling blue eyes but there was something wonderfully warm and sexy about Jesse's blue-gray ones. The way he looked at her made her tingle all over.

"Lucy, I don't care if you're a Northerner. You're my honorary yellow rose of Texas!"

"I'm honored," Lucy said. She looked over at Joel, then back at Jesse. They both made her feel so desired, so beautiful. It didn't matter that it was just a silly game. She thought they were both so sweet and always said such nice things to her that she wanted to return the favor. She supposed they'd eventually force her to choose, but she wanted them both to know how wonderful they each were in their own way, no matter who won.

"You see why it's so hard to choose?" she said to Theresa, who nodded. "Joel is so very handsome..." Lucy began. She felt her face heat up again, but she tried to ignore it. She hated that she blushed so easily!

"She said I'm better looking," Joel whispered hoarsely to Jesse, fully intending for everyone to hear him.

"But Jesse is handsome, too. In a very manly, rugged way," Lucy continued, her blush deepening.

"She called you a pretty boy," Jesse whispered hoarsely back. Both Theresa and Lucy giggled.

"And you're both clever and entertaining, that's for sure. I don't know who to pick!" Lucy said as she wrapped the last pieces of silverware in a napkin. She turned to Theresa. "Are you hungry?"

"Yeah, I called ahead and ordered already. You boys staying for lunch?"

"Well, we already ate, but we'd be happy to sit with you while you grab a root," Jesse said, winking at her. Lucy chuckled.

THEY SAT OUTSIDE at the same table as the last time. Jesse again wondered how long they could possibly get away with this charade. They managed to follow the girls out the door and were able to appear to sit again, but it was getting harder and harder to keep the fact that they were dead hidden. Jesse hated that he couldn't hold the door for the women and couldn't pull out his own chair, let alone theirs.

Once the four of them were settled, Fillis wandered over. She stood right next to the table, just outside the metal railing that separated the outdoor tables from the sidewalk. She was invisible to the living, but Joel and Jesse could see her plain as day. Both soldiers glanced up at her, and she blew them each a kiss. She folded her arms, making it clear that she wasn't going anywhere. She was there to see what her boys were up to. Jesse gave her a quick, almost imperceptible smile, then turned his attention back to Lucy.

"You really have no idea who you're gonna pick?"

Theresa asked after swallowing a bite of her cheeseburger. She looked at Joel and Jesse, making no secret of the fact she was sizing them both up.

"No. It's impossible to choose!" Lucy said, leaning back in her chair.

"What's ridin' on this bet anyway?" Theresa asked.

"Oh, yeah! I kept meaning to ask." Lucy said.

"When I win," Joel said, leaning in with a grin, "Jesse has to stand in Lincoln Square, wearing his raggedly old Confederate uniform, and sing 'The Battle Hymn of the Republic.'"

Lucy laughed. She should have known it would be something Civil War related. She looked over at Jesse. "Oh, I would love to hear you sing, Jesse."

Jesse's ghost heart did a flip inside his chest when she said his name, even if she was talking about his losing the bet.

"And what's he gotta do if you win?" Theresa asked Jesse.

"Then Private Casey here has to wear his bluebelly Yankee duds and sing 'Dixie,'" Jesse said.

Theresa and Lucy burst into laughter.

"Now *that* would be entertaining to see," Theresa said, eying Joel's uniform. Her eyes lingered on his broad chest.

"I'm terrified of the idea of hearin' either one of ya sing," Fillis commented dryly.

Joel and Jesse exchanged a look, trying not to laugh at a joke that only the two of them could hear.

"Ugh! I don't want to be the one who makes either of you sing in public!" Lucy said.

"You're a darling girl, sweetheart," Joel said with a chuckle. "We should have picked someone meaner."

"We won't take it personally, Lucy," Jesse lied, knowing full well it would crush his heart to pieces if she picked Joel.

He felt bad about the position they had put her in. She was so sensitive when it came to other people's feelings. It was one of the things he loved the most about her. "It's just a friendly wager. Just pick one of us!"

Lucy let out a weary sigh. Then she said softly, "Maybe tomorrow."

9

The conversation with Theresa and Lucy was the longest time that Fillis had ever seen her boys be civil with one another. That was one thing this silly contest had going for it. They still argued, but their exchanges didn't devolve into shouting matches. Not with those pretty women around.

Fillis was still worried as she watched the boys talk and flirt with Lucy and her friend. Joel clearly enjoyed the banter, and it made Fillis happy to see him laugh and interact with other people. It was a lot better than seeing that haunted look in his eyes when he was grieving over his wife and children.

Jesse was another worry entirely. While Joel enjoyed the entertainment of flirting, there was something more going on with her rebel boy. Joel was clueless, but Fillis could see that Jesse had feelings for that girl. He'd been inexperienced with women when he went off to war, and Fillis knew he'd never been in love. Her protective mama-bear instincts kicked in, and she decided to check on this Lucy woman. It must be hard enough for Jesse to be enamored of a living woman, which meant he could never be with her. Fillis wanted to make sure Lucy never did anything to hurt him.

After the boys finished their lunch break with the girls, Fillis stuck around to watch Lucy after Joel and Jesse went their separate ways.

Fillis followed Lucy as she worked her shift at the tavern. She eyed her critically as she waited on her customers. Lucy was soft-spoken and friendly and was especially good with children. Knowing Jesse, that was one of the things that drew him to her.

Fillis learned that Lucy was a student when she saw her taking brief study breaks during her shift. Lucy was a hard worker, as she managed to juggle work and school.

It was one thing to be nice when others were around, but the real test was how people behaved when they thought no one was watching. Fillis followed Lucy down the street when she left the tavern to run a quick errand. Out on the street, a man in his forties or so was walking and missed the curb. He fell awkwardly onto the ground and his pants slipped down a bit, revealing a bit of his underwear. Lucy watched the man carefully, just long enough to make sure he was all right. When he looked up to see if anyone had noticed his misstep, Lucy quickly busied herself with her cell phone so the man wouldn't feel embarrassed that she saw him fall. Fillis shook her head and laughed. Lucy was a sweet girl, that was for sure.

Poor Jesse was the thought that ran through Fillis's head all day. His heart never stood a chance. The woman was *perfect* for him. If Fillis had to pick from a lineup of women for her favorite cowboy, she would have zeroed in on Lucy right away. While Joel liked his women sassy and bold, Jesse had always preferred the softer, gentler type. They didn't come any softer and sweeter than Lucy. Even her appearance was gentle, with her long, brown hair and warm brown eyes.

It made Fillis sad as she watched Lucy and thought of Jesse. They would have made a wonderful couple. It was so easy to imagine them falling in love, getting married, and having babies. Jesse wanted to have children so badly, and he would have been the most wonderful father. But he had been robbed of that chance just like Joel. Joel had been a devoted, loving daddy, but he hadn't gotten the chance to raise his children. War was such a wretched thing!

Fillis deliberately chose not to have children when she was alive. She was a lesbian and had no interest in marrying a man, but it was more than that. She was a slave, which meant her children could be sold away from her at any time. She knew she could never have survived a loss like that. She ended up feeling like a mother anyway, since she practically raised her master's children.

When the little ones arrived, three in all, she found it impossible to hate them. They were beautiful children, and she loved the two boys and little girl like they were her own. She felt a kinship with Joel, having lost her babies the day she had to run away, the same way Joel had when he went to war and never returned.

Fillis wondered if Lucy could have loved Jesse if he were alive. Worry clutched her heart when she thought about the bet her boys had made. Joel obviously had no idea how Jesse felt about the girl, which was probably a good thing. Joel was a good man at heart, but oh lord, how he hated Jesse! There was no telling what he would do if he knew about Jesse's feelings for Lucy.

Fillis dreaded to think what would happen when Lucy finally made her choice. If she picked Jesse, Joel would get over it. He'd be humiliated in front of his most hated enemy, but then it would be over. But Jesse would be heartbroken if she chose Joel.

Like any good mother, Fillis could tell how Jesse was feeling just by looking at him. Lucy was harder to read, and she seemed to genuinely like both men. Fillis wasn't sure who she was going to choose. If the boys had to make this dumb bet, Fillis was glad they chose Lucy. A lesser woman might have enjoyed their attention too much, egging them on to fight over her. Lucy was a classy girl and a peacemaker at heart. Who knows? Maybe she could help them get along.

Fillis chuckled at the thought. It would be a miracle if those boys stopped fighting. Not even death had been able to stop them so far.

10

J oel headed toward Meade's Tavern, hoping to get a
chance to talk to Lucy without Jesse hanging around.
It was nearly midnight, and they'd be closing up
shop soon. His plan was to catch her as she walked
to her car, giving them a few moments alone to talk.

Though Lucy wasn't exactly his type, Joel was very fond of
her. He spent so much time being invisible, or at least keeping
a safe distance from the living, that it felt good to have
someone actually look him in the eye and talk to him like he
was a real person. It didn't hurt that Lucy was pretty, either.

Except for Fillis, Joel rarely got the chance to talk to
women anymore, save for the occasional tourist. Even when
he was alive, his last few years had been spent in the
company of men. He loved the way Lucy made him feel
when she looked at him. He felt like a man again. Lucy had
no idea that he was just a wispy spirit; she looked at him like
he was big and strong. Lucy was so petite that it made him
feel even more masculine when he towered over her.

Joel remained invisible when he got to the tavern so he

could drift right into the restaurant to see if Lucy was working. If she was, he would go back outside and wait until she got off work.

He floated through the wall of the tavern, only to find the stupid hick there. Jesse was standing in the back, invisible to the living, watching Lucy as she worked.

"What the hell are you doing here?" Joel demanded.

Jesse shot him a look of disgust. He hated having Joel invade his hallowed space at the tavern. This was *his* spot. His and Lucy's. Jesse wished Joel would just go back to wallowing in misery at Devil's Den.

"I'm just enjoying the view," Jesse said, looking over at where Lucy was wiping down a table.

Joel's expression softened as he looked over at Lucy. "It is nice."

Jesse didn't like the way Joel looked at Lucy. Was he falling for her, too? That would be horrible. Jesse would never stand a chance. He had to remind himself that neither one of them actually had a chance with her. They were dead, for God's sake.

"What are *you* doing here?" Jesse asked.

"I wanted to talk to her without your hillbilly ass interfering. No rule says I can't talk to her alone," he said.

Jesse glared at him, then turned back to Lucy. Both soldiers watched as she wiped down the rest of the tables and cleared off the remaining glasses and silverware.

A small creaking noise came from somewhere inside the old tavern. It was the normal cracking sound of an old place settling, but it made Lucy jump. She looked around nervously.

"What's wrong with her?" Joel asked, concern in his voice. "She looks upset."

"She doesn't like working late at night," Jesse said. He glanced over at Joel. "Turns out she's petrified of ghosts."

"Oh," Joel said, looking even more worried.

"She hates when it's dark and quiet."

Another creaking noise from upstairs startled Lucy. She jumped, then let out a nervous sigh as she heard Craig stomping down the stairs. He passed through the dining room and went into the kitchen.

"Wow, you weren't kidding." Joel said. There was sadness in his voice. "Too bad. I was really hoping we could tell her the truth about us someday. I don't know how we could do it without terrorizing her."

Jesse nodded. He'd thought about it a million times. Would it ever be possible for her to stay friends with them if she knew they were ghosts? Could they somehow break the news to her without scaring her half to death?

Craig came back through the dining room and went upstairs. Joel and Jesse watched Lucy as she finished her work.

"I wish we could help her," Joel said. It was another thought Jesse had had a million times before.

"I just wish we could walk her to her car at night. That part scares her the most," Jesse said, realizing as he spoke that he'd better be careful in revealing to Joel just how much he knew about Lucy. "I guess we could sometime... I mean, I doubt anyone would bother her if it looked like she had two men walking with her. Still, if something were to happen..."

Joel nodded and said quietly, "We couldn't stop it."

Jesse winced. The idea of watching someone hurt Lucy and being powerless to stop it was horrific.

As Lucy swept the floor at the front of the room, the back door to the dining room slowly opened. It was Craig. He crawled silently behind the bar. He crouched on the floor and picked up two wineglasses from under the bar and clinked them together a few times, making a soft, tinkling sound. It was barely audible, but in the still of the night, Lucy heard it loud and clear. She gasped and looked over at the bar.

"They do this shit to her all the time," Jesse said bitterly.

"Bastard," Joel said, glaring at Craig.

Lucy went pale. "Craig, is that you?" She bit her lip and took a shaky step back. She said louder, "Craig?"

Craig chuckled and crawled out from behind the bar.

"I knew it was you," she said, and went back to her sweeping. Jesse could see she was still shaken. He wanted to punch Craig even more than he wanted to punch Joel.

Still snickering, Craig walked back toward the kitchen. "You know I love ya, Lucy!" As always, he thought he was being witty and charming by teasing her. Both dead soldiers glared at him.

Then Joel followed him to the kitchen.

Jesse floated through, too, to see what Joel was up to. As Craig tidied up the kitchen and put some dishes away, Joel became visible for a split second. It was a quick flash of light, then it was gone. Just enough for Craig to see him from the corner of his eye. It startled Craig at first, but then he shrugged, convincing himself it was just his imagination.

Then Joel did it again. Craig drew in a deep breath as he stared at the spot where Joel had been standing. Hands shaking, Craig dropped a plate on the floor where it shattered at his feet.

How does it feel to be scared, you sorry sonofabitch? Jesse thought, thoroughly enjoying Craig's terror.

Joel appeared one more time to ensure that Craig was well and truly scared. Craig gasped and took a step back toward the wall. He took a few deep breaths to steady himself.

"I'm gonna go check on Lucy," Joel said, once he was done messing with Craig.

Jesse was glad to see Craig finally get a dose of his own medicine, but he was jealous that Joel had been the one to do it. Jesse was supposed to be Lucy's protector, not that piece of Yankee garbage. He also hated having Joel watch Lucy without her knowledge. Sure, he felt guilty sometimes doing it himself, but he felt it was different when he did it. He loved her so much and he just wanted to be close to her. Joel just wanted to win the stupid bet. It was one thing to have Jesse quietly watching her from afar, but having both of them do it seemed like an invasion of her privacy.

They went back to the dining room where Lucy was humming softly as she put the broom and dustpan away. To Jesse's utter delight, he recognized the song.

It was "The Yellow Rose of Texas."

Jesse cocked his head at Joel and gave him a sly grin. Joel stuck up his middle finger at him.

That's my beautiful rose of Texas, Jesse thought as he watched Lucy. He wondered if she was thinking of him.

"Hope you know all the words to 'Dixie!'" Jesse said gleefully. "It's pretty obvious who she's thinking of right now."

"Because you got that stupid song stuck in her head? Get real." Joel said, sounding defensive. "Yeah, she may just pick you, but only because you're not playing fair."

"How you figger that? Just 'cause I came here without you? You did the same damn thing!"

"I'm not talking about that. I'm talkin' about the way you've been fawning all over her. Telling her she's the most beautiful woman you've ever seen and looking at her like you're about to drop to one knee and propose."

A stab of anxiety and self-consciousness hit Jesse. He hadn't been too good at hiding his feelings. He wondered if Lucy knew.

"She *is* beautiful," Jesse said.

"I know that! But you seem to forget she doesn't know we're dead. You keep looking at her like that, and she's gonna think it's more than just a bet. She's gonna think you're really interested in her. Then what?"

"You flirt with her, too!"

"Yeah, I *flirt* with her. I give her compliments because I like her, and I get the feeling she's been treated bad in the past. She's a sweet girl and I think it's fun to make her blush when I tell her she's pretty, but it's *just flirting*. She knows that!" Joel shot a worried look over at Lucy as she put the chairs back under the tables. "She's already not sure what to make of us. Half the time she still thinks we're making fun of her."

"I know she does," Jesse said softly as he watched Lucy. Sometimes she would hug her arms around her chest, like she was protecting herself, and wore the most heartbreaking, vulnerable expression. Like she was afraid they would suddenly burst out laughing at her and tell her the whole thing was a joke at her expense.

"You're taking the whole goddamn thing too far. You wanna beat me so bad that you're using her, and it's cruel," Joel said angrily.

"I am not using her!" Jesse hollered.

"You keep looking at her like that and saying all that stuff, you're gonna give her the wrong idea. You're gonna break her heart!"

That was the dumbest thing Jesse had ever heard. He rolled his eyes and shook his head. "Ain't you got no horse sense? You think a classy girl like her could ever go for a guy like me?" He gestured down at his ragged appearance. It was a rare display of vulnerability in front of his enemy, but the idea of Lucy being heartbroken over him was ridiculous.

"Good point," Joel scoffed. "But she could fall for you because she doesn't know the real you. She thinks you're some dumb, innocent cowboy. She doesn't know you're a cold-blooded killer."

"You son of a bitch..."

"You can say whatever you want to me, just leave her alone. You're leading her on, and it's cruel. Stop trying to hurt her."

"*I would never hurt her!*" Jesse roared.

Lucy froze. She stopped what she was doing and looked around. She looked over to where Joel and Jesse were standing and screaming at each other.

"She can sense us," Joel whispered. Jesse stood still and nodded. She'd never sensed it when Jesse sat quietly in the back of the room watching her, but anger was a loud and violent emotion. She could feel their fury in the room. Joel watched her, worried but fascinated. "Wow, she's really sensitive." Joel and Jesse screamed at each other all the time while invisible, and nobody had ever batted an eye.

Lucy hugged her arms to her chest and looked all around the room. She let out a ragged and shaky breath.

"We're scaring her," Joel whispered.

"Yeah," Jesse agreed grimly.

With that, they both left the tavern and floated out onto the street. They turned and went in opposite directions without another word.

11

The next day, Fillis went out in search of Jesse. She was fairly certain where she would find him. Sure enough, he was sitting on the ground outside of Meade's Tavern. He was invisible at the moment, and was probably planning on spending some time with Lucy without her knowledge. Fillis remained invisible, too, so she could talk to Jesse privately.

She walked over and looked down at where he was sitting. "Waiting for Lucy?" she asked dryly.

He grinned at her and nodded. He might be hundreds of years old, but he still looked so young to Fillis. It made her sad when she thought of the way he looked at Lucy. He was like a hopeful schoolboy. She wished there was some way to protect him from heartache, but it was too late for any of that.

Fillis sat down next to him, and they watched the people go by for a few moments.

"You know, I'm not as thick-headed about these things as Joel is," Fillis said.

"Well, few people are as thick as Joel," Jesse responded.

Fillis chuckled, then said, "You in love with that girl."

Jesse was silent for a moment, then shrugged his shoulders. "What difference does it make?"

"I 'spect it makes quite a difference to you."

"Yeah, I love her."

"Well," Fillis said gently. "I can see why. She's a lovely girl."

"She *is* a lovely girl. And not just on the outside."

I know, Fillis thought. She'd become quite fond of Lucy, and anyone who was precious to Jesse was precious to her.

Jesse looked off into the distance, waiting for Lucy's approach. He looked a little sad. Probably thinking of what might have been. Fillis understood exactly how he felt. She often joked with her soldier boys about her relationship with Helene, the master's wife. She talked about their secret, forbidden sex life. She told stories about how they'd had to sneak away when the master was asleep, what a great body Helene had, and how great in bed she was. Everyone thought that was all there was to their relationship. Fillis had been caught having a sexual affair with the master's wife, and she had to run away before the master killed her. That wasn't the whole story.

Fillis and Helene had been in love. Not a day went by when Fillis didn't think of her lovely, careworn face. Helene had light brown hair and soft, gray eyes. The master was abusive to them both and was a cruel father to his children. Fillis was Second Mama to Helene's children, too. It was easy to pretend sometimes that Helene was her wife, and the children belonged to the two of them.

That was another reason Fillis felt so close to Joel and Jesse. She understood Joel's agony at losing his children, and she could empathize with Jesse's pain of loving a woman he couldn't have.

"I think she could have loved you. If things were different."

Jesse grinned at her. "You're biased, Second Mama."

"Not at all. You're quite lovable. And you'd treat her right," Fillis said. From watching Lucy's interactions with the boys, it was clear that she'd been treated badly in the past. Though she was friendly with everyone, she was tentative when anyone showed interest in her. Just when she started to relax around Joel and Jesse, she'd get her guard up again. Understandably, Lucy wasn't sure what to make of these two crazy soldiers. Fillis wished she had a way to reassure Lucy that they'd never hurt her. They just enjoyed her company, and she seemed to be good for them.

"Ya think she'll choose me?" Jesse asked with that hopeful schoolboy look of his.

"I don't know," Fillis replied wearily. "'Tween you and me, I hope she does pick you. Means more to you, and there could never be anybody but Emma for Joel anyhow. Not even for a game."

Fillis knew that Lucy was headed their way just by watching Jesse's face. His expression softened and he looked at Lucy adoringly. Lucy couldn't see him, and Fillis was aware of his feelings now, so he didn't have to pretend. Fillis watched him watch Lucy as she walked up and opened the tavern door right next to where they were sitting. He sat there for a moment after she went inside.

"Go on. Go see her," Fillis said.

Jesse grinned and quickly floated into the tavern.

12

Theresa had a little time to kill before her next class, so she figured she'd drop by The Regimental Quartermaster reenactor store to see if either Joel or Jesse was working.

Specifically Joel.

She didn't even know why she was doing it. She had a boyfriend whom she was fairly serious about. They'd been together for three months, which was a long time for her. Besides, Joel was a young widower, and Theresa knew she shouldn't be pouncing on the poor guy. Not that she would.

Would she?

Theresa reasoned there wasn't any harm in just stopping by the store. She hoped Lucy wouldn't be upset, but Theresa doubted she would be. Lucy was quite taken with Jesse, so she likely wouldn't care what Theresa did with Joel.

And there were a lot of things Theresa would love to do with Joel. To him. With him. On him. Under him.

Theresa shook her head as if to shake off those naughty thoughts. *Steven, Steven. I have a boyfriend named Steven.*

Nervous excitement fizzled in her stomach as she opened the door to The Regimental Quartermaster. She tried not to think about the fact that Steven never made her stomach fizzle.

Theresa walked in and scanned the room, looking for one or both sexy men in Civil War uniforms. There was an older man behind the counter who looked like General Robert E. Lee. She was more disappointed to see him than George Meade must have been when he saw the real General.

"Excuse me? Could you tell me if Joel is working today?"

General Lee looked up at Theresa. "Who?"

"Joel Casey. About yay-high," Theresa said, holding up her right hand to show how tall Joel was. "Dresses in a Union soldier outfit. Has blond hair, blue eyes, looks like sex on a stick?" It occurred to Theresa that, for all she knew, Joel was hiding somewhere in the store and could have overheard her. The thought thrilled her rather than making her feel ashamed. She'd tell him he was gorgeous right to his face.

The general glanced around the store, his gaze landing on an employee who was organizing soldiers' forage caps on the shelf. The guy was super skinny with bad acne. The general shook his head. "Don't have anybody like that working here."

Theresa stared at him. "You don't have a guy named Joel Casey working here?"

General Lee shook his head.

"Has he *ever* worked here?

"Nope. Not to my knowledge, and I been here five years.
"

A small knot of fear replaced the fizzle in Theresa's

stomach. "What about a guy named Jesse? Jesse...Jesse I-Don't-Know-His-Last-Name?" Dammit. Lucy would know his last name. The way she looked at him, she probably wanted to share it one day.

"Nobody named Jesse," General Lee said, looking bored with this conversation that clearly was not going to end with his making any money.

"Wears a gray Confederate uniform?"

Lee didn't even look up. He just shook his head again.

The knot in her stomach grew bigger. Both Theresa and Lucy liked Joel and Jesse, but how much did they really know about them? This was a little scary. Why would they lie? Theresa thought of all those serial killers with dashing good looks she'd heard about. Though she knew she was probably overreacting, she figured she'd better give Lucy a heads up.

Theresa left the store and headed back to school. She tried calling Lucy, but she didn't answer her cell phone. Theresa would have felt better if she could go see Lucy and warn her, but she really had to get to class. Theresa left her a voicemail message and also texted her.

Turns out Joel and Jesse don't work at the reenactor store. Never did. Don't know what it means. I'll demand an explanation the next time I see Joel. Or Jesse. In the meantime, you know, just be careful. We really don't know much about these guys...

JESSE STRODE with purpose through the streets of Gettysburg. He remained fully visible as he walked, taking care that none of the tourists and barhopping college students got close enough to touch him. It was after eleven, and there weren't too many people out on the streets. Most of the bars closed at eleven, including Meade's Tavern, which was where he was headed. He was determined to spend a little quality time with Lucy without Joel hanging around. And this time, Lucy would be aware they were spending time together.

Lucy would be closing up the restaurant, and Jesse wanted to play the hero. He would finally walk her to her car.

To keep her safe from ghosts...

Jesse smiled to himself, both excited and nervous. He was always nervous when he first started a conversation with Lucy, but her gentle nature always calmed him and he felt more at ease.

When he reached the tavern, he paused a moment, gathering his nerve. Suddenly, the door swung open and Lucy emerged. Jesse was startled at first, both at the noise and at the surprise of seeing her before he was ready.

Calm down. Don't say anything stupid. This is your one shot without Bluebelly around.

Lucy's face broke into a warm smile when she saw him. She started closing the large umbrellas on the outdoor tables.

"Well, if it isn't my lovely yellow rose," Jesse said. Lucy bit her lip and seemed to be charmed by his words.

"Hello there, Rebel-of-my-heart."

Jesse was surprised and thrilled by her words, but she seemed nervous, like she regretted saying something so brazen. She averted her eyes and blushed.

"Y-y-you're out late."

Jesse had already thought about what to say when she asked why he was out and about at this hour. "Just decided to grab a drink after work." That explained both why he was out and why he was still in his "uniform."

Lucy nodded. She took her time with the umbrellas.

"I don't know if I like seeing you out here late at night," Jesse said with genuine concern. Gettysburg was generally a safe place, but he still didn't like the thought of Lucy being out on the street alone at night, even if it was just for a minute to put the umbrellas away. He also knew how much she hated Gettysburg after dark. On the weekends, there were lots of people around. On weeknights, it was fairly quiet. He knew the silence upset her. "Isn't there somebody else who could do that?"

Lucy shrugged, then shot an annoyed glance toward the tavern. There was no reason why Craig couldn't do it, but he never volunteered. "I don't mind." She made her way slowly back toward the front door. "Well, I guess I better go in and finish up for the night."

"Want some company?" Jesse ventured hopefully.

Her tender, grateful smile melted his heart. "I would love it."

"Not without me, you don't!" Joel's obnoxious voice boomed. Jesse's whole spirit "body" jumped.

"You okay?" Lucy asked.

Joel's image was faint, and Jesse knew he was invisible to the living.

"I'm fine," Jesse said, doing his best to hide his disappointment and disgust at Joel's presence. He forced a smile, then started toward the steps. Lucy opened the door, and Jesse quickly followed behind before the door swung shut.

Joel floated through the door and planted himself right in the center of the room. "Trying to get a leg up on the competition, eh?" He deliberately spoke much louder than necessary, trying to rattle Jesse.

Lucy shyly went about her work. She topped off the salt and pepper shakers and filled the ketchup bottles, acutely aware that Jesse was watching her.

"It's nice having company here. I don't like working by myself late at night. I know it's silly, but I just find it kind of creepy," Lucy said.

I know you do, my darling.

"Well, I'm happy to keep you company," Jesse said.

"Oh, I bet you'd love to keep her company all night long. Look at those luscious curves of hers. She does have some beautiful breasts," Joel taunted. "And those lovely legs of hers. You'd love those legs wrapped around you, now wouldn't you?"

Jesse's expression grew tight. Joel's strategy was working. Jesse had an old-fashioned reverence for women and he simply could not abide disrespect for them, especially a girl like Lucy. His instinct was to vehemently defend her honor, but he couldn't protect her from insults she couldn't hear.

Jesse struggled to keep his face even. He didn't want Joel to see that his words were getting to him, and the last thing he wanted was for Lucy to think he was scowling at her. He did his best to pretend that Joel wasn't there, but it was hard to tune him out. His disrespectful words about Lucy angered him, yet they reminded him of his own fantasies about having sex with her. Quite distracting in either regard.

"I know it's dumb," Lucy said as she added sweetener packets to the tables. "But all those ghost stories around here really get to me, you know? And my coworkers love to play tricks on me because of it."

"Those jackanapes!" Jesse said with a grin.

Lucy laughed and tucked her hair behind her ear. She looked over at him with amusement.

"You love those old-fashioned terms, don't you?" Jesse said.

"I do! I feel like I'm talking to a real Civil War soldier."

"Well, I got all kinds of fun terms for ya," Jesse said. He walked over toward the bar. "Lots of good ones for alcohol. Tar water, Nokum Stiff, How Come You So..."

"How Come You So. That's a good one!" Lucy said.

"Oh, Jesse likes that one, too," Joel said loudly. "I bet he'd love to make you come so."

Jesse couldn't help it. Joel's words conjured up the familiar fantasy of Lucy on her back, long brown hair splayed out, moaning. *Oh, Jesse...*

Damn Joel for getting into his head! Jesse continued, "And there's lots of great Civil War insults. If I was fightin' with someone, say, I don't know, *Joel* for example..." Lucy giggled softly. Turning to face Joel, Jesse said, "I'd say something like 'Go boil your shirt!' or 'I'll knock you into an ugly cocked hat!'"

"And if *I* wanted to insult someone," Joel boomed, glaring at Jesse. "I'd just say FUCK YOU!"

Jesse blinked. It drove him half mad that Joel used that kind of language in front of Lucy—never mind that she couldn't hear it. It was a struggle to keep his cool, but he knew he had to stay calm. Even if they weren't alone, Lucy thought they were. Jesse needed to make the best of it and enjoy the fact that she was there talking to him, and only him.

"Sparking," Jesse said. "Now there's a wunnerful old-fashioned term. It means courting a girl."

Lucy looked up from her sweeping to give him a shy smile. Hope surged inside Jesse when she looked at him like that. Was it possible that she was interested in him?

Jesse shot her a meaningful look. "Sparkin' also means kissin'"

Lucy glanced at his lips before going back to her sweeping. Naturally, she blushed.

"Don't do that," Joel said sharply. "Don't say shit like that to her. You can't kiss her, so stop acting like you're going to. She'll feel rejected when you don't make a move."

Jesse's heart sank. He nodded, almost imperceptibly, acknowledging Joel's words. He was right. Even if Lucy did have feelings for him, the situation was hopeless. It wasn't humanly possible for them to ever be together, and he was wrong to lead her on just because it felt so good to be with her.

"So!" Jesse said, forcing himself to change the subject. "You got people 'round here botherin' ya, do ya?" He looked toward the kitchen door, knowing damn well who was doing the bothering.

"Yep. Sometimes," Lucy said. "I guess I'm just an easy target since I'm such a scaredy-cat."

"Tell me who they are and I'll beat 'em up for ya! I'll make short work of those little gallinippers!"

Without warning, Lucy reached over to swat Jesse playfully on the shoulder, "Oh, you!"

Whooosh! Lucy's hand sliced right through his transparent form.

"Oh, *shit...*" Joel said, horrified, as he watched it happen.

Lucy stood still, stunned. She glanced down at her hand, trying to comprehend what had just happened.

"L-L-Lucy..." Jesse stammered.

Lucy drew in a sharp, shaky breath and staggered backward toward the bar. Jesse stared at her, afraid to move. No matter what he did, he was sure to terrify her further.

"I'm so sorry," Jesse whispered softly.

Lucy's face went frighteningly pale. She looked more dead than the two dearly departed soldiers. She gripped the bar with her hand in an effort to steady herself. After swaying back and forth for a second or two, she fainted. There was a horrible *crack* when her head hit a table as she fell to the floor.

13

J esse rushed to Lucy's side and knelt beside her. "Oh, my sweet Lucy. What have I done to you?"

Joel went to her, too, and crouched down by her side. "Dammit. I'm so sorry, sweetheart. I never meant for you to get hurt..." He'd been so worried about her getting hurt emotionally, thinking that he or Jesse might be interested in her, and now she'd come to physical harm because of their stupidity. He felt terribly ashamed when he remembered all the sexual things he'd just said about her. Lucy was a classy girl and didn't deserve to be talked about like that, even if she couldn't hear him.

Joel felt awful that she had gotten hurt, but Jesse seemed completely distraught. Joel was surprised at the intensity of the anguish on his face. He suddenly recalled all the times he'd seen Jesse staring at Lucy meaningfully. He hadn't thought anything of it before.

My sweet Lucy, what have I done to you...

I would never hurt her!

I think she's the most beautiful woman I've ever laid eyes on.

"Ohhh..." Joel said stupidly, as the truth finally dawned on him. Jesse hadn't been leading her on for the sake of the bet. *He was in love with her.* It occurred to Joel that the two of them would have made a great couple. Lucy's natural sweetness and Jesse's gentlemanly manner were a perfect combination.

"Lucy," Jesse whispered. He was desperate to wake her, but if he shouted her name and she came to, she would be terrified all over again when she saw him standing over her.

Joel couldn't help but feel sorry for Jesse. He imagined how he would feel if that were Emma lying there, pale and unresponsive, her honey-blonde hair spread out on the floor instead of Lucy's darker tresses. *Poor Lucy,* he thought as he looked at her. She looked so innocent, lying there on the floor. She *was* innocent.

"She'll be okay," Joel said gently, trying to reassure Jesse. "She just fainted."

Jesse looked up and shot Joel a panicked look. "But she hit her head! What if she's really hurt? We have to do something!"

Joel shook his head sadly. What could they possibly do? They could yell out for help, but that would likely create a panic. The police would be called as Lucy's coworkers searched for a male attacker who'd hurt Lucy, called out for help, then disappeared.

Jesse stood up suddenly. He closed his eyes and concentrated.

Joel was alarmed. "You can't possibly pick her up! Even if you could, you'd drop her and hurt her worse!" He understood Jesse's desperation to help Lucy, but there wasn't anything they could do.

Jesse ignored Joel. Eyes still closed, he concentrated on

gathering his strength. He opened his eyes. Focusing as hard as he could, he went over to the bar right behind where Lucy lay on the floor. With one violent shove, he pushed a tray of empty glasses and silverware off the bar and onto the floor. It hit the ground with a terrific *crash* and landed right next to Lucy, making it look like she'd dropped it when she collapsed.

Jesse's image became so faint that Joel could hardly see him anymore, the consequence of using up so much of his strength. But his plan had worked. It took only a few seconds for Craig to come rushing in to investigate the cause of the crash.

He looked around for the source of the noise and didn't see Lucy right away. He walked over toward the tables and finally saw her.

"Oh, shit!" Craig rushed over and crouched beside her. He slid his left arm under her back and cradled her in his arms. "Lucy! Lucy!"

He shook her harder, but she was still unresponsive. Lucy's fall, combined with Craig's shaking her, had caused her blouse to slip down. Most of her left breast was revealed, covered in a lacy, white bra. Craig noticed, and stared for a second or two. Then he reached over and tugged at her blouse, pulling it over her chest to protect her modesty.

Joel and Jesse exchanged a look that said *Good thing...* They'd have haunted Craig for the rest of his days had he dared to grope Lucy.

Brayden came in from the kitchen, and the manager, a woman in her forties named Mandy, came in at the same time from the door on the other side of the dining room.

"Lucy! Lucy! Can you hear me?" Craig said.

Mandy rushed over. "Oh, my God. What happened?"

"Not sure. I think she fainted. I didn't see it happen. I just heard the noise when she dropped a tray and I found her like this. Come on, Lucy. Come on!" Craig pleaded. "Okay, girl. You got three seconds to wake up before I call an ambulance. Lucy. Luce!"

He sighed. With his free hand, he pulled his cell phone out of his pocket and entered the unlock pattern with his thumb. Just as he was about to dial, Lucy moaned softly.

Jesse walked around and crouched down next to Lucy while Joel stood just behind her. Jesse's image, while still invisible to the living, was starting to get a bit stronger.

Lucy's eyes fluttered open, and she drew in a deep breath. It took her a moment to make sense of her surroundings, then she shot a terrified look in the direction where she'd last seen Jesse.

Craig saw her frightened expression and tried to comfort her. "Hey, it's okay. It's okay, it's just me," he said softly.

Joel watched Jesse, who was watching Craig take care of Lucy. He could see relief in Jesse's eyes that help had arrived, but also pain as he watched another man hold Lucy in his arms in a way he never could.

Lucy looked up at Craig as he held her. She looked relieved to see that she was no longer alone in the tavern, but she was still afraid. She was shaking.

Mandy crouched down next to Lucy, and, unbeknownst to her, next to Jesse as well. "You okay, honey?"

"I think so," Lucy responded in a small voice. She reached around and touched the back of her head. She winced. "I must have hit my head."

"Hey, Brayden," Craig said. "Go get her some water, will ya?"

Brayden nodded, and seemed grateful to be able to help.

Craig pressed his hand firmly on Lucy's back and helped her to sit up. She took a few deep breaths.

"She's getting her color back," Joel said to Jesse encouragingly.

"Your color looks a bit better," Mandy said.

Brayden returned with a glass of ice water with a straw. He handed it to Craig, who held it to Lucy's lips. She drank a few sips, and the coolness of the liquid seemed to help calm her a bit.

Lucy looked around at all the people who were staring at her. Brayden, Craig, and Mandy. Lucy's cheeks turned pink.

"Yeah, that's her usual color," Joel said, laughing softly and with affection.

"I'm all right, you guys. Really." Lucy started to get up. Craig took the glass of water from her and handed it back to Brayden before helping Lucy to her feet.

"What happened, Lucy? Were you feeling sick?" Mandy asked with concern.

"No. I don't think so. Not really. I guess maybe I just didn't eat enough today. I-I-I just suddenly felt a little lightheaded." She glanced again at the corner where she'd last seen Jesse. She swallowed hard and looked away.

Joel and Jesse looked at each other. She clearly wasn't going to tell anyone what she'd seen, which was probably for the best. For them, anyway.

"I feel fine, now. Really."

"Why don't you head on home, sweetie. Go home and rest," Mandy said, sounding like a mother hen. "Give me a call tomorrow if you don't feel up to coming in, okay?"

Lucy nodded.

"You gonna be okay to drive?" Craig asked, sounding worried.

"Oh, yeah. I'm okay, really," Lucy said, uncomfortable with being fussed over.

"I'll walk you to your car," Craig said, and Mandy nodded her approval.

Craig walked to the back of the room where all their coats and jackets were hanging on hooks. He grabbed his jacket as well as Lucy's.

Jesse watched sadly as Craig helped Lucy on with her jacket. Both Joel and Jesse followed as Craig led Lucy to her car. Lucy looked more terrified than ever as she looked out at the blackness of the night.

"Are you sure you're okay to drive?" he asked. "If you pass out again, you're gonna have an accident."

"No, I'm fine. Really. I just need to go home and get some rest."

All three men watched with concern as she drove away. Craig watched her until she was out of sight, then trudged back toward the tavern.

Jesse sat down on the sidewalk. Instead of going off on his own like he usually did, Joel sat down next to him.

"You're in love with her!" Joel said.

Jesse just stared straight ahead, a grim expression on his face. So Joel finally knew the truth. He would probably laugh in Jesse's face, mocking the very idea that a backwoods guy like him had fallen in love with a beautiful woman like Lucy, but he didn't care. Nothing Joel could say could possibly hurt him. His taunts were nothing compared to the fresh, raw pain he felt when he pictured Lucy's face as her hand passed through him. She was terrified of him. He'd never be able to go near her again.

"I didn't know," Joel said softly. "I didn't know."

Jesse looked over at him, shocked by his tone of voice.

Joel actually looked sympathetic. "What the hell do you care?" Jesse asked, his voice rising.

"Well, I know what it's like when you can't be with the woman you love!" Joel exclaimed. "I wouldn't wish it on my worst enemy. Which would be, well, *you*."

Jesse decided he might as well tell Joel the truth. He had nothing left to lose anymore. "I already knew her when I picked her for our bet."

Joel looked annoyed at Jesse's confession.

"She didn't know me. I swear," Jesse said, holding up his hands. "It's like she said, she only saw me that one time when I was playin' with that little kid." He chuckled softly. "Still can't believe she remembered that. But really, she didn't know me at all. I just knew her. I used to, you know, watch her."

Joel nodded. Ghosts often stuck around people they liked, watching them just for something to do.

"I was already in love with her when I picked her. I jus', ya know, figured I'd finally get the chance to talk to her."

"Weren't you afraid she was gonna pick me?" Joel asked dryly.

Jesse laughed. "Of course. She prolly woulda."

"Nah. I don't think so," Joel said quietly. "Guess we'll never know now."

Jesse closed his eyes, overwhelmed at the prospect of having to go on with his existence without Lucy. He couldn't even watch her in secret anymore. Not without recalling how frightened she had been. She probably thought of him as some creature from a horror movie.

"Did you see the way she looked at me?" Jesse asked, the agony evident in his voice.

"Yeah. I know. I guess it was bound to happen. We both knew we were pushing it."

They sat in silence for a while. They would both miss Lucy terribly.

Jesse stood up. "I'm just gonna, ya know, go for the night. I'll come back tomorrow and check on her. I have to make sure she's all right."

Jesse vanished for the night so he wouldn't have to be conscious and suffer the agony of worry over Lucy. He disappeared, from sight and from consciousness, for a short respite from his pain.

14

T he moment Lucy walked into her apartment, she could feel the quiet stillness in the air.

Oh, no...

Theresa was obviously spending the night at Steven's house, which meant that Lucy was in for a long night. She couldn't imagine how she was ever going to get any sleep.

Wearily, she hung up her jacket, then proceeded to turn on every light in the apartment. She still didn't feel safe, and she wondered if she ever would again. Her head was spinning with the implications of what she had learned.

Jesse was dead. *Dead.* And Joel must be, too. So many things made sense now. The way they always wore their so-called costumes. Why they never ate anything. The way they fought with each other. Lucy realized they were *actual* enemies, having fought against one another in the Civil War.

Lucy went into the bathroom to brush her teeth and get ready for bed. She washed her face, then looked up at herself in the mirror. She hardly recognized her pale, terrified reflection. She started to feel dizzy again, then took a few deep breaths to steady herself. Ghosts were *real*. It was like her worst nightmare coming true. She tried to remind herself of how kind Joel and Jesse had seemed. How human. They were nothing like horror-movie ghosts.

Picturing their kind faces didn't help. They were dead. Ghosts. Spirits. And Lucy knew they weren't the only ones. She remembered all those times in the tavern when she'd felt like she was being watched.

It turned out she *was* being watched.

Lucy shuddered as she slipped on her nightgown. How would she ever be able to go to work again, especially at night?

As she pulled out her cell phone and placed it on the nightstand to charge, she saw she'd missed a call and a text from Theresa. She read her friend's message, warning her that Joel and Jesse didn't work at The Regimental Quartermaster. She let out a sarcastic chuckle.

"Yeah. I can explain that..." she said aloud.

Lucy turned off the lights and lay down. She wrapped her arms around herself. A fresh wave of terror washed over her as she remembered her hand going right through Jesse, leaving behind a frigid chill. Cold. Jesse was cold and dead.

She lay there in the dark, listening to the silence, and began to cry.

JESSE CAME to the tavern the next afternoon to check on Lucy. He remained invisible; he didn't dare let her see him. What he saw filled him with sorrow. She looked exhausted. Her eyes had circles under them and looked puffy, as if she'd been crying. She smiled as usual and was kind to the customers, but her smile didn't look the same. Jesse could see the fear in her eyes, and he hated himself for causing it.

Throughout the day, Lucy kept glancing at the corner of the room where she'd last seen Jesse, and she often looked apprehensively toward the front door as if she expected Joel or Jesse to show up at any moment. Jesse desperately wanted to talk to her, comfort her, reassure her that he was nothing to be afraid of, but he knew better than to even attempt it. Not yet anyway.

Jesse watched Lucy's anxiety grow as darkness fell. She always dreaded closing up the restaurant at night, and he couldn't imagine how petrified she felt now.

Closing time finally came, and Lucy locked the door after the last customer had left. Jesse tried to keep his distance from her as he watched over her. He imagined what would happen if she accidentally walked through him. Sure, she'd done it before, and had written it off as a sudden chill. If it happened again, she would know that a ghost was present. She might faint again, or worse. Jesse anxiously wondered if it was possible to have a heart attack from fright. How could he have been so careless around her?

Lucy began refilling the salt and pepper shakers. She gasped and her whole body jerked as the door to the kitchen swung open. Craig walked in and started gathering up the dirty glasses to take to the kitchen.

"Craig," Lucy said, her voice quavering. "Please don't play any tricks on me tonight."

He looked at her with unusual tenderness. "I wasn't going to, Luce," he said softly. "You all right?"

"Yes. I'm fine. I'm just not feeling that well."

"You want to go home? I'm sure Mandy would let you," Craig said.

"No, that's okay."

"Okay. Let me know if you change your mind. And tell me if you start feeling worse. I don't want to find you on the floor again. That was awful."

"I'm sorry about that, Craig. Thanks for helping me."

"You bet," he said. He finished picking up the dishes and went back into the kitchen.

Lucy wiped down the tables and straightened out the ketchup and mustard bottles. Jesse could see that her hands were shaking. She kept looking around the room, expecting the worst.

Her breaths became shallow, and tears started to fall.

"Oh darling, please don't cry..." Jesse said.

Lucy wiped her face with her hand and continued her work. Jesse watched her, agonizing over his powerlessness to comfort her.

Then he got an idea.

Jesse remembered that Lucy had sensed it when he and Joel were yelling at each other. She'd felt it because anger was such a strong emotion. Well, love was a powerful emotion, too. Maybe if he could somehow get her to sense his presence, feel his love and protectiveness of her, she might calm down.

Jesse followed her to the tables as she set rolls of silverware down. He began to sing softly to her.

"There's a yellow rose of Texas, that I am gonna see..." Jesse watched her carefully for any reaction, any sign that she could sense him. What if she did feel his presence and it frightened her?

"Nobody else could miss her, not half as much as me," Jesse continued to quietly serenade her. Lucy's hands still shook as she wiped the tears from her eyes. "She cried so when I left her, it almost broke my heart... And if I ever find her, we never more will part."

Jesse followed Lucy as she walked from table to table, careful not to get too close to her in case she made any sudden moves.

"She's the sweetest little rosebud that Texas ever knew. Her eyes are bright as diamonds, they sparkle like the dew. You can talk about your Clementine and sing of Rosalie, but the yellow rose of Texas is the only rose for me."

Lucy stopped at another table to straighten out the bottles of steak and barbecue sauce. Jesse took a risk and stood right in front of her. He looked at her brown hair that fell all the way to her waist, wishing he could run his fingers through it. He imagined what it would feel like to comfort her, hold her in his arms, stroke her hair, tenderly telling her not to be afraid.

"I love you, Lucy," he whispered.

It could have been Jesse's imagination, but it seemed like Lucy paused for just a brief instant. He couldn't tell whether or not she had sensed him.

Lucy finished with that table and then got to work sweeping the floor. Jesse listened intently to her breathing, which had become noticeably calmer and more even.

She had stopped crying.

15

Lucy arrived back home to her apartment and collapsed on the couch, relieved that she had survived her shift at Meade's Tavern without fainting again or having a stroke. She knew a lot of her fear was her own fault, the way she psyched herself out. Still, she couldn't help that she was terrified of ghosts. A touch of anger broke through her fear. Why did those soldiers have to come and torture her like this? Just so they could settle some bet because they hated each other? Why couldn't they have just left her alone?

Theresa walked in from the kitchen.

"Thank God you're home!" Lucy said.

"Awww. It's so nice to be loved," Theresa said with a sigh.

"We have a lot to catch up on, girl," Lucy told her.

"Really," Theresa said, her eyes wide. "Do tell!" She flopped down on the couch next to Lucy and looked at her expectantly.

"I don't even know where to begin," Lucy said. "First of all, you have to promise that you're gonna believe me."

"This is gonna be good, isn't it?" Theresa said enthusiastically.

"Well, that's a matter of opinion I suppose," Lucy said. "Hasn't been too great for me. It's about Joel and Jesse."

Theresa's face fell. "Oh no, honey. Does Jesse have a girlfriend?"

"No. That much I know for sure. I-I just... You *will* believe me, right?" Lucy asked.

"Lucy! Of course I will. How can you even ask that?"

Lucy nodded. "Okay. Well, you were right. They don't work at that reenactor store."

Theresa nodded, looking worried.

"So, Jesse came to see me at the restaurant. At night. When I was closing up."

Theresa's eyes grew wide. "Oh, my God. He didn't try to hurt you, did he?"

"No, no. Nothing like that. We were just talking, joking around, you know. And I went to swat him on the shoulder, like this..." Lucy swatted Theresa on her right shoulder. "And-and my hand went right through him," she whispered in a shaky voice. "I-I mean, my hand went *right through his body*. And-and-and it felt really cold but there was nothing solid...nothing at all..."

Theresa stared at Lucy. What she was saying was crazy, but the fear in Lucy's eyes made it clear that it had really happened.

"What?" Theresa asked, still trying to process Lucy's words.

"They're not reenactors, Theresa. I think... I think they're really Civil War soldiers."

Theresa slowly sank back into the couch.

"I mean, think about it. Have you ever seen them eat anything? They always sit with me at lunch but they never eat. And I've never seen them wear anything but their Civil War uniforms. And-and you know, when I ask them about themselves, they kinda laugh it off and tell me they're soldiers who fought in the war. And when they fight, which is *all* the time, they argue about the war and stuff."

"Oh, my God..." Theresa said, her mind spinning.

"Oh God, 'Resa. I've never been so scared in my whole life. The last thing I remembered I was just staring at Jesse, then the next thing I knew I was on the floor and Craig was trying to wake me up. I must have fainted. And then last night I came home and you weren't here and I was by myself and—" Lucy covered her mouth with her hand and started to cry.

Theresa sat back up and put her arms around her. "I'm so sorry, Lucy. I know how much this stuff scares you. You should have called me! I would have come home. I could have brought Steven over so you'd feel safer!"

Lucy nodded. She grabbed a tissue from the coffee table and wiped her tears. "It's okay. It was so late by the time I realized you wouldn't be home. I'm so glad you don't think I'm crazy."

"No. I know you're not crazy." Theresa squeezed Lucy's hand. She drew in a deep breath. "I've never told this to anyone in my entire life, but...I saw my dead grandmother once."

Lucy's eyes grew wide. "Are you serious?"

Theresa nodded. "It was the day of her funeral. I was seventeen when she died. We were really close. Anyway, it was late at night on the day we buried her. She came and sat down on my bed and told me that she was okay and not to worry."

Lucy drew in a shaky breath, and Theresa squeezed her hand again.

"It wasn't even scary. Really! She made me feel better. And I'm sure Jesse didn't mean to scare you."

"No. No, I'm sure he didn't. The last thing he said before I passed out was *I'm so sorry.*"

"You know what this means, don't you?" Theresa asked. "Jesse really *is* a sweet farm boy from Texas."

Lucy nodded. She'd been so overwhelmed with fear that she hadn't thought much about that yet. Her head was reeling with everything she knew about Jesse. His life as a Texas farmhand, his Southern manners, his accent...it was all *real.* She felt stupid for thinking he might have been interested in her romantically. She was grateful that she'd never told him anything about her feelings for him. Except for that time she'd called him Rebel-of-my-Heart.

"I feel like such an idiot for thinking he might ask me out sometime."

"Well, jeez, how the hell were you supposed to know?" Theresa said. She looked at Lucy curiously. "Do you think we could find anything about them online? Did they keep records of soldiers back then?"

"I'm not sure."

Theresa picked up her laptop from the coffee table and flipped it open. While she waited for it to boot up, she asked Lucy, "Do you know which regiments or whatever they were in?"

"Jesse fought with the First Texas Infantry. Joel was... um...I don't remember." Theresa shot her a wry look. Lucy sighed deeply. "Yes. Of course I would have picked Jesse. And you'd have picked Joel if it were up to you."

"Hell, yeah. He's got a face and a body to die for. Get it?" Theresa nudged Lucy, making her groan at the horrible pun.

"Ugh. I don't know. He was in some regiment in New

York. Oh, I know! They were nicknamed the Orange Blossoms. I remember Jesse calling him a delicate Orange Blossom."

Theresa nodded. She looked up *Orange Blossoms Civil War.* "124th New York Infantry?"

"Yeah. That sounds right."

"Okay, cool. Here's a search engine from the National Park Service. You can search by regiment and by name." Theresa typed *124th New York Infantry,* then typed in *Joel Casey.* She took a deep breath.

Lucy's hand flew to her mouth when the name got a hit. There it was. Joel Casey. There really was a Joel Casey in the 124th Infantry.

"Now do Jesse!"

"Bet you'd like to do Jesse," Theresa quipped. Lucy was too shaken up to respond. Theresa typed in *First Texas Infantry,* then typed in the name *Jesse.*

Private Jesse Spenser came up.

Lucy dropped her hand from her mouth. The room started spinning. She drew in a deep breath and put her head between her knees.

"Lucy? Lucy?" Theresa said. She shut the laptop and tossed it onto the coffee table. She put her hand on Lucy's back. "Lucy? You all right?"

Lucy took in a few more deep breaths, then lifted her head. Pale and shaken, she said, "They're dead, Theresa. They're *dead.*"

16

Fillis hadn't seen Jesse in over a week, and she was worried. Whenever one of her boys went missing, there was always the possibility that they'd crossed over. That wasn't likely with Jesse. Fillis usually had a sense of when the time was coming for someone to finally pass on to the other side. She'd seen it happen dozens of times over the years. When a spirit was finally at peace with himself, his past, his life, he experienced self-acceptance and a sense of belonging to the Universe. The main things that kept a soul earthbound after death were feelings of guilt and unworthiness. You crossed over to Paradise when you finally realized you were worthy.

Nothing had changed in Jesse recently to make Fillis think his time was near. It was far more likely that his disappearance had something to do with Lucy. Fillis hadn't talked to Joel recently, either, but she'd seen him around and knew he was all right.

As Fillis wandered around Gettysburg, looking for Jesse, she met up with another one of her boys.

Adam Conrad, a private from the First Maryland

Infantry, was sitting on the ground on Cemetery Hill. He had dark brown hair, dark brown eyes, and a permanent five o'clock shadow. He looked up at Fillis' worried face.

"Who you fussin' over now, Mama?" he asked, smiling at her. Though most soldiers called Fillis Second Mama, Adam's real mother had been cruel and abusive. He considered Fillis his only real mama.

"Jesse. Ya seen him?"

"Not in a bit, no," Adam said. "He still pinin' over that girl?" Most of the ghosts in Gettysburg knew about the bet between Jesse and Joel, and that Jesse had fallen hard for the girl in the contest. Nothing much new or exciting happened with spirits around here, so gossip ran rampant when something interesting transpired.

"More than ever. You doin' all right?"

"Yep. Just fine."

"Good. You see Jesse, you let me know. Ya hear?"

"You got it."

Fillis continued her search and finally found Jesse way out on Constitution Avenue, near Gettysburg College. It was close to the limit of how far he, or any of the ghosts who'd died in Gettysburg, could travel.

Jesse looked up at her from where he was sitting, which was under a tree not far from the busy road. Occasionally, there was some foot traffic as students walked to class, but for the most part it was cars that whizzed past.

Fillis stood over him. "You hidin' from me, boy?"

"I'm hidin' from everything," Jesse said forlornly.

Fillis sat down next to him and waited until he was ready to talk. They watched the vehicles fly down the road. Cars, tour buses, and big trucks. When there was a lull in the traffic and the air grew still, Jesse broke the silence.

"She knows."

Jesse didn't have to elaborate. Fillis knew exactly what he meant. "Did you guys tell her?"

Jesse shook his head. "She found out the hard way. She tried to touch me."

"Oh," Fillis said, wincing. Both boys had voiced their concerns about what would happen if Lucy found out they were dead, especially if she discovered the truth by accident. It was one thing if they told her themselves, gently breaking the news that they were dead and then, *carefully*, proving it. "What did she do?"

"She looked at me like I was a serial killer who was about to murder her. Then she passed out and hit her head on a table."

"Oh my... Is she all right?" Fillis asked. *Oh, that poor little girl.* Fillis had already begun to think of Lucy as one of her many adopted children, and it pained her to know how scared she must have been.

"Yeah. We stayed with her, you know, until somebody came to help."

"I'm so sorry, honey. I guess it was bound to happen 'ventually, but I'm sorry it happened like that." Jesse looked so sad that Fillis could hardly bear it.

"I know she could never love me. But now she thinks I'm a monster," Jesse said.

They sat again in silence for a while. Fillis wished there was something she could do or say to fix this. "It's possible she'll come around. She got to know you both a good while before this happened. She's got to know you don't mean her no harm."

Jesse nodded.

Fillis shot Jesse a sly grin.

"Whut?" he asked.

"Where did she try to touch you?" she asked salaciously.

Fillis's words and expression made Jesse burst out laughing. "My *shoulder*," he responded.

Fillis smiled. It felt good to hear Jesse laugh again.

"Hmm. It's a start."

"God, can you imagine if she really could touch me? I mean, *touch* me? And I have imagined, and I mean a *lot*." He paused for a moment. "She would have been worth waiting for, you know what I mean?"

Fillis nodded. "Yeah. I know."

Jesse watched the cars whiz past. "Wanna head back to town?"

"Sure, honey."

They both got up and started walking back to the main, touristy part of Gettysburg. There was more to see, more people to watch in that area. There wasn't much else for spirits to do than to watch the living.

"I was thinking. I might want to vanish for a little while, you know?" Jesse said quietly. "It jus'...it hurts too much."

"I unnerstan," Fillis said. She would miss him while he wasn't around, but maybe some time away from Lucy was what he needed.

Joel spotted the two of them as they walked down Steinwehr Avenue. Fillis and Jesse sat down in their usual spots on the street, and Joel went over to them. He just stood there, looking down at Jesse.

"Whut?" Jesse asked abruptly, narrowing his eyes as he looked up him.

"I miss her," Joel said sadly.

"Me, too," Jesse said mournfully.

"Do you think there's any way she'd ever talk to us again?" Joel asked hopefully.

"I don't know. I guess we could go try to see her. Ya know, in broad daylight when there's other people around."

Joel brightened. "That might work. I could try to go see her. Your ugly mug would just scare her off."

"No way. I don't want you going to see her without me."

"Well, I don't think we should both gang up on her," Joel said. "We have to approach her carefully."

"No. Not we. *Me*," Jesse insisted.

"Oh, 'cause you fell in love with her, you own her now?"

Fillis looked at Joel in surprise. So he'd finally figured out that Jesse loved Lucy. Fillis glanced over at Jesse, who was miserable enough without Joel causing more trouble.

"No, I don't own her. And neither do you. But I know her better than anybody, so I should be the one to try to talk to her."

"Since you did so well the last time?" Joel asked angrily.

"You think it's my fault she found out about us?"

"Yeah, it's your damn fault. You shoulda known better than to get so close to her!" Joel exclaimed. "You traumatized her!"

"Joel!" Fillis intervened. "Stop it, now. That's enough!"

"You think I like that she's afraid of me?" Jesse yelled. "You think I like that she prolly wakes up in the middle of the night screamin' havin' nightmares about me?"

The pain in Jesse's voice was so raw, so real, that Joel fell silent for a moment.

"I never wanted to hurt her," Jesse said quietly. He glared at Joel. "*I* will go see her. If for no other reason than to see her one last time. I need to say goodbye."

Without another word, he trudged off toward the tavern. The idea of saying goodbye to Lucy was unbearable, but he didn't see any other choice. He couldn't continue to torture her. If she was still afraid of him, he couldn't ever let her see him again. He'd never again be able to visit her, even without her knowledge, without remembering the terrified look on her face.

It had taken him 175 years, through life and through death, to find a woman like Lucy. He had a feeling he'd need another two centuries to forget her.

17

J esse ducked behind the back of Meade's Tavern, in the parking lot, so he could turn visible without anyone seeing him. Then he walked back around the front and waited for someone to go into the restaurant so he could walk in through the open door.

A million scenarios of what could happen swirled through his head, and few of them ended with Lucy rushing toward him telling him how much she'd missed him.

What if she saw him and screamed? What if she fainted again?

A young couple finally walked to the front door of the tavern. Jesse did his best to look as non-threatening as possible as he followed them inside.

The hostess, Janine, greeted the couple warmly. As she led them to a nearby table, Jesse scanned the dining room. He knew Lucy's schedule and knew she was working that day, but she wasn't in the room at the moment. His ghostly stomach tingled with nervousness and excitement. He wanted so badly to see her again, but he didn't want to scare her.

Janine smiled at Jesse, but otherwise ignored him and went back to work. She knew he was a friend of Lucy's and wasn't there to dine.

Lucy walked into the dining room carrying a huge tray of entrees for her customers. Jesse hoped to God that she would be able to put the plates down in front of her customers before she caught sight of him. He had a horrible vision of her panicking, dropping hot food, and burning herself or someone else.

She smiled warmly as she set the food down on the table. After she ensured they had everything they needed for their meal, she started to head to the back of the room.

Lucy caught a glimpse of Jesse just as she turned to head toward another table. She slowly, methodically turned back around. She locked eyes with him from across the crowded dining room.

Jesse didn't move an inch. He knew that anything he did or said could frighten her.

Lucy's hand flew to her lips. She paled, just as she had when she first realized he was a ghost. She looked terrified, as if she might burst out crying.

Jesse's heart sank. She was still afraid and probably always would be. He didn't want to hurt her anymore. He gave her a sad smile, then pressed his right hand to his lips and blew her a kiss. The door opened behind him as more customers came in, and he used that opportunity to turn and walk away.

Lucy stared at the door after Jesse had left. Adrenaline pumped through her system, and she put a hand on the bar to steady herself. His sudden presence had taken her completely by surprise. She was scared, but also happy to see him again. She hadn't realized how much she'd missed Jesse until she saw him.

Jesse's smile was so sweet and so sad. It was hard to be frightened when she thought of his gentle face. Lucy recalled Theresa's words: *He really is a sweet farm boy from Texas.* Standing in the doorway, he looked like a poor soldier, a kind young man, and not something to be feared.

Lucy had the sudden urge to run after him.

"You okay, honey?" Mandy asked. She stood behind the bar and saw how pale Lucy had become.

"Y-yes. Yes, I'm fine," Lucy responded. She glanced back at the doorway, then went back to tending to her customers. For the rest of her shift, she couldn't stop thinking about Jesse. He'd seemed so lost, so lonely. She pictured how he'd looked before she found out he was dead. How happy he seemed when he talked with her, joked with her.

Jesse had obviously given her a few days to recover from her shock before trying to visit her again. The poor guy was doing his best not to scare her, but she'd freaked out anyway. Why the hell did she have to be so scared all the time? He'd never done anything to hurt her. He was lonely and just wanted to be her friend, and Joel likely wanted the same thing.

Lucy worried that she had completely ruined her chance at ever seeing either one of them again. She thought of Jesse blowing her a kiss as he stood in the doorway. It was a goodbye kiss. Her heart ached at the thought.

DESPONDENT, Jesse trudged down the street. Joel watched Jesse as he walked right by him, staring at the ground. He didn't even see Joel sitting on the steps of one of the historic buildings. Jesse's dejected expression told him everything he needed to know. Lucy was still afraid. It would be cruel to continue to haunt her with their presence, so they had no choice but to leave her be.

Joel felt terribly, utterly alone. It had been wonderful to have someone as kind as Lucy to speak to every day. It was something to look forward to in an otherwise empty existence.

He watched as Jesse continued to walk aimlessly down the street. He couldn't help but feel sympathy for him. Joel understood the heartbreak of being separated from the woman you loved.

JESSE FOUND a place to sit in the busiest part of town. He watched the crowds for a bit. He flirted with some of the women, but his heart wasn't in it. Even watching the children running around didn't cheer him. It simply reminded him of the family life he'd never have.

His plan had been to vanish for a long time, to simply cease consciousness for a while to escape the pain of losing Lucy, but he knew that was only a temporary solution. When he came back, he'd still be faced with the same problems.

The only other solution was to cross over. If he'd known how to do that, he'd have done it long ago. It had been a long time since he'd even tried to work through the issues that were keeping him earthbound. Now Jesse had more motivation than ever. The only way to escape this hellish existence was for his spirit to be released.

18

Lucy lay in bed that night thinking of Jesse. This time, however, it wasn't fear keeping her awake. She found she couldn't stop thinking of his face, his sad smile. She remembered the way she had felt when she was with him. Before she knew he was dead. No one had ever made her feel the way Jesse did when he spoke to her.

He'd called her his honorary yellow rose of Texas.

Lucy wondered if he really meant it, or if he was just bored and wanted a friend.

She also thought about Joel. Where was he? Was he lonely, too? Joel and Jesse were enemies, so they didn't even have each other to talk to. What did ghosts do all day? Where did they go?

Lucy didn't have to work the next day. As she drifted off to sleep, she wondered if she could find the two soldiers again. They knew she was afraid of them and would probably never come back to the tavern. It was up to her to go look for them.

～

JESSE SAT, invisible, on the steps of the Pennsylvania Monument on Hancock Ave. The monument was off the main, busy streets of Gettysburg, but was a big tourist attraction nonetheless. Over one hundred feet high, it was the biggest monument in the historic town. It was made of granite and had stairs that led all the way to the top, offering an amazing view of the battlefields. Jesse sat somberly on the steps as the tourists, especially the kids, climbed up to the top. It was mid-afternoon on a weekday, so it was mostly mothers with little ones who were too young for school.

It was not uncommon for people to trample right over, or through, Jesse as he sat. It was a windy, somewhat cool day, so the shiver they felt was simply attributed to the weather.

Jesse stared out at the vast battlefield before him, contemplating his next move. He still couldn't decide whether to concentrate on trying to cross over, which seemed pointless after all these years, or vanishing for a while to escape his sorrow.

As always, his thoughts were consumed with Lucy, so at first he thought he was seeing things when he caught sight of the woman walking in the distance, her long, brown hair whipping around in the wind.

Lucy.

Jesse would know her anywhere. He knew all her mannerisms; the way she walked, the way she brushed her long hair out of her face. He jumped up from his spot on the stone steps, carelessly charging through a tourist, a man in his sixties. The man zipped up his jacket, then continued on up the stairs.

Jesse stared at Lucy as she walked on the freshly cut grass. In all the time he'd known her, he had never seen her on any of the battlefields. Lucy was fascinated by history, but she'd lived in Gettysburg for several years now because she attended Gettysburg College. Jesse figured she'd toured all the battlefields when she first arrived, and had long ago seen pretty much everything the historic town had to offer. These days, she mostly concentrated on work and school.

Jesse walked a little closer, but was still a distance away from her. Lucy glanced around, looking a little scared, but nowhere near as frightened as she had been before.

Was it possible that she was looking for them?

Jesse's heart surged with hope. He knew she had the day off, and she rarely came into town when she wasn't working. He stared at her, afraid to let himself believe that she was searching for them. For him.

Jesse got his answer when he followed her to her next stop, which was just down the road. Gettysburg National Cemetery. Creeped out as she was by all things ghostly, there was only one possible reason why she would choose to go to the cemetery on her day off from work. She *was* looking for her dead soldier friends.

Jesse followed Lucy as she walked around the cemetery. She looked at the rows and rows of graves, many of which simply had numbers on them instead of names as they contained the unknown dead. Jesse's heart ached when he heard her let out a shaky, nervous breath. How he hated seeing her afraid! He remembered how terrified she'd looked when her hand had sliced right through his ghostly body. He'd never be able to get the image out of his head. He knew he had to tread carefully when he approached her. She did seem to be looking for them, but that didn't mean she wouldn't freak out again if she actually found them.

Jesse watched in astonishment as Lucy walked over to grave number 495. She stood right over it, staring at it like she'd been drawn to that spot. She shivered a bit and hugged her arms around herself the way she did when she was feeling self-conscious. Or frightened.

There were no other people around, so Jesse became visible. He stood in front of Lucy a short distance away. She still stared down at grave 495. He watched her face and could pinpoint the millisecond when she became aware of his presence. She drew in a sharp, nervous breath. She moved her eyes slightly, from the grave to Jesse's worn, dirty shoes. She swallowed hard and slowly raised her head to see his face.

Jesse looked into her soft, brown eyes. He didn't say a word and didn't dare move. Then he smiled at her.

It took Lucy a moment to find her voice. When she did, it was small and timid. "Hi."

"Hi," Jesse replied quietly.

She glanced down at the grave. "Is this you?"

Jesse nodded. Lucy's eyes opened wide with astonishment. "I-I don't know how I knew. I just knew!"

Jesse smiled again. "You're sensitive. I don't really understand it either, but some people are just sensitive to things like that. You know...paranormal things. I seen some tourists over the years go right to a grave and say they think it's their relative or somethin'. I don't really know, but I 'spect they're right."

"So it wasn't just an act," Lucy said, gesturing at his Confederate uniform. "You really are..."

Jesse touched the tip of his hat and bowed to her. "Private Jesse Spenser of the First Texas, at your service. Born May 26, 1839. Died July 2, 1863."

Lucy went a bit pale.

"You all right?" Jesse asked, looking worried. "You're not gonna swoon again, are you? I can't catch ya, ya know."

"I think I need to sit down," she said, looking slightly

woozy. She slowly lowered herself to the ground and sat just in front of Jesse's grave. He sat down across from her, but still kept a safe distance. Lucy ran her fingers over the number 495, gently, and with great respect.

"Weren't supposed to be any rebels in this cemetery, but a few of us goobers snuck in on 'em," Jesse told her.

Lucy smiled, looking calmer. "Yeah. I remember reading that there are supposedly nine or ten Confederates in here with the rest of the Union soldiers."

They were both silent for a moment.

"Please don't be afraid of me," Jesse said softly, almost a whisper.

"I'm trying," Lucy said quietly. She looked into his gentle blue-gray eyes.

"I can't hurt you. I mean, I would *never*...but even if I tried..." He held up his ghostly hands.

Lucy nodded. Then laughed suddenly. Jesse looked at her curiously.

"Whut?"

"That's why you wouldn't pick up the silverware for me."

Jesse laughed and nodded. He threw up his hands again. "I couldn't."

Lucy chuckled again. "Joel is such an ass."

"That's what I've been trying to tell you!"

"So, Joel...is he...?"

"Yeah," Jesse said carefully, taking care not to frighten her. "He died in the battle, too."

Lucy nodded. She glanced around the cemetery. "Where did he end up?"

Jesse winced, not knowing how to put the truth delicately. "They, uh...they didn't find enough of him to bury."

"Oh," Lucy said, looking a bit nauseated. Then she just looked sad. "Poor Joel. So you guys really are enemies."

"Yeah, you could say that," Jesse said. That was a bit of an understatement. "At least now you know why I never take off my hat in your presence. I feel bad about that. It's very disrespectful not to take off my hat around a lady."

Lucy laughed. "You're so sweet. I never noticed, really. But thank you. The world needs more gentlemen like you, Jesse."

He grinned and nodded in thanks. He loved hearing Lucy say his name.

Lucy looked at him with wonder. "There're so many things I want to ask you guys!"

Jesse's heart sank. He enjoyed having Lucy's attention all to himself and didn't relish the idea of bringing Joel back into the mix. "You really want to see that Yankee Doodle again?"

"Of course! After all, I haven't made my decision yet."

"Ah. That's true."

"Is there somewhere the three of us could meet? You know, talk in private? I don't want to blow your cover by asking about ghost stuff when I'm at work." Lucy second-guessed herself for a moment. Perhaps she was being presumptuous. "I-I mean...not that you have to answer my questions about your personal life. I mean death. I-I mean..." She blushed as she stammered awkwardly.

Jesse found Lucy adorable when she blushed, but he didn't want her to feel uncomfortable. "You can ask me anything you like, my lovely rose."

Lucy bit her lip and looked at him shyly.

"We could meet tomorrow morning," Lucy said. Jesse nodded, so Lucy asked, "Where do you want to meet?"

"Anywhere you like! Well, anywhere within the town of Gettysburg. We're not physically able to go any farther than that."

"Really? Wow."

"Anyplace around here is fine—the battlefields or whatever. Just not... I prefer not Devil's Den."

Lucy nodded somberly.

"Okay. What about near the college? Is that too far to walk for you? I mean..."

"Not at all. We don't get tired anymore. At least not physically. It's easy for us to get there."

"Okay. How about we meet at one of the gazebos?"

"Sure. The one in the main square or the one behind the athletic building?" Jesse asked. When Lucy looked at him curiously, he added, "We been here a long time. We know where *everything* is." He remembered when the damn gazebos were *installed.*

"Yes, I suppose you do," Lucy said. "How about the athletic building one. About nine a.m.?"

"It's a date. Even if you do insist that I bring another man along," Jesse said, making a face.

Lucy laughed. She smiled shyly and let out a nervous breath.

19

J esse wandered around, reluctantly looking for Joel. Part of him hoped he wouldn't find him so he could keep his appointment with Lucy to himself. Guilt took over, and he knew he couldn't leave Joel out. He knew Joel missed Lucy, but he didn't care much about that. Lucy wanted to meet with them both, and God knows she didn't ask for much. He owed it to her to honor her request.

Joel hung out at Devil's Den a lot, and Jesse hoped he wouldn't have to hunt him down there. He finally ran into him along a quiet stretch of Confederate Avenue. Joel shot him his usual look of annoyance mixed with disgust.

"I talked to her," Jesse said.

"You did?" Joel asked, his eyes lighting up.

"Yeah. She was really scared at first. I tried to see her at the tavern and she looked upset, so I figured I best leave her alone."

Joel nodded.

"Then she went looking for us."

"No way!" Joel said. He looked happy, almost childlike. Jesse felt a twinge of guilt for thinking of leaving Joel out.

God knows he understood the crushing loneliness of being a spirit.

"Yeah. She walked to the battlefields and then to the cemetery. Joel, she went *right up* to my grave. She knew it was mine. She knew it was me!"

"Damn. She really is sensitive. That's incredible!"

"I know. She wants to see us again. She wants to talk to us—you know, ask us about everything."

Relief washed over Joel's face. "That's wonderful. I'd love to talk to her again."

"Yeah. It was so good to see her. I talked to her a little at my gravesite."

Joel's eyes opened wide. "Wow. She's come a long way already."

Jesse laughed. "I know. But we still gotta be careful, be gentle with her. She's still scared. I tried to keep my distance a bit—you know, ease her into it. She said she wants to talk to both of us, but having two ghosts with her might be overwhelming."

Joel nodded. "Yeah. You're right. "

"We're supposed to meet at the Gettysburg College gazebo, nine o'clock tomorrow mornin'. The one outside the athletic building."

"Okay," Joel said. "Okay! Sounds good!"

Joel looked so excited that it was hard for Jesse to hate him.

LUCY SAT NERVOUSLY in the gazebo, waiting for Joel and Jesse to meet her. Though she was much calmer about ghosts than she'd ever been before, she was still frightened.

A shot of adrenaline exploded in her body as she saw

the two soldiers walking toward her in the distance. She thought she was ready, but her instinct was to run. Lucy drew in a breath, trying to steady her nerves. She knew they wouldn't hurt her, *couldn't* hurt her, but the idea that she was meeting with two dead people was a little creepy.

Lucy felt dizzy when Joel and Jesse got close enough to make eye contact with her. Fear gripped her until she looked into Jesse's eyes. He smiled at her, and she remembered how comfortable she'd been talking to him yesterday.

"I told ya," Jesse said to Joel. "The lovely rose of *Texas* has returned."

Joel shot him an annoyed look. Lucy was struck by how familiar their exchange was. They were still the same two men she used to talk with before she knew the truth, and the familiarity of their arguing was comforting.

Standing outside the gazebo, Joel turned his attention to Lucy. "You okay, sweetheart?" he asked.

Lucy nodded, touched by his concern. "Yes. I'm fine," she said in a small voice.

Jesse entered the gazebo and sat down, choosing a seat a little distance away from her.

Joel hesitated at the door. "Is it okay if I come in with you?"

Lucy smiled, and her shoulders relaxed a little. She felt a little silly being afraid, but was grateful for his tentative approach. "Of course."

Joel quietly entered and took a seat across from Jesse and an equal distance away from Lucy.

"I'm sorry," Lucy said to Jesse. "I know I completely over-reacted when, you know, that night at the tavern. I was just... so scared." Her voice shook a little.

"You have nothing to apologize for," Joel told her. "It was

completely our fault." He shot a look at Jesse, making it clear that he blamed the Rebel for what happened.

"Yes, it is," Jesse agreed, looking at Lucy and ignoring Joel. "I'm so terribly sorry I scared you. I don't blame you one bit for swoonin'. You scared the heck outta *me* when you fell, I don't mind tellin' you."

"Me, too," Joel said.

Lucy looked at him curiously, and he looked guilty. "Yeah," he admitted. "I was there that night, too. But, you know, you couldn't see me."

"Really?" Lucy asked, more curious than afraid. "Where were you?"

"I was there in the room. Yelling at Jesse the whole time you were talking to him," Joel said, smirking.

"So you can be invisible?"

"Yeah," Jesse said. "Ghosts can always see other ghosts, but we can be invisible to the livin' when we wanna be. I was invisible to you after you fainted. I stayed right by you the whole time, though. When you hit your head, I was so afraid you were hurt."

Both men looked guilty and sad, and Lucy felt the last remnants of her fear fade away.

"We both stayed with you to make sure you were okay," Joel said. "Jesse was able to get help for you. He managed to knock over the tray next to you, and that's when Craig came and found you."

Lucy's eyes grew wide. "You can touch things? But I thought—"

"Well, *sometimes* we can touch things. If you concentrate real, real hard," Jesse told her. "I just got all my strength together, and all I could manage was one quick shove. But it worked. Thank God."

"Thank you, Jesse."

"No need to thank me, ma'am. I'm the one responsible for you gettin' hurt in the first place. I'm real sorry about that." He lowered his head, and she could no longer see his face under his hat.

"It's all right," Lucy said. She thought about what they'd just told her. "It's so odd to think you could be there without me knowing. Have you guys ever done it before?"

Joel sent a pointed look at Jesse. Lucy gasped, horrified.

"You have, haven't you?" she cried. "You've watched me without me knowing!" She hugged her arms around herself like she always did when she was feeling self-conscious or, in this case, violated.

"Yes. I won't lie to you, Lucy," Jesse admitted, wincing a bit. "We have watched you before."

"How could you do that? Why would you do that?" Lucy asked, looking down. She refused to look at them. She couldn't bear to think of what they might have seen or heard when she was unaware of their presence.

"Lucy, I swear to you. It was only at the restaurant and usually when there were lots of other people around. I never watched you in your private time, like at home or anything. I-I can't travel that far anyway, and even if I could, I would *never* do that."

Lucy tentatively looked up at him. She remembered him saying that he was physically unable to travel outside the town of Gettysburg, and she also knew he was a true gentleman. He would never violate a woman by watching her inappropriately, even if he had the opportunity. But Lucy was still uneasy with the knowledge of having been watched. Especially by him. Lucy looked up at Jesse, her face reddening with anger and embarrassment.

"People act differently when they think no one is

around. H-how could you spy on me when I didn't know?" She had been so careful about how she acted around him. She'd always tried to put on her best face, both with her physical appearance and in the way she acted. Now there was no way she could ever know what he had seen and heard.

"I'm so sorry, Lucy. I remember the first time I laid eyes on you." Jesse said looking at her tenderly. "It was a few months ago. There was this group of kids that came to the tavern on a school trip. I was bored, like usual, and I love watching kids, so I followed them inside."

Looking down, Lucy furrowed her brow. She remembered that day, that large group of kids. Her mind whirled as she tried to remember what she'd said and done while Jesse was there.

"Nobody wanted to deal with all those messy kids, but you did. You walked right up to 'em, smiling all sweet and lookin' so pretty, and you took care of them. You talked to them about history. You told them the Confederates weren't necessarily bad guys."

Lucy finally looked up. "I remember that."

"That meant so much to me, Lucy. To hear you tell them that the Southern soldiers weren't bad. We were just tryin' to protect our homes and our families."

Lucy felt her shoulders relax a little. As far as she could remember, she hadn't done anything foolish to be ashamed of that day. Thank God.

"You're gonna make a wunnerful teacher, Lucy," Jesse told her. Lucy looked a bit unsettled that he knew so much about her, so he added, "You told the kids' teacher about being at Gettysburg College studyin' to be a teacher yourself."

Lucy let out a small sigh. She felt slightly better.

"I'm so sorry I upset you, Lucy. I promise you that most of the times I saw you, there were lots of other people around."

"And the other times?" Lucy asked, feeling her anger rise again.

"Sometimes I'd come look after you late at night. When I knew you were scared, closin' up the restaurant by yourself." Jesse laughed. "You know, when you were afraid there might be ghosts nearby."

Even Lucy chuckled at the irony. She glanced over at Joel.

"It was only a couple of times for me," Joel admitted. "There was one time when I think you had a feeling we were there."

"Really?"

"Yeah. We were there at night when you were closing up. We were yelling at each other, acting like idiots as usual. You stopped what you were doing and looked around, like you knew you were being watched."

Lucy shivered a bit. "Yeah. I do get that feeling sometimes. Now I know why!"

"We felt really bad," Joel continued. "So we left so we'd quit scaring you."

"I already knew how scared you were of ghosts, so I can't imagine how you felt when you found out about us," Jesse said sorrowfully. "I felt so bad about that. I was worried 'bout how you'd fare that first night closing up after you found out we were...you know. So I went to check on you."

"You did?" Lucy asked.

Jesse nodded. "It was terrible. You were cryin' and terrified and it was all my fault."

He looked so sad, so concerned, that Lucy's anger started to fade.

"I figgered, you'd sensed we were there that one time, so mebbe you'd know that I was there again. Watching over you. I hoped you'd sense I was there and feel better. I even sang to you."

"You did?" Lucy asked incredulously.

"I was hopin' it would calm you down."

"Did it work?" she asked.

Jesse shrugged and said quietly, "You stopped cryin'."

Lucy thought for a moment. "What did you sing to me?"

Jesse grinned and sang with gusto and a little off key, "She's the sweetest little rosebud that Texas ever knew!"

Lucy laughed and clapped her hands. "Of course. You know, you're making it impossible to stay mad at you!"

Jesse shot her that impish grin that made her heart skip a beat.

"I promise you, my beautiful rose, it was almost always at the restaurant when I watched you. Then sometimes when you were out in public, on the street, I'd catch sight of you. I was sittin' there on Hancock Avenue when you walked by yesterday. I followed you to the cemetery 'cause I thought you might be lookin' for us."

"I was."

"I know." Jesse grinned, and Lucy blushed.

"Okay. Thank you for explaining it all to me. I guess I'm glad you were honest," Lucy said, not sure that it was the truth. She still felt horribly unsettled that they had watched her in secret. "I know the truth about you now. I know... what you are." She looked at Joel, then at Jesse. Then she said forcefully, "*Don't ever watch me like that again.* If you want to talk to me, come see me. And I need to be able to see you. Got it?"

"Deal. I promise," Joel said. "No more stalking you."

Lucy looked at Jesse.

"Cross my heart and hope to *die*," Jesse said, making a cross over his heart. Lucy looked irritated, and not amused. Jesse nodded solemnly and said, "I promise, Lucy. I swear. I'll never do it again. And I'm so sorry that I upset you. I never meant to hurt you, darlin'"

"We're sorry to put you through all this, sweetheart. Truly. We were trying to figure out how to tell you about us," Joel said. "We hadn't planned on hanging around with you so much. I figured we'd ask you to choose, you'd pick me, and it'd be over and done with!" He puffed out his chest and displayed his manliness.

Lucy laughed, and Joel smiled back.

"We never counted on getting so attached to you," Joel said warmly. "As you might imagine, we don't have too many people to talk to in our situation."

"No, I guess you don't," Lucy said with sympathy. "You must be very lonely." Joel and Jesse nodded. "So, spirits can be invisible," she said, her mind spinning with the implications of that. "There must be ghosts everywhere around here. Does that mean they're wandering around all the time even when we can't see them?"

Joel and Jesse exchanged a look.

"Well, kinda," Jesse began carefully. "There are a fair amount of ghosts around—lots of soldiers in this area, of course, because so many of us died here."

Lucy swallowed and nodded. The thought of thousands of dead soldiers wandering around scared her, even if she was no longer afraid of the two she was talking to now.

"It's not as creepy as it sounds, Lucy. Really. I know you're probably picturing something out of *The Walking Dead*."

Lucy looked at him, surprised. "How do you know about *The Walking Dead*?"

"Days Inn," both soldiers answered.

"We watch TV over there sometimes," Jesse explained.

"You do?" Lucy asked.

"Oh, yeah," Joel said. "We get bored so we go over there and watch TV if people have it on. I especially love *Real Housewives.*"

"So you just go sit with people when they don't know you're there?" Lucy asked, looking uncomfortable with the idea.

"Yeah, we do. But it's not like we watch people in the shower or anything," Jesse said.

"Right," Joel said. "I can't promise you that no ghosts ever do that, but we don't."

Lucy still didn't look thrilled with what they were telling her.

"There are a lot of spirits around here," Joel told her, "but they won't hurt you."

"Truth is, most ghosts don't bother much with the living. Most of them kind of keep to themselves. They have their own problems to deal with," Jesse told her.

"Like what?" Lucy asked.

"Dealing with the past, mostly," Jesse said sorrowfully.

Lucy looked at him with concern, wondering what had happened to him.

"Is that why you're still here? You have...things you have to deal with?" Lucy asked.

"Yes," Jesse told her with a sad smile. "We all do. Otherwise, we would have crossed over."

"You mean, you're waiting to cross over to heaven?" Lucy asked.

"Yes," Joel told her. "We've seen it happen to others."

"You have?" Lucy asked, her eyes growing huge. "How? What did you see? How does it happen?"

Lucy was clearly fascinated by this discussion, and Jesse wanted to be the one explaining it all to her. Joel opened his mouth to talk, but Jesse cut him off.

"It's amazing, Lucy." Jesse smiled when Lucy turned her rapt attention to him, hanging on his every word. "It's like this big, brilliant light shinin' all over. And you know, the person goin' just looks so happy. We usually get a feelin' when somebody's gettin' ready to go home. They just seem more peaceful. Then you see this bright, white light and then, well, I wish I could explain what the person looks like. It's like...I dunno, *peaceful* is the only word I can come up with, but it's more than that. You just look at the guy and you know he's going home to all his loved ones and with God and...he's jus'...he's finally going where he belongs."

"So there really is a God...a heaven," Lucy said with wonder. "What about...I mean, is there a..."

"Hell?" Joel asked. "I don't know. If there is, we've never seen anybody go there."

"Hell is here," Jesse added. "Life can be hell. Death can be hell. Being just a spirit is hell. Well, it was until I met you."

Lucy rewarded Jesse's kindness with a smile. "Well, I'm glad I can help." She wondered if there was anything else she could do. What if she was able to help them cross over? She wanted to know what had happened in their pasts to keep them stranded here, but it seemed such a personal thing to ask.

"What do you need to do to cross over?"

"Hard to say," Jesse said wearily. "If we knew, I suppose we'd have done it by now."

"It seems to have to do with accepting yourself somehow. Accepting your past. Forgiving yourself," Joel said. He spoke with an even heavier sense of weariness than Jesse had. Both Joel and Jesse seemed so kind, so good, it was hard for Lucy to imagine what they could have possibly done that was so horrible that they'd been unable to forgive themselves. They might have done things in the heat of battle that they'd never have done in their ordinary lives.

It was hard for Lucy to imagine either of them killing anyone, but she had little doubt that they had. They'd died in the war and must have been forced to kill others. The thought was sad instead of frightening.

"Joel," Lucy said, turning toward him. "You said you were a widower. Do you mind if I ask what happened?" She was a little apprehensive about asking him such a personal question, and she watched him carefully for his reaction.

"Not at all." Joel said. "I wasn't exactly a widower. I just said that because you didn't know I was dead. Truth is, she was alive when I went off to war. But, you know, she's long gone by now."

"Did you have children?"

Joel grinned proudly. "Yes, I sure did. Two little boys. David and Mathew. It's been so long, but I still remember those faces. Their little voices."

"You'll see them again when you cross over," Lucy said softly.

"I suppose," Joel said, sounding tired. "I guess it will happen eventually, but it feels like I've been stuck here for an eternity."

"What was your wife like?" Lucy asked.

Joel turned to her with a look of surprise on his face. At first, she was afraid she might have upset him. Then he smiled at her thoughtfully.

"Nobody's asked me that in a really long time. I think

everyone's sick of me talking about her." He paused for a moment, thinking of how to describe the love of his life to someone who'd never known her. "She was the boss's daughter. Emma. Her name was Emma."

"I worked in a shoemaker's shop, and one day in comes this *gorgeous* woman with long, blond hair. She didn't like to wear her hair up like most women did back in the day. She was rebellious that way."

"She was so beautiful and had this killer smile. I was completely smitten with her right away. Then I found out who she was, and I was like, *Oh no. She's Mr. Arlow's daughter!*"

Lucy laughed again. "Was Dad upset when he found out how you felt about his little girl?"

"No! That's the thing! He was like, 'What took you so long, boy?' when I finally asked about her." He paused again, lost in thought for a moment. "Emma was very sweet. She had a huge heart, just like you, Lucy."

Lucy was honored to be compared to this woman who was obviously Joel's whole world.

"But she was also brazen, bold, outspoken."

"*Not* like me," Lucy said.

"Right. She was beautiful in a different way than you're beautiful, sweetheart."

"You're very kind, Joel," Lucy said with her usual bashfulness. She turned to Jesse. She wanted to know about his past, but she knew it would hurt if she found out that he'd had a wonderful wife, too. Even if she was long gone, Lucy knew it was going to be hard to hear Jesse talk about a woman he loved. "What about you, Jesse?"

"Welp! Back in the war days, when we came 'cross some poor dead soldier, we'd say 'there's somebody's darling.'" Jesse chuckled. "I was nobody's darling."

Lucy was relieved that she didn't have to hear stories about the love of Jesse Spenser's life, then immediately felt guilty. Jesse had died with nobody waiting at home for him and no one to write letters about how much she missed him while he was away. She felt ashamed that she was happy to hear that Jesse hadn't been married.

"I didn't have a sweetheart back home waiting for me," Jesse continued.

"Well, there's a surprise," Joel said, his voice dripping with sarcasm.

Lucy shot Joel a look of annoyance. *Poor Jesse.* She thought.

"Well, you must have had some family back home in Texas."

"Yeah. My mother and father lived on the farm. I didn't have any brothers or sisters," Jesse said with a touch of sorrow. "I can't even imagine what it was like for my mother to get the news that I was killed in battle."

"You were her baby," Lucy said with great compassion.

Jesse nodded sorrowfully. "I signed up to fight because I thought it was the right thing to do. I thought I was protectin' my family, but I can't help but think it must have ruined my mother's life. Father, too."

Lucy didn't know what to say to that. She wondered if Jesse's regrets about going to war were part of the reason he hadn't crossed over.

"I don't even want to think about what it was like for Emma to get the news. To think of how she had to explain it to the kids," Joel said, looking devastated. His pain was so raw, even after all these years. "God, we're depressing company. I'm sorry, Lucy."

"Me, too," Jesse said. "Enough about us. Tell us about you! What do you plan on teaching when you graduate?"

"I think I want to teach elementary school, or maybe junior high school. You know, that age group where you still have a chance to get kids excited about learning. I want to make learning fun for them, you know what I mean? History is so fascinating. It doesn't have to be just memorizing boring facts. It's about people and stories and adventure, and even heartbreak," Lucy said, looking at both soldiers. She spoke quickly, animatedly. "If we can learn from the past, we can make the future better! I want to help the kids understand the history of our country, of our world, you know? I want them to be interested, involved, you know what I mean?"

Both men stared at her, and she suddenly felt extremely self-conscious. "What?" Lucy asked, hugging her arms around herself.

Jesse smiled at her. "You're even more beautiful when you get all excited and talk about your dreams."

Lucy looked at him like she wasn't sure she believed him. She turned to Joel, who nodded, indicating he'd been thinking the same thing.

"Jesse's right," Joel said. "For *once*. You're going to make a wonderful teacher."

"Thank you," Lucy said, genuinely touched.

"She will be an amazin' schoolteacher, but I don't know how well I'd be able to concentrate on the lesson if she were my teacher," Jesse said, grinning.

"That's a good point," Joel said, chuckling.

Lucy just waved them off. She was quiet for a moment, thoughtful.

"What're you thinkin' about, darlin'?" Jesse asked.

"You guys. I was just wondering...what do you do all day? When you're not spying on unsuspecting women like me," she said dryly. "Where do you go?"

"Well, we can't go far, that's for sure. Like I told ya, we're pretty much trapped inside the town of Gettysburg," Jesse told her.

"What happens if you try to leave?" she asked.

"We just kinda disappear," Jesse said. "Just fade out. Then ya got no choice but to go back."

"So you just hang around Gettysburg all day and all night? Not being able to touch anything or do anything? That does sound like hell. How do you not lose your mind? You can't even sleep to escape!" Lucy said, looking horrified.

"Yeah. It's bad, but it's not as horrible as it sounds," Joel told her. "You're right that we can't sleep. But what we can do is kind of disappear for a while. In our ghost circles, we call it vanishing. It's different than turning invisible. If we're just invisible, the living can't see us, but we're still there. Vanishing means we're not there at all." Joel wrinkled his nose. "It's kind of hard to explain."

"When you vanish, you're not conscious," Jesse added. "You still exist somewhere, but you're not awake and thinkin'. It's a lot like sleep, I s'pose. You're right when you say we'd probably lose our minds if we had to drift around twenty-four hours a day and not be able to do anything. When you vanish, you kinda get a break from existence for a while."

Lucy nodded, taking in the information. It still seemed fairly awful.

"You can even vanish for years at a time," Joel said.

"Really?" Lucy asked.

"Yeah, we all vanish on a regular basis," Jesse told her. "Sometimes several times a day, a week, ya know. So though we've been around for over a hundred and fifty years, it doesn't always feel like it's been that long."

"So, can you feel anything?" Lucy asked.

"You mean physically?" Joel asked. Lucy nodded. "Not really. We have all our memories and still feel emotions and everything, but we don't feel anything physical."

"So if I tried to touch you, you wouldn't feel it?" Lucy asked.

Joel shook his head sadly. "No. I wish I could. Do you want to try to touch me?"

Lucy looked a little nervous, but was curious. She'd been so shocked when she first tried to touch Jesse that she didn't remember much about what it felt like.

"Maybe," Lucy admitted.

Joel grinned at her. "Give it a try. It's okay. Don't be afraid."

Joel held up his hand, palm out, in front of her so she could try to touch it. He held eye contact with her to reassure her, to make sure she wasn't scared. "It'll feel very cold," Joel gently warned her.

Lucy nodded and took a deep breath. She held up her right hand and placed it against Joel's left palm. She jumped a bit when her hand went through his.

Joel laughed softly. "It's okay, sweetheart."

Lucy pushed her hand all the way through and felt a cold chill run up her arm. Then she dropped her hand back into her lap and smiled.

"I did it!"

Joel laughed again. "You sure did! Good job. You've come a long way."

"I'm proud of you, Lucy," Jesse said. He looked annoyed, maybe even a little jealous.

"Thanks," she said, smiling at him. She felt like she had accomplished something huge. If anyone had told her that someday she would willingly reach out and touch a ghost, she never would have believed it.

Lucy pulled out her cell phone from her purse and glanced at the time. "Well, I better get going. I have to get to work."

When she looked up, she saw that both Joel and Jesse looked disappointed. She felt guilty, but she had no choice but to leave.

"You can't go yet," Jesse told her. "You still haven't chosen a winner."

Lucy chuckled, having nearly forgotten about the bet. "Maybe tomorrow."

"Come on, darlin'. Sooner or later you're gonna have to acknowledge the corn."

Lucy giggled like she always did when Jesse used 1860s phrases.

"Are you planning on eating lunch outside tomorrow?" Jesse asked hopefully.

"I think that can be arranged." Both men grinned at her. Though Lucy felt sad for them and their current situation, it felt nice to be needed. Now she understood how much her companionship meant to them. They had no one else, at least no one else alive, to talk to.

"Hunkey dorey!" Jesse said with enthusiasm. Joel rolled his eyes, but Lucy giggled again.

"See you guys soon," Lucy said. She gathered her purse and cell phone and then stepped out of the gazebo. Both soldiers watched her walk away.

Joel suddenly got up and went after her. He jogged up to her and said quietly, "Lucy."

"Yeah?" she asked, looking at him with concern.

"I just wanted to thank you for asking me about my family. It meant a lot to me to be able to talk about them again. You have no idea how much."

Lucy smiled warmly at him. "Well, I'm not done asking.

I'd like to hear more tomorrow." She reached over and put her hand on, or through, his shoulder. "I would give you a hug if I could."

Joel smiled at her wearily. "I would've liked that."

20

Joel and Jesse were already sitting at a table outside of Meade's Tavern when Lucy came out carrying her tray of food. She smiled as she set down her tray and sat with them.

"Are we coming across as totally needy and pathetic?" Joel asked.

"Not at all," Lucy said kindly. "I enjoy your company." She took a bite of her turkey wrap. It still felt a little weird to be eating around them, but at least now she understood why they never actually ate lunch with her.

"Is it good?" Jesse asked.

Lucy nodded. "Yep. Pretty much everything here is good." She lowered her voice, since there were a few other diners nearby. "Do you guys miss eating food?"

"Nah, not really," Joel answered. "We never get hungry, and we can't smell the food, so it's not like it's really tempting anymore. Sometimes I do miss the idea of food, you know? Meals are something to look forward to. Something to *do*, for God's sake!"

"That makes sense." She couldn't imagine the tedium of

being a spirit who couldn't smell, touch, or taste. Seeing and hearing were all they had. Lucy never realized how much she'd taken the other three senses for granted.

"Ya know what I miss?" Jesse asked. "Coffee. And I mean *real* coffee. Not that stuff we had in camp."

Joel grimaced. "Oh, man. That stuff was awful. It tasted like liquid dirt."

"Did you choke it down anyway? Just for the caffeine?" Lucy asked.

"Yeah. At least I did. It was called 'essence of coffee,' and it's kind of like what you'd call instant coffee nowadays. Was more like essence of garbage." Jesse said. He glanced over at a group of women eating lunch. One of them had a cup of coffee. "I can hardly remember what coffee smells like."

Lucy looked up from her lunch and smiled, but not at Jesse. She was looking past him out to the street where Theresa was approaching. Lucy had told Theresa that she would be eating lunch with the boys, and she wasn't surprised in the slightest to see that she'd found the time to drop by. She hadn't seen the guys since finding out they were dead.

Theresa strutted over to where they were sitting. She leaned over on the railing that separated the outdoor tables from the street, revealing an impressive amount of cleavage in the process. She looked at Joel.

"What's up, Casper?" Theresa said.

Joel chuckled, amused that Theresa was clearly unafraid of the two dead soldiers in her presence. She looked approvingly at Joel's physique. She glanced around to make sure no one was looking, then she poked a finger right into his chest. Naturally, her hand went right through. She didn't even flinch.

"Too bad," Theresa said with a sigh. "You would have been absolutely delicious to touch."

Joel looked unabashedly right into her cleavage, then looked up at her face. "Likewise," he told her.

"Is she always like this?" Jesse asked Lucy.

"Always," Lucy replied. "Especially around men in uniform."

"Hey!" Jesse said, sounding wounded. "I'm in uniform, too. Kinda." He was in a gray Confederate uniform, but his worn and tattered clothes were a far cry from Joel's crisp, blue Union attire.

Theresa glanced at him, looking him up and down. "I'd do ya."

"Gee, thanks," Jesse said wryly.

"That was a pity compliment, you know. She's just trying to be nice," Joel told him.

"It matters not!" Jesse said, with a dramatic toss of his head. He looked across the table at Lucy. "I'm only interested in winning the fair Lucy's affections."

Jesse looked into Lucy's eyes in a way that made her shiver with delight. She'd always felt so plain, especially around Theresa. Theresa was so beautiful and vivacious that men rarely gave Lucy a second look when she was around. Jesse made Lucy feel like she was the only woman in the room.

Lucy looked at Jesse, fascinated. "It's funny how I never noticed before that nothing moves on you. Like when you toss your head." Lucy mimicked the way Jesse had dramatically tossed his head a moment ago. "Nothing moves. Not your hair and not your hat."

"Nope," Jesse said, a little sadly. "Nothing works anymore."

"Your mouth still works, that's for sure," Joel said.

Lucy glanced at Jesse's mouth, his lips. *If only...* She wondered what it would have felt like to kiss him. She imagined his kiss would be tender and gentle. She quickly looked up before Jesse saw her staring at his mouth. She turned to Joel.

"Joel. You promised to tell me more about your family."

"So I did," Joel said, grinning. "What do you want to know?"

"What did your little boys look like?" Lucy asked.

"Me!" Joel said proudly.

Jesse shook his head. "Those poor babies."

Joel narrowed his eyes at Jesse, but then brightened when he resumed talking about his children. "They both had my eyes. It was funny to see these little tiny babies with these big, bright blue eyes lookin' at you. I could have stared at them for hours. I probably did!"

Lucy, Theresa, and even Jesse fell silent as they listened to Joel talk. You would never know that it had been well over a century since Joel had seen his children. He spoke as fondly of them as if he'd seen them last week.

"Did Emma like being a mother?" Lucy asked.

Joel smiled at Lucy. "Oh, yeah. Emma was the most wonderful mother. The thing I remember most was the laughter in our house. Emma and the kids laughed all the time. I don't know what they did all day when I was working, but the kids were always so happy. God, they adored her. She was like a kid herself with them. But she was a good mother, too, you know? She raised 'em right. Sure, they had fun, but she made sure they behaved. God help 'em if they talked back to her!"

Lucy laughed. "Good for her!"

Joel paused for a moment, looking rather melancholy. "I always wondered what it was like in that house when I didn't come home. I can't imagine there was much laughter there after I was gone."

"That must have been so hard for her," Theresa said softly.

"It sounds like she was a strong woman," Lucy said. "I can't begin to imagine her heartbreak, but I know she must have been strong for the children."

Joel nodded. "I think so, too. I hope so. Do you want to have kids someday?"

"Oh, yes!" Lucy said. "I would love to be a mother. I want to get through school and teach for a few years, but I would really love to get married and have a family."

"Well, you're going to make a wonderful mom someday," Joel told her.

"She is gonna be a great mama," Theresa said. "And I'm gonna be a kickass Auntie Theresa. So did you have a wife and kids back home, cowboy?"

Joel opened his mouth to give a smartass answer, but Lucy cut him off before he could speak.

"Jesse had a doting mother and loving father back home," Lucy said, giving Joel a pointed look. He grinned at her. "He was an only child, and his parents must have missed him terribly."

"Well, if I'd had a beautiful girl like you back home, I'd probably never have gone to war," Jesse said, looking into Lucy's eyes.

Theresa raised an eyebrow and said seductively, "Oh, yeah. Lucy would give you good reason to stay home."

Lucy blushed deeply. "Stop."

Theresa shot her an apologetic look. She hadn't meant to make her uncomfortable.

"You remind me so much of my wife," Joel told Theresa. "She always spoke her mind just like you do."

"I'm honored, Joel," Theresa said with a soft smile.

"I know you both miss your families so much. That's why I'm going to help you get back to them," Lucy said, her voice full of determination and confidence.

"You are?" Theresa asked.

"Yes," Lucy said forcefully. "I'm going to help them cross over whether they like it or not.

"Well, you're welcome to try," Joel said. "Just don't get your hopes up. We've been stuck here for a very long time."

"We'll see about that," Lucy said, a twinkle in her eye. Though she would miss them terribly if they crossed over, she hated the thought of them being trapped here, alone and away from their families. Lucy glanced around at the other diners. "I think we should meet somewhere more private tomorrow. Where we can really talk. I get the feeling there's a lot of stuff you guys avoid talking about, but it might help if you opened up about it. Might help you work out some of your issues."

"Oh, you're playing amateur therapist now?" Theresa asked, grinning. "I thought I was the psychology major."

"There's an awful lot of psychology in teaching, too, you know," Lucy said wryly, looking at the soldiers. "I have to figure out how to teach stubborn students who don't want to learn."

"I'll learn anything you want to teach me, Ms. Westbrook," Jesse said seductively.

Lucy chuckled. "Good."

"Where do you want to meet?" Jesse asked. "Anywhere, you know, but Devil's Den."

"You yellowbelly!" Joel said. "I died there, too, you know, and I go there all the time."

That comment got some strange looks from nearby diners, but his Union outfit seemed to explain his "death."

"We can avoid Devil's Den," Lucy said gently. "For now."

"Wuss," Joel mumbled.

"Why don't we meet at the Eternal Light Peace Memorial?" Lucy asked, but it didn't sound like a request. It was more of an order.

21

J   esse sat on the steps in front of the Eternal Light
        Peace Memorial. The large monument was located
        on Oak Hill overlooking Gettysburg National Park. It
        was intended to be a testament to everlasting peace;
the coming together of the North and the South into one
perfect Union. The memorial was made of materials from
Maine and Alabama and was funded by donations from
both sides. Atop the monument was a flame that shone
twenty-four hours a day, a light to shine in the hope for
continued peace.

Jesse had gotten there early, hoping to spend a few
moments alone with Lucy before Joel showed up and ruined
everything like he always did. It was a quiet weekday morning, and there weren't any tourists out yet.

Jesse groaned as he saw Joel, invisible to the living,
walking toward the memorial. Couldn't the guy ever be late?

"Delightful to see you, as always, Secesh," Joel said.

"Likewise, Yankee Doodle."

"Bet you were hoping to have some time alone with the
lady," Joel taunted.

"Nope. I was hoping to be alone with you, you sweet young thang."

"You know she's gonna try to make us get along," Joel said.

"I know. Good luck with that," Jesse said, scowling. It wasn't humanly possible to get along with that despicable Lincoln Boy.

Jesse's expression softened as he saw Lucy approaching in the distance. She was wearing blue jeans and a lacy, white blouse. Her long hair blew gently in the wind. "God, she's so damn beautiful," Jesse said softly, mainly to himself. When Lucy got close enough to see his face, Jesse would have to wipe that dreamy look off his face and act like he wasn't desperately in love with her. For the moment, though, his devotion was written all over him.

Jesse put on his charmer face and smiled at Lucy. "Good morning, my lovely rose."

Lucy smiled warmly at him. The morning sun highlighted her hair, and she looked like an angel standing there. The first few buttons of her blouse were undone, and the outfit was more revealing than her work uniform was. She wore a dainty, gold, heart-shaped necklace that glinted in the sun, drawing even more attention to her breasts. It took a lot of willpower for Jesse not to look, but he behaved. At least while she was looking at him.

Still looking at Lucy, Jesse said bluntly, "You're still invisible, jackass."

Joel faded in, and Lucy jumped a bit, startled. "Sorry," Joel mumbled guiltily.

"It's okay," Lucy said. She glanced up at the steps. "Let's move up a little closer."

Lucy walked up the steps of the memorial, and Joel followed. Jesse trailed them, glaring at Joel's back. He wished he could smack him right on the back of that big, blond head of his.

Lucy sat down on the ledge at the top of the stairs facing the monument. Both Joel and Jesse sat opposite her, their backs to the huge structure. Lucy shielded her eyes from the sun as she looked up at the Eternal Flame.

"Such a beautiful testament to peace," Lucy said.

Joel and Jesse exchanged a wry look.

"Real subtle, Lucy," Joel said wryly.

Lucy giggled. "I know, I know. I'm laying on the symbolism a little thick here, but really. Look at it!"

The boys obligingly turned around and looked at the Eternal Light Peace Memorial. They were unimpressed.

"I remember when they put that thing up," Jesse told her.

Lucy sucked in her breath. "1938."

"Yup. For the 75th anniversary of the battle. Old Franklin Delano was here and everything," Joel said.

"You saw President Roosevelt?" Lucy asked with astonishment.

"Yep, we sure did," Jesse said, not wanting Joel to get all the glory.

"That's incredible. I can't imagine how much history you guys have witnessed!" Lucy's eyes lit up with excitement.

"Yeah, it was kinda neat. They had thousands of Civil War veterans show up to help dedicate it. It was kinda nice to see all those guys from the North and the South come together," Jesse said. He looked up at the memorial, specifically at the flame that burned eternally. He quoted the inscription from memory, "*An enduring light to guide us in unity and fellowship. With firmness in the right as God gives us to see the right.*"

Lucy looked pleased, but the moment didn't last.

Joel smirked at Jesse. "You know who said that, right? Lincoln. Abe Lincoln. Good ole honest Abe himself!"

"Yes, Joel. I know. You won the War to Suppress Yankee Arrogance. Bully for you."

"Did you guys see anyone you knew at the reunion? Anyone you fought with?" Lucy asked.

"No," Joel said abruptly. "Everyone I fought with and cared about was already dead." He glared menacingly at Jesse.

"I think you guys really need to talk about what happened. I know you're still angry after all these years. You must have your reasons, and I really can't begin to imagine what you've been through," Lucy said. "But thousands of people died violently, tragically here, and most of them have crossed over. Be honest with me, and with yourselves." She looked from one to the other. "Do you know why you're still here?"

Joel stared at the ground.

Lucy chose her words carefully, spoke gently. "Do you mind if I ask how you died?"

Jesse raised an eyebrow. "Oh, hadn't you guessed? Joel killed me."

Jesse relished the look of shock on Lucy's face. He couldn't help it. He wanted Lucy to see Joel for the murderous monster that he was, not some good-looking guy in a Yankee uniform. Joel stared daggers at Jesse, but he couldn't argue with the truth. He had killed him. And would probably do it again if it were possible.

"Oh," Lucy said. "Well, I guess I'm not really surprised."

"You're not?" Joel asked. He looked a bit offended.

"Well, I suppose I figured one of you had probably killed the other and that's why you hate each other so much."

"Yep. That's why. Joel's a killer," Jesse said, enjoying being able to make Joel the bad guy.

"Oh, so you're going to conveniently leave out the fact that you murdered my best friend?" Joel snarled.

"Murdered as in...killed in the battle?" Lucy asked, trying to understand.

"Yeah, it was in battle, but it was still cold-blooded murder!" Joel shouted.

Jesse's eyes flashed, and his good-natured disposition disappeared. He actually looked dangerous. He said menacingly, *"Don't yell at her."*

Joel looked at Lucy apologetically. "I wasn't yelling at you, sweetheart. I'm sorry. You wanna know what happened? My friend Charles, my best friend from childhood, *surrendered*, and Johnny Reb here killed him anyway just for sport. Took his bayonet and rammed it into his belly." With that, Joel made a violent, thrusting motion. Lucy winced, visualizing Charles's violent death.

"He was not surrendering!" Jesse yelled suddenly, making Lucy jump.

"Don't yell at her," Joel mimicked.

"I swear to God, if I only had the strength, I'd wrap my hands around your neck so hard your face would match your outfit, Bluebelly."

"Yeah, well, you can't, you backwoods rube. You're dead 'cause I killed you, and you can't kill me back." Despite the gravity of the conversation, Joel's words sounded like a silly schoolyard taunt.

"It's your damn fault I'm stuck here. Maybe if my death hadn't been so *violent* I wouldn't be trapped here for eternity!" Jesse hollered, leaning forward right into Joel's face.

"Oh, poor baby. Your death was violent, as opposed to the rest of us who were licked to death by kittens?"

"At least you went quickly," Jesse said, his voice suddenly going quiet.

Lucy looked at Jesse sorrowfully. "What happened?" she asked in a quiet voice.

"First, I was shot in the shoulder," Jesse said, running a ghostly hand through the top of his right shoulder.

Lucy glanced at Joel, but Jesse shook his head. "Joel wasn't 'sponsible for that one. Somebody else shot me. I didn't see the guy. It was hard to see anything on the battle-field with so much smoke and confusion."

"Oh, gimme a goddamn break," Joel seethed.

"Shut yer mouth, you dirty Mudsill. I'm tellin' this story," Jesse said angrily. "You'll get your chance to slander me soon enough." God, how he hated talking about this in front of Lucy. As painful as it was when she had been afraid of him, her thinking of him as a killer was worse.

"Then, according to Yankee Doodle here, his best buddy was holding up his hands in surrender, plain as day, and I just bayoneted him to death because I just had nothin' better to do that day."

"But you did kill him," Lucy asked, as gently as possible.

"Yes," Jesse said softly, his heart heavy. He felt terrible for killing Charles, but the man was at peace and had been since the day he died in battle. His grieving family was long dead, too, so there was no one left to mourn him except Joel. Regardless of what Bluebelly thought, Jesse had always carried a huge weight of guilt over Charles's death. Now, though, his sorrow was centered on the way Lucy was looking at him. Her expression was a mixture of sadness and disappointment. He feared that she thought less of him now, and the ache in his heart grew stronger.

"Did you know he was trying to surrender?" Lucy asked. Joel was ready to explode, but she silenced him with a look.

Jesse looked deeply into Lucy's eyes. He wanted her to see the truth of his words. "No, Lucy. I didn't know. There were bullets flyin', smoke in my eyes and nose, and the sound of cannons was deafening. I *did not know* he was trying to give himself up."

Lucy nodded. She believed him. Relief flooded through Jesse.

Jesse glared over at Joel. "Then I was shot in the head."

"Yeah. I shot him. I had to avenge my friend. Plus, Secesh was standin' there with a loaded musket and woulda got me if I hadn't gotten him first."

Lucy nodded again.

"You're not gonna leave out the rest, now, are ya?" Jesse asked, glaring fiercely at Joel.

"Oh, I wouldn't want to rob you of the pleasure of telling your favorite part," Joel said. He shot a worried look at Lucy, clearly afraid of what she would think of him when she heard the rest.

"Old Lincoln boy here just happened to grab his regiment's flag when the color bearer got shot down right next to him. And well, he was so completely nuts about his friend bein' killed, that he thought it would be a great idea to impale my corpse with the flagpole. Stabbed my body all the way through my stomach."

Lucy looked horrified and slightly nauseated. It was such a ghastly image, to think of Joel stabbing Jesse's dead body all the way through. She looked over at Jesse, her face filled with compassion and sorrow.

"Thing was, though," Jesse continued, his face becoming an almost unrecognizable sneer as his eyes bored into Joel's, "I wasn't dead yet."

Lucy gasped and she covered her mouth with her hand. Joel continued to stare at Jesse, not wanting to look at Lucy.

Jesse was thrilled to think she'd never look at him the same way again. Joel's being a ghost might be scary, but it didn't make him a monster. Impaling someone alive certainly did.

"W-were you still conscious?" Lucy asked, hoping to hear that he hadn't been. "After having been shot twice?"

"Oh, yeah. I felt it. It was…"

Jesse stopped himself for a moment. He wanted Lucy to be horrified because he wanted her to hate Joel as much as he did. To see Joel for the horrible person that he really was. At the same time, he wasn't trying to upset her. He'd thought about going on and telling her what it was like to die in such a gruesome way. However, there was really no way to describe the agony of being impaled to death by a flagpole, and there was no reason Lucy needed to know what it felt like.

"It wasn't just the pain," Jesse said, thinking that *pain* didn't even begin to describe it. He spoke more quietly now. "But to die by the Union flag when I gave my life for the Rebel one."

Lucy nodded and spoke in nearly a whisper, "Yes. I know how much you love the South. Your home and your family." She took a moment to compose herself, she looked like she might burst into tears. "Thank you for telling me what happened. I know this is very hard for you to talk about."

Joel finally lifted his head to look at Lucy. Jesse was disappointed and even a little angry to see that Lucy looked at Joel with as much compassion as she had with him. She gave Joel a sad but reassuring smile.

"I-I know it sounds so horrible…" Joel began, faltering. He didn't have the words to explain why he did what he did.

"War is horrible," Lucy told him. "That doesn't mean you're horrible."

Joel nodded, looking relieved. "I was angry. I mean,

angry isn't even a strong enough word." He glared over at Jesse. "I hated him. I still hate him. But I thought he was dead when I stabbed him."

"Like hell," Jesse said, his voice still low and menacing.

"You really think I woulda done that if I knew you were still alive?"

"Course you would have!"

"Well, maybe I would have, you goddamn redneck. But I *didn't* know you were still alive," Joel yelled in his face.

Jesse yelled right back. "You 'spect me to believe you can't tell the difference between a live guy and a dead one?"

"Not in the middle of a battle with people dropping all around me and with...with..."

Jesse laughed cynically. "Oh, you tryin' to say you couldn't tell what was goin' on, what with all the smoke and cannon noise? You can use that as an excuse but I cain't?"

Lucy could see that this discussion was going nowhere fast. "Guys..."

"You'd been shot in the head. You were lyin' on the ground in a pool of blood. How the hell was I supposed to know you were still breathin'?" Joel demanded.

"I know you loved seeing that, boy," Jesse said, his face inches from Joel's. Good thing they were already dead, or this conversation would have already escalated into a bloody fistfight. "Me lyin' there, bleeding all over your shoes. But you didn't think I'd suffered enough."

"Guys, why don't we--" Lucy tried to intercede.

"That is not true, you motherfuckin' hick. There is no way I'd have--"

"The *hell* you--"

"*Boys!*" Lucy shouted. "*That's enough!*"

Stunned, both Joel and Jesse turned to look at her, taken aback, having never heard her raise her voice.

"Sorry, Lucy," Jesse mumbled, ashamed.

"Sorry," Joel said, looking equally contrite.

Lucy stifled a laugh at their hangdog expressions. They sounded like two brothers who had just gotten scolded by their mother.

"It's all right. You're allowed to be angry. I think it's good that you're finally talking about it."

"It's not like we haven't talked about it, Lucy. I've known this clown since 1863. We've had this discussion a time or two," Jesse said, glowering at Joel but determined not to lose his temper in front of Lucy anymore. So much for being a gentleman around her.

"Well, I'm not sure I would call this shouting match a discussion," Lucy observed wryly. "I'm sure you've screamed at each other a lot, but you may want to have a calm, rational talk about it someday. You know, after you've had some time to cool down." She sighed and looked from one angry soldier to another. "Maybe another hundred and fifty years."

"At least," Jesse mumbled.

Lucy looked at Joel somberly.

"What?"

"How did you die?" she asked softly.

"I never saw it coming," Joel said wearily. "That's why it took me a bit to figure out that I was dead, you know? Being a spirit like I am now, I was still conscious so it was kind of confusing. I didn't know what happened, but another dead soldier told me what he saw."

Lucy nodded, giving him time to finish. She looked a little sick to her stomach. Jesse remembered telling her that Joel's body had been too mangled for a grave, so she knew his death wasn't pretty.

"I was hit by a cannonball that was fired from a long

distance. I kinda vaguely remember a sharp, searing pain but then it was over." Joel grimaced. "Was pretty awful to witness from what I understand. Must have been quite a mess."

Lucy swallowed hard. "I'm so sorry."

"That was a goddamn cakewalk..." Jesse muttered.

Lucy turned to Jesse. "I'm very sorry for you both. I'm glad that I know now, though. I understand why you're so upset with each other."

"Not upset," Joel said. "Hate. We hate each other."

"I know," Lucy said sadly. "But I like you both so much, and I wish you would get along. I think you're both wonderful."

Jesse grinned. "Who does that remind you of?"

Lucy looked surprised to see that Joel actually smiled back at Jesse. "Fillis."

"Uh...who's...who's Fillis?" Lucy asked Jesse, looking a little worried.

"She's, you know, like us," Joel answered.

"Fillis is wonderful. She's like a mother to us," Jesse said.

Lucy let out a breath and smiled.

"She was a runaway slave. She got as far as Gettysburg when she died. She was here, you know, as a spirit, during the battle," Joel explained. "Fillis witnessed everything that happened, and she has a soft spot in her heart for soldiers. She takes good care of us. We call her Second Mama."

Lucy looked over at Jesse. "She's that way with all the soldiers? I mean, even..." She wasn't sure how to put her thoughts forward tactfully.

"You mean does she even love the idiots who were fighting to keep people like her in bondage?" Joel said, shooting Jesse a disdainful look.

"I was never fightin' to keep people in slavery. And quit actin' like you was fightin' for some noble cause, because you weren't!" Jesse said, his temper rising again. "I heard the way you Yanks talked about black people, and it wasn't any better than the stuff our guys said!"

"What a bunch of bull!" Joel fired back. "You know what your problem is? You-"

"I've read about that," Lucy said. She gave Joel an apologetic look for interrupting, but continued. "It was a very different time. Most people were just brought up to believe that blacks were inferior, no matter what side they fought on. Sure, there were some staunch abolitionists, but I've read that many soldiers on the Union side were pretty resentful that they were fighting and dying for the rights of black people. Is that true?"

Joel looked into her eyes, not wanting to admit the truth.

"I think we can take that as a yes," Jesse said smugly.

"Even so," Lucy said, shooting a look of reprimand at Jesse. "The South fought for many reasons, but keeping slavery was one of the main reasons they went to war. To preserve that way of life."

Joel stuck his fingers in his ears and waggled his tongue at Jesse, which made Lucy burst out laughing. Jesse looked angry instead of amused. He was about to argue, but Lucy interrupted.

"So tell me more about Fillis!" Lucy said.

"To answer your question, Lucy," Jesse said, "Fillis loves the Confederate soldiers, too. She knows me well enough to know the real reasons I fought in the war, despite what this Little Coot says."

"That's nice," Lucy said. "I'm glad you have her to lean on."

"Yeah. She's an amazin' woman, that's for sure. She'd been dead a few months by the time the fightin' started at Gettysburg, so she was able to help the soldiers adjust to being dead. She..." Jesse stopped for a moment, overcome with emotion. "She jus'...she saw right through my Confederate uniform and saw me for who I was. A lost young man who'd just been killed in battle. In life, most of us couldn't see past that brown skin, but Fillis? She saw us for who we really were. She didn't hold nothin' against us. She just comforted us the best she could."

"She just went from soldier to soldier, talking to 'em, comforting 'em, telling us it was gonna be okay," Joel added with tremendous affection.

Jesse glanced at Lucy, debating whether to confess the next part. Lucy's face was so full of kindness and understanding that he decided to tell her everything, even though he was afraid it might make him appear weak.

"I remember I jus'...I just broke down. I kept talkin' 'bout my mama and what she would do when she found out I wasn't coming back." There was a quiver in Jesse's voice as he spoke. "I knew she was gonna be heartbroken, and there was nothin' I could do about it. Fillis...my Second Mama, jus' sat there and cried with me."

Joel looked at Jesse with uncharacteristic compassion. "Yeah, that's our Second Mama. And she let me talk on and on about Emma and the boys, and she never seemed to tire of it. I don't know how we would have made it this far without her."

"Wow," Lucy said softly. "She sounds amazing."

"Fillis hates when we fight, too," Jesse said. "And we should warn you, she's been tryin' to make us get along since the 1860s, and it ain't happened yet. You got your work cut out for you if you think you can do it!"

"Is that a challenge, Private Spenser?" Lucy asked, looking in him in the eye.

"Damn, you're sexy when you're determined," Jesse said, grinning at her.

Lucy's cheeks reddened, but she held his gaze. "Challenge accepted."

22

Lucy had ordered Joel and Jesse to meet her at the picnic tables at the Gettysburg Visitor's Center the following afternoon. She seemed to be getting more aggressive now that she was on a mission to help them, and Jesse found her newfound assertiveness extremely sexy.

It was a warm Saturday afternoon, and the Visitor's Center was fairly crowded. Joel and Jesse were treated like celebrities in Gettysburg, particularly here at the Center. People took photographs of them as they walked by, and the two soldiers smiled and waved at people. If these tourists had any idea they were looking at men who actually fought in the real battle...

"Sorry we're late," Jesse said with a grin as they approached Lucy where she sat at a picnic table. "Just dealing with our adoring fans."

"I see that," Lucy said. "Do photographs of you actually come out?"

"Oh, yeah," Jesse said. "So long as we're visible when they're taken."

"And sometimes when we're not," Joel added.

"Yeah. Sometimes the camera will pick us up—or part of our image anyway—when we're invisible. That really freaks people out," Jesse said, sounding a little sad.

"That must be upsetting," Lucy said with sympathy.

"Depends on the tourist," Joel said. "Some people love that shit. Sorry. Stuff. They love that stuff."

Lucy smiled. "That's for sure. Must be thousands of people who come to Gettysburg just to hunt ghosts. What do you guys think of all this? All this hype over the battle? It must seem so strange to you."

Joel and Jesse followed Lucy's gaze and looked over at the crowd of people going in and out of the Visitor's Center.

"It is strange, for sure," Jesse said, thoughtfully. "I 'spose it's good that people remember all the lives lost, but..."

"Sometimes the circus atmosphere does get to be a bit much," Joel added.

Jesse nodded. "Yeah, the way they sell souvenirs and stuff, like the battle was some kind of show for entertainment. And you get a lot of real Civil War nuts around these parts. I mean, some people are just obsessed."

"Yeah, I know what you mean. I see people like that in the restaurant all the time. They come from all over the world to visit the battlefields." Lucy looked at them curiously. "So, how do you guys feel about all the ghost tours around here?"

Joel and Jesse looked at each other before answering.

"I don't know," Jesse began. "Most of the time it doesn't really bother me. I mean, I get it. People are curious about life after death. It's only natural."

"Yeah, for the most part it's pretty harmless. People come out to get a good scare, especially around Halloween." Joel said.

"Do you ever scare people? I mean, on purpose?"

"Sometimes," Joel answered, and Jesse nodded in agreement. "And only people who seem to really, really want a ghost encounter. Sometimes I'll try to touch somebody, but it's hard. You gotta really concentrate on it, and it doesn't always work. But if I hear somebody talking 'bout how they want to see a ghost, I'll appear visible real quick. So they'll have a story to tell when they get home."

"Yeah, it's easier to appear to someone than to try to touch them," Jesse explained. "But it can really freak people out."

"Yup," Joel said. "Sometimes people *think* they want to see a ghost, but when they do, boy..." He laughed, but sounded a bit sad.

"Some other spirits aren't so nice. Some of them are mean and are out to scare people." Jesse's expression hardened. "And some of 'em have scared little kids."

Lucy smiled softly, and she seemed pleased to hear how Jesse was protective of little kids. He remembered her lovely smile the day she caught him playing with the little boy in the Yankee cap. *She'll make the most wonderful mother,* Jesse thought. He felt a sharp pain in his chest when he pictured her having a child with another man.

"We've pretty much seen it all," Joel said. "We've seen people cry, laugh, *faint...*"

Both Joel and Jesse looked at Lucy and smiled. She laughed self-consciously and tucked her hair behind her ear.

"You sure it doesn't bother you? All the ghost stuff?" she asked with concern.

"Maybe a little," Jesse said. Leave it to Lucy to realize how they really felt about the subject. "I don't know. I guess I don't like people to be afraid of me. I never wanted to be a ghost, you know? I'm still a man, and it's hard to feel like it sometimes when you're like this." He gestured with annoyance at his body.

"Exactly," Joel said. "I never wanted to be some freaky... *thing*...to be feared. I wish I could be a real man again, you know?"

"Well, I-I-I've always thought of you both as real men," Lucy said. "When I look at you, I see two very handsome, strong men."

Both Joel and Jesse gazed at her tenderly. She was blushing fiercely, and they could see it was hard for her to be so honest about her feelings.

Lucy spoke nervously, her words rushed. "And-and you're still, *you*, you know what I mean? The essence of who you were--and are. Does that make sense? Your souls, the most important parts of you, are still here. And-and I think you're both wonderful."

"Thank you, Lucy," Joel said softly.

Lucy looked at Joel, then at Jesse. "I mean you guys are both so...I mean, look at you. If you weren't dead, guys like you wouldn't give me the time of day." She glanced over at the crowd of people milling around the Visitor's Center. "People probably look at the three of us and wonder what two gorgeous guys like you are doing with someone like me. You could have any woman you want, dead or alive!"

For just a brief moment, Jesse let his guard down and looked at her the way he did when he knew she couldn't see him. "Oh, Lucy you have no idea..."

Joel exchanged a look with Jesse as if to say, *This is your chance.* It was the perfect opportunity for Jesse to tell Lucy how he felt about her.

Jesse looked longingly at Lucy, wanting to tell her everything. How he had watched her work for months. How he'd admired her gentle sweetness, her beautiful smile, and how he adored her enthusiasm and dreams of making the world a better place when she became a teacher. How he'd fallen in love with her.

Joel hesitated a moment or two, giving Jesse the chance to say what he felt. He didn't.

"Sweetheart, we've been roaming this earth for well over a century, and you're the first living woman that we've really had contact with," Joel told her. "You're the one who caught our eye, and you're the only woman who was kindhearted enough to give us a second chance, even though you were really scared. Anybody looking at the three of us should wonder what a beautiful, classy girl like you is doing with a couple of idiots like us."

Lucy looked gratefully into Joel's eyes, and he smiled at her. Pain seared Jesse's heart as he saw the way she looked at Joel. He hated himself for not speaking up when the moment was right. He just didn't know what to say or how to say it. He didn't know how to express how much he loved her, so like an idiot, he said nothing.

"So!" Lucy said. "Tell me about life in camp. What was it like to be a soldier?"

"Who wouldn't be a soldier?" Jesse said with a smile. "There's another Civil War slang term for ya. It kinda means *who cares?* Hmmm. What was it like to be a soldier... Most of the time it was boring. Really, *really* boring."

"That's for sure," Joel agreed. "The fighting was every bit as horrible as you've heard, but we actually spent very little time on the battlefield. Most of the time we were in camp or marching."

"Dear God, the marching," Jesse said with a groan. "Marching, drilling all the time. Hours and hours and hours of it and during all kinds of weather."

"That sounds just awful," Lucy said, but she was smiling. She loved it when she got Joel and Jesse talking about something, anything, that they could agree on. She was so patient, so kind. Jesse didn't know how she could stand to put up with their incessant arguing.

"Oh, it really was," Jesse told her. "And the food, what there was of it, was terrible. I know you've heard of hardtack. We also had desiccated fruits and vegetables."

"What does that mean?" Lucy asked. "Desiccated?"

"Means dried out. Dry fruit and stuff." Jesse made a face, and Lucy laughed.

"And we had this stuff called skillygallee," Joel said. "It was like fried pork fat that we mixed with hardtack. Made hardtack halfway edible. It was still gross."

"Our guys had coosh. It was beef fried with bacon grease and cornmeal," Jesse said. "Wasn't half bad, but it was kinda hard to come by."

"Yeah, I know the rebels were awfully short on food. You're so thin," Lucy said sadly.

Jesse grimaced and nodded. It had been a very long time since he'd had a real, nourishing meal. Not that it mattered. He could barely remember what it felt like to be hungry anymore. He just hated that he was so damned skinny, and he hated that Lucy had noticed. She was concerned, which was sweet, but Jesse wanted so much to be strong and muscular for her. He would have given anything to have a physique like Joel's, which just made Jesse hate him more.

"The Union army was much better fed, that's for sure."

"Well, if you and your raggedly old rebels hadn't started the fight in the first place, maybe your scrawny ass wouldn't have half starved to death!" Joel said with a dismissive wave at Jesse's body.

"Oh, we started the fight? It was you guys who were tryin' to trample all over our rights!"

"Gimme a damn break, ya redneck," Joel said, his eyes flashing angrily. "That war had nothing to do with states' rights. That is such a crock of--"

"Anyway!" Lucy interrupted sternly. "Life in camp."

Joel and Jesse glared at each other for another moment, then turned softer gazes toward Lucy.

"It was mostly men, men, men all the time," Jesse said. "Even before we died, it had been a long time since we'd seen any beautiful women. That's another reason we love being around you, my lovely rose."

Jesse loved the way Lucy smiled every time he called her his rose.

"That's the truth," Joel said. "We were around a bunch of dirty, filthy men twenty-four hours a day. We sure missed the company of women. In more ways than one..."

"Well, there were some women around if you, ah, missed that kind of company. You know...for a price, if you know what I mean," Jesse said.

"I'm pretty sure I do," Lucy said.

"We had a great nineteenth-century term for, you know, *enjoying* that kind of time with a lady, but it would probably make you blush," Jesse said with a mischievous grin.

"Oh, everything makes me blush," Lucy said irritably as her face turned that familiar shade of red.

"It's cute!" both Joel and Jesse said at the same time.

"You're very becomin' when you blush, my rose." Jesse said.

Naturally, Lucy's blush deepened. She glanced at Joel. "I bet Emma never blushed."

Joel laughed heartily and shook his head. "Not very often."

"Well, I'm already blushing so you might as well tell me."

Jesse grinned and said, "Horizontal refreshments."

Lucy laughed and clapped her hands. "I love it."

"Don't forget ridin' a Dutch gal," Joel added.

Lucy laughed again. "That's awful! And hilarious."

"Joel, I know you were married and devoted to Emma, but should I dare ask if you..." She glanced at Jesse, then blushed more deeply and looked away.

"No, no. Not me," Jesse answered. He shook his head and actually grimaced. "I mean, I'm not judgin' guys who, you know, did that kind of thing. Life in camp was rough. Lonely. Frightnin'. You did what you had to do to keep from going crazy, you know? Ya gotta do something to help you forget the stuff you seen. The stuff you did. That kinda thing 'jus, ya know, ain't for me."

Lucy smiled shyly. Jesse could see that Lucy was impressed that he'd behaved well in camp, so he continued. "I don't know. I guess it's really old-fashioned––even for the time I come from––it jus' seems weird to be so intimate with someone you don't love. I jus', I can't imagine makin' love with some girl that I wasn't *in* love with."

"Oh, that is so sweet," Lucy replied dreamily. She put her hand over her heart to show how touched she was by his sentiment. "Have you ever been in love?"

A panicked look crossed Jesse's face. It took Lucy a moment to understand what she'd said to upset him, but then she must have realized what she was forcing him to admit. Given his feelings about sex and love, if he'd never been in love before, then he was still a virgin. She didn't want to make him admit this highly personal truth about himself, especially in front of his archenemy, Joel. She opened her mouth to stop him from answering before it was too late.

"No. I've never been in love." *Before you.*

Jesse looked down at the ground and awaited the inevitable.

Joel spoke much more loudly than necessary. "Oh, my God, you're a *virgin!*"

Jesse was too ashamed to look at either one of them. He'd been terrified that his secret would eventually come out, and now his nightmare was worse than he'd imagined. Joel's harsh emphasis on the word *virgin* rang in his ears. Jesse had never been so humiliated in his entire existence, and he'd been around for a very long time.

"That makes you even less of a man than being a ghost does!" Joel said, enjoying a hearty laugh at Jesse's expense.

Lucy whipped her head around at shot a fierce glare at Joel. "It does *not!*"

Joel's eyes opened wide at Lucy's sudden anger.

"It's okay, Lucy," Jesse said. "He's right. It's ridiculous that I'm...I'm you know."

"It is *not* ridiculous," Lucy insisted.

Jesse shot her a doubtful look and said, "You *must* think it's pathetic that I've never been with a woman." He figured she was just being her usual, kind-hearted self. She hated seeing anyone suffer, and she was just trying to save him from further embarrassment. Lucy would never see him as a real man now. He was just a scrawny, scraggly wisp of a spirit who'd had no sexual experience and never would.

"Of course it is!" Joel said. He couldn't resist chiming in but had stopped laughing since he knew it made Lucy mad.

"It's *not* pathetic!" Lucy said, shooting another furious look at Joel. She turned to Jesse, looking at him with tender affection. "You wanted to wait to have sex until you were in love? That's not pathetic, Jesse. I think it's the most romantic thing I've ever heard a man say."

Jesse stared deeply into Lucy's beautiful, brown eyes. It was the longest time he'd ever held her gaze, and as they looked into each other's eyes, he could see she was telling the truth. She was always saying something nice, but he knew her well enough to know when she was speaking from the heart. She really didn't think he was pathetic. She thought he was *romantic.*

"Most men don't care about love when it comes to sex," Lucy said, the pain clear in her voice. "Usually a man tells you he loves you just to get you in bed."

Jesse knew she must be talking about Eric. Jesse knew about him from Lucy's conversations with Theresa at the restaurant. Eric had been her first and only boyfriend, so he must have taken her virginity. Jesse wished to God he had the strength and ability to punch that bastard for hurting her like that. No wonder she had such a hard time believing him and Joel when they talked about how lovely they thought she was.

Joel just stared at the two of them, stunned at the reversal that had just occurred.

Lucy looked over at Joel, still irritated. "I still haven't made my choice, you know." She looked over at Jesse and smiled. "Jesse gets major points for this."

"You can't be serious!" Joel said.

"And you lose points for being an *ass*, Joel Casey," Lucy admonished.

Both men were shocked at Lucy's words. Then Jesse stuck his tongue out at Joel and Lucy laughed. She looked into Jesse's eyes again, and didn't look away this time.

Jesse could scarcely believe the way she was looking at

him. His virginity had *raised* his estimation in her eyes, that much was clear. He couldn't believe it.

Lucy finally broke away from staring at Jesse. "Well, I suppose that's enough catharsis for one day." She stood up to go. "I still think you boys need to work harder on getting along. I think making up with each other, forgiving each other, is a really important step in crossing over."

The two looked at her skeptically.

"I'm not giving up on you." With one last smile at Jesse, she turned and walked away.

Once she was out of earshot, Jesse knew Joel was going to make fun of him. He didn't give a damn.

"I can't believe it. The rebel is as pure as a lily. I better watch what I say around you. Wouldn't want to make *you* blush, what with your innocent, virginal ears."

Jesse grinned at him. "You heard the lady. I'm *romantic*. And you're an *ass*."

"You're pathetic," Joel said, but with much less enthusiasm than before. Jesse had won this round, and they both knew it.

"Hers is the only opinion that matters. Yours means nothin', Blueballs."

"Hah! Seems to me *you're* the one with the blue balls."

Jesse couldn't help but chuckle at that. "Guess I kinda walked into that one."

Joel grinned. "Yeah, ya did."

23

L ucy had put a lot of thought into how to make Joel and Jesse get along. They'd been enemies for a long time, and that was putting it mildly, but she truly believed that the key to getting them to cross over was to forgive each other. And to forgive themselves.

She'd also thought a lot about Fillis ever since the boys had mentioned her. She sounded like a wonderful woman. Lucy thought it was adorable that they called her Second Mama, and she must be an amazing lady since she loved both the Union and Confederate soldiers.

It occurred to Lucy that she might have seen Fillis before. There were lots of people dressed in costumes around here, but she seemed to recall a black lady in her forties or fifties hanging around Steinwehr Avenue. She was often near The Regimental Quartermaster, where Joel and Jesse had once claimed they worked, which was right next to The Gettysburg Ghost Lab. Lucy chuckled at the irony. She thought back to the day she first saw Jesse when he was playing shoot-'em-up with that kid. Was Fillis there that day? Lucy vaguely remembered seeing someone who could have been her.

Lucy ventured out on her lunch break a few times, and one day she finally saw a woman who might be Fillis sitting on the front steps of one of the historic buildings.

Lucy looked down at the older woman where she sat with a Confederate soldier. If this lady was Fillis, then the soldier beside her was probably dead. The woman smiled encouragingly at Lucy, waiting patiently for her to speak.

"Are-are you...Fillis?" Lucy asked uncertainly.

"Yes, I sure am!" Fillis said warmly. "And you must be Lucy!"

Lucy exhaled with relief. "Yes. Yes, that's me."

"So you're the famous Lucy!" the soldier said. "We've all heard so much about you."

"You have?" Lucy asked. Though she was getting used to speaking to the deceased, it was still a little unnerving to be talking to two more people who had passed on. But here they were, sitting out in broad daylight.

"Oh, sure. You're big news around these parts," he said with a grin. "And you're every bit as pretty as they said you were."

Lucy blushed and looked down.

"I'm Adam," he said. "Friend of Joel's. I know Jesse, too, but not real well. Nice guy, no matter what Joel says."

Lucy chuckled, still feeling a little nervous. Fillis smiled and gestured at the steps. "Come. Sit down. You know we won't bite," she said with a wink.

Lucy nodded and sat next to Fillis. "It's so nice to meet you. Joel and Jesse both speak very highly of you. They love you to death! I-I mean...I didn't mean—"

Fillis and Adam both laughed good-naturedly, and Lucy felt more at ease. She was learning that most ghosts seemed to have a good sense of humor about their situation. After all, humor was one of the only things they had left.

"That's one of the few things they have in common," Lucy said.

"Ain't that the truth!" Fillis said, shaking her head. "I don't know what to do with those two."

"Do you think it's possible for them to ever get along?"

"Anything's possible, I 'spose."

"I think they have to make up in order to cross over," Lucy said thoughtfully. "And that's the thing. They seem to be able to get along when they're not talking about the war and what happened. There's times I can almost imagine them being friends."

Adam snorted loudly. Lucy giggled and looked over at him. "I know, I know. But *really*. When they're distracted, when they get to talking about other things, they kind of get along. But when they talk about what happened and how they died..."

"They lose their shit!" Fillis said.

"Exactly!" Lucy said with a laugh. "I just wish there was some way to get them to actually talk about what happened. Talk, not scream at each other."

"Been a long time," Fillis said wearily. "Hard to imagine they'll ever get it together. Guess they have to eventually. Can't be spirits floatin' around forever."

Lucy looked at Fillis thoughtfully. "You've been here a long time, too. Do you know why you're stuck here?"

Fillis smiled at Lucy with great affection. "Don't you worry about me, honey." Her tone was soft, but it was clear that she did not want to discuss this any further.

Lucy nodded, but was already determined to help Fillis if she was ever successful in getting Joel and Jesse to cross over. Fillis always looked out for everybody else, but who was taking care of her?

"Jesse never wants to go to Devil's Den," Lucy said. "I mean, I can understand why."

"You know what happened then?" Fillis asked.

"Yes. They told me."

"Bet *that* was a fun conversation," Fillis noted sarcastically.

"Oh, yeah. There was a lot of yelling involved. I just think maybe if I can get them both to go to Devil's Den and really hash it out, it might help. They need to talk about what happened, and maybe my being there will help them get through it."

Fillis nodded. "Maybe."

"I don't know," Adam said. "I don't think it would go over too well."

"Maybe not," Lucy agreed. "But it might be worth a shot. I wouldn't even try it if they had the physical ability to hurt each other." They both behaved like gentlemen around her most of the time, but if she put them in the volatile environment of where they'd died, they might really get crazy. But they couldn't throw punches or anything, and they were already dead so there was only so much they could do to each other.

"Joel goes to Devil's Den all the time," Fillis said, looking worried. "But I don't know if we could get Jesse to go there."

"You could get him to go there, Lucy," Adam said with a sly smile. "He'd do anything for you."

Fillis shot Adam a warning look and Lucy wasn't sure why.

"I think he'd do anything for his Second Mama, too," Lucy said. "I mean, if you think it's a good idea, would you be willing to help me get them to go?"

"Of course. I'd do anything if I thought it might help them," Fillis said. "But you really want to go with them to Devil's Den?"

"I do," Lucy said with determination. "I think it will be good for them."

"Well, all right then. I say we corner them and order them to go to Devil's Den to work out their issues!"

"Sounds like a plan!" Lucy said.

Fillis looked at Lucy with great fondness. "You're a sweet girl. You're very patient with them. They're lucky to have you around."

"I should say the same to you, Fillis! They'd be lost without you."

"I mean it, honey. You've got them talking somewhat civilly to each other, and that's more than they done in the last hunnert years. They usually just avoid each other, and I agree that's no good. I think they both feel bad about what happened, and they won't admit it. They're good boys. Both of 'em, and they were forced to do some horrible things. Things they're reminded of every time they look at each other."

Lucy nodded sadly.

"They need this, Lucy. It's been too long. They need to go home." Fillis looked tired. Lucy figured it had been too long for her, too. "But girl?"

"Yes?"

"Don't get your hopes up too high. Them two are damned stubborn!"

"I know," Lucy said, sounding worried. "I know."

24

I
t was a Friday night, and Jesse was wandering around the Gettysburg College campus. He had nothing better to do, and it was always entertaining to see what college kids got up to on the weekends.

As he drifted invisibly across the campus grounds, he caught sight of something that made his heart jump. He'd know that long, flowing brown hair anywhere. He'd spied Lucy on the front lawn of a fraternity house. There was a loud party going on, and Lucy was there with Theresa and her boyfriend, Steven.

Jesse paused a moment on the front lawn, watching her. Lucy looked somewhat uncomfortable. No doubt Theresa had talked her into going.

Lucy stood awkwardly on the lawn, a red Solo cup in her hand. Jesse looked longingly at her. His heart ached as he watched a good-looking college guy chat her up. To his delight, she smiled politely but appeared uninterested. She clearly planned to let the situation go no further than polite conversation.

Jesse was confident that Lucy could handle herself. She

was shy, but she was no pushover. She didn't need Jesse to come rescue her, but he still wished he could. For a second he contemplated becoming visible and walking right up to her. He could start talking to her, and college guy would get the hint and go away.

Jesse looked down at his ragged Confederate uniform. His clothing looked impressively "authentic" during the day when tourists were around, but he would look like a complete idiot at a college party. Worst of all, he would embarrass Lucy.

He wanted so desperately to be close to her. He thought about staying invisible and going to stand beside her at the party. Then he remembered his promise. He had solemnly sworn to her that he would not watch her without her knowing. He had no choice but to leave. With one last look at her, Jesse sadly turned and walked away.

Unaware of Jesse's presence and departure, Lucy smiled wearily at the college guy prattling on and on about how wasted he'd been the previous weekend. She couldn't even begin to fathom why he thought she would be impressed by such a feat.

Lucy spied Theresa sprinting across the lawn toward her. *About time*, Lucy thought with irritation. Theresa had talked her into coming to the party and then had abandoned her.

"Hey! Mind if I grab my friend for a minute, thanks!" Theresa said to college guy. She spoke so fast that the whole sentence sounded like one long word.

Theresa tugged on Lucy's shoulder and pulled her away from the guy. Lucy glared at her.

"Sorry, sorry, sorry! I got cornered, too. Won't happen again," Theresa said, sounding appropriately guilty.

Lucy's expression softened a bit. She never could stay mad for long, especially at Theresa.

"Want another drink?" Theresa asked.

"No, thanks. I've barely touched this one," Lucy said, peering into her plastic cup of cheap beer. She wasn't much of a drinker, and when she did imbibe, she preferred wine or a girly kind of fruit drink.

Lucy looked around at the guys at the party. It seemed like they were all trying to find a hookup, and most of the girls seemed more than willing to oblige. Some of these frat boys were really gorgeous, yet it was difficult for her to summon any attraction for them. This wasn't her kind of scene, so she was unlikely to meet anyone she had anything in common with. Besides, she wasn't the type of girl who always needed to have a boyfriend. She might be the quiet type, but Lucy prided herself on being a strong woman. She refused to buy into that garbage that you weren't complete without being part of a couple, and she had every intention of being a strong role model for her future students. She especially wanted to encourage her female students, empower them to pursue their dreams first and worry less about having a boyfriend. She always thought the best relationships were the ones where you met someone naturally while you pursued other things in life.

Lucy glanced over to the corner of the lawn and saw the guy she'd been talking to puking in the bushes. She closed her eyes and let out a breath. She couldn't help but think of Jesse. Now there was somebody wonderful who'd just happened to come along out of the blue. She opened her eyes and looked around at all the partying and drinking going on, and couldn't help but think what Jesse would do if he were here. He'd probably be content to stand in the corner, talking quietly with her.

Steven jogged over to where they were standing. "So this is where you got to," he said to Theresa, sounding a little irritated. He had longish brown hair, blue eyes, and was built like the linebacker he was. He played for the Gettysburg Bullets, the college football team.

Lucy narrowed her eyes as she watched Steven grab Theresa by the wrist. His possessiveness annoyed her. Theresa was such a strong woman, and Lucy didn't understand why she put up with the guy. She was much better off alone than with a guy like Steven.

"I think I'm gonna head home," Lucy said.

"No, don't leave!" Theresa said. "I'm your ride anyway."

"Come on, Theresa! Let's go back inside. They're playing my song. Let's dance!" Steven said. Theresa was hot, and he loved showing her off to his frat brothers. Lucy always suspected that was the only reason he dated Theresa. Because she was pretty. Theresa's outspokenness annoyed him, and he was always trying to suppress her personality. She was like a different person when she was with him.

Lucy winced at the thumping noise coming from inside the house. Steven's "song" sounded like every other song they'd played that night.

"I'll take a cab or something," Lucy said, trying not to grimace at Steven.

Steven grabbed Theresa harder. "Okay, okay. I'm coming." Then, to Lucy, she said, "Wait for me here. *Please?*"

Lucy nodded wearily. She watched Theresa and Steven as they went back into the house. *Jesse would never, ever grab a woman by the wrist like that*, she thought. He'd take hold of her hand gently and probably kiss it. That thought made Lucy smile. Joel would never treat a woman like Steven did either. She could picture Joel grabbing Emma's hand and pulling her to the dance floor, but in a playful, spirited way.

Lucy had a fairly clear picture of what Emma looked like from Joel's description, and she could imagine the two of them dancing together. Joel twirling her, Emma's long, honey-blonde hair flying. Joel would probably dip her, then pull her up into his strong arms. They'd look so happy, so much in love.

Theresa was every bit as full of color and life as Emma was. Lucy couldn't figure out why she was with a guy like Steven. Shaking her head, Lucy looked around for a quiet place to go where she could get away from all the noise. She walked around the back of the house and spied a porch swing. There were only a few people hanging around out back, so she sat down.

Lucy's thoughts drifted back to Jesse, as they did more and more often these days. She looked out into the night and wondered where he was, what he was doing. Was he lonely? It must be awful, drifting aimlessly all night with nowhere to go.

More than a half hour later, Theresa found Lucy out back.

"There you are! I was worried that you left without me."

"I'm here," Lucy said, sounding tired.

"You okay? You looked lost in thought out here."

Lucy smiled self-consciously. "I guess I was."

"What are you thinking about?"

"Jesse," Lucy answered honestly.

"Why does that not surprise me?" Theresa asked wryly. "You're making yourself crazy, you know. Thinking about him like that."

"I know," Lucy said softly.

"All the best men are either gay or dead," Theresa said. Lucy laughed.

"That's the truth," Lucy said. "There's something I've

been dying to tell you about Jesse, but I'm not sure if I should."

"Ooh! Of course you should!"

"It's really personal, though. I don't think he'd want me telling anyone."

"Did you he swear you to secrecy?"

"Well, no," Lucy said.

"Then it's fair game. Spill it!"

"I guess. Well...he's never... He's a virgin. He'd never been with a woman before he went off to war, so..."

"Oh, wow!" Theresa said, her eyes lighting up with interest at good gossip. "He's so cute, that's hard to imagine. Well, I guess it's really not all that unusual, considering the time period he's from."

"True. But there's actually a reason he's never done it."

"What? His junk not work or something?"

"No!" Lucy said, then burst out laughing. "No. Nothing like that. Don't ask me how, but we got on the topic of prostitutes in the war, and he said he could never be with one. He said he didn't want to have sex with someone he didn't love. And oh, my God, Theresa, I felt so bad afterwards, but I asked him if he'd ever been in love. He hasn't, so I pretty much forced him to say he was still a virgin right in front of Joel."

Theresa winced. "Oh, man. I bet that didn't go over too well."

"No. He looked so embarrassed. I felt awful, but I told him I thought it was romantic that he felt that way. And I do, Theresa, I really do. I mean, guys never say stuff like that. You feel like most guys just want sex however they can get it, and they'll say whatever they have to to get you in bed."

"I know," Theresa said gently. Lucy had been reluctant to sleep with Eric at first, but he kept insisting he was in love with her. He'd lied, pure and simple, and had hurt Lucy to the core. A man like Jesse, who was genuine and honest, would never do such a horrible thing. "That is sweet. But sad. He died before he ever found love."

"Exactly." Lucy fell silent for a moment.

"Boy, you know how to pick 'em, you know that?" Theresa said, shaking her head.

"I know, right?" Lucy said, laughing. "I finally find the perfect guy and he's a ghost. That could only happen to me."

"That's the truth. I don't blame you, Luce. Jesse's wonderful. They both are, really."

"Yeah, they are." Lucy knew Theresa was right when she said she was making herself crazy by thinking about Jesse all the time. She needed to stop torturing herself. Being with him wasn't humanly possible, and he probably wouldn't be interested in her anyway. She was the only woman, besides Fillis, that he could talk to. That was the only reason he flirted with her and called her his lovely rose.

Instead of fantasizing about Jesse, she needed to concentrate on helping both Joel and Jesse cross over. Nothing would make her happier than to help Joel return to his beloved wife and precious children, and she wanted to help Jesse reunite with his parents. Still, she would miss Jesse terribly when he was gone. She'd only known him a short while, but it was hard to imagine what life would be like without that impish smile and the sexy accent that drove her crazy.

Lucy couldn't help but worry that for the rest of her life she would compare every man she met to Jesse. She couldn't imagine ever finding anyone as sweet and charming as he was. No one had ever made her feel he way he did, and she wondered if anyone ever would again.

25

F illis and Lucy patiently waited together in Fillis's usual spot near The Regimental Quartermaster. They were ready to present a united front in order to help the soldiers. It was for their own good. The guys finally showed up to find both women standing, arms folded, looking determinedly at the boys.

"Oh, man. I think we're in trouble," Jesse said as he approached. The affection he had for both women was clear by his smile and the look in his twinkling blue-gray eyes.

"It was Secesh who broke the window, Ma. I swear!" Joel said, throwing up his hands, showing his innocence.

Lucy struggled not to laugh. She straightened up, putting her determined face back on.

"Okay. What'd we do now?" Jesse asked, waiting for his inevitable punishment.

"Lucy thinks it would be good for you both to take a trip to Devil's Den, *together*, and I agree," Fillis said.

The soldiers looked wearily from Fillis to Lucy. They could see they had little chance of getting out of this assignment.

"I don't see what good it would do," Jesse said. "We'll just be yellin' at each other there instead of here."

Joel nodded, his expression tightening.

"You might as well just agree to do it, because we're not gonna stop hounding you about it," Lucy said firmly.

Joel shot a grim look at Jesse, who nodded.

"Good!" Fillis said with a grin. "And you two need to behave yourselves around the lady. I know how you boys get when you're together. I don't want no screamin' and yellin' and carrying on, and you watch your language."

"Of course we will!" Jesse said indignantly.

"I don't even mind if you scream and yell, and I'll even let the language slide. Just this once," Lucy said with a sly smile aimed in Jesse's direction. She was a grown woman, and she didn't mind bad language. It was doubtful the boys could say anything she hadn't heard a hundred times before, but still. She found it sweet that Jesse was careful to behave like such a gentleman around her. He treated her like a lady. Most men didn't.

"Good thing. I really can't promise I won't scream at Rebel Boy here," Joel said, glaring at Jesse.

"It's okay to be angry. The whole point is to go back to where it happened and say what you need to say. You need to get it out of your systems. Talk about it. Yell about it. I don't care. But stop avoiding it!" Lucy said.

Jesse looked at Lucy and nodded. He looked miserable and Lucy knew he didn't want to go through this torture, but he was willing to do what she asked.

"You sure you don't want me to go with you?" Fillis asked Lucy, looking concerned.

"No. It's all right. I can handle them," Lucy said.

"Okay," Joel said wearily. "Let's get this over with."

THE THREE MET up on Sykes Avenue around Little Round Top. Lucy parked her car there so they could walk together. There were plenty of places to park right in front of Devil's Den, but she said she wanted to have some time to walk and talk with Joel and Jesse, kind of ease them into the situation.

They greeted her with a smile when she got out of her car, but the tension was clear on their faces.

"You guys aren't going to hate me for making you do this, are you?" she asked.

"Of course not, sweetheart," Joel said.

"We could never hate you, Lucy," Jesse said. His tone was gentle but full of distress. It was a sad place for Joel, too, but he visited so often it was familiar.

Jesse looked ahead, his dread growing by the minute. As much as hated this journey, he wondered if finally facing what had happened at Devil's Den would free him from some of his anxiety. He was worried how he and Joel would react, though, being on the battlefield together. Jesse always tried to be respectful when Lucy was around, but there were many times he'd almost forgotten she was there when he got to fighting with Joel. His anger took over and he felt out of control.

There were few people out on the road as it was late afternoon on a Tuesday. They'd deliberately chosen that time because there was likely to be nobody out on the rocks of the Den. On weekends, particularly if the weather was good, there could be dozens of tourists visiting and climbing on the huge rocks.

They approached Devil's Den in silence. Lucy took a deep breath as she looked out across the land, up at the mountainous rocks, then back down at the boulders below. She closed her eyes.

"You all right, Lucy?" Jesse asked, looking at her with concern.

She opened her eyes and nodded. "Yes. It's just...so sad. I'm sorry for what happened to you both."

"Thanks, sweetheart," Joel said. Though the men hated being near each other, especially here, Lucy's presence helped soften their mood.

They stood looking around for a moment, both taking the time to reflect and being unsure of what to do next.

"Where did it happen?" she asked quietly.

Jesse looked over to his left and gestured with his hand. "Over there," he said in a small voice.

"I'm sorry, Jesse. I know this is very hard for you."

Jesse smiled at her. "Well, you know I would do anything for you, my lovely rose."

Jesse walked slowly over toward some of the large boulders. He stood in the middle of the huge outcropping of rocks. He put his head down. Lucy let out a shaky breath, then walked over to where Jesse was standing. Jesse looked up and offered her a sad but grateful smile.

Joel's expression hardened, his fury quickly bubbling to the service. Lucy's attempts to comfort Jesse made him angry. As far as Joel was concerned, Jesse was the bad guy.

"Joel," she began gently. "Will you come over here with us?"

Joel's anger softened. It was impossible for him to stay mad at her.

Joel walked over to Jesse and Lucy.

The two men stood, face-to-face, eye to eye. Their emotions were raw, the anger between them making it hard for either of them to put their feelings into words, even after all the time that had passed.

Lucy gasped suddenly. The sound of air rushing into her lungs as she took a sudden, huge breath was startlingly loud in the stillness of the battlefield.

It was clear that something was horribly wrong the moment they turned to look at her. Her face drained of color, and she looked like she did the night she found out that Jesse was a ghost.

"Lucy?" Jesse asked, alarmed at her sudden paleness and pained expression. "What is it? What's the matter?"

"I-I don't know..." she said. She grabbed her right shoulder with her left hand. "My-my shoulder hurts. It's really bad..." Lucy moaned and slumped against one of the rocks, holding on to her shoulder like she'd been shot.

Like she'd been shot.f   •

"Oh, God, no..." Jesse said, staring at Lucy in horror.

Jesse looked up at Joel, a panicked look on his face. They locked eyes, and Joel realized what was happening to her.

It was around five o'clock, the time Jesse had died, and they were standing on the exact spot where it had happened.

Dear God, Jesse thought, his ghostly body suddenly heavy with dread. *I knew she was sensitive. How could I not have realized this could happen to her?*

Even though both Joel and Jesse had seen it before, it was extremely rare for a person standing on one of the battlefields to experience the mortal wounds of a long-dead soldier. They'd witnessed it maybe three or four times in the fifteen decades they'd been in Gettysburg. Rare, but not impossible.

Jesse leaned in close to where Lucy was slumped against

the rock for support. He tried to stem the rising panic in his voice as he spoke. "Listen to me, Lucy. It's gonna be okay. You're gonna be all right, I swear to you. We've...we've seen this happen before." Guilt dripped from his words.

"What's happening to me?" Lucy shrieked. She looked into Jesse's eyes, terrified.

My death. You're experiencing my death.

"It's...you're....you're experiencing phantom pains...from the battle."

"Phantom?" Lucy said, her eyes wide with terror. There was nothing *phantom* about the agonizing pain she was in.

"I know it feels real," Jesse said with great anguish. "It's... it's my death, darling. You're feeling what I felt because you're very sensitive and you're standing right where I died... but-but it's not going to hurt you. I-I mean, when it's over, you're not gonna be hurt. It'll all stop. I swear to God, Lucy, it's going to stop, and you're going to be fine."

Jesse tried his best to keep eye contact with her to keep her from panicking further. The only time he broke away from her gaze was to look over at Joel, who shot him a terrified look. They both knew exactly what was going to happen to Lucy over the next few minutes.

Lucy held onto her shoulder, taking huge breaths as she tried to cope with the pain of being shot. "Why-why didn't you tell me this could happen? Why didn't you warn me?"

"Oh, Lucy, I'm so sorry," Jesse said, his voice barely a whisper. "I've only seen it happen a few times, and it must be thirty or forty years since I last seen it. I-I just didn't think..."

Lucy looked up at him, tears spilling from her eyes. Her breaths came in great gasps.

Goddammit, I should have known. My fault, my fault, my fault. I should have known. I should have known...

"This is what happened when you died?" she asked, looking into his eyes.

Jesse nodded. A fresh sense of horror filled him. He didn't want to see it in her eyes, the moment she remembered exactly how he'd died and what was coming.

"How-how long did it take you to die?"

"Not long, darling. Not long. I promise," Jesse said, looking into her pleading eyes. She was in too much pain to think clearly, to remember the details. He knew, no matter how much he didn't want to, he had to warn her about what was coming. God, he didn't want to see her face when he reminded her of how he died.

"Lucy, I was shot again. After the shoulder. Right here..." Jesse sorrowfully pointed to his left temple.

Lucy gripped her shoulder tighter and her eyes filled with tears of horror. "It's--it's going to happen again? Jesse, please...no, please...."

Jesse wanted to squeeze his eyes shut. Her torture was too much for him to bear. But he knew he had to stay with her.

Joel went over to Lucy and leaned down so he could look into her eyes.

"Joel," she pleaded weakly. "Please help me."

Joel clenched his cursed ghost hands, and Jesse could see Joel felt as helpless as he did. Joel was so strong in life. It would have been nothing for him to pick up Lucy and carry her away from here if he were still alive.

"Sweetheart, try to lie down. Right over here." Joel got up and pointed to the flat rock. She was going to have to practically drag herself there.

"Good idea!" Jesse said, sounding relieved that there was at least *something* they could do. Lucy looked dizzy and seemed to have trouble focusing. *"Lucy!* Come over here, my love. Lie down."

Lucy's entire body was shaking, but she managed to stand up. She unsteadily followed Jesse's lead. She stumbled over and was about to climb up on the flat rock when the phantom bullet struck her in the head.

Joel watched in horror as Lucy grabbed her temple and her agonized scream echoed across the rocky terrain.

"Lucy," Jesse croaked weakly.

Jesse looked up to see Joel staring at her. Joel's voice was barely a whisper. "Jesus fuckin' Christ, how could we let this happen to her..."

It was their worst nightmare come true. They'd always worried about walking her to her car, all the while knowing if something happened they couldn't save her. Now, it was like Lucy was being brutalized by an unseen attacker and they were powerless to stop it.

Jesse was frozen in terror. *Goddamn it, pull your shit together. Help her. Do something!* He knew he had to get his own panic under control if he was going to get her through this.

"Lucy, try to get up on the rock. Please. You gotta try to lie down."

Lucy was sobbing openly now. She tried to grab onto the rock, but she slid down, tearing the skin on her leg in the process.

Jesse tried to focus on helping her, pretending his heart wasn't ripping in half as he watched her suffer. *She's so pale. Dear God, she's so pale...* He winced as he saw the blood from her cut start to run down her leg.

"My love, try to lie down. Please. You can do it. Pull yourself up and lie down," Jesse told her.

Lucy somehow managed to get on top of the boulder and lie flat on her back.

"That's it, darlin'. That's it. Rest."

Lucy stopped shaking when she lay down on the rock. She stopped crying, and her sudden silence scared Jesse. She was even paler than before, and her lips were turning blue.

"She's not getting enough oxygen," Joel said, rushing to her side. "Breathe, Lucy. Please, breathe! Try to take a deep breath."

Lucy struggled to take a breath and she said in a frighteningly weak voice, "It hurts...it hurts..."

"I know, darling. I know," Jesse said as he stood over her. "Look at me. Please. Look at me!"

Lucy looked up at him but she couldn't focus. Her eyes fluttered shut.

"Lucy!" Jesse pleaded. "*Please!*"

Jesse pressed his hand to her forehead. The chill of his ghostly touch startled her, and her eyes opened.

"Good!" Joel yelled. "Do it again!"

Jesse touched his hand to her cheek, and the cold seem to revive her a little more. Then he closed his eyes. Concentrating, he gathered all of his strength the way he had when Lucy had collapsed at the restaurant.

Joel watched him, trying to figure out what he was planning to do.

Jesse opened his eyes, then bent down and kissed Lucy on her forehead.

Lucy gasped. "I felt that. I felt *you!*" His lips had actually felt *warm*. She was so shocked at being able to actually feel him that she regained her focus.

Jesse smiled sadly and nodded. Then he faded from view.

"No!" Lucy shrieked. "Don't leave me, Jesse!"

Joel leaned down close to her face. "He didn't leave you, sweetheart. He used up most of his strength when he touched you. He's not strong enough to be visible to you right now, but he's still here, you understand?" Joel glanced up at Jesse. "He's still here. I can see him, okay?"

Lucy nodded weakly. She kept looking at where Jesse had been standing until he finally appeared again. She drew in a breath when she saw his faint image.

Jesse stood over her and looked into her eyes. "I won't leave you. I would never leave you. I'm here. Look at me. *Please* stay with me."

Lucy let out an agonized moan and touched her temple again, but managed to nod weakly. "Is-is it almost over?"

Jesse knew he had to tell her.

"One more, Lucy. One more and it will all be over. I swear to God, it's almost over. One more."

Her hand over her left temple, trying in vain to stop the pain, she asked, "Where?"

I can't I can't I can't I can't tell her I can't I have to tell her I have to I have to...

"The stomach."

Lucy's eyes opened wide with horror. She remembered. She knew. "The flag..." she whispered.

"Yes." Jesse wanted to look away, but he didn't. No matter how much seeing her torture would tear him apart. *I won't leave you. I'll never leave you.*

"No!" Lucy wailed, somehow finding the strength to cry out loud. "No!" Her voice became a pleading whimper, which was so much worse. She looked into Jesse's eyes, desperate. "No, please. Please, Jesse...no...I can't...help me! Please! Help me, Jesse. *Help me!*"

"I can't..." Jesse said with hopeless desperation. He wanted to look up at the sky and scream at God. *Why are you doing this to her? Why? Do it to me! Kill me, torture me, a hundred times! Why are you doing this to HER?*

Jesse's final, fatal wound struck Lucy, and she let out an ungodly shriek of agony. Jesse had heard that anguished cry of the dying many times on the battlefield, but never before had the sound been so horrifyingly female.

Jesse never took his eyes off the love of his life as she screamed through the deepest throes of the final, torturous blow.

Joel had never seen a man look so utterly destroyed as Jesse did at that moment.

Lucy finally fell silent. Her eyes were closed. She let out a long, shuddering breath.

"Is it over?" Jesse whispered.

Eyes still closed, she nodded. Her screams had stopped. There was nothing but eerie silence. The silence that fell when the fight was over, days later when there was nothing left but the dead on the battlefield.

Joel looked down at Lucy. She looked so small, so fragile, lying there. Her feet looked so tiny in her sandals. Her pale blue sundress was spread out, and her long hair hung over the edge of the rock. This innocent waitress, this sweet future schoolteacher, now knew what it felt like to be slaughtered on the battlefield. Her petite body had just endured wounds that had been enough to kill a full-grown man. Joel felt a deep ache that seemed to come from his soul. He couldn't even begin to imagine Jesse's anguish. *Dear God, if it had been Emma...*

Joel looked up at Jesse, who was standing over Lucy. He looked so grief-stricken, he might as well have been standing over her grave. As he watched Jesse mourn Lucy's suffering with a look of pure, raw heartbreak, Joel was struck with a sudden realization. It was something he should have figured out long ago.

Jesse Spenser was a good man.

Jesse loved Lucy with all of his heart. Joel knew he would have willingly, gladly endured the battle pains for her if he could have. He would die for her if he weren't already dead. Jesse was a good, honorable man who, except for his screaming fights with Joel, never had a bad word to say about anybody. He loved his Second Mama, loved children, and was a gentleman through and through. He was a kind-hearted man who'd gotten trapped in the madness and horror of the war, just as Joel had. As Joel looked at Jesse's face, so full of sorrow, regret, and compassion, Joel thought, *this is not the face of a man who would kill someone in cold blood.*

For the first time, Joel believed what Jesse had been telling him all along. He only killed Charles because he felt he had no other choice. And seeing Lucy's agony as she endured Jesse's death, Joel realized for the first time exactly what he had done to the Confederate soldier. The torture Jesse had endured in his final moments. A sharp stab of pain, guilt, and sorrow sliced through Joel. His heart hurt for Lucy, for Jesse, for everyone who had suffered so horribly in that wretched war.

Jesse looked over at Joel and was startled by his agonized expression. In that moment, Jesse realized that Joel was almost as distraught over Lucy's suffering as he was.

A look of silent understanding passed between them. They were both sick of the pain and the violence and the memories. Watching Lucy suffer had brought them back to the first time it had happened. The churning emotions of fear and anger and sorrow. It reminded them both of how helpless they'd been to stop the blood and the death, and how much they hadn't wanted to die. They'd been victims of war, and now Lucy was, too. Too bad she had to undergo physical torture before they understood what she'd been trying to tell them. Nobody was at fault. In times of war, nobody wins.

Lucy opened her eyes and saw Jesse standing over her. She looked relieved, but also angry. The boys knew that this kind of thing was possible, yet they hadn't warned her of the danger they'd put her in by allowing her to stand right where Jesse had died. Jesse didn't care if she was angry with him. As long as she was no longer suffering.

"My rose," he said, his voice heavy with sorrow.

"I'm all right, Jesse," Lucy said, her face softening as she tried to comfort *him*. Seeing the anguish on his face, she must have understood that he never meant to hurt her. She moaned softly, then turned to curl up on her right side, almost in a fetal position. She began whimpering as the tears began to flow. Soon, Lucy was sobbing violently, her tiny shoulders shuddering. The physical pain was gone, and now the mental anguish was taking over.

Jesse and Joel exchanged a weary, helpless look. They didn't know what to do to comfort her. Joel knew how much Jesse must have ached to gather her in his arms, to hold her, to comfort her. But he couldn't. He couldn't do a goddamn thing.

"Jesse," Lucy cried out between sobs. "Jesse."

"Yes, my love. I'm here." He'd called her *my love* several times that day, but she'd been too distraught to notice. "I'm here." He crouched down to look into her eyes.

"I'm so sorry. I'm...I'm so sorry you had to die like that..."

Lucy managed to say before bursting into a fresh round of tears.

"Please don't worry about me," he said mournfully. "It's my fault. It's all my fault this happened to you."

"No, it isn't," Joel said, standing a short distance away from where Jesse stood. "Lucy, he would never in a million years do anything to hurt you."

Jesse looked down at her. Her eyes were red from crying. The pain was gone, but she still had the exhausted and terrified look of a woman who had been suddenly attacked and beaten within an inch of her life.

"I will never, ever forgive myself for letting this happen to you, Lucy," Jesse told her, his voice catching as he spoke.

"That's not what I want, Jesse," Lucy said. She took a deep breath, finding it exhausting just to speak. "I brought you here to make you two feel better, not to add to the burdens you already carry. Joel," she said, her voice so soft that he didn't hear her call his name at first. "Joel! Come here."

Joel came closer to her, knowing he could not possibly find the words to tell her how sorry he was for what she'd been forced to endure. With great effort, she struggled to sit up so she could face him.

"Lucy, I--"

"Shhhh," Lucy said, putting a finger close to his lips. "Please. Both of you. If you want to make it up to me, do what we came here to do. Talk about it. *Finish it.*"

Joel looked over at Jesse and said quietly, "I know you didn't kill Charles on purpose. You didn't--you're not that kind of man."

Joel saw relief in Jesse's eyes. The relief that comes from long-overdue forgiveness.

"I was so angry when you killed Charles. I killed you

because I was angry and because if I didn't, you would have killed me," Joel said, his voice cracking with the pain of the awful memory. "But I really thought you were dead. My God, you'd been shot in the shoulder and shot in the head. Who could possibly survive that?"

Joel winced as he looked over at Lucy, knowing she had somehow just lived through the same horrific ordeal.

"I...I had never, ever been so filled with rage than when I saw Charles die. That's why I... I had the flag and I...I-- thought you were dead. You were bleeding... God, there was so much blood... Then...th-th-then I-I stabbed you...and... and I heard you scream. I still hear that scream... I didn't know. I was still angry, but I didn't know you were still... I-I felt like some kind of wild animal...a sick monster. It was so gruesome, so horrible, I couldn't believe I'd actually done it. I didn't know you were still alive, Secesh. But if I had, in that moment...with Charles dead..." Joel struggled to meet Jesse's eyes. "Even if I had known, I don't know if I would have done any different. I-I just don't know."

After a moment of silence, Lucy said softly, "Jesse."

Jesse nodded. He took a moment to gather his thoughts, knowing it was his turn to explain what happened. To take Joel through Charles's last moments. "I know...I know you think I didn't care but...I remember the face of every man I had to kill. Maybe there were more, more guys that got hit by bullets I fired but... I remember the ones I saw up close." Jesse looked at Joel. "Charles had dark hair...dark, curly hair and dark eyes. Square jaw, a kind face."

Joel nodded, his lip trembling, as he still grieved for his childhood friend.

"He was standing right in front of me. It was hard to see...there was so much smoke and so much noise..."

Joel nodded. This was the point in Jesse's tale where Joel

usually yelled at him, telling him that not being able to see or hear was no excuse, but Joel knew deep down that it was the truth. The thudding boom of the cannons, the thick smoke in the air, the crush of bodies, both living and dead; the atmosphere was chaos, bedlam. You really couldn't see a goddamn thing.

"I-I couldn't see well. When the smoke cleared for a second, I saw Charles standing just inches from me. I-I thought he had a musket, loaded and ready to fire at me." The terror of the memory was written all over Jesse's face. "I thought he was going to kill me...I thought he was going to kill me...I thought he was going to kill me..." Jesse looked up at Joel and whispered, "I didn't want to die."

Fresh tears spilled down Lucy's face. "Oh, Jesse..."

"I had half a second to make a decision. So I...I killed him. I took my bayonet and I...I..." Jesse could hardly get the words out. He closed his eyes. "I can still feel...I remember what it felt like when the bayonet went into him. You don't forget somethin' like that. I can't feel anything physical anymore...but I can still feel *that*."

Jesse opened his eyes and looked at Joel. For the first time, Joel's expression was one of understanding and not judgment.

"When he fell...it wasn't until he fell to the ground that I saw his hands were empty. He didn't have no weapon. That was the last thing I remember thinkin'. He couldn't have killed me after all. Then...then I got shot..." Jesse glanced at his right shoulder, then down at Lucy.

"Oh, Lucy, I'm so sorry..." Jesse said, bowing his head. "You didn't deserve this."

"Neither did you," Lucy said with great emotion.

"I'm sorry, too, sweetheart," Joel said.

"I know you are, Joel." Lucy looked at Jesse, then back at Joel. "Then stop fighting. Start healing."

Joel smiled sadly at her. Lucy was recovering from being shot twice and impaled, and here she was, still worrying over them. No wonder Jesse loved her so much.

"I'm going to get you home to your wife and children if it's the last thing I do. And I want to help you go home, too, Jesse."

Home is wherever you are, Lucy, Jesse thought. It was hard for Jesse to imagine being happy, even in heaven, without her.

Lucy let out a deep breath.

"Are you all right?" Jesse asked.

"Yes," she answered. "I'm all right. I'm just very, very tired. I need to rest." She lay back down on the rock and closed her eyes.

Jesse nodded. He figured they would let her rest for a little while before they walked her back to her car. She should be safe here for a bit. After all, she had two soldiers standing guard over her, even if they were just spirits. They'd wake her before dark so she could get back safely.

Lucy was nearly asleep when a sudden, horrifying thought dawned on Jesse.

"Joel!" he said sharply, startling Joel and jolting Lucy awake. "When did you die?"

Joel's eyes opened wide with fear. "It was around seven p.m., I think."

Jesse nodded. "Okay, we still got a little time, but we gotta get her outta here. Lucy, darlin', I'm so sorry but you gotta get up. We gotta get you out of here 'fore you feel Joel's death, too. Don't ever come back here in the evenin' time. In fact, just don't ever come back here."

"Don't worry," Lucy said. She slowly pushed herself up into a sitting position on the rock.

"Oh, Lucy. I would give anything in the world if I could just carry you out of here," Jesse said, his voice full of tired desperation. He stood helplessly next to her as she wearily got to her feet.

Lucy smiled warmly. "That's kinda romantic, Jesse." She turned to Joel. "He gets extra points for that."

"Fair enough," Joel said with a smile, having lost all interest in winning the bet. Lucy might never be able to return Jesse's love, but he deserved to hear her at least say the words, *"I choose you, Jesse."*

Lucy's legs were a bit shaky, and she looked utterly exhausted. Joel looked at her with great concern. "You all right?"

"Yes, I'll be fine. I just need some rest and I'll be okay."

"You know, we could probably flag down a state trooper to help get you to your car."

Jesse's eyes lit up, happy that there was finally something they could do to help her. "Hey, yeah! That's a great idea. They're always patrolling the battlegrounds. We could get one of 'em to drive you back to your car."

"It's all right," Lucy said. "It's not that far. Just walk with me, and I'll be fine."

The soldiers walked on either side of her, back to Little Round Top. They got Lucy safely to her car and watched as she drove off.

Joel and Jesse started the walk back to town. Without verbalizing it, they both knew where they were headed. They needed comforting from their Second Mama.

"So..." Joel began to speak after a few moments of silence. "I guess...I guess we're not allowed to fight in front of Lucy anymore."

"Nope. I guess not," Jesse agreed.

It was their way of saving face, claiming that Lucy was the reason that they couldn't fight anymore. The truth was, neither one had the desire to argue any longer. The day had been traumatic—and cathartic—for everyone involved.

"God, that poor girl," Joel said, his voice filled with regret. "I know that must have been horrible for you, Secesh."

Jesse winced, still hearing Lucy's screams in his head. "It was harder the second time."

Joel nodded. "I know. I'd rather die a thousand times than have Emma suffer it once."

"I've seen it happen before, but, you know, never like that. Never that bad," Jesse said.

"I know! I mean, I'm sure it hurts. I've seen people grab their chest or their head or whatever, but then it passes. This time was so awful...it's like..." Joel glanced at Jesse, not wanting to make him feel worse.

"It's like she really felt everything that I felt when I died."

"Yeah," Joel said. "Well, I guess it makes sense. Usually, it's somebody's distant relative that someone's connected to that makes them experience this. With her, I mean, shit, she knows us personally...you were standing right next to her when it happened. I guess that's why it was so intense."

Jesse nodded sorrowfully, fell silent for a moment, then finally spoke again.

"I never...I never told you how sorry I am that I killed your friend. I mean...I...I did what I thought I had to do, but I'm sorry I had to kill him. And I'm real sorry you had to see it."

"Thank you," Joel said quietly. "And I'm, you know, I'm sorry I killed you."

Jesse was quiet for a second, then suddenly burst out

laughing. He couldn't help it. The absurdity of what Joel had said struck him as hilarious. He looked over at Joel with a good-natured smile to show that he meant no offense.

Joel started laughing, too.

"Pish posh!" Jesse said. "Think nothing of it, my friend!"

They both burst into a fresh round of laughter as they headed to town to look for Fillis.

26

J oel and Jesse found Fillis in her usual spot. She could tell something was wrong the moment she saw them.

"So...how did it go?" she asked. The boys looked so upset that she was afraid to hear the answer. Fillis knew it couldn't have been easy to visit the spot where they died, but she also knew it was something they needed to do.

"It was...it was..." Jesse said, faltering. "Lucy...Lucy..."

"What happened to Lucy?" Fillis asked, alarmed at Jesse's expression. She glanced down the road behind where the boys were standing, suddenly worried as she realized that Lucy wasn't with them. Fillis noticed that Joel looked at Jesse with uncharacteristic sympathy.

Joel could see that it was too rough for Jesse to talk about, so he took over. "Well, you know how sometimes we've seen tourists experience battle pains? Like they feel how a soldier died?"

"Oh, no," Fillis said. She looked at Jesse, whose devastated expression confirmed it.

"Yeah," Jesse said quietly.

Fillis looked up at Joel and asked hopefully, "Your death?"

Joel shook his head somberly. "No. Secesh's."

Fillis's hand flew to her mouth out of humanly instinct, even though it was no longer possible to cover her mouth with her hand in shock. "Sweet Jesus. Sweet Jesus! Is she all right?"

"Yeah," Joel answered. "Yeah, I think so. We tried to explain what was happening to her and we took care of her the best we could. But it was...it was pretty awful. Worst I've ever seen."

"Oh, my God," Fillis said mournfully. "That poor little lamb." Fillis couldn't imagine what it was like for her to suffer through Jesse's death. Lucy was like a daughter to Fillis already, and she had to fight the instinct to run off and try to find her, to see with her own eyes that she was okay. Lucy was most likely home by now where Fillis couldn't go. For now, she needed to concentrate on comforting the boys, especially Jesse.

"You all right, honey?" she asked him.

"She kept...she kept beggin' me to make it stop. And I couldn't...I couldn't..."

"And there wasn't anything you could do. I know, honey. I know," Fillis said gently.

"I couldn't help her," Jesse said in barely a whisper. Then his voice got louder. "I should have known. I knew she was sensitive to this shit, and I knew we were going right to where we died. How could I not have realized? How could I have done this to her?"

"Baby, I know, lookin' back now, you think you shoulda known, but honey, none of us thought of it. We all seen it happen and none of us thought about it. It's so rare, honey. It's so rare. Must be forty years or so since I seen it happen. Jesse. *Jesse.*" Fillis spoke firmly, loudly, until Jesse finally raised his head to look at her. "We all love her, baby. None of us would ever do anything to hurt her. We didn't know. You didn't know. She'll be all right, okay, honey? She gone be jus' fine."

"Well, there was one good thing to come out of all this, Second Mama," Joel said with a smile. "Lucy said we're not allowed to fight anymore."

Fillis knew her boys well enough to notice the change already. At first, she thought Joel was being kind to Jesse because of what had just happened to the woman he loved, but now she saw there was more to it than that. Fillis could sense the change in them. There was a feeling of understanding between them. She never thought it would happen, but the hatred between them was gone.

"Oh, I see how it is! I been tellin' you boys for a hunnert years to get along, and some pretty little thing comes along and you listen to her all of a sudden."

"Yep," Joel said.

"Pretty much," Jesse said with a smile.

Relief flooded through Fillis. She didn't care how it came about; it gave her such a sense of peace to think that her boys might finally start getting along. She felt awful that Lucy had to suffer so much, but her pain just might be what finally helped to set them free. Mending old wounds was a vital step toward crossing over. And by some miracle, Lucy had helped them to heal.

LUCY MADE IT SAFELY HOME, then collapsed onto the couch in exhaustion. She had never felt so utterly drained in her entire life.

Her mind whirled with the events of the evening. She'd endured more physical pain than she had ever thought possible. Even now, Lucy wasn't sure how she had gotten through it. The trauma was still so fresh in her mind. She began to shake as recalled the searing throbbing in her shoulder, the sharp, blinding pain in her left temple, and the ungodly agony in her abdomen when she'd endured the flagpole impaling her. Lucy had truly felt like she might die. Thank God Jesse had stayed with her for the entire ordeal.

Jesse.

Lucy's heart ached as she thought of him. When the agony of enduring his death wounds had finally subsided, she'd been furious. She had had no idea that feeling phantom battle pains was even humanly possible, but Joel and Jesse knew. She was so damned angry at them for allowing this to happen to her.

Until she opened her eyes and looked at Jesse. His agonized expression told him how sorry he was and how much he blamed himself for her pain. As she looked into his sweet, blue-gray eyes, so full of tenderness and sorrow, she knew she couldn't deny the truth to herself any longer.

She was in love with him.

Lucy hadn't wanted to admit the truth to herself because it hurt too much. She loved Jesse, and he was dead. That was why she had started sobbing all over again once the physical pain had abated. She'd been overwhelmed with the emotional pain of loving a man she couldn't possibly have, and she was utterly distraught at knowing how horribly Jesse had suffered when he died.

As she had lain on the rock in Devil's Den, she'd thought

of all the horror stories she'd heard about the battle of Gettysburg and its aftermath. There were bodies strewn across the land for weeks afterward. The thought of Jesse's suffering, dying in a Northern town so far from his beloved South, and the idea that his precious, broken body lay on the battlefield was too much sorrow for her to bear.

When Lucy had looked up at his face, she was consumed with love for him. Jesse Spenser was the kindest, gentlest, most wonderful man she had ever known. How she adored that boyish smile of his, and the way he always called her his rose literally made her knees weak. That look of pure compassion on his face as he looked down at her on that rock was heartbreaking. Jesse cared so much about everyone. Lucy knew she would never find another man as tender and loving as him.

And she nearly told him so. She'd been such an emotional wreck that she nearly professed her love right there on the battlefield. She went so far as to open her mouth before she came to her senses, realizing she would regret blurting out her feelings later.

Lucy moaned aloud as the tears began to flow again. Finally, exhaustion overtook her and she fell asleep.

Lucy slept for a few hours, and awoke when Theresa came home around nine p.m. She opened her eyes and rolled over, meeting Theresa's worried gaze. Lucy looked exhausted and stressed.

"You all right?" Theresa asked.

"No. Not really."

"You look like hell! What happened to you?"

"That's going to require some explanation." Lucy took a huge breath and let it out slowly. "I need you to do something for me."

"Anything!" Theresa said, sitting beside Lucy on the

couch and looking at her with great concern.

"I need you to get me drunk tonight."

It was an unusual request coming from Lucy. Aside from the glasses of wine they shared together in the apartment, Lucy wasn't much of a drinker. If she needed to get drunk, there must be a good reason. No questions asked, Theresa grabbed her keys.

"Let's roll."

They went to an Irish bar not far from the tavern where Lucy worked. Theresa didn't ask any questions on the ride over, either. She knew Lucy would tell her what was going on when she was ready, preferably when she had a drink in front of her.

NOT FAR FROM where the women were headed, Joel and Jesse sat, invisible, outside of Meade's Tavern, even though they knew Lucy had the night off. It was always entertaining to watch people here on a Friday, and there was a lot of foot traffic. In all the time they'd known each other, this was the first time they had hung out together, just the two of them, without Lucy or Fillis forcing them.

Jesse sat up suddenly and looked down the street.

"What?" Joel asked, following his gaze.

"Lucy," Jesse said simply. He could spot her a mile away.

Lucy and Theresa headed toward them on the street. Silently, the soldiers watched the women walk past them and head into the Irish bar across the street from Meade's Tavern.

"She still looks upset," Jesse said, worry in his voice.

"I know. I don't blame her." Joel got to his feet. "We should go check on her."

"No! We can't."

"Why not?

"I promised. We *both* promised we wouldn't watch her without her knowing." Jesse said, looking anguished.

Joel let out a frustrated moan and sat back down. "You're right. She would be really upset if she knew we were watching her again, and Christ knows we've done enough to her already. But that doesn't mean we can't wait for her out here."

Jesse nodded. They both sat and waited. And worried.

THERESA AND LUCY sat at a table for two instead of at the bar so they could talk in private. Once they were comfortably seated with a fuzzy navel for Lucy and a lemon drop martini for Theresa, Lucy was ready to talk.

"Where to begin..." Lucy said. "Well, I took them to Devil's Den today."

"Oh my gosh, that's right!" Theresa exclaimed. "Oh, I feel so bad. I can't believe I forgot to ask you how it went."

"It's okay." Lucy took a sip of her drink. Then another. "It was so weird having them there together. I know they've both gone back to that spot where they died over the years, but I don't think they've ever been back there together."

"Wow. What did they do when they got there?" Theresa asked, eyes wide. She'd already drained half her martini. She could hold her liquor a lot better than Lucy.

"It was intense, that's for sure. We got to this spot between some of the rocks. It was right where Jesse died. The two of them just stood there for a minute, glaring at each other like they wanted to kill each other all over again."

"Wow, that is intense," Theresa said.

"Then...then..." Lucy's voice quaked a little. It was difficult for her to describe the terrifying events that followed. "Then I suddenly got this horrible pain in my shoulder. And I don't mean just a twinge or an ache, I mean *pain*. It was horrible. I felt dizzy and I swear, I felt like I was gonna pass out."

"Oh, my God. What the hell happened?"

"Well, you know how I'm really sensitive to ghost stuff? All that time I felt like I was being watched, and it turned out I really was? And I knew the exact spot where they buried Jesse?"

"Uh huh," Theresa said, spellbound by Lucy's tale.

"Basically, I found out the hard way that it's possible for people who are really sensitive to feel the pain of a soldier who died in battle. What I felt was Jesse being shot."

"You've got to be kidding me!"

Lucy shook her head and took another gulp of her drink before she continued. "It was...horrible. I mean, I felt *everything*. I basically lived through his death."

Theresa took a moment to let that idea sink in. It was a lot to comprehend.

"I-I mean...all of it...Jesse was shot in the shoulder, and then he was shot in the head."

Theresa gasped. "Oh, my God, Lucy. Oh, my God...."

"And then he was...remember....that's when Joel...."

Theresa closed her eyes, remembering how Joel had killed Jesse with the flag. "Oh, Lucy..."

Lucy nodded, tears spilling from her eyes. She was so grateful that she had Theresa to confide in. No one else in the world would believe a story like this, but Theresa would never doubt her.

The server stopped by their table. She hesitated just a moment when she noticed that Lucy was crying. "Would you like another?" she asked softly, gesturing at Lucy's empty glass.

"Yes, please. Thank you," Lucy responded. Theresa nodded at her glass, then smiled at the server, who rushed off.

Theresa reached across the table and grasped Lucy's hand and squeezed it. She was silent for a bit, taking in what Lucy had told her.

"Lucy, I can't imagine how awful that must have been for you."

"It was. It was, Theresa. It felt like I was gonna die. But Jesse stayed with me. Joel did, too. They kept telling me to hold on, that it would be over soon. That I would be okay." Lucy wiped her eyes and tried to calm down.

"Oh, man, I bet they both felt pretty bad."

"Yeah, they did. They said it was all their fault. That they should have known it could happen if I stood right where Jesse died. They'd seen it happen to other people before."

"Damn right should have known!" Theresa snapped angrily. "They knew it could happen, so what the fuck?"

The server returned with their drinks. She set them down and departed quickly, probably to less volatile tables.

"I know. That's what I thought, too. But they've only seen it a few times. It's really rare. They would never do anything to hurt me on purpose."

Theresa took another sip of her drink. She still looked severely pissed off.

"The thing is, I think having me go through it really helped them in a way."

"Oh, goody for them!" Theresa said irritably. "You got to experience being shot and brutally murdered, but they're better than ever!"

Lucy laughed out loud, the alcohol clearly taking effect.

"You better take it easy on that, hon," Theresa said, looking at Lucy's glass.

"I'm fine!" Lucy said much more loudly than she usually spoke. "But really. It helped. It did help. It was like they had to live it all over again, too. Trust me, Theresa they feel bad. Like, *really* bad. But seeing how horrible it was made them kind of realize they both suffered a lot. They realized that nobody's really the bad guy."

"You mean they made up?"

"Yeah. They did. I mean, I don't know if it'll last, but I think it will. They just seemed different." She looked at Theresa with a smile. "They don't hate each other anymore."

"That's incredible. And very hard to imagine."

"I can't believe the difference it made. I mean, knowing what I know now... If I'd have known it would happen, I wouldn't have..." Lucy thought about it. The experience was horrific and terrifying, but what if it helped them cross over? "I don't know--maybe I would still have gone. For them." *For him.*

Theresa looked at her with renewed concern. "Is that all that's bothering you? Wait, that didn't come out right. I didn't mean, *oh, is that all, you were shot and stabbed.* I just mean, I get the feeling there's something else."

Lucy fell silent for a moment, staring at her nearly empty glass. As always, Theresa gave her time and space to talk when she was ready.

Finally, Lucy lifted her tear-filled eyes and said softly, "I love him."

Theresa smiled sadly. There was no need to elaborate on who "him" referred to.

"I might have known," Theresa said. "I can understand

why, Lucy. He's so sweet and cute and perfect for you. You know, aside from being dead."

Lucy laughed loudly again, a sound that was dangerously close to a sob. She took a sip from her third fuzzy navel. "You really think he's perfect for me?"

"Oh, yeah. Definitely."

Lucy absent-mindedly ran her finger along the outside of her glass. "If things were different...do you think he could have loved me?"

"Of course. He's crazy about you now! I can't imagine how he would feel if you two actually had a chance. I think he'd fall for you in a minute. You know what they say; in another time, in another place..."

Lucy nodded sadly, but there was sorrow and doubt in her eyes. She thought if Jesse were alive, he would have met some tall, beautiful Southern girl to spend his life with. A *real* yellow rose of Texas, not a short Yankee like her.

"I really want to help them, you know? I want to help them cross over. I want to reunite Joel with his wife and those precious babies of his. I want to help Jesse, too. Wandering aimlessly around Gettysburg for an eternity is no kind of life. It's not a life at all! It's just that..."

"What?"

"I'm going to miss him so much if he crosses over..." Lucy closed her eyes and tried not to cry.

"I know, honey."

Lucy opened her eyes. "But I can't let that stop me. I'm going to help them."

Lucy looked so tired, the alcohol and the traumatic events of the day catching up to her.

"Let's go home. You need rest," Theresa told her. She paid the bill, ignoring Lucy's protestations, and helped Lucy to her feet.

WHEN THEY GOT out onto the street, it became apparent that Lucy was in worse shape than she had thought. Theresa put her arm around her and gripped her tightly to help her to walk. It was a good thing they hadn't parked too far away.

Jesse sat up the moment he saw them. "There she is!"

Now visible to the living, both Joel and Jesse stood up and walked over to the women. Lucy spied Jesse, and she let out a deep, mournful sigh.

"He *had* to show up right now," Lucy muttered, her heart breaking just looking at him. She'd been drinking all night to try to forget the pain of loving a man she could never have, and here he was.

Jesse could see that Lucy was not happy to see them. Fear struck his heart. She was finally sick of them, and who could blame her? She'd tried so hard to help them and all they did was cause her grief. From that time in the tavern when he'd terrified her so much that she'd passed out to the horror she'd experienced at Devil's Den, why *should* she be glad to see them?

"It figures you would be here," Lucy said, slurring a bit. Theresa gripped her tighter to keep her standing.

Joel and Jesse exchanged a worried look. They weren't used to seeing Lucy like this. She rarely drank, and they both knew damn well they were the reason she'd gone out tonight and over-imbibed. It wasn't much different than when soldiers in camp drank to forget the horrible things they'd seen in battle.

"You know, you know, you know...what happened to me at Devil's Den today?" Lucy asked, swaying a bit.

Jesse winced at the mention of what happened to her on the battlefield.

"I'd go through it all over again," Lucy continued. "I would. I'd go through that all over again if I thought it would help you. I'd do anything for you, Jesse. Because I love you."

Jesse's eyes opened wide. He stared at Lucy with astonishment, her lovely brown eyes filled with sorrow. Because she was impaired by alcohol, her feelings were laid bare before him. It was like looking into his own soul. She looked every bit as helpless and heartsick as he always felt when he was with her. Was it really possible that she loved him, too?

He looked over at Joel to confirm that he'd actually heard what he thought he'd heard. Joel looked equally shocked.

"Lucy!" Theresa cried, horrified. "She's hammered. She doesn't know what she's saying." Theresa glared at Jesse, as if he had somehow coerced her confession.

"What?" Jesse asked, his eyes full of hope. He knew he was taking advantage of Lucy during an achingly vulnerable moment, but he had to know the truth. "What did you say, Lucy?"

"Stop it!" Theresa yelled at Jesse. "She's drunk, dammit!" She hugged Lucy closer and pulled her down the street, trying to save her from herself. Lucy broke free and looked back at Jesse.

"I said I love you. I love you even though you're dead. You always say you were nobody's darling. You're somebody's darling now, Jesse." Lucy's eyes filled with tears as she looked at him. Her voice cracked with emotion. "You're *my* darling."

Lucy started to weep openly, and Theresa pulled her to her chest. "Come on, Lucy. Come on, honey. Let's go." Theresa glared fiercely at both Joel and Jesse. "She doesn't know what she's saying. She's upset because of the torture she went through because of you two morons."

Still holding Lucy to her chest, Theresa started walking with her down the street.

"Theresa!" Jesse called after her.

Theresa turned back, her eyes still blazing.

"Get her home safely," Jesse pleaded.

"I will," Theresa promised, her expression softening a bit.

The two men watched as Theresa helped Lucy get to the car. As always, Jesse lamented that he couldn't pick Lucy up and carry her. He looked both ways as if trying to cross a street, then became invisible once he saw nobody was looking. Joel did the same so they could talk in private.

They exchanged stunned looks for a second, then Jesse spoke. "Do you think she meant it?"

"Yes," Joel answered definitively. "Yes, I do."

"I don't know. She was pretty tight," Jesse said, using the old-fashioned term for hammered.

"Exactly! That's why she told you the truth. You know how she is. She could never come out and say something like that if she was sober. And she was so upset. Poor Lucy. But...the way she looked at you...yes. Yes, I think she really loves you."

"I want to believe it. I really do," Jesse said. He glanced down the street where the women had disappeared.

Joel chuckled softly and shook his head. "Poor girl. She's gonna wake up tomorrow and remember what she said and wanna kill herself."

Jesse moaned with empathy for Lucy's plight. "You're right. My poor rose. She's gonna be so embarrassed."

"I know. But not for long. You'll fix it. The second you see her."

"Yes, I will," Jesse said with determination. "I hope she meant it. I really do. But even if she didn't, even if it was just a drunken mistake, I'm gonna tell her that I love her." Jesse smiled, more to himself than to Joel.

27

Lucy awoke the next morning with a headache that would have been much worse had Theresa not forced her to drink a lot of water before allowing her to collapse in bed. Lucy didn't remember everything that had happened last night, but she remembered enough. She felt a rush of humiliation when she remembered crying and sloppily telling Jesse that she loved him. How on earth would she ever be able to face either one of them again?

Lucy showered and eventually made her way to the breakfast table, where Theresa gave her some coffee.

"You feeling okay? Hungover?" Theresa asked.

"A little." Lucy stared at her coffee as she stirred it listlessly. Part of her wanted to avoid seeing Jesse ever again. She didn't want to face him, but the idea of not seeing him made her chest ache. Things would never be the same between them.

"So, how much do you remember from last night?"

"Bits and pieces," Lucy said.

Theresa winced and said, "You told Jesse you loved him."

"I know," Lucy said. "That much I remember." She put her head down on the table and moaned. Theresa sat next to her and put her hand on her back.

"Oh, honey. I know it's embarrassing for you that you told him, but how do you know he doesn't feel the same way?"

"Oh, get real, Theresa," Lucy said with unusual harshness.

"Lucy, he cares about you. I really believe that. What about the way he always calls you his rose?"

"He's just flirting with me because he's dead and he has nobody else to talk to." Lucy looked up at Theresa, her face full of sorrow. "He's so handsome and so charming. He's so sweet. He's every girl's dream come true. I didn't know men like that actually existed. He'd never be interested in someone like me."

"You don't know that."

"I want to ask you something, and I need you to be honest with me, okay? Please?"

"Of course."

Lucy hesitated, not sure she really wanted to know. "How did he look when I said it?"

Theresa thought for a moment. "Stunned. He looked... stunned. I really couldn't tell what he was thinking or how he might feel about you or anything. All I can say for sure is that he had no idea you felt that way about him."

Lucy nodded, and let out a shaky breath. "Thank you." She needed to know what situation she would be walking into when she saw him. She couldn't avoid him because he was bound to show up at the tavern. "God, I feel so stupid! What kind of an idiot falls in love with a ghost?"

"He's not just a ghost," Theresa reminded her kindly but firmly. "He's still a person. I believe it was you who was good about reminding them of that. They're not just spirits. They're men. Very, very handsome men..." she said, biting her lip.

Lucy couldn't but laugh. "I know, but...I still feel stupid. It was just supposed to be some dumb contest, a bet. I wasn't supposed to fall for him! They're gonna laugh at me, you know."

"No, they're not!"

"Yes, they are. I'm sure they'll think it's funny that I got drunk and stupid in front of them."

"You wouldn't say that if you'd seen Jesse's face last night."

"What do you mean?" Lucy asked, a glimmer of hope on her face.

"He didn't think it was funny. He was worried about you."

"He's always worried about me," Lucy said with a soft smile. She didn't remember his expression from last night, but she knew the face Theresa was talking about. That kind face filled with concern. She was right. He would never laugh at her. She tried to remember more of what happened. "Did you...did you call them morons?"

"Damn right I did! I'm so pissed at them for what happened to you yesterday."

"I know. They didn't do it on purpose though." Lucy put her head back down on the table. "I really don't want to see them. What am I gonna say?"

"It probably won't be as bad as you think. Just get it over with." Lucy lifted her head and nodded wearily.

"And if they give you any shit about this, so help me God...." Theresa said clenching her fists.

Lucy smiled. Theresa might not be able to touch them,

but she would figure out a way to kick their asses if they gave her any grief.

28

W hen Joel and Jesse showed up at the tavern, they watched Lucy rushing around to help her customers.

"You know, she may not even remember what she said," Joel said.

Lucy accidentally locked eyes with Jesse. She groaned and put her head down on the bar.

"She remembers," said both Joel and Jesse.

"Poor thing. Go. Put her out of her misery." Joel gestured toward Lucy, planning to stay back and give them some privacy.

Jesse nodded. "Come with me. I'll need backup. You know her—she's not gonna believe me when I tell her."

"Good point." It had taken her a long time to understand that they really liked her and weren't just playing with her. She would probably think Jesse was just being nice when he told her how he felt about her.

Lucy looked over to see the two of them grinning like idiots. *So much for not making fun of me.* She felt a fresh surge of humiliation so strong that she wanted to quit her job and run away. Then her embarrassment fused with anger. *Who told them to bother me with their damn contest anyway? Who told them to come flirt with me every damn day and confuse me and act like they cared?*

Jesse walked toward Lucy, careful to avoid any physical contact with anyone or anything in the middle of the crowded restaurant. Joel followed behind, and Lucy found herself having to face both of them.

"We need to talk, Lucy," Jesse said.

"What if I don't want to?" Lucy said, avoiding eye contact.

"Please?"

Lucy sighed and nodded, resigned to her fate. This was what she'd been stressing out about all day. It was somewhat of a relief that they'd finally shown up. At least now she could get the awkward discussion over with. She still wanted to be friends with both of them, but it would be so uncomfortable now.

"Out back. I don't need the whole restaurant overhearing this," Lucy grumbled.

Lucy walked out the back door and carefully held the door open so the guys could follow. She was relieved to find they were alone in the back parking lot. Servers and busboys often snuck out back for a smoke, but thank goodness there was no one else around now.

Lucy leaned back against the wall of the building. Jesse stood in front of her, with Joel to her left. Though she usually loved Joel's company, she didn't know why he had to be here now to witness this awkward exchange.

Jesse didn't seem to know where to begin. The silence was unbearable for Lucy, so she finally decided to speak first. She forced herself to look Jesse in the eye.

Lucy spoke quickly, angrily. "Look, I know what I said last night. Can we just forget—"

Jesse spoke loudly so he could be heard over her protestations, "I love you too, Lucy!"

Lucy stared at Jesse for what seemed like a full minute.

Joel chuckled softly.

"What?" Lucy asked finally.

"I love you too, Lucy," Jesse repeated with a twinkle in his eye.

Lucy looked over at Joel, who smiled and nodded at her. She saw that his smile was warm and caring, and she realized they hadn't been mocking her after all. They were just excited to tell her how Jesse felt. She allowed herself to believe Jesse's words for just a moment, then her usual doubts took over.

He's just saying that to be nice. He knows I feel like a fool, and he's just trying to make me feel better.

"Jesse, you don't have to say that just because—"

Joel laughed out loud. "Lucy, Lucy. You have no idea…"

"Oh, Lucy," Jesse said, looking at her with adoration. "I've been in love with you for so long. Long before this silly contest ever started."

"But…but…I didn't even know you before then," Lucy said with confusion.

"I knew *you*," Jesse said. "I know you don't like hearing about all those times I used to watch you when you didn't know I was there, but I couldn't help myself. It was always the highlight of my day. I'd come in and watch you wait on people, lookin' so pretty and smilin' so sweet." Jesse arched an eyebrow and grinned at her. "You drove me crazy when I'd see you lean over in that short skirt of yours."

Lucy glanced down at her work skirt and looked back up

at him. She could see the desire in his eyes. She was too stunned to blush.

"And you know how sometimes you'd sneak off to that back room so you could study for a quick bit? Then you'd feel a chill and pull on your sweater? That was me. Sitting next to you. Jus' tryin' to be close to you for a while."

Lucy's eyes grew wide, and she nodded. Looking back, she remembered how often that had happened. She recalled looking around to see if there was an air-conditioning vent blowing on her. Here she'd always thought it was just cold in that room.

"It always made me so happy to come in and watch you talk with people. You were always so nice, 'specially when you were dealin' with little kids. And the way your eyes lit up every time you told anybody that you were gonna be a teacher. You were just so sweet and so lovely..." Jesse threw up his hands helplessly. "I fell in love."

Joel's smile widened as he saw Lucy's expression slowly change from doubt to belief. She was starting to understand that these weren't just idle words. Jesse obviously knew so much about her. He clearly wasn't making it all up to spare her feelings.

"It's true, Lucy," Joel told her. "Not that he told me any of this when he picked you 'at random' for our bet." He made air quotes, then smirked over at Jesse.

Jesse chuckled. "That's right. I knew I could never try to court any other woman, and I knew if I chose you for our wager, I'd finally be able to talk to you. I'm in love with you, Lucy Ann Westbrook."

Lucy took in his beautiful words and finally allowed herself to believe them. "Oh, Jesse," she said softly. She knew she could never express her devotion as eloquently as he just had.

"So. You know how I feel. Now, do you really love me," he asked with a grin, "or were you jus' wallpapered on the bark juice?"

Lucy laughed. Eyes shining, she replied, "I really love you," then added, "my *darling*."

Jesse's handsome face broke into that boyish grin that Lucy adored. She'd never seen him look as happy as he did at this moment. The two looked deeply into each other's eyes, happy to be in love but aching to hold each other.

Joel looked at Jesse, then at Lucy, then back to Jesse. "You win."

With that, he turned and walked down the parking lot, singing Rick Springfield's "Jessie's Girl." Lucy laughed as she watched him walk away, then turn invisible.

Jesse looked at Lucy and said, "I'm sorry you had to say it first. I jus' had no idea..."

"Me neither," she said, shaking her head and gracing him with a lovely smile.

Jesse looked worried. "Are you all right, Lucy? I've been so worried about you since yesterday. I'll never forgive myself for letting you get hurt like that."

"It's all right, Jesse. I'm all right now. Thanks for staying with me. I never could have gotten through it without you by my side."

"I never felt so helpless. I just couldn't stop it. I couldn't protect you. I-I couldn't—"

"It's okay. It's okay," Lucy said soothingly, wishing she could take him in her arms. Now that she knew how Jesse felt about her, she realized how hard it must have been for him to witness her suffering. It would have killed her if she'd had to watch him be tortured like that right in front of her eyes. It was hard enough for her just thinking about him going through it back in 1863.

Jesse moved in closer to Lucy, making her heart race. He usually kept a respectful distance, but now he knew he was welcome in her personal space. Lucy leaned with her back against the wall as Jesse towered over her. She looked up at him adoringly and wistfully imagined standing on her toes to kiss him. *If only.*

Instead, she held up her palm in the same way she had with Joel when she wanted to feel what it was like to touch him. Jesse held up his palm against Lucy's. The sensation was frigid, but it still felt good to have some kind of physical contact with him.

"I'm sorry," Jesse said as his hand went right through hers.

"For what? Being dead?"

"Yes. Because now I have something to live for."

Lucy smiled. She pushed her hand all the way through his palm before putting her hand back down. "I'm sorry, too, but I really have to get back to work. I wish I could stay here with you."

"I know. We'll go somewhere alone soon so we can talk without Bluebelly around."

Lucy's smile lit up her face and Jesse's whole existence. "I would love that."

"We could go to one of the park areas where it's quiet. I wish I could bring you a bottle of wine and flowers. Treat you like a lady like you deserve."

"You always treat me like a lady, darling." That was one of the things she loved most about him. "What kind of flowers would you get me if you could?"

"I don't know. What are your favorite flowers?"

Lucy thought for a moment. Long-stemmed red roses were beautiful, but so common. It was nicer to have something more unusual. The answer was suddenly obvious.

"Yellow roses!"

"Of course!" Jesse said. "I wish I could buy you roses and wine and take you somewhere romantic. Then I'd lay you down on a blanket and make passionate love to you."

Lucy's face colored, but she didn't break eye contact with him. "You would?"

Jesse grinned at her, that mischievous look that turned her on almost as much as his accent did. "Yeah, I would! I'm in love now, so it's okay."

Lucy laughed. "Yes, I guess it is. I would have loved that, Jesse. To be with you. I would have been so honored to be your first."

They looked longingly at each other for a moment, then Lucy sighed and glanced at the door.

"You need to go," Jesse said.

Lucy nodded and turned to go back inside.

"Lucy!" She turned to look at him. "I just want you to know that this is the happiest day of my...you know...whatever this is. See you soon, my lovely rose." He blew her a kiss, then turned invisible.

Lucy smiled at the space where he'd disappeared, then walked back in to work.

She hurried over to check on her badly neglected tables. Apologizing profusely, she hurried to refill empty glasses and check on food orders that were quickly cooling in the kitchen. Lucy wondered if any of her customers had seen her sneak out back with a man and were angry with her. They didn't seem to be, and Lucy didn't care if they stiffed her on the tip.

Lucy spent the rest of her shift in a happy daze. She kept replaying Jesse's words over and over in her head, that deep, sexy voice drawling, *I luuurrrve yoo too, Loosey.*

Lucy's mind reeled as she thought of all the times he'd

called her his rose. She thought back to the day when she first spoke to him. When those two "reenactors" approached her on the street. She recalled the times they'd sat in the tavern, outside at the table, and in the gazebo. He had been in love with her the whole time. It was so hard to imagine, but it was a wonderful idea to get used to. Jesse had fallen in love with her by watching her from afar. It was like something from a fairytale.

Though it had a wonderful beginning with the two of them falling in love, the ending would be much darker. She tried not to think about it, but the harsh facts still remained. Jesse was dead and Lucy was not. They would eventually be separated, either when Jesse crossed over or when Lucy was done with school and had to move away to find a teaching job.

Lucy took a deep breath and concentrated on the immediate future. For now, she could spend time with Jesse, savoring each moment until it had to end.

29

J esse found Fillis sitting, invisible to the living, on the steps of Farnsworth House Inn. Known for being one of the most haunted places in the entire world, Farnsworth was a popular tourist spot in Gettysburg. It *was* haunted, of course, but no more than anyplace else in town. Farnsworth consisted of an old brick building that housed the restaurant and had tavern rooms upstairs where you could stay overnight. Fillis was friendly with all the ghostly inhabitants of the house. She was particularly fond of Mary, who was a motherly type much like Fillis, and Jeremy, a small child who was killed in a carriage accident before the war.

Mary sat beside Fillis on the steps. She got up when she saw Jesse, offering him a friendly wave before disappearing into the tavern, leaving Fillis and Jesse alone to talk.

Jesse looked down at Fillis, a huge, silly grin on his face.

"What you up to, boy?" Fillis asked, pleased to see that Jesse was excited about something. He'd looked so drawn and worried ever since Lucy's traumatic experience on the battlefield.

"Lucy said she loved me. She *loves* me, Second Mama."

A wide smile broke out across her face. "Now o' course she does! That's wunnerful, Jesse, just wunnerful. So you finally told her how you felt about her!"

"No, she told me first!" Jesse said.

"You're kiddin'! That shy little thing came right out and told you she loves you?"

"Well, she had a little help."

"From who?"

"Oh-Be-Joyful," Jesse quipped.

"Oh!" Fillis's eyes opened wide. "Sit your ass down, boy, and tell me everything!"

Jesse chuckled and sat down next to Fillis.

"It was kind of sad at first, actually," Jesse said, turning a bit somber as he recalled how upset Lucy had been. "She'd been cryin', ya know, over what happened earlier that day."

Fillis nodded, sad to see that worried look back on his face. She knew Jesse would never be able to forget that nightmarish experience.

"So her friend Theresa took her out for a few drinks. Joel and me were waitin' outside to see 'em when they came out. Lucy'd had way too much to drink. She saw me, ya know, and started cryin' again. She kinda poured her heart out. She told me she would do it all over again for me. She said she'd...you know...experience my death all over again if it would somehow help me."

"I believe she would," Fillis said, deeply touched. It was obvious now that the two of them would do anything for each other. That was what made their love so tragic. It was doomed from the start. Fillis tried not to think about it for the moment. Right now she wanted to celebrate Jesse's happiness.

Jesse spied Joel walking down the street toward them.

"I swear. Can't get away from that guy," Jesse grumbled. He tried to look annoyed, but Fillis knew better. It was tough for either guy to admit, but they had started to like each other. For decades, Jesse's eyes had been full of white-hot fury whenever he saw Joel, but now? Now the usual gentleness remained in his face even when his former archenemy was around. He simply wasn't angry with him anymore.

"You can't hide from meeee," Joel said in a singsong voice as he taunted Jesse. Fillis smiled up at him.

"Apparently not. Lucy's workin' all night, so I 'spose I got nothin' better to do than talk to you anyways," Jesse said.

Joel grinned mischievously, and Fillis wondered what he was up to.

The two soldiers chatted and exchanged friendly insults for a while. Joel kept glancing down the road as if looking for someone. Joel had been joking about how Jesse had somehow suckered Lucy into falling for him when Fillis saw her approaching.

"Well, well, well. Speak of the devil. Or angel, as the case may be," Fillis said when she spotted Lucy walking toward them. She relished the look of pure delight on Jesse's face as he whirled around and saw her coming.

The three of them watched as she walked up to the steps. She stopped right in front of Farnsworth House Inn and looked around.

"Oh, shit," Joel said. "She got off work early and wanted to surprise you, but I forgot she can't see us." All this time he'd eagerly been awaiting her arrival, but he'd completely forgotten that they were all invisible.

There were people milling around all over. On the street, dining in the open garden area, driving by in cars. Jesse looked around frantically for a place to turn visible, like Superman looking for a place to change.

Lucy looked down right at the spot where Jesse was sitting. "You're here, aren't you Jesse? I think...I think I can feel you..." She spoke softly so passersby wouldn't think she was completely nuts.

Joel grinned at Jesse, who looked up at Lucy with wonder. It was fascinating that she not only sensed a ghostly presence, but she knew it was him. Jesse jumped to his feet, then touched Lucy on her arm.

She jumped in surprise, then laughed. "I knew it," she whispered.

Jesse quickly ducked around to the side of the Farnsworth building. Joel watched, mesmerized, as Lucy looked in the direction where Jesse headed. She knew when he'd left her side and even knew the direction he went. *Incredible.*

Jesse turned visible, out of sight of the tourists, then walked back to the front of the building. Lucy greeted him with a joyful smile.

"I thought you had to work!" Jesse exclaimed.

"Someone else needed the hours, and I wanted to see you more than I wanted the money."

Jesse glanced around. "Fillis and Joel are here, too." He didn't want Lucy to say anything that was meant to be private without knowing the others were close by.

Lucy nodded and smiled. She clearly didn't mind that they were near.

Fillis and Joel followed Jesse's lead and became visible by discreetly ducking behind the building and then walking back to the front. They both walked toward Lucy.

"So," Fillis said. "You finally made your choice. You love my Jesse boy, now do you?"

"Fillis..." Jesse moaned, sounding like a teenage boy who was embarrassed by his mother.

Lucy smiled. "Yes, ma'am. I love him very much."

Fillis laughed, the sound almost a girlish giggle. She was so happy for both of them she could burst. It took a very special girl to love a ghost. Jesse had absolutely nothing to give her. He couldn't buy her flowers, take her on a date, or make love to her. But she loved him anyway. She loved him for the very essence of who he was, the most selfless kind of devotion Fillis could imagine.

"It was the accent, wasn't it?" Joel asked glumly.

"Oh, yeah," Lucy said, a seductive lilt to her voice. "That accent, that smile, that handsome face..."

Jesse smiled shyly and looked down. Fillis suspected he would have blushed if he still had a beating heart to pump blood to his face.

Lucy knew Joel was joking, but she didn't want to leave him out. "I love you, too, you know," she told him sincerely. "Just in a different way."

"Friend-zoned!" Jesse said with great zeal.

Lucy laughed. "Well, sort of..."

"Feeling's mutual, sweetheart," Joel said with great affection. "I hope you know that."

"Well! The fair Lucy has made her choice! For some crazy reason, she chose the raggedly ol' cowpoke from Texas," Jesse said gleefully.

Joel rolled his eyes and shook his head. "Yeah, yeah, yeah..."

"For what it's worth, I never thought she'd pick me over you," Jesse said, trying not to rub it in too much, given their newly brokered peace. "But she did. So it's time for you to pay the piper, Billy Yank!"

"What?" Joel asked, eyes wide.

"We had a deal," Jesse said, a mischievous glint in his eye.

"Are you serious?"

"Time to pay up, Lincoln Boy!" He whistled for a few seconds, then said, "And I ain't just whistlin' Dixie!"

Joel looked over at Lucy for help. She threw up her hands as if to say, *This is between you two. Leave me out of it!*

Jesse jabbed a finger at Joel, "And don't you sit there and act like you wouldn't make me do it if you'da won!"

Joel had no retort for that. Everyone knew he would have done the same thing to Jesse.

"All right, all right. I'm a man of my word."

Jesse cackled. "No time like the present! Friday night, too. Boy, Lincoln Square will be crowded!"

Joel closed his eyes and moaned.

THE SQUARE *WAS* CROWDED. It was a Friday night in May, and the weather was beautiful. Lincoln Square was a popular spot among tourists, especially late in the evening or at night when the battlefields and museums were all closed. The square was right in the heart of the town and contained a roundabout on the street where there was usually heavy traffic. The historic Gettysburg Hotel was located in the square, as were several bars, restaurants, and shops.

Joel looked around nervously at all the parents, kids, older tourists, and young people out on dates. This was going to be humiliating. He knew he had to be a man and suck it up. Jesse had won the bet, and that was putting it mildly. Neither one of them could have imagined that the sweet, pretty girl they had chosen for their wager would have fallen in love with him.

Even now, Joel was glad that she had. Jesse had been robbed of a chance at love because he'd sacrificed his life for his home and family. He deserved a wonderful woman like Lucy.

Jesse cleared his throat and spoke loudly, "Attention, everyone!"

"Oh, Jesse," Lucy moaned, and shot a sympathetic look at Joel. Joel chuckled and shook his head.

"Let's get this over with."

Fillis was invisible, but she was there to watch.

"My buddy and I here had a friendly wager..." Jesse's voice traveled across the square. The man in the Confederate uniform easily captured the attention of the people milling around. A hush fell, as people were curious to see what was going on. "If I lost, I would have had to stand here in the square and sing 'The Battle Hymn of the Republic.'"

Murmurs and laughter came up from the crowd.

"However! Since I *won* the bet, my pal from the Union side now has to pay up. Take it away, Joel!" He gestured grandly toward Joel, who was resplendent as always in his blue Union uniform.

Joel looked over at Lucy, who blew him a kiss. She was supportive, but she was still laughing.

Joel mentally took a deep breath since he couldn't take an actual one. If he had to do this, he might as well do it right. He sang out, loud and strong, "Oh, I wish I was in the land of cotton! Old times there are not forgotten. Look away! Look away! Look away! Dixie land..."

Laughter erupted from the crowd as they realized what Joel had to do to settle the bet. Joel was surprised to find the whole experience wasn't as embarrassing as he had thought. He found the happy laughter of the crowd invigorating. It almost made him feel alive again. Joel was never one to take himself too seriously, so it wasn't that big of a deal.

"In Dixie land, where I was born," Joel made a face after

singing that part, which elicited even more laughter. He looked over at Jesse, who offered him a cheerful thumbs up. Joel would have given him another finger, if not for the kids in the crowd. "Early on one frosty morn, look away! Look away! Look away! Dixie land. Oh, I wish I was in Dixie," Joel rolled his eyes as he sang, "Hooray! Hooray! In Dixie land I'll take my stand, to live and die in Dixie. Hooray, hooray, away down South in Dixie!"

Joel threw up his hands, and took a theatrical bow to the delight of everyone watching. There were cheers and whistles from all around, and Joel laughed good-naturedly.

When the laughter and noise died down, Jesse stood before the crowd again. Lucy looked at him curiously, then looked over at Joel, who shrugged. The crowd hushed again, eager to see what would happen next.

"Ah, what the hell!" Jesse said with enthusiasm. He suddenly dropped to one knee and dramatically threw up his right hand in the air. In his loudest and best Elvis impersonation, he sang out, "Glory, glory hallelu-u-u-u-jah! Glory, glory hallelu-lu-jah... Come on, Joel!"

Jesse beckoned to Joel, who went to his side and dropped down right next to him in the same position. Both on one knee, arms in the air, the two sang loudly, "Glory, glory, halleulu-lu-lu-jaaaaah! His truuuuuth isssss marchinnnnnng ONNNNNNN!"

The crowd went wild. Jesse looked over at Lucy, who was laughing so hard she was wiping tears from her eyes. That made it worth it right there. He'd gladly make a fool of himself anytime if it made her smile.

"Good job, Bluebelly," Jesse said to Joel, bowing slightly. Had they been alive, Jesse would have given him a hearty handshake.

Joel looked him in the eye and said sincerely, "Congratulations."

Lucy walked up to the boys. The crowd dispersed, sensing the show was over. Joel and Jesse offered smiles and waves to those who shouted "Good job!" and "Nice singing!" but were careful not to make too much eye contact, lest anyone try to clap them on the back or try to shake their hands.

"That was great, guys," Lucy said, laughing.

"Thanks, sweetheart," Joel said. "You chose wisely. He's a good man."

Lucy looked into Joel's eyes and smiled warmly. It was amazing to see how far the two had come in the short time she'd known them. She also noticed a deep sadness in Joel's expression.

"What is it, Joel?" she asked. Lucy felt another presence and turned to her right.

"Fillis is here, too," Jesse explained.

Lucy smiled at where she now knew Fillis was standing, then turned back to Joel.

Joel looked around and saw three pairs of supportive eyes looking at him. Even Jesse looked concerned. Joel knew the time was finally right.

"I...I know why I'm still here. Why I haven't crossed over yet. I've always known. And I think I'm finally ready to talk about it."

Lucy nodded, offering him a sad but encouraging smile. Whatever it was, it was hard for him to talk about.

"It's something nobody knows about. I've never told anyone and...well, because of you, Lucy, I'm ready to finally try to deal with it. You've given me hope again that I really can cross over and be with my family. Your friendship has meant everything to me."

Lucy placed her hand over her heart.

"Anything I can do, Joel. Just name it."

"I think we should meet somewhere private. All of us," Joel said. He looked at Lucy, at Fillis, and tentatively at Jesse.

"Anything you need," Jesse said solemnly. His tone and expression made it clear that there would be no jokes, no insults at Joel's expense. He was willing to help, too.

"Not tonight. It'll be dark soon, and I don't want Lucy out by herself late at night," Joel said.

"Agreed," Jesse said.

"How about tomorrow morning?" Lucy offered. "I don't have to be in to work until eleven."

"Okay," Joel said. "We need to go somewhere private. Lucy can't be invisible, after all. We could meet on one of the battlefields. They're usually pretty quiet in the morning."

"No," Jesse said firmly. "No battlefields. Lucy's getting more sensitive by the minute. She could have had relatives that died in the war. I don't want her anywhere near where any fightin' took place."

"Good thinking," Fillis said.

Lucy turned her head toward where Fillis stood. She couldn't hear the words, but she sensed something. Joel noticed Lucy's perception, and nodded grimly at Jesse.

"What about the Eternal Peace Memorial? Where we met before?"

"No," Jesse said. "It's on a battlefield. Absolutely not."

Lucy smiled gratefully at him. She loved how protective he was of her. Lucy turned her head again. She knew Fillis had said something, and she looked at Jesse to translate. Jesse nodded at Fillis, then turned to Lucy.

"That playground that's not far from the college. There's

plenty of open space there, and it's not near the battle-grounds."

"Yeah. I know exactly where you mean. We can meet there tomorrow. Around nine o'clock?"

Joel nodded, nervous but also somewhat relieved.

"And you want all of us there?" Lucy asked gently. Joel always confided in Fillis, and he'd said he specifically wanted to talk to Lucy. She just wanted to make sure that he was comfortable with Jesse's presence during such a personal conversation.

Jesse looked at Joel. "Whatever you want. No pressure, okay?"

Joel searched Jesse's eyes and saw only support. Not judgment. Not hate.

"Yeah. Yeah, I'd like you to be there, too," Joel said.

30

J oel, Jesse, and Fillis showed up at the playground first and chose a quiet spot under a tree. It was close enough to the playground where they could watch the kids play, but far enough away so they could talk without being overheard.

Joel was nervous. He'd always known he would have to come to terms with what had happened if he were ever to cross over and be with Emma and the boys, but it was painful just to think about. He wasn't even sure how he was going to say it out loud.

All three smiled when they saw Lucy approach. Her mere presence was such a breath of fresh air, metaphorically anyway. They all felt blessed to have her around, after so many years of being around only other spirits.

Lucy smiled warmly at all of them. Her eyes lingered on Jesse. "Hello, Rebel-of-my-heart."

Jesse grinned, honored to be singled out. "Hello, my beautiful rose." He stood up, like a gentleman should when a lady is present. He bowed and tipped his hat, still annoyed that he couldn't remove it for her.

Joel wrinkled his nose, but couldn't hide the amusement in his eyes. "Aw, man. You two aren't going to get all gooey and lovey-dovey on me, are you?"

"Count on it," Lucy said, blowing Jesse a kiss. Jesse "caught" it with his hand, then placed his hand dramatically over his heart.

Joel leaned over and made a loud, exaggerated vomiting noise. Lucy burst out laughing.

Lucy sat down on the grass, and Jesse sat next to her as close as possible. She felt his eyes on her as she straightened out her black work skirt to cover her legs. She also caught him looking down her blouse, trying to catch a glimpse of her cleavage. Had anyone else done it, she would have felt self-conscious. With Jesse, she felt desired. Though Lucy loved when she caught Jesse looking at her body, she was careful not to tease him too much. She didn't know how strong the sex drive was for ghosts, but she knew he had no physical way to satisfy his urges.

But Lucy did. Many times, late at night, she would close her eyes and think of Jesse. She'd imagine unbuttoning his uniform and finally being able to see his manly chest. She fantasized about what it would feel like to run her hands down his chest, then stroke him between his legs. It would be so wonderful to touch him in ways that no other woman ever had. Her favorite fantasy involved Jesse pushing her down on the bed, kissing her passionately, then finally spreading her legs and pushing himself inside her. *Hard.* Often, Lucy would close her eyes and stroke herself, imagining what it would feel like to have Jesse pounding into her. When she gave herself an orgasm, she quietly cried out his name.

Lucy looked into Jesse's eyes. He grinned at her, unabashed at being caught looking at her figure. She also caught Joel grinning at the two of them, as if he could read their minds. Lucy blushed and looked away.

"Thank you, guys, for being with me today. I feel like I can trust you with what I have to say, even though it won't be easy to talk about."

"Take your time, Joel," Lucy said softly.

Joel smiled gratefully. Then he looked down at the ground, not wanting to look at anyone while he made his confession.

"I cheated on Emma," Joel said, barely audible. He continued looking down as he waited for the news to sink in.

Lucy exchanged a stunned look with Jesse but was quick to change her expression. Her mind was reeling with Joel's words, but she didn't want to make him feel worse. He needed help and support, not judgment.

"I did it three times," Joel said, his voice thick with emotion. Lucy didn't know if spirits could cry real tears, but Joel was definitely on the verge. "I-I mean it wasn't three women. It was all in one week. Three times. Same girl. A fancy girl."

"Prostitute," Jesse quietly explained to Lucy.

Lucy nodded. She stared at Joel, who was still looking at the ground. She couldn't help but feel disappointed. The love of Joel and Emma Casey was the stuff of legend around here. Theirs was a fairytale, if tragically doomed romance. Joel lit up every time he spoke of her. Lucy had been so inspired by Joel's marriage. It had helped make her believe in love again after the psychological damage that Eric had done to her. What did this mean? Was nothing sacred?

The pain on Joel's face was excruciating. Yes, he'd cheated. And he'd clearly spent the last 150-plus years torturing himself for it. Compassion flooded through Lucy. He'd suffered enough as far as she was concerned.

"That's why you're still here," she said gently.

Joel finally dared to lift his head. He looked immensely relieved to hear her gentle tone, as if he'd expected her to be angry with him. That plaintive look of gratitude and relief in his eyes broke her heart.

"Yes," Joel said. "Emma was a perfect angel. I left her with two little boys to take care of, to raise all on her own. I loved her—" His voice broke and his chest heaved. "I loved her more than life. More than anything. And then I went and fucked some other woman."

The look of pure, vile hatred and self-disgust on his face made Lucy's chest ache. She loved Joel dearly and could never hate him, and she knew Emma couldn't have either. No matter what.

"I think it's good that you told us," Jesse said, the compassion on his face and voice matching Lucy's. "I think it'll help you. I can't imagine how hard it was to keep that to yourself all this time."

"You shoulda told me, honey," Fillis said. "I woulda understood. You didn't have to suffer with this secret all this time."

"I know, Second Mama. I just...I didn't want anybody to know. All anybody knows about me is how much I love my wife...and I do! I do, goddammit. That wasn't a lie. I love her every bit as much as I always say I do."

"Nobody doubts that," Lucy said firmly.

"I don't deserve her," Joel said miserably. "I'll never be worthy of her."

"Never?" Lucy asked. "You think no matter how many years you're trapped here on Earth, there's no way you can ever be good enough again?"

"I don't see how. It's not like I can make it up to her."

"Not hanging around here, you can't!" Lucy said. "You need to go to her. When you cross over you can be with her, make her understand why you did it. Why...why did you do it?" She felt bad for asking, but she needed to understand. Why would a good man like Joel do something like this? It was scary. If he could cheat, anyone could.

"I was a fuckin' idiot."

Jesse winced, and Lucy fought the urge to crack a smile. He got upset when anyone used bad language around her. It was nothing she hadn't heard before. With Theresa as her roommate, she'd heard it all.

"Me and my regiment, we'd been traipsing all over the damn country for months on end and hadn't really seen battle. You wouldn't think it, but being a soldier is *boring*. Like mind-crushingly *boring*."

"Got that right," Jesse said.

You cheated on your beautiful wife because you were bored? Lucy tried to withhold her judgment, but it was hard.

"Then we fought at Chancellorsville. And people... people I knew...died. And all of a sudden, the war wasn't a game anymore. It was real. People died and...I had to kill some of 'em," Joel said, looking nauseous. "We had...you knew when it was one of our guys, even if you couldn't recognize his face anymore..." Joel's face twisted into a grimace as he remembered some of the horrible things he'd seen. "We were from Orange County New York, so we put orange ribbons on our uniforms, you know, in case...in case..."

"In case you didn't survive the battle," Lucy finished for him.

"Yeah. When you saw a dead guy with an orange ribbon, you knew it was one of our guys. And we lost a lot. A lot of good guys. My friends. Playin' cards the night before. Dead the next day."

Joel looked into Lucy's eyes, bolstered by her compassion. She nodded, encouraging him to let it all out.

"And as we're marchin' off to the next...whatever...we didn't know what would happen to us. I kept thinkin' of all the friends I lost, and I kept thinkin' about the guys I killed. Somebody's else's friends. Somebody's husband, maybe. Somebody's...child..." Joel broke down in a tearless sob. "I thought of my little boys...and did I...did I kill someone else's baby?"

Lucy put her hand over her mouth as her own tears started to spill. Jesse put a hand on her knee, the cold sensation was oddly comforting to her.

"It was suddenly so real...so permanent. Lots of men were dead, and there would be more. It was like...it was like I couldn't turn off my own brain. I couldn't sleep without thinkin' of the guys I had killed. I just couldn't stop thinkin'. And then, when we were in camp..." Joel laughed bitterly. "On our way to Gettysburg. There were some girls who would...who were willin' to...you know, for money."

Lucy nodded. This was hard enough for Joel to talk about, and less he had to spell out, the easier it would be for him.

"And-and I hardly even thought about it. I just wanted to do it. I just wanted something...anything...to get my mind off what was going on. What had happened, what I was afraid was going to happen. Jesus Christ, why the fuck couldn't I have just kept it in my pants for just a little while longer? I got killed at Gettysburg. I'd made it all that time without...and then I died at the very next battle."

"You died before you ever had a chance to atone," Lucy said.

"Yeah. As if there was anything I could ever do to make up for something like that. I never in a million years could have imagined doing something like that to her. We loved each other so much. We were so happy. I mean, some of the guys weren't so lucky. Some of 'em were kinda relieved to get away from their wives. So, I don't know, I mean I know they were foolin' around, too, but it just didn't seem as bad, you know? God, how could I do something like that to Emma?"

"War makes you do crazy things," Lucy said gently.

"But it's not like it was just the one time. I did it three times that same week. It was like...I knew I was gonna do it, too. At least after the first time. You can't think about much else when you're havin' sex, you know? I was lookin' forward to it, you know? Gave me something to be excited about." Joel looked at Lucy apologetically. "Sorry. I don't mean to be indelicate."

Lucy smiled. She really didn't mind. She thought it was probably good for him to be so honest about what had happened. Still, it was painful to watch him expose himself so emotionally in front of all of them.

"It's all right." Lucy shot a pointed look at Jesse. "I understand what it feels like to really, really want to sleep with someone." She turned bright red, but still looked back at Joel and smiled.

Joel and Fillis chuckled softly. Jesse's surprised and delighted expression only made Joel laugh harder. Lucy was happy to have taken some of the pressure off Joel.

"But you're in love. That's different," Joel said, looking at Lucy, then at Jesse. "I never should have made fun of you for sayin' what you said back at the Visitor's Center. You were right, Secesh. Sex without love is very empty. You were right to wait on the right woman. You had the same opportunities I had in camp, but you still didn't do it. Now that you've met the perfect woman—well, I'm just real sorry that you'll never have the chance to...be with her."

"Thank you," Jesse said, the sadness evident in his voice. He was sorry, too. He looked at Lucy sitting next to him. He smiled at her and held out his hand. She put her hand on his and felt the familiar cold sensation. When they looked at each other, it was easy to forget that anyone else was there.

"Could you have forgiven him?" Joel asked suddenly, looking at Lucy with a desperate, plaintive look in his eyes. "If he slept with someone else?"

"Joel, that's an impossible question to answer!" Lucy said. She knew what he wanted to hear, of course, but the answer was different for everyone.

"You can't expect her to answer something like that," Jesse said, but not without sympathy.

"Of course not. You would never have done such an awful thing," Joel said.

"That's not what I meant, Joel," Jesse said, even though it was impossible for him to imagine cheating on Lucy. "I just mean—she's not Emma. She can't speak for what Emma would have done."

"I know. I know. I'm sorry, sweetheart."

"Don't be sorry, Joel," Lucy said. She wanted so much to say something comforting to him, something to help him come to terms with what he'd done. "But...I'd like to think that, if I was lucky enough to have you come back home safe from the war, and you came home looking at me like that..." She gestured to his mournful, pitiful expression. "I'd like to think I could have forgiven you."

The look of relief on Joel's face was so intense that Lucy wished she had the power to forgive him on Emma's behalf.

"You two loved each other so much. I don't think she would want to end it all over one mistake."

"Three," Joel said bitterly.

"Joel. You've been torturing yourself over this since 1863. Haven't you suffered enough?"

"I don't know. Have I?"

"Lord, *yes*, child," Fillis said. "Emma knows how much you still love her. You think she can't see?" Fillis lifted her eyes to the heavens. "You think she likes seeing you like this?"

"No," Joel said. "She wouldn't want this for me. That's the way she was. She had such a good heart. She didn't want anyone to suffer. Ever."

"Especially not you," Lucy said. "Your Second Mama is right. I believe that Emma sees this"—she gestured at Joel's sorrow—"and I think it breaks her heart. You want to tell her you're sorry? Go to her. Go home to her and the boys, and you can spend eternity making it up to her."

Joel looked down at the ground and smiled. There was a small change in his demeanor. It wasn't the dramatic epiphany that Joel and Jesse had experienced at Devil's Den, but there was a subtle change. Joel was starting to feel better.

"Thank you for listening to me." Joel looked up at all three of them. "And for not hating me."

"We could never hate you, sweet boy," Fillis said. "I jus' wish you'd told me sooner. Ain't no reason for you to be carryin' this burden alone."

Joel looked at Fillis and saw the unconditional love of a mother in her face.

Lucy got up and walked over to Joel. He stood so he could look her in the eye. He had to look down at her, just like Jesse did, since she was so much shorter. "I would give anything in the world if I could just give you a big hug right now," Lucy said. She sighed deeply. She raised her hands and placed them on his shoulders, feeling the chill go right through her.

"I'll take what I can get," Joel said with a smile. "That's the closest thing to a beautiful woman's touch that I've had in a very long time."

Lucy smiled at him, savoring the sweet moment. Then she sighed and said, "I'm sorry, guys, but I've got to get going to work."

"I know. Lucy I—" Joel faltered, not knowing what to say to thank her.

"I know," Lucy said with a smile. "You don't have to say anything. Just keep working, Joel. I know it's hard. You've been through a lot, but you're getting better. Every step of the way you're working toward going home to be with Emma. Don't give up."

Lucy turned around and smiled at Fillis, who smiled warmly back. Lucy loved teaming up with her to help the boys. It was such a comfort to Lucy to know that Second Mama was always there to stay with the boys any time Lucy couldn't be with them.

Lucy looked at Jesse, who was still sitting on the ground. "I love you," she said softly.

Jesse looked at her with a pained expression, hating that she had to go. "I love you, too."

It was such a tender moment that Joel didn't have the heart to tease them. Yes, they were all lovey-dovey now, but words were really all they had to express their feelings. Joel couldn't begin to imagine being near Emma and not being able to touch her.

"Here, lemme walk with you a minute," Jesse said, getting up and walking beside her.

Joel sat down next to Fillis as they watched Jesse and Lucy stroll together.

"She loves him so much," Joel said. "If he crosses over…"

"She'll be devastated," Fillis said softly.

Jesse walked Lucy to the edge of the playground, where they stopped to talk before she continued on to work.

"That was really wunnerful, what you did for you him back there," Jesse said to her.

"I hope it helps him."

"I still wanna be with you, ya know. *Alone*," Jesse said.

"Me, too. We'll have to find somewhere quiet to go by ourselves."

"But *not*—"

"On a battlefield," Lucy finished for him.

"*Right*," Jesse drawled.

"There's a good place right behind the Arts building at the college."

"Good idea. Tomorrow afternoon?" Jesse asked hopefully.

"Yes. I'll see you then," Lucy said. She held up her palm, and he touched it with his. "It always feels cold when I touch you. Can you feel anything?"

Jesse shook his head sadly. "No. But I like doing it anyway. It's as close to touch as I can get."

"But you were able to touch things before. You pushed the tray to the ground at the restaurant, and you were able to kiss me on the forehead at Devil's Den." Lucy looked at him hopefully. She would have given anything to have him kiss her on the lips.

"Yeah, but it only worked then because I was all charged up and upset. You were in danger, and I was scared to death. I can't seem to do it any other time," Jesse said sadly.

Lucy nodded and touched his hand again.

Joel and Fillis watched as Jesse and Lucy said their good-byes, and Jesse walked back to the tree to rejoin them.

Joel looked at Fillis. "I think I want...I need to go back to Devil's Den for a little bit."

"Joel," Fillis began, looking worried.

"No. No, it's not like that. I think...I think it'll be different this time. It's just something I need to do. I need to try to talk to Emma," he said, glancing up to the sky.

"Want us to walk with you for a while?" Jesse asked.

"Yeah. Yeah, that'd be good."

Joel looked around to make sure none of the kids or parents were looking, then turned invisible. Jesse and Fillis did the same.

They walked quietly together for a little while. Finally, Jesse spoke.

"Lucy's gonna get hurt," he said. Joel and Fillis looked at each other as Jesse echoed the concerns they'd been discussing earlier. "She's trying so hard to help us cross over, but now it's like I don't even want to. I don't want to be without her, and I don't want to hurt her."

"I think that ship has sailed," Joel said as they weaved their way through the crowd. No one could see them, but they still evaded touch in case someone felt a cold spot and realized what it was. "It's pretty much inevitable in this situation."

"Sometimes I think I should just disappear and leave her alone," Jesse said miserably. The idea of being without her was worse than death, but he'd do it if it helped spare her feelings.

"No. Don't do that," Joel said. "You'll break her heart."

"It's gonna be broken anyway!" Jesse said. "Sooner or later—"

"Then make it later." Joel insisted. "She's the first good thing to happen to you in forever. She's a wonderful woman, and she loves you. I know, eventually, something has to happen. You'll either cross over or she'll graduate and have to start her new life, but it's okay to love her until then."

"I'll love her longer than that," Jesse said.

"I know," Joel said. "Believe me, I know."

Fillis walked behind them, listening. It was wonderful to hear the two talking and confiding in each other. It was good for them. They needed each other, and Fillis was starting to believe their time was finally coming. Especially Joel's. He was making good progress in dealing with his demons, and he just might make it home soon.

Jesse was another matter. He loved Lucy. He wouldn't leave her willingly, but it was no good for him to be trapped here for another hundred years because he'd fallen in love. If they could be together, that would be one thing, but it was impossible.

Fillis's motherly concerns turned to Lucy. She would be the one who suffered the most. Fillis had no doubt that she loved Jesse enough to put his needs above her own. She might be shy and quiet, but Lucy was a strong woman. She'd been terrified of Joel and Jesse at first, but she faced her fears and eventually welcomed them as friends. She'd endured the agony of Jesse's death, but her dedication to helping them never wavered. Lucy would help him cross over, and she'd encourage him to be at peace, crushing her own heart in the process. The notion of her grieving, just like Joel had, for the rest of her life made Fillis's heart hurt. Thank God she had her friend, Theresa, to confide in. No one else in Lucy's life even knew Jesse existed.

They reached Devil's Den and left Joel alone there. Well, not exactly alone. It was a sunny Saturday afternoon in May, and the place was literally crawling with tourists. Kids were climbing all over the rocks as their parents took pictures.

"Good luck with your quiet contemplation," Jesse said.

Joel laughed. "It's okay. Gives me some entertainment while I'm here."

They had long since gotten used to the fact that people used Devil's Den, also known as the Slaughter Pen, as a playground. It was strange at first to see people laughing and climbing over the rocks that had once dripped with blood. But watching the kids and all those living, breathing people helped block out some of the horrible images of dead bodies lying all around. There was no sense keeping the Den around as some kind of graveyard. Better to have it crawling with life.

Jesse shot a pained look over at the flat rock where Lucy had lain after suffering his battle wounds. A small kid, maybe four years old, was trying to climb up on it. His struggle brought back the horrific image of Lucy trying to pull herself up on the rock after feeling like she'd been shot. Jesse quickly turned away. He gave Joel a quiet, supportive smile, then he and Fillis left to give him some privacy.

31

"How's your sexy cowboy?" Theresa asked when Lucy got home from work. The day after her drunken confession, Theresa had worried all day about what was going to happen when Lucy had to face Joel and Jesse. The moment she'd arrived home that night, Lucy's look of elation said it all.

"He said it back, didn't he?" Theresa had said. Lucy had cried, tears of joy this time, and told her everything Jesse had said to her.

"He's wonderful and perfect as always," Lucy replied dreamily as she set down her purse. She sat down on the couch and put her feet up. "I saw him this morning before I went to work. We met up with Joel and Fillis. It was good. Really good. Joel opened up a lot about the war and everything. He's really trying now, you know?"

Theresa nodded thoughtfully. Lucy knew her friend had the hots for Joel. She never denied it, not even really to Joel himself. She flirted openly with him, and Joel playfully flirted back. Still, Lucy had no intention of repeating what

Joel had revealed about cheating on Emma. That was intensely private and painful, and it wasn't Lucy's place to go blabbing about it.

"That's good," Theresa said.

"I'm finally gonna meet up with Jesse tomorrow morning, just the two of us."

"That'll be nice," Theresa said. "You guys could use some alone time." She fell silent for a moment.

"What?" Lucy asked.

"Nothing. Just thinking."

Lucy was a little worried, but didn't press her.

"Oh! I almost forgot!" Theresa said, her eyes wide.

"What?" Lucy asked, looking at her curiously.

"You got a flower delivery. Lucy," Theresa said, a look of astonishment on her face. "They're yellow roses."

LUCY ARRIVED before Jesse at the designated spot behind the Arts building. She brought a picnic lunch for one. She wanted to spend the whole day with him outside, so she knew she'd better be prepared for when she got hungry.

She looked off in the distance, eagerly awaiting his arrival. Her whole body tingled when she saw his familiar form come walking toward her, clad as always in his handsome gray uniform, white shirt and suspenders, and slouch hat. His mere presence excited her, and she could hardly imagine what he could do to her with his hands and the rest of his body if he were alive. *If only,* she thought as usual. She would have to settle for that killer smile and devastatingly sexy accent.

Jesse sat down next to her on the blanket. He looked into her eyes. "Alone at last, my rose."

Lucy laughed. "Yes." She held up her palm and he pressed his hand to hers.

Lucy noticed the look of apprehension that crossed Jesse's face as he looked around at all the students walking around on campus.

"What is it?" Lucy asked with concern.

Jesse looked down at his clothes, the same ones that Lucy had been admiring just a moment ago. "Aren't you embarrassed to be seen with me at your school in this...costume?"

"Of course not!" Lucy said. "And it's not a costume, darling. It's the uniform you bravely fought and died in. Of course I'm not embarrassed to be seen with you. Are you kidding? A gorgeous guy with a drop-dead sexy accent? I wish I could parade you up and down the halls and show you off to everyone!"

Jesse still looked unsure.

"I've never seen anyone look so handsome in a uniform, Jesse. Although..." She looked critically at his clothes.

"What?" Jesse asked, looking down.

Lucy waited to finish her sentence until he looked back up at her. "As much as I love the way you look, sometimes I wish I could just rip those clothes right off you..." Her eyes flashed with desire.

Jesse laughed with pleasure and relief.

"Guess what?" Lucy asked. She reached into one of the big bags she'd brought with her for the picnic. "Someone sent me flowers."

Jesse watched her with confusion and a hint of worry. "What?"

Lucy pulled out the beautiful bouquet of yellow roses from the bag. She also pulled out an empty vase and opened a bottle of water. She got the flowers all set up, then turned to Jesse and smiled.

"They're from you," she said. "You said you would get them for me if you could, so you did. I just helped you a little."

Jesse looked at the flowers wistfully. "I wish I could have bought them for you."

"As far as I'm concerned, you did." Lucy pulled out the blank card that came with the flowers. "Now, what would you have written on the card?"

Jesse thought for a moment, then said, *"To my beautiful rose, All my love, Jesse."*

Lucy smiled as she wrote his words down on the card. "Perfect. I'm sure your girlfriend will love it, Private Spenser."

"Are you really my girlfriend?"

"I should hope so," she responded. She held the card up to Jesse's lips, and he pressed a kiss to it the best he could. Lucy opened her purse, pulled out her wallet, and slid the card inside.

"By the way," Lucy said. "Happy birthday."

"What?"

"It's May 26."

"It is?" Jesse asked. "I don't pay much attention to dates anymore. But how did you—"

"That day when we stood at your grave. You said, 'Private Jesse Spenser of the First Texas, at your service. Born May 26, 1839. Died July 2, 1863.'"

"You remember that?" Jesse asked.

"Of course I remember. I remember everything you say. I was quite smitten with you even then. Even when I found out you were dead."

"Wow," Jesse said, genuinely surprised. "Thanks for remembering. People like us...we don't think much about birthdays anymore. I don't think anybody really knows my birthday around here. Well, except..."

"Second Mama," Lucy said with a smile.

Jesse nodded. He stared at the yellow roses.

"What if you meet someone else?" he asked.

"Jesse!" she said sharply.

"Well, I can't even touch you," he said, his voice full of frustration. "And I want to so badly."

Lucy looked at him, remembering what he'd said about wanting to lay her down on the blanket and make passionate love to her. It hurt so much that she couldn't wrap her arms around him, and it was incredibly frustrating that they couldn't have sex, but it made her feel good to know that he wanted to. Jesse wasn't like Eric. Jesse really did love her.

"It's not fair to you. You deserve a real man. One that can touch you and hold you and protect you," he said.

"You are a real man, Jesse, and you came along at a time when I didn't think there were any real men anymore. A real man is good and kind. You always treat me like a lady. I still can't believe that you love me."

"I know you can't," Jesse said. "Why is that? For the longest time you were afraid me and Joel were makin' fun of you or something. Like you thought we were tryin' to play a mean trick on you. Why did you think that?"

"I don't know. I guess...I guess it's because of some stuff that happened when I was in school. Earlier, I mean. Grade school, high school. There were people who I thought were my friends and weren't," Lucy said. It felt good to confide in Jesse about these things. "It's hard to describe, but it's like...I don't know. They would talk to me and ask me questions and act like they were my friends, but they were making fun of me behind my back. And...and I guess I just didn't realize it until it was too late."

Jesse's eyes flashed with anger, and Lucy loved how protective he was of her.

"I used to be really skinny, ugly."

"You could never be ugly," Jesse said in a harsh tone, still furious with the little bastards who had made Lucy feel that way. "Your soul is too beautiful."

"I feel the same way about you. I mean, people talk about having soulmates, but that's really what we are," Lucy said, sounding tired. "Because that's all we have. And speaking of souls...I understand why Joel is still here. Now it's your turn."

"I don't want to talk about it," Jesse said.

"Why? Don't you trust me?"

"Of course I do!"

"Then why won't you talk to me? Do you know why you're still here? If it's, you know, some kind of secret like Joel has, I'll understand. You know I will," Lucy told him. She wondered if maybe Jesse had some dark secret he was hiding.

"No, not really. Nothing like that. I just...don't want to talk about it."

"But why?"

"I just don't want to deal with it," Jesse said, his temper rising again. He wouldn't meet her gaze.

"Jesse—"

"*I don't want to cross over!*" Jesse roared, startling her. He felt terrible for yelling when he saw the tears in her eyes. "Lucy, I—"

"I understand," Lucy said without a trace of anger. "I can't bear the thought of being without you, either. But you can't stay here like this. When I graduate school next year, I'll have to go back home. I won't ever be able to rest if I know you're out here, aimlessly wandering around."

"Then I'll wait until you graduate. We'll sort through it all then."

"There's no sense prolonging the inevitable, Jesse. It'll only hurt more. Let me help you. Please. I'm not going to give up, so you might as well give in."

Jesse saw the determination in her face and knew she was right. She wasn't going to give up trying to help him.

"Why are you still here?" she asked gently.

"Isn't it obvious?" he asked. Her perplexed expression made it clear that it wasn't. "I fought for the wrong side."

Lucy let the words sink in. The pain of regret on Jesse's face mirrored the look that Joel had when talking about his transgressions. Jesse was so passionate about the South that his words came as a surprise to her.

"I mean, I look back at everything that happened. I had to kill people, too. I mean, you know that, right?" He looked up at her, worried about what she might think of him.

"You did what you had to do. Just like Joel did. Just like all the soldiers did. You didn't ask to go to war."

"But I volunteered! I didn't wait 'til conscription. I took up arms and went to war straight away. I left my family. My mother..." He closed his eyes. "I jus'...I can't imagine what she went through when she got the news that her only child was dead." He opened his eyes. "I wish I could just see my mama one more time. She was so good to me. I was her pride and joy, that's for sure."

Her heart ached when she saw the pain in his eyes. He

needed to go home. He needed to be with his family, too. Every bit as much as Joel did.

"She was proud of me for fightin', but she was worried sick that I wouldn't come home. And I didn't. Probably ruined the rest of her life. And for what? For what?"

"Why did you go to war?" Lucy asked. She already had a pretty good idea from her history books of why Confederate soldiers fought, but she wanted to hear it from him. He needed to talk about it and, truth be told, she needed to know why he fought. How could anyone think that slavery was okay? How *could* anyone fight and die to keep slavery in practice?

"I thought I was doing right, Lucy. I really did!" Jesse had a pleading look in his eyes. He needed her to understand. "I didn't know no black people. Not personally anyway. And I never really got to know any of 'em, until..."

"Fillis," Lucy said.

"Yeah," Jesse said, his expression softening as he spoke of the woman who had mothered him far longer than his biological mother had been able to. "Can you imagine the kind o' heart that woman has? She loves me, Lucy. She loves me like I was her own. After everything I did..."

"That's what good mothers do. They love their children unconditionally. Why did you think fighting for the Confederacy was right?"

"We was told that the Union guys were fightin' to take away our way of life. They were big, bad, mean city folk, and we were simple farmers." He laughed bitterly. "Not so simple for them people pickin' the cotton. But that's what we were told, and that's what we believed. I mean, it sounds terrible now, but I didn't think about it. We was taught that black folks were like animals. They didn't think like us, didn't feel like us. We were doin' them a favor givin' them a purpose in life. And those horrible Northerners were tryin' to modernize everything and take away our way of life. So they stirred us up, got us all wrathy and fired up, and said it was our duty to fight! We had to fight! For our families! For our homes!" Jesse shook his head. "And we...never...questioned it."

"Sounds familiar," Lucy said.

"What do you mean?"

"I mean some things never change. You know all about September 11, right?"

"'Course. That was terrible. We all...lots of spirits around here, we saw on the TV when it was happening. The streets were real quiet that day. Was awful."

"It certainly was. Then the government did the same thing they did to you back in the day. Stirred everybody up. Patriotism! Gotta fight to protect our way of life! Then they talked us all into invading a country that had nothing to do with what happened."

"You're right," Jesse said somberly. "Lots of men and some of the women, off to war. Came back in lots of flag-draped coffins."

"Yeah. The Civil War, the Iraq War, so often it's the same old thing. Rich man's war, poor man's fight. They get the poor ones to do their dirty work so the rich can stay rich. Cotton. Oil. Blood money."

"Yeah. But still. Ain't I 'sponsible for my own actions? I'm not the smartest man in the world, but I ought to be able to think for myself. Nobody forced me to fight. I don't know. Maybe if they had...maybe if I'd had to be a conscript and had no choice. Most of the spirits that are stuck around here chose to fight."

Lucy nodded, and couldn't help but wonder why Fillis

was stuck here. Whatever it was, it didn't seem tied to the war.

"There's a reason why thousands of people down South fought for one reason and the Northerners fought for another. It has to do with the way you were brought up," Lucy said. "When you're taught that anyone different from you is wrong, bad, you can't help but believe it. Especially when it's your parents, your grandparents telling you these things."

Jesse looked up at her. "I wanna be proud of who I am, where I come from. Sometimes I don't know how to be, or even if it's okay."

"Of course it's okay! You should be proud of who you are and where you're from. Your Southernness is a big part of who you are."

"But is it really anything to be proud of?"

"Yes! You don't have to accept everything about it. In fact, you shouldn't. There are good things about the South, Jesse. There is something to be said about a simple way of life. The farm life, family, church, community. Those things are still strong in the South."

Jesse nodded.

"But so is racism, so is homophobia. It's fine to love a simple life, but it can be a narrow-minded life. Sometimes it's hard for people to accept their differences. If we could just learn to accept each other, celebrate our differences instead of railing against them, I think we'd all be okay."

"Sounds so simple, don't it?" Jesse asked wearily.

"It's not as hard as people make it out to be. Look at us. I'm a Yankee gal who fell in love with a handsome Southern rebel."

Jesse laughed.

"And it's not like things in the North are always so great.

Ugh, you look at all the greed on Wall Street. So many people worship money above all else."

Lucy watched Jesse as he contemplated her words. She could see that she was getting through to him. He seemed a bit calmer.

"I feel like people still argue and fight as much now as they did back in your day. It's funny how things never seem to change. Now it's not blue and gray anymore, it's blue and red."

"Yep. Blue states hatin' on red states, and the other way 'round. Hear so much of that around here. People visit from all around the country, so people like me and Joel have pretty much heard it all."

"I'm sure you have. There's still a lot of racism, a lot of hate in this country."

"And I contributed to it. I really did," Jesse said mournfully.

"It's never too late to change your mind, Jesse. Even after death. You have a good heart. That's why Fillis loves you. That's why I love you."

Jesse looked into her eyes. If someone as wonderful and good as Lucy could love him, maybe he was worthy of forgiveness.

"Look at me and Theresa. You talk about blue and red. I'm pretty blue, politically, and she's about as red as they come. She's a Christian—the good kind, not the crazy kind —but she's Republican all the way. And we're best friends! She votes her way, I vote mine, then we go have a drink together!"

"So I saw," Jesse said.

Lucy blushed deeply and looked down. "I made a complete fool of myself, didn't I?"

"No," Jesse said firmly. "Not at all. Joel and I felt just

awful, seeing you so upset. God knows we were the reason you needed to drink."

"Well, yeah, kinda..." Lucy said. "I was drinking to forget you, and then we come outside, and there you were."

"I'm glad, Lucy. I'm so glad. If you hadn't said somethin', I probably never would have had the guts to tell you how I felt."

Jesse looked around the fairly empty campus, then up at the American flag waving high up on a flagpole.

"It's a holiday today, ain't it? I didn't know the calendar date, but it's Memorial Day, right?"

"Yes," Lucy replied. Meade's Tavern was closed for the day, so she was able to stay with Jesse as long as she liked.

Lucy could feel Jesse's sorrow as he looked at the flag. "What is it, Jesse?"

Jesse watched the flag flap in the breeze. "Memorial Day is all about service men and women who died protecting the flag. Days like this I just...I feel like such a traitor. The USA ain't perfect, but it's a good country. It's a good place to be. And I took up arms to help tear it apart."

"You know, there are lots of memorials and remembrances for Confederate soldiers, too. Maybe, you know, not a lot around here. But down South? Believe me, you guys are revered."

"But ought we be?" Jesse asked.

"It's a complicated issue. Slavery is bad. Keeping the United States united is good. But to die fighting for what you believe in is good. You fought to protect the South. Your family, your friends, your family's farm in Texas. You were so young, Jesse. And you were strong and brave. I'm proud of you."

Jesse smiled at her gratefully.

Lucy reached into her bag and pulled out a small Bose

sound system, one that could play music she had stored on her phone.

"I forgot I brought music to listen to. I've got some old Civil Wars songs in there, too, in case you're feeling nostalgic."

"Nice," Jesse said.

Lucy cued up the music and put her music mix on shuffle. The first song was a fast, spirited instrumental version of "Dixie."

"Love it!" Jesse said.

Lucy laughed. "I know this song ought to make me think of you, but I'm afraid now all I can think of is Joel singing!"

Jesse grinned mischievously. "Oh, man that was sweet, wasn't it? I can't believe he actually did it."

"I liked your singing, too." Lucy said with a giggle.

"You know I only did that 'cause I was showin' off for you. I like hearing you laugh."

The next song on the mix, "Wildwood Flower," began to play.

"Oh, this is a good one! Now this one reminds me of you. 'Specially the part in the beginning. *Oh, I'll twine with my mingles of waving black hair, with the roses so red and the lilies so fair...*"

Lucy smiled, finding his off-key singing somehow more charming than if he could actually carry a tune like Joel could. "He dumps her at the end of the song, you know," she observed drily.

Jesse waved her off. "Details, details..."

Jesse's eyes lit up when the next song came on. "No way!"

"Well, of course I had to put this one on there."

It was "The Yellow Rose of Texas."

"Dance with me!" Jesse said.

"What?"

Jesse jumped up and held out his right hand. "Ma'am, may I please have this dance?"

He glanced around to make sure Lucy wouldn't be embarrassed by the spectacle of the two of them dancing together on the lawn of her school. Lucy made it clear that she had no qualms about dancing with the love of her life in public by reaching over and turning the sound up before joining him. He grinned at her, then stood directly in front of her, his right arm up to lead. They danced joyfully, holding their arms up together, moving their feet, doing everything but touching.

They laughed and danced, not caring who was watching. It was the happiest single moment of Lucy's life. She realized she'd never known true joy until now.

When the song ended, Jesse looked at Lucy and said, "You know, there's a song I've heard—it's one of the newer ones—and every time I hear it I think of you."

"What is it? Maybe I have it on there," Lucy said, glancing down at her phone.

"It's called 'True' by Ryan Cabrera."

"Oh, I think I have heard that one. I don't think I have it but I can download it now."

Jesse smiled at her as she picked up her phone, located the song, and downloaded it.

Lucy cued up the song, then stood up so she could dance with Jesse. The lyrics in the beginning of the song mentioned not breathing, and Jesse winked at her, making her laugh.

They slow-danced together, looking into each other's eyes. It was sweet and sensual; it was wonderful how they could feel so close even without touching. Jesse softly sang along with the song. He knew every word and sang with great passion as he looked lovingly at her.

Lucy looked up at him, into those beautiful blue-gray eyes. He knew the song so well, and she realized that he must have thought of her every time he heard it. She could never have imagined that any man could feel that way about her. She was overwhelmed with love for him.

"This will be our song," Lucy whispered when the song ended.

"Always has been," Jesse answered, reminding Lucy again of just how long he'd loved her. "It's good to know there's still some nice modern songs out there. Seems like every other song is about somebody's booty nowadays. What's that about?"

Lucy laughed. "You sound like an old man."

"I am an old man. A very, very old man." Jesse looked Lucy up and down, admiring her. "Jeez, talk about robbin' the cradle."

Another tune came on. Lucy had been listening to Civil War music a lot lately, and she recognized the song immediately from the opening chords. Her breath caught in her throat and her heart clutched. It was a beautiful song, but it hurt so badly to hear it.

"Now this one definitely reminds me of you," Lucy said.

"Yeah," Jesse said somberly. "I ain't heard this one in a while. It's real pretty, though."

The song was "The Legend of the Rebel Soldier." It was a slow, sad song about a Southern soldier, passionate about the South, who was dying in a Yankee prison. The song tells of how the Rebel grabs a preacher by the hand, asking him if his soul will pass through the South when he dies. The lyrics describe how much the soldier loves the Southland, the church house where he made his wedding vows, and his precious daughter. All the good things about the South. The kind of things that Jesse missed desperately.

The song tells of dying for loving Dixie, which Jesse surely did.

In the last stanza the preacher blesses the soldier as he dies. He raises his hand and says a prayer, imploring the Father to grant the soldier's wishes and let his soul pass through the South one last time before he goes to heaven.

Jesse and Lucy had been dancing slowly, somberly to the song. As the song reached the last verse, Lucy's emotions overwhelmed her. She began to cry. She covered her eyes with her hands, her shoulders shaking, tears flowing.

"Oh, Lucy," Jesse said. He longed to wrap his arms around her and hold her close. "I won't leave you."

"You have to," Lucy said, trying to talk while taking deep breaths as she sobbed. "You can't stay here." She looked up at him with tear-filled eyes. "I hope that happens for you. I hope you can pass through the South one last time before you—"

Lucy broke down crying again. She took a few moments to compose herself while Jesse helplessly watched.

"I wish I could hold you, Lucy."

"Me, too. I need you to hold me right now."

Jesse looked into her eyes and held up his palm. She touched it with her hand. She sighed. It just wasn't enough. She loved him. She loved him, and she needed to touch him. She felt like she needed to touch him like she needed food and water and air.

The next song came on. It was a slow, almost sensual version of "Dixie" with a woman singing the lyrics instead of just instrumentation.

"Now, you better think of me when you hear this song. Not Joel," Jesse said, trying to break the somber mood a bit.

Lucy smiled sadly. She held up her arm and he did the same. They danced together to the song.

Jesse stopped dancing as they listened to the last part of the song. The woman sang slowly, somberly as Jesse looked mournfully into Lucy's eyes.

With one kiss she acted the foolish part...and died for a man that broke her heart. Look away, look away, look away...Dixieland....

32

Theresa had hinted around, asking where Lucy thought Joel might be while she and Jesse were having some alone time.

"Do you want me to just tell Joel you want to see him?" Lucy had asked.

Brazen as usual, Theresa had responded, "Sure, why not?"

"Just what exactly are your intentions with the poor man?" Lucy asked.

"Don't worry. I'm not planning on trying to break up his marriage from beyond the grave. I just like him is all. And I'm sure he's lonely now that you've made it abundantly clear you prefer the Rebel to him. Poor guy. He's probably heartbroken."

"Yeah, right," Lucy said with a chuckle. Then she sighed. "Well, just be careful. As much as I adore Jesse, I know what it's like to be in a relationship with a dead guy and I wouldn't recommend it."

～

LUCY ARRANGED for Theresa and Joel to hang out at one of the battlefields.

"So, I hear you were dyin' to see me," Joel said as Theresa approached him on the battlefield.

"Oh, absolutely," Theresa said. "I came to throw myself at you. Well, you know, *through* you."

Joel grinned.

"Oh, don't get too cocky, Little Blue Boy. I figured you might be bored now that Lucy's thrown you off for the sexy cowboy."

"I see. How kind of you to visit me in my fortress of solitude," Joel said, enjoying her company already.

"I hear I missed a hell of a singing performance the other day," she teased. "You know, there was really no question who Lucy was going to pick. Right from the beginning. She fell head over heels for Jesse straight away. No contest. Not even close."

"Thank you for clarifying that, Theresa."

"And I would have chosen you straight up. No question there, either." She looked right into his eyes, having no qualms about his knowing she found him attractive.

"Why?" Joel said, raising an eyebrow.

"Because you're hot. You're funny, too, and that's sexy as hell."

Joel smiled. He had a faraway look in his eye.

"You're thinking about your wife again, aren't you?" Theresa looked a little sad, and Joel wasn't sure if it was sympathy or jealousy. Perhaps it was both.

"I'm sorry. You're just so much like her. It's a compliment, I promise. She was the smartest, sexiest woman I've ever known."

"Tell me about her."

Joel looked at Theresa skeptically. "You really want to sit here and listen to me drone on about some other woman?"

"She's not just some other woman. She's the love of your life. It makes you happy to talk about her, and that makes me happy." Theresa smiled, exuding warmth and sincerity. It was obvious that she cared about him. Joel looked at her with a mix of gratitude and admiration. He didn't know what he'd ever done to deserve to have wonderful friends like Lucy and Theresa to lean on, but he would be forever grateful.

Theresa sat down on the grass and looked up at Joel expectantly.

"I'll never forget the first thing she said to me." Joel put his hand on his side and jutted his hip out effeminately. He spoke in a high voice, mimicking Emma. "You're quite a handsome man, Joel Casey."

Theresa giggled. Joel looked down at her. "Emma was fearless. So much like you. She wasn't afraid to speak her mind. God, she turned me on."

Joel sat down in the grass across from Theresa. "Every time she came into her father's store, she would just give me this look. I-I can't even describe it."

"A come-hither look?" Theresa suggested.

"Yeah. Yeah, exactly! But only when her father's back was turned. Can't tell ya how many times I had to stand behind the counter to hide the raging hard-on my boss's daughter gave me."

Theresa threw her head back and laughed. Joel knew it would be perfectly acceptable to say such things to her. Lucy would have turned crimson and lowered her head. Besides, Jesse would be furious if Joel spoke that way around his beloved.

"She loved to tease me, that was for sure."

"I'm sure you gave as much as you got," Theresa said.

"Oh, I did," Joel said, wonderful memories of his marriage filling his head. He certainly did tease her, especially in bed. He loved to climb on top of her and press his cock against her opening, teasing her until she pleaded with him to give her what she needed. How he relished her first cry of pleasure when he slammed into her after taunting her for a few moments. It was a wonderful memory, but far too private to share with anyone. Lovemaking with his wife was sacred.

"I'm jealous," Theresa said. "You and Emma had the perfect marriage. So rare nowadays. I don't know—it was probably rare back then, too."

Joel suddenly looked sad, and Theresa could see it was more than just missing Emma.

"You all right?" Theresa asked.

"Lucy didn't tell you, did she?"

"Tell me what?"

"We all had a long talk yesterday," Joel began uncertainly.

"Yeah. Lucy told me you all sat and talked awhile about the war and everything you guys went through. Said it seemed to do you good to talk about it."

Joel searched Theresa's eyes and could see Lucy hadn't told her about his confession. Of course she hadn't. Lucy was no gossip, and she never would have told anyone about something so personal.

"We did have the perfect marriage. Until I fucked it up. I cheated on her."

Theresa's eyes went wide with surprise and disappointment. Joel hated telling her the part where Prince Charming had betrayed the beautiful princess, but she deserved to know the truth.

"I cheated on Emma while I was away at war. With some cheap hooker. Next to killing people in battle, that was the worst thing I've ever done. That's why I'm still here. I could hang around here for another million years and still not be worthy of Emma."

"So you think because you made a bad mistake you should be punished by never seeing your wife and children ever again?"

"Don't you?" Joel asked, looking up at her.

"No!" Theresa said, and Joel was never so happy to see a pretty woman looking at him like he was the dumbest man on the planet. "You think because you did something stupid that you should be condemned to aimlessly wander the earth alone for all eternity? That's a bit melodramatic now, don't you think?"

"I never thought of it that way."

"You think Emma would want this for you?" Theresa said, gesturing at Joel's pitiful expression.

"That's what Lucy said."

"Lucy's right, as usual," Theresa said. "So, why don't you just travel back in time and fix it?"

"What?"

"Just go back in time and undo what you did," Theresa said, as if time travel was as simple as hopping a train to New York.

"What do I look like, Marty McFly? I can't do that!" Joel looked at her like she was a madwoman.

"Then why are you still here?"

Joel gave her a weary look, finally understanding.

"You can't change the past, Joel. You can't fix it from here. You need to go to her. You can spend the rest of eternity making it up to her, but there's not a damn thing you can do while you wander around here."

"You're right, I guess." Joel got quiet for a moment. "So what's up with you and your love life?"

"What?" Theresa was surprised but not offended by the question. She rather liked his bluntness.

"I forget you even have a boyfriend half the time because you barely ever mention him. I can't go five minutes without talking about Emma. So what's up with this Stevie guy? He don't do it for ya?"

"I don't know...I guess—" Theresa began.

"Ehhhh!" Joel said, making a wrong-answer buzzer sound. "If you have to think about it, then he's not right for you."

"Really? You think it's that simple?"

"Yes. I do. You either want to be with a person or you don't. If you're all wishy-washy about it, then it's doomed."

Theresa's face fell. Joel didn't like seeing her upset, but he thought she was a wonderful woman and knew she deserved better.

"I knew the moment I laid eyes on Emma. I really did. Not everybody knows right away, though. That's okay, too. But the more time you spend with a person, the more you should like them. I was so hot for Emma in the beginning. Oh, my God..." Joel shook his head, laughing. "But she was Daddy's little girl, and she made me wait until we got married."

Theresa laughed, too. "That must have been hard. I can't imagine."

"It was, but she was well worth the wait. But, you know, even after the kids came along, we were still so crazy about each other. It was like she got more and more beautiful the longer we were together. I used to run my hands along the stretch marks on her belly," Joel said with tremendous affection. "I just knew I'd still be chasing after her even when we got old, you know?"

Theresa nodded sadly.

"I know Jesse feels the same way about Lucy. He fell for her right away, just like me and Emma."

"They're perfect for each other," Theresa said.

"I know. They would have made the most wonderful family, you know? Can you imagine Jesse as a father?"

Theresa laughed. "Yeah. He would have been such a fun daddy."

"And Lucy... She's gonna make a great mom someday..."

"Yeah, she will."

"You'll take good care of her, won't you?" Joel said, his face full of worry. "Whatever happens with Jesse?"

Theresa nodded, touched by Joel's concern for Lucy. "Yes. I'll do whatever I can."

"Don't settle," Joel said suddenly.

"What?" Theresa asked.

"Don't settle for just any man. Either find someone who's worthy of you or stay single."

"Okay, Dad."

Joel laughed. "I'm serious! You're damn sexy, and not just because of your body, either. You're smart and sassy. Passionate. And you're also kind and thoughtful."

"Thanks," Theresa said, sounding a little doubtful.

Joel looked into her eyes for a moment. "Theresa...you know I'm devoted to my wife. Even if I never get back to her, she's the only woman I could ever love. But I want you to know...if that wasn't the case..." Joel looked at Theresa with affection. "I would... you know...go for you in a heartbeat."

Therese smiled gratefully. "Thank you, Joel. I really needed to hear that."

"You deserve a guy who can keep up with you. I want you to promise me you won't settle for just any guy."

Theresa thought about cracking a joke, but she was too honored by Joel's words to make light of them. "Yeah."

"I mean it," he said sternly. "Otherwise, I'll have to haunt you."

~

LUCY DIDN'T HAVE to work the next day, so she was able to spend more time with Jesse after her classes were done. They met at the same spot behind the Arts building at school.

They talked about all sorts of things. They talked about how well Joel seemed to be doing lately. Between making amends with Jesse, confessing his secret about his infidelity, and confiding in Theresa, he seemed so much happier. His face just looked more peaceful, and that haunted look was almost gone.

Jesse had told Lucy before that appearing more peaceful was nearly always a sign that a spirit would soon cross over. Lucy was thrilled to know that Joel might finally go home soon. She'd also seen how much happier Jesse seemed these days. She knew part of it was due to being in love, but she felt there might be more to it than that. He was more at peace. His time might be coming, too.

They spoke of their families and homes. Lucy told Jesse all about her older brother, her younger sister, and her parents. She had a wonderful, close-knit family, but she had felt she needed a fresh start at college after all her troubles in grade school and high school. Jesse told her all about life on the farm, his parents, and the dog he'd had to leave behind.

The groundskeeper was mowing the lawn off in the distance. Lucy took a deep breath, taking in the smell of fresh-cut grass as she sat close to Jesse on the blanket.

"I miss the smells of the earth, you know?" Jesse said. "It's so hard to remember what grass and dirt smell like."

"Yes, I imagine it must be hard to remember things like that after so long."

JESSE ADMIRED HER LONG, brown hair. "I wish I knew what your hair smelled like."

Lucy smiled at him. "I wish I knew what it felt like having you run your fingers through it."

"I wish I knew what your hair looked like spread out on the bed while you're on your back and I'm on top of you."

Lucy laughed with delight, surprised at his boldness. Jesse grinned at her. He loved how he could say things like that to her and she didn't blush anymore. That meant she was comfortable with him. They couldn't be physically intimate, but it made him happy that he could tell her all the things he wished he could do with her, to her. He wanted her to know how much he desired her.

Something moving in the distance caught Lucy's attention. Jesse followed her gaze.

"Is that...Bluebelly?" Jesse asked.

Lucy nodded. Joel came running—or gliding, really—up to them where they sat on the blanket. He'd been dashing at full speed, and Lucy half expected him to be out of breath even though that was impossible.

"There you are! I've been looking all over the damn town for you!" Joel said, a wild look in his eye.

"What's the matter, Joel?" Lucy asked with great concern.

Joel glanced at the blanket where Lucy and Jesse were settled. "I-I'm sorry to interrupt. Really! But you've got to help me, Lucy. Please?" Joel pleaded, looking desperate.

"Of course. Anything! What can I do?"

"They-they found Emma's diary!" Joel said.

"What? Who?" Lucy asked.

"The-the-one of the historians over at the Visitor's Center. He has an office upstairs. He was going through all the new arrivals last night. Even after all this time, they still find letters and cards and diaries when people die and other people clean out their attics and stuff."

"You're sure it's Emma's?" Lucy asked.

"Yes! It says Emma Casey on it, and believe me, I know her handwriting. I used to live for her letters back in camp. Help me, Lucy. Please!"

Lucy stood up and looked up at him. "What can I do?"

"I-I can't read it! I-I mean, I can *read* it but I can't turn the pages. And George—that's the historian—he-he-he put it back on the shelf and I can't get it. Lucy, please...." Joel looked at her with pure desperation as he clung to this precious connection to his wife.

"But how can I—I mean, what do I do, break into his office?"

Jesse stood up. He looked at Joel and at Lucy with equal concern. "Joel, this could be really dangerous for her. She could get arrested..."

"Of course I'll do it!" Lucy said.

Joel nodded rapidly. "The Visitor's Center closes at six o'clock. Usually by eight o'clock everybody's gone. We know the security codes, we know the security guard's schedule..."

Jesse saw Lucy's look of determination and knew there would be no stopping her. His only choice was to help her in any way he could. He was worried that Lucy could get in big trouble for doing this, but he understood how important this was to Joel. Jesse loved Lucy every bit as passionately as Joel loved Emma. God knows, he understood.

"You sure you're up for this?" Jesse asked Lucy uncertainly.

Lucy glanced over at Joel and knew there was no way in hell she could possibly refuse him. She nodded.

"Let's go," she said without hesitation.

33

"**I**f you get arrested, this could really mess up your teaching career," Jesse said, already regretting his decision to help Lucy do this. "Trespassing on government property?"

"I know," Lucy said, her look of determination fiercer than ever. She wasn't kidding when she said she wanted to help her boys cross over. She would do whatever it took.

Jesse looked at Lucy as the three carefully walked up the steps to the Visitor's Center. He had never seen Lucy look so strong, so determined. It was a huge turn-on, as if he needed another reason to find her sexy.

The soldiers remained visible so that Lucy could see them, even though it made them more conspicuous overall.

"We need to go 'round back. Much easier to get in." Jesse said.

"Right," Joel said, understanding the plan. The front doors to the Gettysburg Visitor's Center were locked up tight with two different locks. The employee entrance in the back wasn't quite so secure. It had one simple lock, and the key was always resting on top of the doorjamb. This was to allow easy access for the employees who stepped out for smoke breaks. Employees also used this exit to leave for lunch breaks or when they left for the day.

The three crept around back to the employee entrance. "The key's up there," Jesse said, pointing to the top of the door.

Lucy stood on her tiptoes, but she was too short to reach. "Damn," she said. It wasn't like either of the tall soldiers with her could give her a boost. She looked around and saw some crates lying near the dumpster. Jesse watched with amusement and admiration as she stacked the crates and stood on top to get the key. He especially admired the way her stretching revealed more of her legs as she strained to reach the top of the door.

Jesse caught Joel admiring her figure, too, and gave him a stern look. Joel held up his hands and mouthed "sorry."

Lucy got the key and stepped down. "Isn't there an alarm?"

"Yes," Jesse said. "Okay, here's the tricky part. Once you get inside, you gotta run all the way to the front entrance. You got thirty seconds to put in the code."

Lucy nodded. She looked nervous, but still determined.

"You're so brave, Lucy," Jesse said with a smile. He was worried, but still incredibly aroused by her boldness. It was a side of her he wasn't used to seeing.

"We'll run with you. We'll show you where to go and we'll be right beside you, okay?" Joel said, looking guilty for putting her at risk. He was so desperate to read Emma's words, though, that he would have done just about anything to make it happen.

"You ready?" Jesse asked as Lucy stood poised with the key at the back door.

"Yes," she said. Her hands shook a bit, but she turned the key and opened the door.

"This way!" Jesse yelled into the silence of the still Visitor's Center as he took off running. Lucy couldn't run quite as fast, but she did her best to keep up. They reached the front door with Lucy gasping for breath. The alarm system was beeping.

"Okay, hit Disarm!" Jesse instructed. Lucy complied. "Now Three! Seven! Nine! Two! Seven!"

Lucy quickly, carefully put in the code. They all breathed a sigh of relief—Lucy's breath real and the soldiers' figurative—as the beeping stopped.

"Great job, darlin'!" Jesse said.

"Thanks!" Lucy said, smiling and tucking her hair behind her ear. She looked at Joel. "Now what do we do?"

"Follow me," Joel said. He led them to the stairs, and they walked to the second floor. He showed Lucy the door of the historian's office. "There. It's in there!"

Lucy opened the door and went inside the dark office. She found the light switch and turned it on. Joel dashed over to the bookshelf where Emma's diary was carefully wrapped in plastic to preserve the pages, which were over a century old.

"Be careful with the pages," Jesse warned. "They'll tear real easy."

Joel eagerly stood behind Lucy as she gently removed the diary from the shelf. She carefully took it out of the plastic. Sure enough, the name *Emma Casey* was scripted in delicate, feminine handwriting.

"It's hers all right. Come here," she said softly.

She pulled out the historian's chair for him. Joel sat down, and Lucy placed the book right in front of him. She gingerly opened the first page. She turned her head, not wishing to invade Emma's privacy by reading the pages. If Joel wanted to share what he read, he would.

Joel read the first page, then said quietly, "Okay," so Lucy would know when to turn the pages. He read on, occasionally chuckling at something Emma had written.

Jesse and Lucy exchanged looks from where Jesse stood in the office doorway. He looked at her with tender affection, grateful for her kindness. Sometimes it was still hard to wrap his head around the fact that such an amazing woman was in love with him. But there was no denying it from the way she gazed at him.

Lucy stood patiently as Joel read for a long time, his only words being "Okay," when he was ready for a page turn.

Joel felt a sense of warmth and comfort as he read his wife's words. She wrote the way she spoke—bold, sassy, funny, sweet, loving. Reading her thoughts was almost as good as hearing her voice.

I love Joel more with each pasing daye. He is the most wonnderfull husband. He is never more handsom then when he plays with our boys. The way he slings them over his strong shulders, teasing them, telling them he will feed them to the neghbor's farm animals. Oh, how they laugh when daddy is home!

Joel stopped reading occasionally to take a moment to control his emotions as they threatened to spin out of control. "Oh, my babies," he said softly. "My little boys..."

Lucy put her hand over her heart as she looked at Jesse. Jesse nodded. It was an incredibly emotional experience just to be here with their friend, to be present and actually feel him reconnect with his wife.

He is most wonderfull in the bedroom, too. Oh, it is so hard to keep quiet when we make love. It's a job not to yell out his name when he does his thing to me. But I caint frightin the boys!

Joel chuckled. "She writes some good, dirty stuff about me in here..."

Lucy laughed, too delighted to blush. Jesse exchanged an amorous look with her.

It was hard for Joel to read Emma's thoughts during the time he prepared to go to war and after he left. She expressed her pain and heartache so much more in her diary than she had in her letters to him. Emma had tried to keep her letters upbeat. Her diary told the real story.

Each day is harder than the last. I miss his smile so much, I feel I could fall to pieces. I caint be too sad. I must think of Mathew and David. I broke down in teers the other day when the children asked where daddy was. I don't know...I don't know was all I could say until I puled myself tigither. Daddy is being brave, I told thim. He's fightin and bein brave, ,

And sleeping with another woman, Joel thought bitterly. He'd been screwing another woman while his wife cared for their children and patiently waited for his return. Joel read on and was stunned with what Emma wrote about next.

"Oh, my God..." Joel said as he read. "Oh, my God, oh my God..."

Jesse and Lucy exchanged concerned looks.

"Emma...she...she...." Joel looked up at Lucy, the agonized look on his face almost more than she could bear. "She had another child after I was gone."

Lucy gasped and put her hand over her mouth. Joel looked so distraught as he continued reading that she couldn't help but think the worst. After a moment of disbelief, she dropped her hand, and whispered, "She was unfaithful, too."

"NO!" Joel roared, startling Lucy. "Don't ever say that. She would *never* do that!"

"Joel," Jesse said, his tone one of warning as he walked over to his side. He knew Joel was upset, but he'd be goddamned if he'd let him take it out on Lucy.

"I'm sorry, sweetheart. I-I just...she wouldn't do that. She's not like me. She was a saint," Joel said, his eyes full of anguish. "The baby was mine. We made love right before I left and...and we must have made another baby. It-it-it was a girl. I had a daughter. I had a baby girl..." Joel broke down, sobbing waterless tears as he covered his face. These weren't tears of joy. It was pure, unadulterated grief. "I left Emma with three children to care for...I had a child I never knew..."

Lucy's tears flowed freely, too. It hurt so goddamn much to bear witness to Joel's pain.

"Turn back, please. One page. Please."

Lucy flipped the page back.

"*I wanted to tell you, my darling,*" Joel read aloud. "*Oh, Joel, my love. I wanted you to know. But I heared stories, terrible tales of men dying of homesickness at camp. Soldiers worry themselves to death over thoughts of home. You would, my love. You'd be sick if you knew there was another child here. One you caint see. I new that you'd be so happy, Joel, if you arrived home and saw me with a new baby but if you new while you were away...*"

Joel frantically gestured for Lucy to turn the page. "*If you was away and you new what you were missing you would die. You would jest die so I didn't tell you. She's so beautifull, Joel.*" His voiced cracked. "*She lookes like me, not you. Our boys look like you, those blue eyes. I see you every time I look at our sons. But the girl don't. People say she looks like somebody else was her daddy. People talk, but I don't care. I don't care what people think. She's ours, my love. My body is only for you, forever for you...*"

Joel closed his eyes and Lucy could feel his heart ripping

apart. He opened his eyes and managed to croak out one more sentence written by his wife, *"My love for you is undying. If you don't come home again, I shall see you again when we are reunited with the Good Lord."*

And there it is, Lucy thought. That says it all. *Right there.*

Jesse looked down at Joel where he sat, completely shattered and broken.

"I'll never be worthy of her," Joel whispered, his eyes taking on a dull, hopeless look. There was no way to atone for leaving his beloved wife to care for three children when he went off to fight in that pointless war. A war where he'd killed people and screwed around with a whore, desecrating his wedding vows.

Lucy could see all the progress Joel had made recently slipping away right before her eyes. She'd be damned if she was going to let that happen.

"So that's it?" Lucy asked, her voice rising and her eyes blazing. "You're just gonna give up again?"

"What can I do?" Joel asked, his face looking more haunted than ever.

"Don't you think this is one *hell* of a coincidence that they happened to find Emma's diary now? Now, after all these years? Now, when you have me to help you read her words?"

"What do you mean, darlin'?" Jesse asked.

"This is a message from Emma, Joel. She's crying out for you! She's telling you what you're missing by hanging around here!" Lucy's voice was choked with emotion. "Don't you see? She's *waiting* for you. She's been waiting for you! You have another child to love, Joel. David and Mathew probably grew up and had kids of their own. You probably have grandchildren and great grandchildren. There's probably a whole clan of people up there waiting for you to get your *shit* together and go join them!" Lucy screamed.

Joel and Jesse stared at her, stunned into silence by her outburst.

"Sorry," Lucy said, shooting a wry look at Jesse. "I shouldn't use such language in front of a gentleman."

Jesse grinned at her.

Lucy touched Joel gently on the shoulder, even though she knew he couldn't feel a thing. "It's time, Joel. It must have been hard for her to raise three kids on her own, but she did it. Her work on Earth is done and has been for a long time. Now you have to go see how they turned out. You didn't know about your daughter. So don't blame yourself. She was a product of your love for Emma, just like those beautiful boys were."

Joel nodded, his face twisting up with pain again. Lucy sighed. "I would give anything in the whole world if I could just give you a big hug right now."

"Hell, even I'd hug him," Jesse said gruffly. "I know this is rough, man, but Lucy's right. Now you know you're missing out on even more by staying here."

"Everybody keeps telling me I need to go home, I gotta go home, like it's some kind of choice. I don't know what to do to cross over. It's not like I can make it happen, you know? I mean, what do I do?" Joel looked helplessly at Lucy.

"I think for one thing, you have to feel worthy. You have to know in your heart that you're worthy of crossing over, of seeing her again."

"Am I?" Joel asked.

"You know what I think," Lucy told him firmly.

"You really think this was a sign from Emma? This diary, you being here to help?"

"Yes," Lucy said. "I believe that with all my heart. Sometimes I think she sent me to find you, to help you."

"Finding Emma's diary isn't the only coincidence." Joel said, the pain in his eyes finally starting to ease as he smiled warmly at her. "My daughter's name was Lucy."

34

Before sunrise, Jesse walked the silent streets of Gettysburg alone. He knew Lucy must still be sleeping, and he longed to be there next to her in bed. Holding her close, feeling the warmth of her body. As he wandered aimlessly, he found himself headed toward Devil's Den. Normally, he would have turned around and headed the other way, but something made him continue on toward the place where he had died.

It was a good time to visit for quiet reflection because it was deserted at this hour of the morning. The sun was just coming up as he walked over to where he had drawn his last breath. He stood right in the spot where he'd first been shot in the shoulder and thought of the events that had immediately preceded that bullet. He thought of Charles and closed his eyes.

I'm sorry, Charles, he thought. *I'm sorry for you, I'm sorry for your mama. I'm sorry if you had a girl like Emma or Lucy waiting for you to come home. I'm sorry.*

Jesse felt his sadness over killing Charles ease greatly. It

felt good to apologize, and it felt good to know that he had
Joel's forgiveness for killing his friend.

After spending so much time avoiding Devil's Den,
today he spent hours there. He took his time contemplating
everything that had happened. His life. His death. He'd
been around for so long that there was much to think about,
to sort through. He thought of his life on the farm in Texas,
his friends back home, and even the dog he'd had to leave
behind. And he remembered his mother. The way she'd
doted upon him as a child, and the way she'd looked when
he told her goodbye when he joined the First Texas
Infantry.

As if the battle had not been ghastly enough, Devil's
Den now held fresh horror for Jesse as he recalled Lucy's
traumatic experience there. He stared at the rock where she
had lain while feeling his mortal wounds. He felt a tight,
squeezing sensation in his chest as he pictured her eyes
filled with terror and agony, her tears, and her screams. *Dear
God, her screams...*

Jesse forced himself to sit on the rock where Lucy had
suffered. He closed his eyes and lowered his head, remembering everything she'd endured. It was as if he thought he
could atone for causing her such pain by torturing himself
with those horrible memories.

*"I'd go through it all over again if I thought it would help
you..."*

He heard her voice almost as clearly as if she'd been sitting
right beside him. Yes, she'd been drunk when she'd said those
words, but Jesse knew in his heart that she had meant them.
Just as he would endure any amount of suffering for her, he
knew she would do the same for him. Suddenly, his horrific
memories of Lucy were replaced with much sweeter ones. He

remembered the tender way she'd gazed at him when he'd confessed that he'd never been with a woman because he'd been waiting for the right one. He knew now that she'd been falling in love with him then. He thought back to the way she'd looked at him when they danced together and he sang *their* song to her. He remembered when Lucy had confessed her feelings for him. *I'd do anything for you, Jesse. Because I love you. You're somebody's darling now, Jesse. You're* my *darling...*

Jesse opened his eyes and smiled. "She loves me," he whispered out loud. It still seemed impossible, but it was true. Lucy knew all of his flaws, his deepest secrets. He was dead, nothing more than a wisp of the man he had once been in life. And she loved him anyway. He longed to kiss her, hold her; he physically ached for her touch. When he looked into her loving face, he knew she yearned for him just as much.

Jesse closed his eyes. For once, he allowed himself to let go of his guilt over the past. The events of the war, the pain Lucy had endured, all the mistakes he had made. He allowed himself to be happy. *She loves me,* he thought again. *Lucy Westbrook is in love with me.*

Suddenly, an immense sense of peace washed over Jesse. It was a feeling of euphoria, an abrupt yet all-encompassing understanding that everything was right. With him, with the world, with the entire Universe. Suddenly, somehow everything made sense.

The odd yet wonderful sensation continued to grow, filling him with love and light. Jesse's whole body felt strange. Something was different and it took a moment for him to understand what it was.

Cold, was Jesse's first thought. Something felt very cold.

It was the rock. He could feel the cold, hardness of the rock where he sat.

Jesse gasped suddenly, and his hands flew to his throat where he'd felt air rushing into his mouth, down his windpipe, filling his lungs.

Oh, my God, I think I'm breathing.

Jesse jumped up from the rock. Instead of floating freely as he had done for the last century and a half, his feet got tangled underneath him and he fell, crashing hard onto the ground.

He cried out with surprise when he hit the dirt. He could feel the hardness of the earth underneath him. He jumped to his feet, then turned and reached out to touch the flat rock where Lucy had lain. He could *feel* it. He darted around, touching rock after rock after rock, amazed as he felt each one with his hands.

Jesse stopped and stood in the middle of Devil's Den, where he had died so long ago.

"I'm alive," he whispered into the stillness of the battlefield.

JESSE RAN toward the main part of town, adrenaline surging throughout his body and propelling him forward. He couldn't remember the last time he had run so far and so fast. He should have been exhausted by the time he reached Steinwehr Avenue, but he wasn't. He was exhilarated. Relief washed over him when he found Fillis and Joel just where he'd hoped they be in the usual spot in front of The Regimental Quartermaster. There weren't many tourists out on this weekday morning, and the two were alone on the street when Jesse came running up to them.

It was immediately apparent that something incredible

had happened to Jesse, based on his stunned expression and the fact that he was audibly gasping for breath.

Joel stared at him. "Are you...are you fucking *breathing*?" His question was nearly a shout.

"Y-yes. Yes. Yes!" Jesse managed to say, his lungs burning from his lengthy sprint from Devil's Den.

Fillis jumped up. "Jesse! What's goin' on?"

"Mama, Mama, Second Mama, I don't know!" Jesse said, his eyes wide. "But...but...I'm...I can..." Jesse whirled around, looking for something to touch to show what he was trying to say. He didn't see any objects on the ground that he could pick up. He spied a tree, then dashed over to it. He grabbed a low branch and snatched some leaves from it. He threw the leaves in the air, scattering them like confetti, giving Fillis and Joel a wide-eyed look as he did so.

Fillis stared at him. After recovering from her shock, she hurried over to him. "Jesse," she said, holding out her hand to touch him. He reached for her, but his hand went through hers. After all, she was still dead.

Jesse and Fillis exchanged a sad smile. It would have been so wonderful to be able to touch his beloved, honorary mother.

"What's happened to you?" Fillis whispered.

"I don't know. I-I was sitting over at Devil's Den just thinkin'. Just thinkin' bout everything that's happened and about Lucy and-and-and next thing I knew, I could touch everything. Second Mama, you ever seen anything like this happen?"

Fillis shook her head. "Never...never in all my days...."

Joel stared at him. "Me neither...and we've seen a lot of days...."

Jesse nodded, still looking wide-eyed and confused. "So we got no idea what's going on..."

"Or how long it will last," Joel said. "One thing's for sure. You better go see her *right now*."

"Yes," Jesse said, nodding rapidly, still panting but more from the shock of being alive than from his long run from Devil's Den. That was all he had thought of as he ran. *Lucy, Lucy, I can touch Lucy.*

"She working today?" Joel asked.

"Yes, thank *God*. I only got a vague idea of where she lives 'cause it's outta my reach. Or, at least it was. I gotta go!"

With that, Jesse turned and started to run toward Meade's Tavern.

"Hey, Secesh!"

Jesse whirled around.

Joel smiled and said, "Give her a hug from me."

Jesse grinned. "You got it."

∾

JESSE RAN ALL the way to the tavern. He arrived huffing and puffing and out of breath. It was an incredibly strange feeling, to be sure. It was agony to have to stop in front of the tavern for almost a full minute to catch his breath. He didn't want to frighten his beloved by running in all wide-eyed and crazy. He had to calm down for a moment.

Jesse paused in front of the tavern door. He stared at the doorknob. Would he be able to turn it? He reached out and grasped it, the metal cool against his hand. He let out a breath of relief and walked inside.

Jesse scanned the room and saw Lucy right away. She caught his eye, looking surprised and delighted to see him. It thrilled him to see that her reaction to seeing him was sheer joy. He gestured frantically for her to meet him out back. She nodded, suddenly looking worried.

Lucy was waiting for him around the back. He saw her visibly relax when she saw his smile.

"Lucy," he said as he jogged up to her. "Something's happening to me. I don't know what it is, okay? I don't know. But..."

Jesse held up his left palm like he usually did. Lucy held up her right one, fully expecting to feel the familiar icy sensation when she tried to touch him. Jesse grinned at her, then suddenly grabbed her hand and squeezed it.

Lucy gasped, looking more shocked than she had when her hand had gone through his shoulder and she first realized Jesse was a ghost.

"J-J-Jesse...what?" Lucy stammered, utterly stunned.

"I don't know, darlin'. I don't know! I just all of a sudden felt strange and..."

Lucy looked at his chest, rising and falling. "You're breathing..." she said, her voice almost a whisper.

"I-Yes. I think I am!"

"Do you have a heartbeat?"

"I don't know. I don't know!"

Trembling, Lucy reached over and slipped her hand inside his shirt and pressed it to his bare chest.

Jesse and Lucy stared at each other as they both felt it. With her fingers pressed against his heart, they could both feel it beating.

"Jesse. You do. You have a heartbeat. You're breathing and you have a heartbeat! Oh, my God, Jesse," Lucy said. She flung her arms around him and squeezed him as hard as she could.

Jesse closed his eyes and held her. "My love, my beautiful rose..." He held her tight and stroked her back. He breathed her in deeply as he savored the sensation of finally touching her. Jesse released her from his embrace, but refused to let go of her. He held onto her shoulders as he looked down at her.

"Jesse, how is this possible?" Lucy asked as tears filled her eyes.

"I don't know, my love. I don't know what happened or how long it will last, but I'm here now." Jesse gently wiped her tears. "Oh, no darlin'. You can't cry. You can't be crying when I kiss you for the first time."

Lucy's eyes lit up. It was all so overwhelming. She'd been so desperate to get her arms around him that it had not yet occurred to her that he could kiss her.

Jesse took a small step backward. Lucy looked at him, eyes shining with anticipation. He reached up and *finally* removed his hat. Lucy laughed softly as she admired the way he looked without it. He placed the hat over his heart and bowed respectfully to her. Then he dramatically tossed the hat aside. He cupped her face with his big hands, then dipped his head down to kiss her.

Jesse's passion for her overtook him. He pushed her against the wall so he could kiss her harder. Lucy hit her head against the brick wall. Jesse broke off the kiss and looked into her eyes, ready to apologize. She was so small, and he really didn't know his own strength yet. He certainly hadn't meant to push her that hard.

Lucy looked deeply into his eyes with an expression that could only be described as *hunger*, then grabbed his suspenders and pulled him toward her for another kiss. She made it clear that his sudden strength was a huge turn-on for her.

Jesse's sex drive had been muted—somewhat—while he was dead, but now it was back with a vengeance. He could practically feel the testosterone coursing through his veins and his blood pumping through his heart, his head...and everywhere else. He pressed his hardness against her rather than try to hide his erection. It felt so good to feel like a real man again, and Jesse wanted her to know how badly he wanted her.

Between kisses, Lucy managed to look him in the eye and murmur, "It would seem all your parts are working, Private Spenser..."

Jesse grinned at her and leaned in for another kiss, then nuzzled her cheek and kissed her neck. He inhaled deeply.

"Coconut," he said with a smile. "Your hair smells like coconut."

The back door swung open, and Craig walked out to sneak a cigarette. He shook his head as he saw Jesse and Lucy kissing passionately against the wall of the tavern. "'Bout time you made a move on her," he muttered as he walked a little ways down the parking lot to give them some privacy.

"Oh," Jesse said. "I nearly forgot. This is from Joel." With that, he wrapped his arms around her in a warm yet chaste embrace.

"Aww," Lucy said, as she hugged him back as if he were Joel for a moment.

"Okay, more from me..." Jesse said as he dipped his head down for another kiss. He was becoming more aroused by the second. He had never wanted any woman so badly, and yet... Jesse growled with frustration.

"What?" Lucy asked.

"I swear, my love," Jesse said between kisses. "I could do this all day." He kissed her again, then ran his fingers through her long hair. "But...God, I hate to ask!"

"What, Jesse? What do you need?" she asked, eager to help.

"Could you get me some food?" he asked, looking like an earnest little boy.

"Of course!" Lucy said, grateful there was finally something she could do to help him. "I know just the place." She grabbed him by the hand and pulled him inside.

Lucy seated him at a table in the second dining room of the restaurant, the one not in use at the moment because it was early in the day and not crowded.

Jesse sat down at the table, marveling at the solid feel of the wood under his bottom. He rested his hand on the table, amazed at how *real* everything felt.

"What do you want? A burger? A sandwich? A steak?" Jesse's eyes lit up at the last one. "Of course my Texas boy would want a steak," Lucy said warmly. "Steak it is. Do you want a beer to drink? A soda?"

"No. Water. Please. I haven't had clean water in so long," Jesse said. His throat felt as parched as it had the day he died. It had been scorching hot out on the battlefields, and he'd had precious little to drink that day.

Lucy nodded. She squeezed his hand before she ran off to the kitchen to place his order. Jesse saw the worry in her eyes as she turned to leave. She was probably afraid he might disappear or go back to being a spirit while she was gone. He had the same fears. So much was unknown right now.

Jesse took in several deep breaths as he looked around the quiet restaurant. He adjusted his pants a little to ease the discomfort down there. His penis was still rock hard from making out with the most beautiful woman he'd ever known. He desperately wanted to be with her, to take her to bed, but he didn't want to pressure her. These were extraordinary circumstances, but he was still a gentleman and she'd been hurt in the past. He would not make any demands of her, but would follow her lead instead.

Lucy rushed in with a glass and a pitcher of water. She sat down at the table across from him and quickly poured the water. He grabbed the glass and downed the ice water in just a few gulps. She refilled his glass, and he drained that too. His thirst finally sated, he let out a deep breath of relief.

They talked quietly for a few moments while they waited for his food. Lucy had to get up a few times to check on her tables in the other room, but thankfully it was a slow time of day. Each time she sat back down, she tangled her leg with his under the table. She couldn't bear not to touch him.

Jesse suddenly untangled his foot from hers and got up from the table, then reached out his hand to her. Sitting with her was not enough. He needed to hold her. He pulled her to her feet and held her close to him. He ran his fingers through her hair, kissed her neck, her lips, wanting to touch all of her at once.

"Dear God, it's so incredible to finally be able to hold you," Jesse murmured in her ear.

"Jesse," Lucy moaned softly.

Jesse pulled back a bit so he could look her in the eye. "Darlin', it hurt so bad that I couldn't hold you like this at Devil's Den. I couldn't help you, I couldn't touch you..."

"I know, honey. It's okay. I'm all right, now. It's never too late to kiss it better, though," Lucy said seductively.

Jesse grinned at her, then bent down to kiss her mouth. He slid her blouse off her shoulder, revealing her bra strap. He kissed the spot on her shoulder where the first phantom bullet had struck her. Then he stood up and gently kissed her left temple where the second battle wound hit. Next, he stared deeply, sensually into her eyes, then he reached down and untucked her blouse from her skirt. He crouched down and kissed her stomach where the final blow had wounded her.

Lucy moaned softly as he kissed her all over. Jesse stood up and looked her in the eyes. He kept his hand underneath her blouse and slowly slid his hand up her shirt. She looked into his eyes, breathlessly waiting for him to touch her breasts.

"Hey, now, kids. Keep it PG in here!" Craig joked as he burst into the dining room with the tray of food for Jesse.

Lucy blushed deeply as she tucked her blouse back into her skirt. Jesse chuckled. Though he hated for Lucy to be embarrassed, he couldn't help but be proud to be caught feeling up his girlfriend. It made him feel like a real man again.

Craig set down a huge platter of steak, French fries, and cole slaw in front of Jesse. "There you go, buddy. Enjoy!"

"Thanks," Jesse said with a smile.

Craig winked at Lucy, making her blush harder, then went back into the other dining room.

Though it was around lunchtime, Lucy was too excited to eat anything. She was just happy to watch Jesse enjoy his food. He ate the first bite of steak, then closed his eyes and moaned. The sound was deep and sexual, like noises he might make in bed while making love to Lucy.

"This is amazing, Lucy," Jesse said.

Lucy nodded. The food was great at the tavern anyway, but it was especially delicious to someone who was near-starving like Jesse was.

Jesse devoured his food, then looked up at Lucy. "Oh, no. This must be so expensive. They're gonna take it out of your check, aren't they? I can..." He thought for a moment. He hated to make a lady pay for his dinner, but what could he do? "I don't know...I could—"

Lucy laughed and grasped his hand. "Jesse. I love you. Let me take care of you!"

Jesse saw how happy Lucy was to be able to help him. He realized that she'd been feeling as helpless as he had, not being able to do anything for him. It clearly made her feel good to feed him.

When he'd finished his meal, he stood up and so did she. He grabbed her and kissed her, feeling himself get hard all over again. He pressed himself between her legs, and she let out a soft cry of pleasure.

"Jesse," Lucy said in a soft, sensual voice. "We need to be...*together*. As soon as possible. We don't know how long this will last or if you're here to stay or—"

"Are you sure? Are you sure you're ready to..." Jesse said, searching her eyes. Lucy always joked about how much she wished she could have sex with him, but now that it was physically possible he wanted to make sure she was ready.

"Yes. Of course!" Lucy said. "I want to be with you more than anything in the world."

"I feel the same way," Jesse said, running his fingers through her hair. "It's funny—I always thought if I could come back to life, the first thing I'd want to do is punch Joel." Lucy laughed, then locked eyes with Jesse as he gave her a look of pure lust. "Now all I want to do is make love to you. I wish I could take you right here and now."

"Oh, Jesse," she moaned in the way Jesse always fantasized she would. He thought of his favorite sex-on-the-bar fantasy, but he knew that wasn't possible now. And it wasn't right, especially for the first time with a classy girl like Lucy.

"I get off work at seven p.m. I can try to get done early."

Sudden panic gripped Jesse as he realized how soon this

was going to happen. He was going to have sex for the first time, with the woman of his dreams, *tonight*. He'd been so worried about her being ready that he didn't realize that *he* wasn't. He had no idea what he was doing.

"Okay, okay," Jesse said, trying to hide his fear. "I'll meet you here a little before seven. That'll give me some time to go see Joel and..." He realized what he'd almost said out loud. "You know, to...to... So he and Fillis will know where I'll be."

"That's a good idea." She stood on her toes to kiss him. "Until then, darling."

Jesse nodded, then left the restaurant. Lucy's face broke into a smile. She chuckled softly and put her hand over her heart. She knew exactly why he was rushing to see Joel. He needed advice on how to make love to a woman.

35

After another quick check of her tables, Lucy ducked out back to call Theresa. Now that she'd had time to think about what was happening with Jesse, her emotions overwhelmed her. She was crying by the time Theresa answered the phone.

"What? What is it? Where are you?" Theresa asked in a panicked voice, ready to jump in the car and go to Lucy if she needed her.

"I'm sorry," Lucy said, trying to calm down. "I'm fine. More than fine. It's Jesse. I-I don't know what's going on, but I think he's alive again."

"What?"

"I touched him, Theresa. I could touch him and hold him, and he kissed me. And he has a heartbeat and..." She broke down crying again. "He's breathing, Theresa. He's *breathing!*"

"That's impossible!" Theresa said.

"I know! I know it sounds insane. If I hadn't witnessed it for myself, I'd never believe it. But it happened. I felt him. I put my arms around him and––"

"That's crazy," Theresa said, her voice barely a whisper. After a moment of contemplation, she added, "Well, I am a Christian after all. I believe Christ rose again, so why not Jesse? That's amazing, Lucy. Just amazing. I'm so happy you got to finally touch him."

"Me, too." *And I'm planning on touching him a lot more tonight.* "Look, I really need you to stay at Steven's tonight."

"Ohhhh, I see..." Theresa said in a knowing voice.

Lucy rolled her eyes. She knew Theresa would tease her, just like Joel was bound to torture Jesse.

"You're going to deflower him, aren't you?"

"Yeah," Lucy laughed. "I guess I am. So I need you to make yourself scarce."

"No way! I wanna be there when you rock his world!"

"Theresa!"

Theresa cackled. "Of course. Of course I'll stay with Steven." She didn't sound thrilled at that idea.

"Thanks."

"I'm so happy for you, Lucy. Really," Theresa said sincerely.

"Thanks, 'Resa."

"Have fuuuun," she said in a singsong voice. "I want *details* tomorrow. And Lucy? Be gentle with him." Theresa giggled before hanging up the phone.

JESSE WAS grateful that he found Joel right away. He wasn't surprised to see Fillis sitting with him at their usual spot on Steinwehr Ave, but he wasn't sure if he would be able to get through this conversation with her there. Sure, they girl-watched together and joked about sex, but she was still like his *mother*. Jesse needed Joel to tell him exactly what to do to pleasure Lucy, and the discussion would probably get rather graphic.

Jesse ran up to the two of them. Fillis looked at him with concern at his haste until she saw his expression. He looked happy, so she calmed down.

"Didja kiss her?" Joel asked, grinning and getting right to the point.

Jesse's grin spread even wider. "Yes! I got to kiss her and hold her...and she feels just as soft as she looks."

"Bet you weren't soft when you touched her," Joel said with a chuckle.

With a slightly uncomfortable look at Fillis, Jesse admitted with a slight blush, "No, I wasn't." He looked down at Joel sitting on the steps. "I really need your help. I'm gonna make love to Lucy!"

"Oh, honey, that's wonderful," Fillis said, her face filled with love for Jesse. "What a gift this is. How lovely for you both."

"And you need my help?" Joel asked with amusement. "Hate to break it to you, but this is something you're gonna have to do on your own." He waved a hand through his crotch area, not even looking to see if anyone was watching. Nobody screamed, so he figured he was safe.

"As if I'd let you *touch* her," Jesse said, before remembering he'd better be nice if he wanted Joel's help. "I just...I need your help. I need your advice on what to do. I-I-I mean, I know what to *do,* I-I just mean..." Jesse stammered as he glanced over at Fillis. His face felt hot.

"You're blushing more than that lovely girlfriend of yours!" Joel laughed heartily.

"Okay, okay," Fillis said, getting up. "I can see you don't need your Second Mama here for this discussion."

Jesse smiled gratefully at her.

"You didn't ask for my advice, but I'm gonna give it to ya anyway. *Listen*," Fillis said, making sure Jesse looked her in the eye even though she knew how embarrassed he was. "That girl loves you. She just wants to be with you. I don't want you puttin' all kind of pressure on yourself 'bout this, ya unnerstand? Don't worry about what does or doesn't happen, ya hear? Remember what this is all 'bout. You finally have a chance to express your love physically. Love her, hold her, touch her, be sweet like ya are. That's all she needs from you."

"Thank you, Second Mama." He took her words to heart, and felt a little less nervous. "You're right."

Fillis smiled at him, then murmured to Joel, "Now you teach him how to treat that girl *right*."

Joel stifled a chuckle and nodded.

Fillis left them, and Joel grinned at Jesse. Jesse groaned inwardly. Joel wasn't going to make this easy on him.

"Not here," Jesse said. "I can't go invisible anymore, and we don't need to scandalize innocent tourists with this kind of talk."

"Right. Let's go sit up at Little Round Top."

Little Round Top was a good place to go. They could sit up there and look down on some of the battlefields, including Devil's Den. It might be crowded, but they could find a private spot.

It took them longer than usual to get there, because now Jesse had to actually walk. When they arrived, they perched up on the hill and under some trees, far enough away from the tourists so they wouldn't be heard.

"Okay!" Joel said. "Where to begin. Well, young man, you're old enough to know how it works. When a man and a woman love each other very much..."

"Spare me the grade-school lesson," Jesse said, and Joel

cackled at his own wit. "I know where babies come from, okay? I know the basics. But...I need to know...what to do... for *her*. How do I, you know, make her..."

Joel grinned, amused by Jesse's sudden shyness. It made him want to be as blunt as possible. "Climax. Come. Orgasm. You want to make her scream, don't you?"

"Yeah. I do." Jesse smiled wickedly, his embarrassment fading the more Joel taunted him. He was determined not to let Joel get the best of him.

"All right, *Secesh!*" Joel couldn't help but be impressed by Jesse's can-do attitude. "Do you smell?"

"What?"

"Think about it, Pinocchio. Since you're a *real boy* now, do you stink? You know what life was like in camp, all sweaty and gross. We never bathed."

Jesse smelled his armpits. "Oh, God!"

Joel waved him off. "Don't panic. Go to the Days Inn when we're done talkin'. You can't walk through walls anymore, but you know all the security codes, when the maids come through and all that. Go in and have a shower. Be careful with the knobs and don't burn yourself."

"Okay, okay. Good idea."

"And while you're in the shower, you need to touch yourself."

"What?" Jesse said, his face turning red.

"Read my lips. *Jerk off*. Repeatedly. She's a beautiful woman, and you're a 175-year-old virgin. How long do you think you're gonna last with her?"

"Yeah," Jesse admitted. "Good point. Okay, but what... what do I do when I'm with her?"

Jesse looked so earnest and afraid that it made it hard for Joel to make fun of him. *Be nice,* he reminded himself. *Charles taught you how to please Emma, and he wasn't a dick about it.* Joel had slept with two women before Emma, but he hadn't really known what he was doing. He doubted those girls had all that much fun with him. Emma was different. He loved her so much, and he desperately wanted to make her feel good. Joel knew Jesse felt the same about Lucy.

"First thing's first. Is she a virgin, do you know?" Joel asked.

Jesse shook his head. "No. She's been with one other guy before me."

"Okay, good."

Jesse cocked his head and looked at Joel quizzically.

"Trust me, that's a good thing. The first time can be painful for a woman, and believe me it's no fun when you have to be the one to hurt her."

Jesse nodded. He looked stressed out, overwhelmed at all the things he didn't know.

"Relax. A lot of this is just common sense. Take your time undressing her. Kiss her neck, her shoulders, down her breasts..."

Jesse perked up at that.

"You like that idea, don't you?" Joel teased.

"I just...I can't believe she's gonna let me touch her, ya know?"

"I know what you mean. She *wants* you to touch her," Joel said kindly. "Remember, she'll probably be very emotional. I mean, you both will, but you know how tender-hearted she is."

Jesse smiled, grateful that Joel knew Lucy so well. He would be able to tell Jesse just what to do, what was right for her.

"Make sure you kiss her, especially when you're inside her."

Jesse nodded, still not quite believing that he was going to get to be inside his beloved Lucy. And soon.

"Get her naked," Joel continued matter-of-factly. "Then there's a few different things you can try to make her feel good. Like when she's on her back, you can take these two fingers"—he held up his forefinger and middle finger together—"slip them inside her and stroke upward like this." He made a stroking motion in the air with his fingers.

Jesse looked uncertain.

"What? You can't be a wuss about pleasing your woman."

"No, no. It's just...you wouldn't give me bad advice, would you?" Jesse asked. They'd come to trust each other lately, but their friendship was still a bit tentative. Jesse wouldn't put it past Joel to try to humiliate him by telling him the wrong thing.

"I hate you," Joel said, but in a light tone that made it clear that it was no longer true, "but I get how important this is. Even I wouldn't do that to you." He shot Jesse a serious look. "And I sure as *hell* wouldn't do that to her."

Jesse nodded, convinced. That much he knew was true. Joel would never do anything to ruin this experience for Lucy.

"Trust me. Put your fingers in her, and stroke up. When you do that, you're hitting the same spot that you'll hit when you've got your cock in her. It's her G-spot or whatever."

Jesse nodded. That sounded easy enough.

"Okay. Next lesson. You know about a woman's clit?" Joel asked.

Jesse shook his head, and Joel groaned with annoyance. Jesse looked worried, and Joel reminded himself again to be nice. "Okay. Say this is her vagina," Joel said, making a circle with his fingers. Jesse winced. "What now?"

"If she had *any* idea we were talking about her like this..."

Joel grimaced guiltily, then nodded. "I know it's weird, Secesh. I mean, guys talk about sex all the time, but it's different when you're talking about the woman you love. I get that, okay? I love her, too. And you know that I would never disrespect her, right?"

"I know."

"It's not like we're talking bad about her. I'm just trying to show you how to take care of her."

Jesse nodded. He still felt guilty, but he really wanted to know how to please Lucy. "Okay. If this is her vagina, this is her clit." Joel pointed to the top of the circle. "This little spot right here—that's where a woman feels most of her sexual pleasure. If you want to give her an orgasm, that's where you need to touch her."

"Okay. Good to know." Jesse nodded, paying close attention. He clearly had had no idea about such things.

"Thing is, you gotta be gentle. When you're inside her, whether it's your fingers or your penis, you can stroke pretty damn hard and it won't hurt. Usually feels really good to a woman when you thrust hard inside, but the clit is a different story. If you press too hard, you can hurt her. So be gentle. Think of how sensitive your balls are, and that'll give you some idea."

"Okay, so what do I do?"

"First of all, you gotta forget all the pornos you've seen at the Days Inn. It's all bullshit," Joel explained. He stopped talking for a moment as a mom walked by with a toddler in tow. He continued once they were out of earshot. "All those X-rated movies where the woman is screamin' and having an orgasm with the guy on top of her. It just doesn't work like that."

Jesse looked a little disappointed to hear that.

"You gotta massage her clit to get her to come, and you usually can't get to it when you're on top. Sometimes if the girl is on top it can work, but you usually have to pleasure a woman separately. If you're any kind of gentleman, you take care of her needs first."

"Got it," Jesse said. He would be glad to take care of Lucy first. He wanted so much to be a good lover to her.

"Now you can rub her clit—*gently*—with your finger or thumb...or...how shall I put this...think lesbian porn."

"What?" Jesse asked, more confused than ever.

"Use your tongue," Joel said bluntly.

"Ohhhh. I get it," Jesse said, recalling the lesbian stuff he'd seen on TV. "It all seems so complicated."

"It's not, really. Touch her gently on that spot. Do it however you want, but I'm telling you, if you go down on her, it'll be the most pleasurable thing you can do for her."

"How will I know if I'm doing it right?" Jesse asked, looking stressed out at all this new information.

"Trust me. *You'll know.* She'll probably be screaming your name."

"Really?" Jesse asked with great interest.

"You'd like that, wouldn't you, Secesh?" Joel then spoke in a high-pitched voice, "*Oh, Jesse, Oh, Jesse!*"

Jesse blushed furiously and waved him off. Joel chuckled. He'd behaved pretty well so far, but he still felt the need to give Jesse a hard time.

"Seriously, though. Do this for her. It'll make her crazy, I swear."

Jesse looked completely overwhelmed.

"Fillis was right, ya know. Try not to stress about it. Lucy knows you've never done it before. She just wants to be close to you. She's not gonna expect you to be a great lover, but you're gonna surprise her, now, aren't you?"

Jesse looked at Joel hopefully, like maybe he really could do this well after all.

"*Jesse*," Joel said, calling him by his real name for the first time *ever*. "You can do this."

The Texas soldier took in a deep breath. "Thank you. I mean it."

"No problem," Joel said. "Somebody once gave me the same advice before my wedding night."

"Charles?" Jesse asked.

"Yeah," Joel said with a fond smile.

Jesse looked Joel in the eye and a look of understanding passed between them. Jesse was sorry that he'd killed Joel's friend, and Joel wasn't angry anymore.

Joel gestured at Jesse's dirty clothes and said, "Now, go get cleaned up and go take care of your woman."

36

Armed with security codes and knowledge of the maids' schedules, Jesse found it easy to slip into a vacant room in the Days Inn for a quick shower. Though he'd never taken a shower with actual running water before, he'd seen enough TV commercials to know how they worked. He was careful to get the temperature right before he stepped in.

The clean water felt wonderful against his skin. The shampoo and soap smelled so good, and he was so glad he wouldn't have to meet Lucy tonight smelling like a filthy, sweaty soldier. You got used to the smell of other soldiers in camp, but a delicate flower like Lucy deserved so much better. He was grateful that Joel had suggested he take a shower.

Jesse remembered his other suggestion. He closed his eyes and thought of Lucy. He fantasized about what would happen that night. He reached down between his legs and began stroking himself as he thought about what it would be like to undress her. He thought of unbuttoning her blouse, revealing those lovely, milky-white breasts with soft, pink nipples...

Jesse grunted as the force of his first orgasm in forever took hold of him. The sensation was so intensely pleasurable that it almost hurt.

What was that, ten seconds?

So far, Joel's advice was spot-on. It would have been humiliating to finish so quickly with Lucy. She would have understood, but she deserved a man in bed, not someone with the endurance of a sixteen-year-old boy.

Jesse continued washing up in the shower for a while, then masturbated again as soon as he was physically able to. It took him much longer to come this time, which made him feel more confident. His third orgasm of the day would happen with Lucy later that night, preferably after he'd given her one.

He turned off the water and toweled off. Jesse rinsed his mouth with the tiny hotel bottle of mouthwash on the sink, then went into the other room. He looked at his dirty uniform shirt and gray pants and knew he had no choice but to put them back on. His clothes didn't seem to smell all that bad and, with luck, he wouldn't be wearing them for long anyway.

He looked up and stared at his reflection in the hotel mirror. He definitely looked cleaner, better. He looked into his own eyes for a moment. He'd suffered with so much guilt and self-doubt for so long, but Lucy made him feel better and more at peace. He thought of his beautiful rose, with her soft skin, pretty brown hair, and gentle brown eyes. That amazing woman was in love with that man in the mirror. Maybe he wasn't such a bad guy after all.

~

JESSE SHOWED up at the Tavern at 6:30 p.m., and Lucy was ready to go. She'd managed to get done a little early.

"Look at you!" she said admiringly when he showed up at the front door of the tavern. "You're so clean!"

Lucy ran her fingers through his fluffy brown hair. She was still getting used to seeing him without his slouch hat, which he now held in his hand since he was in the presence of a lady.

"Yeah. I had a shower."

"How did you manage that?"

"Days Inn." He lowered his voice and added, "I know the door codes there, too,"

Lucy laughed, still touching his hair with great affection. "I bet a shower felt pretty good to you."

"Yeah, it sure did." *And not just because I jerked off twice thinking about you.*

"Let's go!" she said, eagerly taking his hand and leading him to her car, which was parked down the street. She opened the car door on the passenger side for him.

"Dangit!" he said. "I should have opened the car door for you. I jus' didn't think of it."

"You're forgiven, darling. It's your first car ride, isn't it?"

"Yeah. A lot of firsts for me today," he said with a nervous smile.

Lucy slid behind the wheel. She helped him with his seatbelt, then squeezed his hand before starting the car. They rode in silence for a few moments, and Jesse kept his hand on her knee the whole time. They both wanted to touch each other as much as possible.

Jesse suddenly stiffened a bit, staring straight ahead. Lucy glanced over and saw him white-knuckling the car door handle with his right hand.

"You all right, Jesse?"

Jesse nodded, still looking ahead. "We're about to leave the town of Gettysburg. I ain't gone this far in 150 years. I'm jus'... I'm not sure what will happen."

Lucy drew in a breath as they drove over the town line. She exhaled as soon as they crossed the road out of town. Jesse looked over and grinned at her.

"I'm still here!" he said with relief. He looked out at the scenery. It was nothing exciting, but it was *different*. It was wonderful.

Jesse was excited, but was getting more nervous by the second. He wanted so badly to please Lucy. He wanted to try all the things Joel had taught him, but what if he messed it all up? He remembered the look of desire in Lucy's eyes when he pushed her against the wall to kiss her. She obviously loved it when he was strong, dominant, masculine. He wanted to be like that in bed for her. He needed to appear confident no matter how scared he was.

They entered her apartment and she put her keys down. "This way," she said and led him straight to the bedroom.

Jesse glanced around the apartment as he followed her to the bedroom. It was quiet, so he figured Theresa wasn't home.

Once inside her bedroom, Lucy stood in front of Jesse and wrapped her arms around him. She looked up at him. "Are you nervous?" she asked.

He considered lying, but figured she would know the truth anyway. "Extremely," he admitted.

Lucy caressed his cheek and said, "Please don't be afraid of me."

Jesse smiled as they shared a knowing look. She was repeating the same words he'd said to her as they stood at his grave.

Jesse leaned down and kissed her, and she eagerly kissed

back. Her lips still on his, she managed to kick off her shoes.

Lucy ran her fingers through his hair as she kissed him. He began to unbutton her blouse, then slipped his right hand over her breast and she moaned softly. She reached around back and unhooked her bra for him. Good thing, because Joel hadn't told him how to take off a woman's bra.

He slid off her blouse, then pulled her bra the rest of the way off. He looked down at her breasts, then back up at her face. "You're a beautiful woman, Lucy."

She smiled shyly, then reached over and slid down his suspenders. She slipped off his white shirt and admired his naked chest. Jesse saw the hint of worry on her face as she looked at how thin he was. He would have given anything to be more muscular for her, but there was nothing he could do about that now. She took off his pants and underwear, and he gently stripped away the rest of her clothes.

Jesse guided her toward the bed, still kissing her. He pushed her down and lay on top of her for a moment. She looked into his eyes with breathless anticipation. Next, he climbed off her and lay down next to her.

This was the moment of truth. He steadied his breath, determined not to let her feel how nervous he was. He kissed her again, then slid his hand down the length of her body. He rested his hand on the mound between her legs. Lucy took a deep breath. Next, Jesse slid two fingers inside of her. She let out a soft moan, then closed her eyes and spread her legs wider to let him get deeper inside. Jesse's confidence soared. He stroked upward, gently at first, then a bit harder.

"Oh, Jesse," Lucy said in a sultry voice.

Her eyes were still closed, and Jesse used it as an opportunity to look at her down there. He gently spread the folds outside of her vagina, and saw the spot Joel had told him about. Women's bodies were *fascinating!* As gently as possible, he ran his thumb across that special area.

"Ah!" Lucy cried out as her eyes·flew open. For a moment, Jesse wasn't sure if he'd pressed too hard. Was that a cry of pleasure or pain? "Oh, Jesse...it feels so good when you touch me there."

Jesse smiled at her, continuing to rub her with his thumb.

"Ah! Ah!" Lucy cried again. She looked up at him, her lovely brown eyes pleading with him to keep going. "Oh, Jesse. I need you..."

Lucy looked up into Jesse's handsome face. She saw the unmistakable pride as he stroked her between her legs. She'd fully intended to encourage him during their first time together, to call out his name and tell him how good he was no matter what. Now she found she didn't have to fake anything. His touch felt *divine.* He was so attuned to her, so intent on pleasing her that it didn't take him long to figure out how to touch her in just the right way.

Jesse kept rubbing her with his thumb, fairly sure that he could give her an orgasm just by doing that. He didn't want to, though. He couldn't imagine how frustrating it must have been for her to have a boyfriend who couldn't touch her, and the last thing he wanted to do was tease her, but he really wanted to go down on her. He wanted to give her as much pleasure as he could. He pulled his hand away before he pushed her too far over the edge.

There was a flicker of disappointment on her face, but then she whispered, "I want to touch you, too." She sat up. She reached down between his legs and stroked his penis, then gently massaged his testicles.

Jesse lay back on the bed and groaned, a deep, manly sound that turned Lucy on even more. She stroked him up and down and asked, "Has anyone ever touched you there before?"

He opened his eyes and looked at her. "Besides me? No."

Lucy laughed gently as she continued stroking him. Jesse realized if he hadn't touched himself so much already today, he would have exploded the moment her gentle, feminine fingers began massaging him. Her strokes were perfect, almost too good. No question that she could finish him off just like this, and he wasn't about to let that happen.

Jesse sat up on the bed and pushed Lucy down on her back. He climbed on top of her and she looked up at him with that same look of lust she'd had back at the tavern when he pushed her against the wall.

"Are you ready?" she whispered, her face full of love and tender concern.

"Almost," Jesse said, nuzzling her neck. "Something I gotta do first..."

He kissed down her neck, her shoulders, her breasts. His kisses traveled farther south, until he reached the mound between her legs. He heard her suck in her breath. His tongue explored her body. It was harder to find the spot now than it had been earlier with his fingers. But he found it.

"Oh, God, Jesse. Right there!" she cried out.

Jesse gently massaged her most intimate spot with his tongue. "Ah! Ah! Ah!" Lucy cried out. Jesse loved that sound she made when he touched her just right.

"Oh Jesse, oh Jesse," she pleaded. "Don't stop, darling. Please don't stop...Jesse...Jesse..."

She'll probably be screaming your name....

Lucy lay back, legs spread, lost in the blissful pleasure Jesse was giving her. She could hardly believe the sounds that were coming out of her mouth; they were completely involuntary. She felt out of control in the most wonderful way. She could only let go and be so expressive with a man that she loved and trusted completely. The pleasure was more intense than anything she had ever known, and his strokes were *almost* perfect.

"*Faster*," Lucy pleaded, and Jesse eagerly complied. Her pleasure intensified, and the rapid flicks of his tongue pushed her over the edge. She threw back her head and surrendered to the most glorious orgasm she'd ever experienced. The sensation seemed to go on forever, and she gripped the sheets in her fists and passionately cried out his name. She gently pushed Jesse's head away when she couldn't take any more.

Jesse climbed back up to her while she caught her breath. "My God, Jesse!" She looked at him with a mixture of surprise and relief. He was overjoyed that he'd been able to please her. "That was *incredible*. No one's ever done that for me before."

He gently stroked her cheek with the back of his hand. "Well, I'm honored to be your first." He nuzzled her neck, relishing the warmth and comfort of her soft skin.

Lucy could feel his hardness pressing against her. He'd been such a generous lover, and she didn't want him to have to wait another second for his own pleasure. She looked into his eyes. "Take me, Jesse."

He grinned at her. "Oh, yes, ma'am."

Jesse slowly, sensually slid himself into position on top of her. They looked into each other's eyes, knowing what a significant moment this was. He pressed himself against her opening, then slid himself inside. He didn't get all the way in at first, and Lucy saw the flicker of panic on his face.

"It usually takes a few tries to go all the way in," Lucy lovingly explained. "I'm small, and..." She glanced down between his legs. "And you're pretty big."

Jesse smiled, grateful for the compliment and comforted that she never made him feel like less of a man because of his inexperience. He pushed a few more times, then slammed into her harder than he meant to. He was about to apologize but Lucy interrupted.

"Ah! Oh yes, Jesse. Just like that." She closed her eyes and moaned.

Jesse remembered that Joel said he could stroke pretty hard and it would probably feel good to her, so that was what he did. The harder he thrust, the more she cried out with pleasure. He was sure to lean down and kiss her while he made love to her. He felt slightly guilty for driving into her so hard. His intention had been to make love to her slowly and tenderly, at least for their first time. But now it seemed his hormones had taken over, and it felt so damn good to finally be strong and masculine for Lucy. At long last, he was able to make passionate love to the woman he'd waited for all his life...and beyond. Her hair was spread out on the pillow, her arms and legs were wrapped around him, and she was crying out his name. Except for the fact that they were in bed instead of on top of the bar, it was just like his fantasy.

Making love with Jesse was as wonderful as Lucy had fantasized, too. She wrapped her arms around his neck and shoulders as she surrendered herself to him. He felt so *strong*, so in control. She'd hungered for his touch for so long, and now her senses were overloaded as she finally experienced all of him. She savored the contours of his arm muscles, relished the sound of his breathless panting, and felt the heat of his sweat as he pounded into her. She cried out in ecstasy, reveling in the pleasurable feel of the hardness of his body inside the softness of hers. She closed her eyes and drowned in the blissful sensation of finally being intimate with the man she loved.

Gasping with effort, Jesse kissed Lucy's neck, cheek, then mouth. His pleasure intensified and he knew he was getting close. "Lucy, Lucy," he drawled in her ear. With one final thrust, his whole body shuddered as he experienced his first orgasm with a woman. He grunted aloud as he came, and Lucy gripped him tighter.

Lucy held him tight, relishing the warmth of feeling his seed inside of her. She'd deliberately dispensed with using a condom. Consequences be damned; she'd wanted to feel all of him.

They lay together for a moment, sweaty, satisfied, and more in love than ever. Having sex with the woman he loved was even better than he'd imagined. No doubt about it. Lucy had been worth waiting for.

They held each other close. After exchanging soft "I love yous," there was no more need for words. After a few moments, Lucy shivered a little, so she got up to put her nightgown on. Jesse remained naked. She climbed back into bed, and Jesse reached for her, pulling her close.

They fell asleep wrapped in each other's arms. Jesse awoke once during the night, not sure where he was at first. Then he saw Lucy sleeping beside him. He felt like he was finally at home. At peace. He gazed at her as she slept. She looked so delicate, so fragile. *I can protect her now,* he thought. Now he could be the one to get her safely to her car at night, and he could finally hold her, love her the way she deserved. He drifted back into a restful sleep.

It was morning when he woke again. He was happy to find Lucy awake as well.

"Good morning, soldier," she said as she wrapped her

arms around him. He smiled at her and couldn't help thinking that she had the happy, satisfied look of a woman who'd been made love to last night. He couldn't wait to do it again.

It turned out he wasn't the only one.

Lucy rubbed his shoulders, then his chest, then reached down and stroked him between his legs, getting him hard. He'd been such an incredible lover that first time. She was proud of him. He must have been so nervous, but he didn't show it much. This morning, Lucy wanted to take charge, take care of him, and give him a stress-free sexual experience.

She slipped down between his legs and put her mouth where her hands had been. Jesse moaned out loud with pleasure. It amused Lucy that even his deep-voiced moans during sex seemed to have that Texas accent.

Jesse closed his eyes and surrendered as Lucy pleasured him. He wasn't sure how he felt about his beautiful rose doing such a thing to him, but it felt too good for him to tell her to stop. Besides, he knew she wouldn't do anything that made her uncomfortable.

Jesse felt himself getting to close to orgasm. That was where he drew the line. He would *not* finish in her mouth. Not now, not ever. He gently tugged on her shoulders, "I'm too close, darlin'. I don't want to...not like this."

Ever the gentleman, Lucy thought. She respected his wishes and climbed up to look at him. He started to get up, to get on top of her, but she pushed him back down. "No no, cowboy. I'm not done with you yet."

Jesse grinned at her with anticipation. Just when he thought Lucy couldn't possibly get any sexier. She slipped off her nightgown, then straddled him. She relished the look on his face when she slid on top of him, putting him inside her.

"Lucy. That feels so good," he said. "You're so beautiful, Lucy..."

She loved how he said her name. She loved how he said everything. She moved herself up and down on him a few times, then leaned down and said, "I love that deep, sexy voice of yours, Jesse," then she leaned closer and murmured in his ear, "and that accent of yours turns me on like you wouldn't believe."

"It does?" Jesse asked, once she sat back up and started moving on top of him again.

"Oh, yeah," Lucy said in a sensuous voice.

"Then I'll just have to keep talkin', darlin'."

He grinned up at her. Lucy's rocking motion on top of him, combined with being able to see all of her lovely, naked form drove him wild. It wouldn't take long for him to finish, that was for sure. He thrust his body upward to meet her motions.

"Ah!" Lucy cried out.

Jesse grinned. He knew exactly what that sound meant. "That's the spot, ain't it?" He jerked his hips twice in rapid motion.

"Ah! Maybe," she said. "It doesn't matter. I'm taking care of you now."

Lucy seemed determined to make this sexual experience all about him, but Jesse had other plans. *Ladies first,* he thought. He jerked his hips upward again. He was already getting to know her body so well that he knew just what to do. Joel had told him that it might be possible for him to hit the right spot when she was positioned on top, and clearly he had.

"Jesse!" she cried, her expression a cross between pleasure and admonishment. "Don't..."

Of course he kept thrusting, pounding her now that he

knew just how to hit that most sensitive spot. He felt Lucy change her motion, grinding differently now. She closed her eyes and moaned as she did it. She'd repositioned herself to maximize her pleasure. She was losing control, and it was the sexiest thing Jesse had ever seen.

"Do it, darlin'," Jesse said. "I want to watch you. You're so lovely, darlin'."

All Lucy could do was moan in between cries of his name. Now that he was hitting just the right spot, he was hopeful that he could give her another orgasm. His own pleasure was so strong, so heightened that it was a struggle to keep himself under control. But she was close, so close... *Please let me get her there....*

The bed slammed against the wall as Jesse continued thrusting upwards into her again and again and Lucy moved her hips in perfect rhythm with him. "Jesse... Jesse... Jesse... Oh, *God!*" She threw her head back and cried out as she came, her long hair touching his knees. Watching Lucy have an orgasm was the most exciting thing Jesse had ever seen. Seconds later, he gripped her hips and groaned as he came, too, emptying himself inside her.

Panting, Lucy climbed off him and collapsed on the bed. "*God*, that was good. Jesse, you're amazing..."

"So are you, my love. So are you." Jesse wrapped his arms around her, and they held each other close. After they caught their breath, he spoke again as he caressed her hair. "I should have been more careful. What if I got you pregnant?"

"Then I'll have your baby." She said it as if it was the most natural thing in the world. To her, it was. If Jesse crossed over, his child would be all she had left of him.

Jesse stroked her cheek tenderly. He couldn't think of a sight more beautiful than Lucy, round and pregnant with his child. *Their* child. But what if he crossed over? He had terrible visions of her working hard as a single mother, taking on extra shifts at the restaurant, maybe even having to give up her dream of being a teacher. And he couldn't help but think of Joel and his anguish over the child he never knew.

"It's okay, Jesse," Lucy said, seeing his worry. "It's not likely that I'm pregnant, and we'll use something next time, okay?" She knew it was a risk to have unprotected sex with him, but she had wanted so desperately to feel all of him, in case it was her only chance. She also knew it was the wrong time in her cycle to get pregnant, but it was certainly possible.

Jesse nodded. Lucy got up and started to get dressed. "I got you a toothbrush and some stuff to shave with." She'd run out to the local pharmacy on a quick break during her shift yesterday to get everything she thought he might need.

"That's very thoughtful, love. Thank you."

"They're in the bathroom. Let me know if you need help, okay?"

"Okay." He'd never used a modern toothbrush before, but he was pretty sure he could figure it out. He ran his fingers over his rough chin; his beard had come in a lot since yesterday. *Incredible,* he thought.

Lucy went to the kitchen. She started the coffee and made pancakes while she waited for Jesse to join her. He appeared in the kitchen, naked from the waist up. He wore only his pants, not wanting to put on the rest of his filthy uniform.

"Mmmm," Lucy said, admiring his chest.

Jesse put a hand over his heart. "I've never seen a sight more beautiful." With that, he walked right past Lucy and put his hand lovingly on top of the coffeemaker. Lucy burst out laughing. "This...*this*...is an incredible invention. It smells *so* good."

Lucy walked over and grabbed the biggest mug she could find and filled it for him. "How do you take it?"

"Sugar," he said simply.

He sat down at the table, and she gave him the mug and a bowl of sugar. Her eyes widened as she watched him heap seven full spoons of sugar into it. Jesse took a big sip, then held the mug to his cheek like it was precious to him. Lucy chuckled and went back to work on the pancakes.

The door opened, and Theresa walked into the apartment. Jesse jumped up from his seat and went to see her.

"Theresa! I'm so sorry we kicked you out of your home last night."

Theresa raised an eyebrow, then looked past Jesse at Lucy. Lucy held a hand over her heart and mouthed, *Oh, my God,* which was her way of reporting on their sexual activity. Theresa stifled a giggle.

Jesse looked down at his naked chest. "I'm sorry I'm not decent!" he said, looking sincerely apologetic for being so inappropriately dressed in front of a lady; at least one he wasn't sleeping with. He put his arms around his torso in an attempt to cover himself.

Theresa looked at his chest admiringly. "You hear me complaining?"

Jesse smiled at her. He knew she was just being nice. He was sure she'd have much preferred Joel's muscles over his scrawny figure.

Theresa stared at his chest for a moment, then jabbed him on the shoulder with her finger. She grinned as she made solid contact with his form. "Welcome back, baby!" She threw her arms around him, and he squeezed her tight.

Theresa was such a nice girl, and it felt wonderful to be able to give her a warm hug. He embraced her so hard he lifted her off her feet for a moment. She laughed as he set her down again.

"I'm gonna go get dressed," Jesse said, leaving the two women to talk. About him, he rather hoped.

"So..." Theresa said in a low voice after he'd gone.

"Oh, my God, 'Resa. He was *amazing*. No one's ever made me scream like that," Lucy confessed, her face coloring a little.

"I knew it. I knew he was gonna be great in bed."

"How did you know? I mean, he was, you know..."

"A virgin?" Theresa said. "Oh, honey. Male virgins feel like they have something to prove! Oh, but it's more than that. He's just so sweet and he loves you so much. I knew he would be really wonderful and attentive."

"Oh, he was..."

"He did it for you, didn't he?" Theresa asked with a twinkle in her eye. She'd been telling Lucy for years that a real man went down on his woman, that there was no feeling like it. She always told her she didn't know what she was missing.

"And how..."

Therese giggled, thrilled for her friend. There was a hint of worry on her face. The unspoken truth hung heavily in the room. Was Jesse here to stay, or was he just one step closer to crossing over?

~

LUCY DIDN'T HAVE any more classes for the summer, but she still had to work. She drove Jesse to the main part of town, then they walked together so he could hang out with Fillis and Joel while she worked her shift. They found the two in their usual spot on the steps.

Joel stood up and pulled Jesse aside while Lucy talked quietly with Fillis.

Eyes wide, Joel asked in a quiet voice, "So? How did it go? Did you make her..."

"*Twass,*" Jesse drawled with pride, a huge grin on his face.

"Bully!" Joel whispered in a hoarse whisper so Lucy wouldn't hear. "Bully for you!" He punched Jesse in the shoulder. It felt like being hit with an ice ball.

The two soldiers joined Fillis and Lucy. Lucy suddenly felt self-conscious. Everyone here was fully aware that she and Jesse had had sex last night. Everyone knew, and had probably even been talking about it. Lucy was also fairly certain that Joel had told Jesse how to do all those incredible things to her in bed. It had been so wonderful, but it was still so embarrassing for her. It was hard for her to know that her private sex life was common knowledge, even among friends like Fillis and Joel.

Jesse noticed Lucy's familiar blush and understood why she stood in uncomfortable silence.

"So," Joel began. Jesse shot him a warning look, but it wasn't necessary. Joel hated seeing Lucy uncomfortable as much as Jesse did, and would never say anything to embarrass her. Instead, he wanted to break the tension. "Lucy."

Lucy looked up shyly, finding it hard to meet his gaze. "I'm so glad you got a chance to be with him. Nobody thought it would ever be possible, and I know how much he means to you. I'm just...I'm really happy for you both."

Lucy smiled shyly, appreciating his tactful candor. Still, she inwardly berated herself for not being more like Emma. Emma would never be shy about sex.

"Thanks," Lucy said. She looked over at Jesse. "He was... amazing." She blushed deeply, but was still glad she'd said it. She wanted to praise Jesse's sexual prowess in front of his friends, especially Joel.

Jesse grinned at her, which made any discomfort she felt totally worthwhile.

"Well, I'd better get to work."

Jesse leaned over and kissed her tenderly, cupping her face in his hands. Joel shook his head, marveling. It was wonderful to see them be able to touch each other! Fillis looked at them the same way, full of happiness for them.

"Oh, by the way," Lucy dug into her purse, then handed Jesse some money.

"But—"

"Take it, darling. You can go to the Gettysburg outlets and pick out some comfortable clothes. Oh, and..." She lowered her voice. "You should get some condoms, too."

Joel chuckled audibly, then regretted it. It was obviously a private comment meant for Jesse's ears only, and he felt awful for laughing.

Lucy felt her face get hot. Then she felt angry, but with herself and not Joel. *This is stupid. We're all adults here. This is ridiculous for me to be so embarrassed.*

Feeling bold for once, she spoke louder. "And be sure to get the right size condoms." She turned to Joel and told him, "It's true what they say..." With a look back at Jesse, she said, "*Everything's* bigger in Texas."

With that, she slung her purse on her shoulder and turned to walk away before they could see her reddened face.

Jesse's deep-throated laughter made her smile.

∾

JOEL AND JESSE came to the restaurant long before Lucy's shift was over. It was around 4:30, and she didn't get off work until eight p.m. As always, she was delighted to see them.

"Look at you!" she cried, as she saw Jesse dressed in civilian's clothing for the first time. The sight of him took her breath away. He wore blue jeans and a black shirt that made his blue-gray eyes stand out. "You look so handsome! I mean, even more than usual!"

"Thank you, my love," he said, his voice full of sorrow.

Lucy had been so preoccupied by his new look that she hadn't noticed how sad he looked. "What's wrong?"

Joel looked at Lucy and said, "I have to go to Devil's Den. *Right now.* I feel...it's like I'm being called there, pulled there. It's my time, Lucy."

Lucy's heart caught in her throat. She gasped. "Oh, Joel. I'm so happy for you, but I'm gonna miss you so much."

"Thank you, sweetheart." Joel sounded sad.

"Aren't you excited? You're going to see Emma!"

Joel's eyes lit up, and she finally saw the joy that was simmering underneath. He was hiding his happiness. But why?

Joel looked at Jesse and said gently, "Tell her."

"I'm supposed to go, too," Jesse said. He didn't look at her as he spoke. He couldn't bear to see her expression.

Lucy felt like someone had punched her in the gut. She stood there, silent, for a moment. She'd always known this day might come, but since he'd become alive she'd dared to hope that he could stay with her.

"Oh," she said. She went numb. It was the kind of sudden, stunned shock you might have when a police officer shows up to your house to tell you someone's been killed in an accident. It took her a moment before she could find the strength to speak. "I-I'll go with you. To say goodbye."

Jesse finally met her gaze. His eyes looked haunted, full of agonized grief. The only time she'd ever seen him look like that was when he stood over her when she lay on that rock at Devil's Den.

"I'll tell my boss I have to go. That I have a family emergency." Still numb, she walked over to Mandy and spoke quietly to her. Mandy looked alarmed at Lucy's expression, then put a hand on her shoulder. Lucy collected her things and joined the soldiers as they walked to Devil's Den.

Lucy walked next to Joel, with Jesse lagging behind like he was trying to resist the call he felt to go back to the battlefield.

"Are you all right, sweetheart?"

"I feel like I'm going to the hospital to turn off his life support," Lucy said dully.

"I won't leave you, Lucy," Jesse said sternly as he jogged to catch up with them.

"It's God's will we're talking about. You can't fight it," Lucy said, struggling to keep her voice even. She wanted to cry out with grief, but she knew she had to pull herself together.

"Damn right, I'll fight it!" Jesse roared.

Lucy suddenly grabbed him and held him close. She willed herself not to cry. Her voice quavered as she spoke. "You have to go. It's your time, Jesse. Your work on Earth is done now. You need to go home."

"My home is with you!"

"No, it isn't. I hoped it would be, but I guess I was wrong. You're obviously being called to your real home now."

Lucy let go of him and started walking with Joel again.

"I won't go!" Jesse stood there, rooted to the spot.

Joel shot him a panicked look, then turned to look

toward Devil's Den. He looked back at Lucy and said, "I have to go!"

Fear and adrenaline shot through Lucy. What if this was some kind of window of opportunity and they missed it? Suddenly, she knew just what to do to force Jesse to come with them.

"Well, I'm going. And if you don't go, Jesse Spenser, so help me God I'll go stand right next to that rock at the Den where you died. *And it's almost five o'clock.*"

"Oh, God, it is almost five. Lucy, no!" Jesse cried out. "You can't go anywhere near the Den right now!"

Lucy charged forward, and she and Joel both picked up speed. They left Jesse no choice but to follow.

"I won't leave you, darling. I won't. I won't leave you," Jesse kept repeating.

Lucy did her best to pull herself together. Jesse would change his mind once he saw the portal, once he stepped into that light. The pull was strong from what they'd told her when others crossed over. She had to hold it together until he was gone, or he might not leave and he'd still be trapped here. Once he disappeared, she could fall apart but *not until then.*

They made it to Devil's Den. It was deserted. This time of day, there should have been dozens of tourists milling around. There was no one but the three of them present. It was eerie.

"Darling, please. Please don't go near that rock, " Jesse pleaded.

Lucy looked over at Joel and was shocked at his transformation. He looked so tranquil, so happy. He had an unearthly calm about him. Lucy was so happy for him. She tried to concentrate on his joy.

"Joel, can you believe you're about to see her?"

Joel spun around and grinned at her, looking giddy as a schoolboy. "No. I just... I can't believe it!" He paused for a moment. "Lucy, I think I'm...I think I can..."

Joel reached over and touched her shoulder, and his face split into a huge smile when he made solid contact with her body. He opened his arms and she ran into them, finally getting the hug from him that she'd always wanted.

"Thank you, thank you, thank you for everything. I never would have made it if not for you," Joel said, as he held her close. He felt huge against her small body, like a big, warm teddy bear. "I love you, sweetheart."

"I love you, too," Lucy told him, fighting tears. She knew if she started crying now, she'd never stop. "Go to her. Go to *them!*"

Joel released her and smiled, gently stroking her hair. "Thanks for not giving up on me. On us. I'll be watching over you. Always."

Lucy nodded, tears spilling out of her eyes.

She glanced over at Jesse. "You-you need to take...take him home. Please. He needs to be at peace, too. I mean it, Joel. Pull him over to the other side if you have to."

"You sure?" Joel asked, still stroking her hair.

"Yes," she said, doing her best not to break down. "Promise me."

"I promise. Will you be all right?" Joel asked, looking at her with tender concern.

"Yes. Emma survived somehow. I will, too."

Joel nodded, then whispered, "Ask her for strength. Call on her for help."

Lucy nodded, then gasped as a huge light appeared over the rocks of Devil's Den. Joel turned to look, his face illuminated not just by the light but by what he saw. Lucy couldn't see into the portal, but she knew what Joel saw just by watching his reaction.

Sure enough, Joel said softly, "Emma..."

Lucy choked back a sob. She cried from happiness and from heartbreak at the same time.

"I'm so sorry," were the first words Joel spoke to his beloved wife, the words he'd needed to say for far too long. Then he smiled, somehow looking even more serene than he had a moment ago. Lucy knew why. He'd finally gotten the forgiveness he'd ached for.

"Jesse!" Lucy called to him. "Come kiss me goodbye."

"No. Lucy, I won't—"

"Please!" Lucy shrieked. "Before it's too late!"

Jesse knew she was right. What if he had no choice and was forced to cross over? He'd never be able to rest if he left without saying goodbye. He rushed over to her and wrapped his arms around her, feeling her body tremble.

Lucy held him close, grateful for the fact that she could still touch him. She held him close, knowing she was only seconds away from having to let go of him forever.

Jesse cupped her face to his and kissed her.

"I love you," Lucy whispered.

"I love you, too," Jesse said. Those words weren't strong enough for what he was feeling, but he didn't know what else he could say.

Jesse suddenly dropped his arms and let go of her. He turned and walked toward the portal as if being pulled there. The force must have been strong, because he didn't even turn to look back at Lucy. The pain that stabbed through her was so severe that for a moment, she thought she might be feeling his death pains again. She'd thought she was prepared for this moment, but how could she be?

Lucy loved him enough to let him go. He needed to be at

peace, and she would not stop him just for her own sake. She would grieve for Jesse like all those Civil War wives and sweethearts did all those years ago. Somehow, she would go on because she had to.

Jesse walked up to the portal. When Lucy saw the look of peace on his face, she knew it was right to let him go. The haunted, sorrowful look on his face was gone.

"Mama," Jesse said tenderly as he looked into the portal.

Lucy covered her mouth and stifled another sob. She knew how much Jesse had ached to see his mother again.

Lucy turned her head when someone called her name. It was Joel. He looked at her as if to say, *it's time.* Joel searched her eyes, nonverbally asking her one more time, *are you sure?*

Lucy nodded. Jesse finally turned to look at her. He still looked peaceful, but she could see he was torn.

"Lucy, my rose..." he said, his voice ethereal, angelic. It was like he was already halfway to heaven. He looked so happy. He wanted, needed to cross over. She had to let him go.

"I love you, Jesse. It's all right to go," Lucy managed to get the words out. She didn't know how she found the strength.

Joel stretched out his hand, and Jesse reached for it.

Lucy closed her eyes. She raised her right hand to the sky and said, "God, please grant my darling soldier's wishes, and may his soul pass through the South!"

That was all she could manage. She finally broke down, sobbing.

Joel grasped Jesse's hand and pulled him to the Other Side.

37

God, grant my darling soldier's wishes, and may his soul pass through the South...

It was like Jesse heard Lucy's words with his head and his heart, rather than through his mortal ears. He could feel her heartbreak as surely as if it were his own. Letting him go was the most selfless, loving act that he could have ever imagined.

You must choose.

It was a voice...*THE* voice from the other side. It was the Creator, the Master, the perfect, all-loving being.

You must decide.

Jesse realized it was up to him. He could cross over to the other side, or he could stay and live.

The pull to the other side was like having the strongest addiction possible. It was so perfect, so joyful, so wonderful there. There was no pain, no sorrow. Only joy.

Make your choice.

Make your choice.

Joel smiled at Jesse, then he tugged on his hand. Pulling Jesse toward the light.

Make your choice.

Jesse could feel Lucy's grief. He felt it deep in his soul.

My rose.

HER! Jesse screamed in his mind. *Her! I choose her! Please! Please!*

So it is done, the all-loving Being said. Jesse felt the Being smile, like He was amused at the situation. Jesse felt His love. For him. For Lucy. For the whole world.

Jesse loosened his grip on Joel's hand and said, "See you on the other side, brother."

Joel slipped away, crossing over, leaving Jesse behind in his earthly body.

All was silent in Devil's Den except for the sound of Lucy weeping. She sat on the same rock where she'd lain after suffering the agony of Jesse's death. She held her head in her hands, her shoulders shaking as she sobbed uncontrollably.

Tenderness overwhelmed Jesse. He thought of all the times Lucy had suffered because of him, all the tears she'd already wept, all the physical and emotional pain she'd endured. *Now I have the rest of my life to make up for it.*

"Lucy," he said gently, not wanting to startle her. He spoke too softly, and couldn't be heard over her sobs. "Lucy."

Lucy slowly lifted her head, afraid to hope. Jesse smiled as he walked toward her.

"J-J-Jesse?"

She staggered to her feet on wobbly legs.

"I told you I wouldn't leave you."

He wrapped his arms around her, and not a moment too soon. Her legs gave out, and he caught her easily in his strong arms.

"It's okay to faint. I can catch you now."

"Why-why didn't you go? You wanted to go!" Lucy stared

at him, wondering if this was all a dream. Was he really still here?

"I wanted to go," he admitted. "But I wanted to spend a lifetime with you first."

Lucy struggled to think clearly, afraid to believe that this was real. That Jesse was still here, still *alive*. She looked over to where his portal had disappeared. "You-you gave up Paradise for me..." She didn't sound flattered. She sounded overwhelmed, frightened even, at the magnitude of his sacrifice.

Jesse gripped her tightly and looked into her eyes. "And you made my heart beat again."

Lucy looked at him gratefully. He was right. Her love had *literally* brought him back to life. Surely, that was worth something. She wrapped her arms around him, sobbing into his chest.

Jesse held her and tenderly stroked her hair. "It's all right now, darlin'. Everything is all right. I'll be back there some-day. We both will. But not for a long time." He lifted her chin with his hand and leaned down to give her a soft kiss. "Now, let's go *home*."

With that, Jesse *finally* swept her off her feet and into his arms. It felt wonderful to finally be physically strong when she needed him to be. He carried her off the battlefield, to safety before his battle wounds could strike her again.

Lucy threw her arms around his neck and clung to his chest, and he could feel her tears soaking his shirt. She snuggled closer to him, next to his heartbeat. He could feel her breathing slow as she began to calm down. He knew she felt safe in his arms.

Carrying her like this made him feel like a groom carrying his bride over the threshold, ready to start their new life together.

The thought made him smile.

JESSE TOOK her straight to her bedroom and had planned on just going to sleep. They were both exhausted and emotionally drained. As they lay together, they started kissing and they realized neither one was ready for sleep just yet.

Jesse just wanted to look at her, to remind himself that this wasn't a dream. He was here to stay. He stared into her eyes, and he slid his fingers down between her legs. She moaned at his touch. He slipped his fingers inside her, stroking upward, then massaged her with his thumb. He knew exactly how and where to touch her now.

It was so slow, so sensual. He continued to stare deeply into her eyes as her pleasure grew. How he loved hearing her panting, her whimpers of delight growing louder as she got closer and closer to climaxing. She only broke eye contact when she reached orgasm, throwing her head back and crying out passionately as she came.

Jesse stroked her face and looked into her eyes. He could hardly believe where he was and what he was doing. He was with Lucy. In *their* bed. Touching her. Loving her. Those days of watching her from afar, aching to be with her already seemed so long ago.

He made love to her slowly and tenderly, the way he'd intended to the first time. It was wonderful knowing they had time together. There were would be more times like this. Many, many more.

Theresa arrived home to the familiar sounds of the bed squeaking and Lucy's cries of *Oh, Jesse. Oh, God...* She rolled her eyes and smiled. Figured they were going at it again.

Theresa didn't mind. She liked having Jesse around. He was sweet and kind and sexy.

All the things Steven wasn't. Which was why she had decided to break up with him.

It made Theresa tired just thinking about it. Once Jesse and Lucy had finished their activities—for now—she was able to get some sleep.

The next morning, Theresa couldn't help but tease them.

"It's like living with the Cinemax channel on all day with you two around."

Lucy blushed, and giggled. "Sorry, I know we're loud."

Jesse shot her a look.

"Okay, *I'm* loud."

"Yeah, ya are!" Theresa said. "That's all right, Jess. That means you're doin' it right."

"We were celebrating," Lucy said, her face glowing with joy. "I get to keep him, Theresa. He had a choice to cross over or stay. He stayed."

"You serious?" Theresa asked, poised mid-pour of her coffee.

"Yep. She's stuck with me now," Jesse said proudly.

Theresa put down the coffee and grabbed Lucy and hugged her. "Oh, honey. I'm so glad. I'm so happy! Oh, my God, I don't know what she would have done if you left, Jesse."

"It wouldn't have been heaven without my Lucy there."

"But, Theresa..." Lucy began gently. "Joel..."

"Oh! He's gone, isn't he?" Theresa asked.

"Yes," Lucy said, squeezing Theresa's shoulders. "I know how much he meant to you."

Theresa smiled sadly. "Yeah. He was a really good friend.

Still, good for him. I'm so glad he made it! I'm really gonna miss him."

"We all will," Jesse said softly.

"Damn. I never got a chance to tell Joel that I'm gonna follow his advice," Theresa said.

"What advice?" Lucy asked.

"I'm gonna break up with Steven."

"You are?" Lucy was rather shocked, but certainly not upset. "Why?"

"I decided I want what Joel and Emma had. And what you two have. Joel told me I shouldn't settle."

"And he's right, Theresa," Jesse told her. "You deserve nothing less than great love."

"Thanks, cowboy." Theresa punched him affectionately on the shoulder.

"And you know, um, I guess I'm gonna have to be stayin' here for a while," Jesse told her uncertainly.

Theresa shot him a stern look. "Okay. You can stay, but I want you to walk around shirtless like you were the other day. I'm gonna need some man candy to look at with Steven gone."

Jesse laughed and waved her off.

Theresa fixed up her coffee and seemed to be lost in thought.

"You okay?" Lucy asked.

"Me? Oh, yeah. I've just been thinking a lot lately... Okay, tell me if this idea is crazy. You did such a great job helping the boys cross over, or at least get to the point where they *could* cross over. What do you think of the idea of me starting some kind of support group for soldier ghosts? I mean, I'm working on my psychology degree and I'm thinking of focusing on PTSD as a specialty."

"Hmmm," Jesse said. "You mean you could form a counseling group for ghost soldiers who fought in the Civil War, help 'em cross over?"

"Yeah."

Jesse seemed touched by the idea. "Theresa, I think that's so sweet. I think it's great. Really, really great. You know who would love that idea?"

"Second Mama," answered both Lucy and Theresa.

"Yeah. She'd love it if you'd help her boys."

"Oh! Poor Fillis. She doesn't even know about Joel yet, does she?" Lucy asked, looking concerned.

"No. We'll tell her today."

"She didn't get to say goodbye," Lucy said, putting her hand over her heart.

"It's all right. Believe me. She knew his time was coming and...well...they said what they needed to say," Jesse put a comforting hand on Lucy's shoulder.

Lucy breathed a sigh of relief. "Thank God for that."

———————

38

Theresa, Lucy, and Jesse headed out to find Fillis and tell her everything that had happened. She smiled serenely when she saw Lucy and Jesse headed toward her, holding hands. Worry pulled at her heart as it always did when she thought about how much Lucy loved Jesse. She'd be destroyed if he crossed over and had to leave her behind.

"Fillis!" Lucy said excitedly. "You won't believe it. I get to keep him!"

"What am I, a golden retriever?" Jesse said.

"Down, boy," Theresa said.

"What do you mean?" Fillis asked.

"He was given a choice to cross over or stay with me. And he chose to stay," Lucy said, looking at Jesse with adoration and gratitude.

Theresa held up her palm toward Jesse. "Stay...stay... there's a good soldier."

"That's wunnerful, Lucy. Jus' wunnerful!" Fillis said, feeling a surge of relief flow all the way through her ghostly form. Lucy wouldn't be heartbroken, and Jesse would lead a happy, contented life with her to take care of him. It was a dream come true. Fillis could see it so clearly. Jesse would spend the rest of his life loving Lucy. Her motherly heart filled to the brim with joy for her beloved adopted son.

Lucy sat down next to Fillis and spoke gently. "Joel made it, Fillis."

"He did?" Her eyes were filled with joy tinged with sadness.

"Oh, Fillis," Lucy put her hand over her heart. "I wish you could have seen his face when he saw her. He's at peace now, I promise you that."

"Thank you, child," Fillis said. She still looked a bit sad, but she also looked more at peace herself. Two more of her soldiers were taken care of now. "Oh, I'll miss my baby, but I'm so glad he's home with Emma and the chillren."

"Me, too," Jesse said.

"Speaking of your babies, Fillis," Theresa said. "I go to school at the college with Lucy, and I'm studying psychology. I think I want to concentrate on helping soldiers after I graduate. You know, especially the ones with Post Traumatic Stress Disorder—PTSD?"

Fillis nodded. She knew all about PTSD, both from what she heard on the news and from seeing herself from some of her boys. All her soldiers were traumatized one way or the other, but she definitely knew a few who suffered with full-blown PTSD.

"I was thinking...maybe I could start helping soldiers even before I graduate. I want to start a support group for the spirits who are still stuck here. Maybe counsel them and help them work out their issues and help them cross over. What do you think?"

"Oh, honey. I think that's lovely. Just lovely. Do it. Please! Many have made it over the years, but there's still a lot left."

"I'm glad you like the idea. Think about who needs help, and you can help recruit them."

"You got it, honey," Fillis said, looking at the two girls with great fondness.

"And I still haven't given up on helping you, Fillis," Lucy told her. "You're so busy worrying about everyone else, you need someone to look after you!"

Fillis waved her off. She didn't want Lucy wasting her time fretting over her.

"I want to get started right away. I'm gonna do some PTSD research and read up on counseling soldiers." Theresa said. She stood up, then looked down at Jesse and Lucy. "Hey, I'll stop at the store to get some more food. Jesse, tell Lucy what you want and she can text it to me. Luce, we need to get your man a cell phone."

Lucy nodded. "You're right."

There were probably a lot of things Jesse needed now that he was alive. Now they could start planning for their future. Jesse was here to stay.

IT WAS wonderful for Jesse to be alive again and to be able to treat Lucy the way she deserved to be treated. He loved being the one to walk her safely to her car at night, and then be able to open the car door for her. He really wanted to learn how to drive, so she could relax after working a long shift.

He felt awful about living in her apartment rent-free and eating food that she and Theresa had to pay for. It wasn't right. He desperately needed a job, a way to provide for his woman.

Jesse was sitting on the couch staring into space when

Lucy got home from work. She could see he was worrying about something.

"What's the matter, Rebel-of-my-Heart?" she asked, sitting next to him on the couch.

"Your boyfriend is a deadbeat, that's what's the matter."

Lucy lovingly stroked his hair. "What are you talking about?"

"I can't have you doing all the work. I have to get a job to pay the bills."

"You will, Jesse. Give it time. You have a lot to catch up on. Theresa and I are fine with money for now."

"But it ain't right! I'm supposed to be a man. It's my job to provide for you."

"Jesse," she said tenderly. "I love that you're such a gentleman. I love that you kiss my hand, open doors for me, take your hat off when I'm around. I adore you and your irresistible Southern charms..."

With that, she pushed him onto his back on the couch. She looked down at his body, then back up into his eyes. She had the look of desire that told him he was about to get laid.

"But let me make something perfectly clear, cowboy..." Lucy said, unbuttoning his shirt as she straddled him. "It's the 21st century. You don't *provide* for me. We take care of *each other*."

Jesse grinned up at her. He knew she was right. He would work hard to find a job and help pull his weight, but he had to be patient. Right now, his number one priority was sexually satisfying his woman.

"Oh, yes, *ma'am,*" he said as he reached for her.

THERESA WALKED DOWN THE STREET, observing the crowd. She still thought of Joel often. It saddened her to think of so many dead soldiers like him wandering around Gettysburg, and she was more eager than ever to help them find peace. She paid extra attention to "reeanactors" on the street, because you just never knew who was alive and who was dead. Even the dead couldn't recognize other dead people for sure, except when they were invisible to the living when their images were more transparent. When they walked down the street in broad daylight, it was tough to know for sure.

Theresa caught sight of a tall, handsome man in a blue Union uniform. He had that big, muscular, sexy kind of build that Joel had. She felt a twinge of sadness. She really missed her friend.

Theresa could tell this guy was dead by the haunted look on his face. Only a real soldier looked like that. He had the look of a man who'd seen and done too many awful things. The man looked lost in thought as he walked near Theresa on the sidewalk. He caught her eye, and her heartbeat quickened.

Damn, he's even finer up close.

Theresa boldly looked into his eyes and smiled. The blue soldier's sorrowful expression eased a bit as he smiled back at her.

He winked at her as he walked past.

Theresa turned and watched him walk away. Even his walk was sexy.

Hmmm, Theresa thought. *I wonder if I could help him...*

THANKS FOR READING!

Beloved Reader,

Thanks for coming along on Jesse's journey to find true love with his beautiful rose, Lucy.

I hope you'll continue with Jesse's return to the land of the living, as well as Theresa's path to find her happy ever after.

Theresa counsels the weary soldiers to help them cross over, and she falls for a dashing Union soldier in the process.

Jesse is the only ghost in Gettysburg to have returned from the grave. Could it happen again, or will Theresa lose her love when Sean's soul finds peace?

If he does make a miraculous return, it would mean Theresa would discover his secret...

Return to Gettysburg now with Darling Soldiers.

If you enjoy the full Gettysburg Ghost Series trilogy, you can also check out the Williamsburg Ghost Series!

WAIT! BEFORE YOU GO!

If you'd like to have a FREE steamy sports romance, you can get STARTING FROM ZERO, the novella prequel to my Boys of Baltimore Series, simply by following me on ANY of my social networks (listed below) and/or joining my email list!

To get your FREE book, FOLLOW me on ANY of the social networks below and then shoot me an email at lindafausnet@gmail.com and ask for your free book:

Join my Author Reader's Group on Facebook.

Follow my Author Linda Fausnet Facebook Page

Follow me on Bookbub

Following me on Instagram

OR join my email list and you will automatically receive the book in your inbox.

This novella is EXCLUSIVELY available to my readers and is NOT available for purchase anywhere!

Why Leave a Book Review? I'll give you 3 good reasons.

You can do it in less than a minute! Just choose a star

rating from 1 to 5 stars and add a sentence or two on how you felt about the book.

Most readers choose the books they read based on the reviews, but only a few readers are kind enough to leave a review.

Most readers are not aware of this, but authors live and die by reviews. We really do.

It only takes a minute to leave a review, but the impact lasts for the lifetime of the book.

Thank you so very much.

ATTENTION ROMANCE NOVEL FANS!

I hope you'll join my romance novel fan club, Romance Novel Addicts Anonymous, on Facebook and Instagram. Join the email list, and you'll receive WHAT'S YOUR PLEASURE? RNAA'S OFFICIAL GUIDE TO FINDING YOUR NEXT GREAT ROMANCE READ.

ACKNOWLEDGMENTS

Special thanks to my wonderful beta readers, Kendall Bailey and Beth Miller, and my fantastic editor, Katriena Knights. Thanks to Chuck DeKett for his fabulous cover design and helping Private Jesse Spenser come to life (pun totally intended. See what I did there??) Thanks to Ryan Pittinger for his insights into what it's really like to work as a server in a restaurant, and thanks to Jack Marahrens and Dwayne Simmons for their help on reenacting and Civil War facts. I assure you, any errors in Civil War history and the battle of Gettysburg are my own....

Thanks to my amazing parents, Cecelia and Bernie Wasiljov, and my fantastic sister, Zann Wasiljov, who have been lifelong supporters and have always been there for me.

Thanks to my lovely children, Celia and Noah. No, you can't read Mommy's book, so don't ask.....

Thanks to my husband, Bill, my real-life handsome, romantic hero. Your love and support of my dreams is the sexiest thing in the world.